Secrets

Satisfy your desire for more.

The Subject by Amber Green

One week Tyler is the hottest game designer in North America, in sight of her first million and signing the deal of her life. The next week, she's on the run for her life. Who can she trust? Certainly not sexy, mysterious, Don't-Call-Me-Werewolf Esau, who keeps showing up right after the hoo-hah hits the fan!

❧⟨⊙⟩❧

Surrender by Dominique Sinclair

Undercover Agent Madeline Carter is in too deep. She's slipped into Sebastian Maiocco's life to investigate his family, a known Sicilian mafia clan. Dark and dangerous, Sebastian unearths licentious desires Madeline is unable to deny, conflicting the duty that honors her. Madeline must surrender to Sebastian or risk being exposed, leaving her target for a ruthless clan. Only, if she surrenders, Madeline's heart will be in immanent danger.

❧⟨⊙⟩❧

Stasis by Leigh Wyndfield

Morgann Right has a problem. Her Commanding Officer—cool, calm, always in control Osborn Welty—has been drugged with Stasis, turning him into a living, breathing statue she's forced to take care of for ten long days. As her hands smooth down soft skin over rock hard muscles, she suddenly sees her CO in a totally different light. She wants him and, while she can tell he wants her, touching him intimately might come back to haunt them both.

❧⟨⊙⟩❧

A Woman's Pleasure by Charlotte Featherstone

After years of enduring a cold and emotionally devoid marriage, widowed Isabella, Lady Langdon is tired of denying her needs and desires. Yearning to discover all the pleasures denied her in her marriage, she finds herself falling hard for the magnetic charms of the mysterious and exotic Julian Gresham—a man skilled in pleasures of the flesh. A man eight years her junior. A man more than eager to show her *A Woman's Pleasure*.

Amber Green

Dominique Sinclair

Leigh Wyndfield

Charlotte Featherstone

Volume 20

Secrets

Satisfy your desire for more.

SECRETS Volume 20
This is an original publication of Red Sage Publishing and each individual story herein has never before appeared in print. These stories are a collection of fiction and any similarity to actual persons or events is purely coincidental.

Red Sage Publishing, Inc.
P.O. Box 4844
Seminole, FL 33775
727-391-3847
www.redsagepub.com

SECRETS Volume 20
A Red Sage Publishing book
All Rights Reserved/July 2007
Copyright © 2007 by Red Sage Publishing, Inc.

ISBN: 1-60310-000-8 / ISBN 13: 978-1-60310-000-7

Published by arrangement with the authors and copyright holders of the individual works as follows:

THE SUBJECT
Copyright © 2007 by Amber Green

SURRENDER
Copyright © 2007 by Dominique Sinclair

STASIS
Copyright © 2007 by Leigh Wyndfield

A WOMAN'S PLEASURE
Copyright © 2007 by Charlotte Featherstone

Photographs:
Cover © 2007 by Tara Kearney; www.tarakearney.com
Cover Model: Chayne Jones and Jill Meyerson
Setback cover © 2000 by Greg P. Willis; GgnYbr@aol.com

Printed in the U.S.A.

Book typesetting by:

Quill & Mouse Studios, Inc.
www.quillandmouse.com

Contents

The Subject

by Amber Green

To My Reader:

Welcome back to the world of Hawkmoor! This time you get to meet Tyler, a woman who's used to making things go her way, and Esau, a shapeshifter who's strong enough to rank his own needs last.

Long ago, overcome by the loss of his mate and children, Esau devoted his entire being to the welfare of his pack. Then he finds a woman who needs him fully alive, and fully alpha. His duty to his pack requires him to track her down and deliver her to her enemies. He can't. Not even if refusing may destroy the pack. To save her, he must give up everything he thought he had, and become more than he ever thought he could be.

Prologue

The earthquake struck at midnight, lifting the streets of West Memphis and dropping them with enough force to break car axles and set off whooping, beeping, blaring alarms. Debris banged against Esau's truck, shooting white spiderweb cracks across the glass. He swerved to stay on more level asphalt.

Help! David's mental scream seared through him. He was close—even absolute panic couldn't make his nephew's cry so clear, unless he was very close.

Vehicles clogged the next intersection, lit by headlights at all angles, but the four-story white building a block ahead should be the lab. David and his young mate Gabie had left a note that this place experimented on involuntary human subjects. They said they wanted to sneak in, get photos to send to the media. They'd been caught.

Another shock slung the truck like a carnival ride, and a flash threw stark shadows on the buildings ahead. Esau braced against the dash.

Another mental scream brought details: David crouched in the dark, shivering against a glass wall. The ceiling came down, and the link broke.

Thrown back into his own head, Esau watched the white building ahead flatten, floor dropping on floor in slow motion. His heart stopped. *David!* His nephew didn't answer. *"David!"*

Dust rose in a cloud, reflecting a dull red from the riverfront fires. Screams, alarms and sirens made a cold stew of meaningless sound.

A subsonic *wumpf,* more felt than heard, brought him back to his senses. That would be the fuel storage tanks at the riverfront, four miles behind. He left the truck and ran, pausing at a fallen billboard to shed his clothes. The fires rimming the horizon stained the gibbous moon like an eclipse, but he hadn't needed moonlight to shift since his teens.

With faint creaks and a burning cramp, his bones shortened and flesh flowed to the four-legged shape he knew best. His wolf nose would find a miracle, if any existed.

Minutes later he found the miracle: David's scent. He squelched the flare of hope. He'd put David on his first bike, led him through his first shift. *If David was alive, I'd know it. But Gabie?*

He lost the scent in a nauseating mélange of spilled gasoline and ruptured sewer lines. Circling a half-buried fire truck, he heard bulkily dressed humans yelling about whether to go to the riverfront on foot. *They need to help right here.* Nothing short of the Mississippi would put out that fire tonight.

Past the truck, he recaptured David's scent. He sniffed madly among shuffled slabs of cement and asphalt to follow it.

At the edge of the lab's rubble, he found a naked woman prying open the door of a car that would never run again. She wore David's scent, and others, in a haze of sex and blood. The moonlight showed numbers and letters painted on her back.

Esau shifted to human and called out.

She scrambled away, but fell on a pile of broken cinderblocks. He pounced without thinking, and pinned her there.

She moaned. Her horror-stricken eyes did not fix on his face or track his waving hand.

The musk and dust-caked blood on her skin, and the dizzying mix of fumes on her breath, tangled his instincts. She was soft, feminine, ripe for breeding, and his skin heated as she struggled under him. But she had been bred; David and two other shifters had left plenty of scent on her.

Gabie would have David's balls for that. If she lived.

Thick lashes fluttered. "Run," the woman breathed. "Got to run."

A different tremor, like a rumble of distant thunder, shook the earth. As Esau looked up, the ruddy fire-stain vanished from the clouds. The rumble continued. *The Mississippi.*

Four miles. A safe distance? What was four miles to the Mighty Mississip?

If he left her to search for his packmates—for the bodies of his pack-mates—she could drown. Forced to a decision, Esau scooped her up and ran to his truck.

Chapter 1

Tyler awoke in a stale-smelling motel room with curling wallpaper and a prominently displayed menu of porn movies available on the TV. *What the blazes?*

From the intensity of the flashing blue-pink-blue neon at the curtain's edge, it was night. She sat up cautiously, registering protests from every muscle, fuzzy vision, and a nasty chemical taste.

I'm sick. But why am I in this dive?

Since she wasn't in her own bed, this couldn't be Atlanta. *Then where? Was I stranded on the way to a seminar?*

Which seminar? Chicago? Detroit? Memphis? Giving seminars on corporate bonding and loyalty in the twenty-first century felt strange now that she'd stopped designing security systems, but Bastian called them crucial to his marketing plan.

Another stupid plan. *Stop it!* His plans always sounded asinine, but she'd made Forbes and the Wall Street Journal based on them. She must be here for one of those seminars.

So where's here?

She remembered dancing with a trumpeter on Beale Street, laughing in the night. After that? Denver. Meeting with lithe, hungry-looking young executives in a room decorated with faux cattle skulls.

She'd looked over the attendees with a distinct feeling that she ought not be here, that these men saw her as Bastian's squeeze, not as the hottest gameware designer in North America, much less as an authority on corporate security and culture.

She frowned, remembering. Bastian had been there, and had proposed again. She'd turned him down again, and this time she'd also told him no more seminars. Her market—markets now—attended cons, not seminars. While half of those hot-eyed young executives probably played her best games, who among them could say so while wearing a corporate tie like a collar and leash?

Bastian had gotten ugly-drunk, and she'd flown home alone.

But this wasn't home.

She stretched. Pain shot through her arms and back.

What the blazes? She flicked on the lamp, squinting against the flare of hard light, and pushed down the sheet and blanket.

Blood-crusted scrapes and scratches marked her arms and legs. She wore a knee-length pink t-shirt she did not recognize. From under the sleeve she traced raised welts lined up in sets of three or four, with the fourth one thinner. *Fingernails.*

Her heart skipped a beat, then restarted with a slow, nauseatingly hard pound. The bruised feeling in her crotch wasn't hormones, but a bruise. Bruises.

She pulled off the t-shirt in front of the mirror. Bruises. Scratches. Bites. A narrow mouth had left arcs of tooth prints on her left breast. A rounder mouth had marked her neck. The shoulder mark showed prominent canines.

Three guys.

She made it to the toilet—barely. The dry heaving ran whip-crack convulsions through her, over and over, while she clung to the bleach-smelling horseshoe toilet seat.

When she finally rinsed her mouth and sagged to the cold floor, she noticed damp towels on the rack. She had bathed; she had washed away the evidence a cop or a prosecutor would need. *No memory; no clue; no evidence. So much for calling the cops.*

She found the phone and hit the button for the front desk.

"Good evening, Room 8!" That Midwest twang sounded maternal and chipper, and wholly bizarre in its normalcy.

"Could someone bring me a newspaper, please?" A paper would give the date and location. Leave her feeling less like she was falling through time with no handhold and no point of reference.

"Sure thing, eh? Glad you're feeling better!"

"Thank you."

She caught sight of her reflection, naked and unreal. *I need clothes.* Wincing, she pulled the oversized t-shirt back on. *I need my brain to function. I'm half-bombed.*

When the knock sounded at her door, she opened it before thinking of the peephole. A man stood in the hall.

Her vision came in focus. *Wow.*

The man loomed over her, all long bone and hard muscle. Glints of silver salted his short, dark hair. His heavy-browed face had a rough, lived-in look.

If I'd slept with you, she thought recklessly, *I wouldn't want to forget it!*

He held something out to her. She took it, belatedly realizing that it was a newspaper.

"Are you all right, miss?"

His deep voice echoed through her, *awl raaht, miyiss?* and for a moment all she could do was admire its rich timbre and molasses accent. Not Midwest at all.

The words penetrated. She groped for an answer that wouldn't reveal unspeakable things to a stranger.

Too late.

His eyes rested on her neck, then traveled down her clawed forearms to her broken fingernails. The lines in his face deepened.

"Are you the manager?" Did this dive have a doctor on call?

"I don't work here, miss. I have Room 7 across the corridor. I just happened to be in the lobby when you called the clerk, and she got busy—"

You're lying. She stepped back and slammed the door, dropping the newspaper to work the lock with both shaking hands. Why lie to a stranger? Maybe he wasn't a stranger. Maybe one of these sets of tooth prints matched his mouth.

Esau stood in the corridor, pressing every nuance of the injured woman's scent into his memory. Last night, when he'd brought her to this rat-hole, the blood and musk had covered her own aroma. She'd washed away those odors to reveal two facts that changed everything: she was not fully human, and she was pregnant.

He backed into Room 7. The woman's scent also said she was ravenous, or would be once she was over being sick. He opened a cup of chicken noodle and set it in the microwave.

As the soup heated, he flipped open his phone and dialed his sister. "What's the news, Addie?"

"Fine, thank you!" she snapped. "You too? Glad to hear it."

"Did you get our people in with the search and rescue teams?" *Did they find a miracle?* The brief silence told him she was composing herself, and something in him quietly died.

"They identified my son and his mate," she finally said. "They also found what might be the Thompson brothers who vanished last year, and two non-local males."

She sounded too calm. They probably both did. But while he'd set the ritual fires last night, Addie had insisted that searchers would find her son alive.

Addie ruled the shifters of Memphis with an airy demeanor, but she had never simply denied such a clearly concrete fact as David's death. And now she couldn't deny it.

David, the only one of Addie's children to survive his teens—gone. Gabie, bought twelve years ago this week and raised to be David's mate—gone. Esau's fangs cut the insides of his lips. Tasting the blood, he smiled bitterly. He could tell himself he had a grip, that his fangs didn't show, but the need to howl and tear things apart kept ambushing him.

The taste did nothing to clear his mind. He ran a glass of water and rinsed his mouth, not caring how much Addie heard. Women did not have fangs that erected with the worst kind of timing, but what a man dealt with, a woman knew about.

"Come home, Esau. You need to help with the announcements."

You need to. Never *I need you to.* But she did need him, if only as a breeder. Now, without a successor of her blood, Addie stood open to challenge by any fertile and ambitious female.

But the injured woman across the corridor also needed him.

"Are you there, Esau? Did you hear me?"

"I heard you," he said gently. "The woman is pregnant."

"So she bears a mule! What's your point?"

He bit back his snarl. As head of the Family, Addie thought generations down the line. To her, this woman was a genetic dead end. Not a person with haunted eyes, soft skin, and a scent that would rouse carnal thoughts in a bronze statue.

"Addie, the woman herself is not fully human."

Addie inhaled sharply, as if testing his scent through the phone.

He let her think it through. Humans did not have to fight the moon to maintain gestation. Human-shifter hybrids with human mothers were not all that rare, but they were effectively human and nearly always sterile. The fertile hybrid, though, could produce shifter children. This one might carry David's get, a potential successor, at least until DNA-testing proved otherwise.

Addie would, he knew, bury the information about other possible sires.

His own thoughts ran a side-track. That lab had held the woman, along with David, four other adult male shifters. And Gabie.

Who else had been trapped there? How long had the lab been active? Once decrypted, the lab's databases might show more about shifter physiology than any human ought to know.

The lab had held a fertile half-breed. Had they known the rarity of that phenomenon? What more did they know? The information in that place was invaluable—and explosive.

If the data still existed. The woman's scent slid through him. She was real, and she was hurt.

"Bring her to me, Esau. I need that heir."

Now that Addie had reached the decision he'd led her to, he realized he did not want her at that point. Not yet.

"She needs time to recover first, Addie. TV doesn't show how bad the damage here really is. Most of West Memphis is a lake of mud. The people are in shock. Don't challenge her whole concept of reality while she's still processing the quake and the—" he could not say it "—what happened to her."

"Don't patronize me! Coming here will be a shock no matter when she comes. Better to combine it with the shock she's already had; she can get over both together."

"No."

He hung up. For a moment he stood in the dark, smelling soup and cheap carpet deodorizer, examining his own reluctance. It was reluctance, he concluded, to let Addie come between him and the injured woman. Not just the knowledge Addie would throw breeders at him in a frantic attempt to get a backup heir, but the knowledge that Addie would quite literally step between him and this female. It was a possessiveness he had never felt before, and almost didn't recognize. At first touch, some part of her had become his, or some part of him had become hers.

Either way, he wasn't sharing. He turned off the phone.

He carried the steaming soup with its rich salty aroma across to her door, and knocked.

No response.

He used the spare key, and slid out a long claw to unhook the chain. Forming claw from bone itched unbearably, spiders with needle-feet dancing across his palm and up his forearm. But he just didn't have the emotional resources to properly rearrange the neural pathways. By the time the door swung open, he knew the room was empty.

"Sir?" The front desk clerk came up behind him, wringing her hands. "I'm so sorry, sir! I have to ask you and your wife to share a room. The sheriff is here with more refugees—and he says if I have fewer than two people per room he'll arrest me!"

"Don't worry," Esau said, hiding the claw as it retracted. "We're leaving now. You can have both rooms back."

Chapter 2

The cash machine refused her code. Tyler stared numbly at it. It'd worked this morning. Or was that a different machine, a different hotel's lobby? Beyond the privacy screen, the polished wood and subdued voices of a well-run hotel stayed resolutely anonymous, out of focus. Then again, what had been *in* focus in the past several days?

Don't go there.

She set her left hand to the scanner and retried her code.

Transaction cannot be completed at this time. Please contact your financial institution. Message authorization B620Z.

She turned. Across the posh lobby, the elevator called to her. Her room called to her. *Can't go anywhere else without money.* Nor could she stay without money.

Who could block her transactions? Celie, maybe. Her secretary broke rules with cheerful vigor. But why would she?

In any case, Celie would know what was going on.

Time to call home.

"*Miss Tyler?*" Celie's voice trumpeted from the handset, an emotional alarm clock that brought all her senses to full alert. "Tyler! Florence Randolph *Tyler*! Is it you?"

Tyler held the phone away from her ear. "Me or a deaf person who looks like me! What's wrong with my debit code?"

"*Tyler!* It's *you!* You're *okay!*"

"Celie, we kind of established that. Or I thought we did. Why is this cash machine refusing to spit out cash for me?"

"We thought you were *dead!* You left your condo in the middle of the night—without having me get your tickets or forward your messages—and you *never* do that. After two weeks, your email accounts overflowed, and I couldn't find *no* way to get ahold of you. High-and-Mighty Bastian Truc said some drifter must have your codes, so he got a court order freezing your account."

A drifter? Yeah, me. Vague impressions of hotels and train stations sifted through her mind. She couldn't focus on any one of them. *Maybe less a drifter than a sleepwalker.* She really had no idea where she had been or, to tell the truth, where she was.

She opened the curtains. Denver. Right downtown.

And dead broke, thanks to Bastian Truc. *Well, he knows how to grab my attention, even if he can't seem to hold it.*

"Celie, dear. You know my old New Orleans account, the emergency one?" No one short of the IRS could freeze a New Orleans account. She coached Celie through the steps of moving the pens-and-pizza fund to that account, and checking to make sure the money was immediately available. "Now, use corporate travel to pay my hotel bill and buy me a train ticket home."

"Don't you want a plane instead?"

"I can't take a plane because I haven't any photo ID." Another option occurred. "Never mind the train ticket, Celie. Get my passport from the safe and have a courier bring it to me. Then book me on the red-eye home. Here's the address." She rummaged through the bedside desk to find the hotel's street address and phone number. Suddenly something Celie had said struck her. "And who said I left home in the middle of the night?"

"Mr. Truc. He said you were to meet him for a late dinner but he got tied up in the Pacific Rim meetings. He went by your place afterward to apologize, but you were gone. Like I said, without telling me! He called the police—I got the report right here."

I don't remember leaving my place late at night.

But something pried at her memory. The doorman calling? A package? The elevator had smelled odd, like canned air. She remembered backing out of it to take the stairs. But the stairs also smelled odd. She remembered falling, and that the fall seemed endless.

Her insides churned as she wrapped up the call. Kidnapped. Not from the street, nor some anonymous hotel. From her home.

Back in her corporate security days, she'd researched kidnapping patterns. Ransom-oriented kidnapers tended to drug the victim and tuck her away with minimal contact, while the rape/torture scene was either a political statement or the mark of a personal grudge. This seemed to combine them in a way that made no sense. Unless the ransom had been refused?

She paced, ordered a BLT with a Caesar salad, and paced some more.

Why me? To destroy the company?

Good thing HandPlus is closely held, or stock prices would've tanked, with me missing so long.

A shower started up in the room next door on the north, and then a passably good tenor launched into a love song Bastian had made his own during a karaoke dare. She listened to the few lyrics she could hear well.

The room to the south was quiet, and she hoped it remained so. She'd taken advantage of the housekeepers' inattention yesterday to stick a little strip of plastic into the lock of the connecting door, so the lock didn't quite seat. The chances she'd ever need that lock to open on command were vanishingly small, but so were the chances she'd ever be kidnapped out of her home in the middle of the night.

Someone knocked on the door. She used the peephole before she opened the door to room service. The elderly bellman smiled as she scribbled a tip on the bill.

The first bite of bacon made her drop the sandwich. The taste didn't make her sick, but one more bite most definitely would.

When did I pick up a nervous stomach?

She paced. Nothing made sense. Outside her window, two jet contrails crept toward one another and crossed in the intensely blue sky. What happened in Memphis had taken over her life, had left her drifting and aimless.

"I want my life back," she said out loud.

But right now she was still stalled, hanging fire. The courier's trip would take at least a few hours. And she was tired, as she had been all day. She had time for a nap. Nothing else seemed worth the energy it would take...

A man wearing a surgeon's mask and bifocal glasses stood over her. "Feet up," he said, and a gynecologist's rack raised her feet. The man checked her ankle straps and tightened one, pressing her calf painfully hard against the cold slick metal.

Some object in her mouth blocked her protest.

The masked man looked up from between her knees. "Raise the dosage. She's trying to come out of it."

A female voice murmured a protest.

The masked man picked up a speculum and smeared clear jelly on it. "Don't worry," he said. "This one isn't quite human."

Tyler woke up, heart pounding.

Rapid-fire knocks rattled the door. "Room Service!"

Huh? She looked about, and saw the plate with the still-uneaten sandwich. *I ordered something else?*

No! I didn't! She scooped up her sack of clothes and ran for the connecting room.

The front door smacked open against the chain.

She opened the connecting door on her side and fumbled with the bit of plastic in the other door's lock. Stepping into the other room, she pulled both connecting doors shut. The sounds of them latching overlapped the sharp snap of the door-chain.

She paused to look around. Nobody here. But a suitcase lay open on the bed. Trespassing in a stranger's room made her feel curiously naked. Then irritated, to waste time and mental energy on the proprieties when, in her room next door, men swore and a dog whined eagerly.

Out in the hallway, she saw that the elevator door stood blocked open by a thick book. Inviting. Too inviting. A game-maker learned to look for traps, whether or not any existed.

She eased open the door to the stairs and ran up two flights to the seventh floor, which had an express elevator.

Express or not, it sank with interminable slowness while she sweated. She waited for the electricity to go off, or an alarm to blare out. Neither happened.

A tone sounded, and a female voice enunciated, "Plaza, plaza," as if it were a code word, or in some foreign language.

She hesitated in the lobby, as green and damp as any fern bar. Staff door, side door or front door?

A shuttle pulled up to the front. She strode purposefully through that door into the cold outside air while the people from the shuttle wrestled with their bags. A porter asked if she wanted a ride to the airport.

Yes! But she smiled and shook her head. Airports were closed to her without photo ID.

Any teenager with the right equipment could fake some ID. With disposable cameras printing instant photos, the tricky part was copying a card or badge without holograms or a magnetic strip. She made a mental list of supplies.

The wind sent icy needles through her sweater, wracking her with shivers as she rounded the corner to find the next shuttle stop. She just missed a shuttle to Union Station, but as thick as the traffic was, another should come by in minutes.

She was not the only person waiting. More people joined the huddled group every couple of minutes. *Hurray for crowds.*

Who's hunting me? Why?

Not quite human. Now that was a concept for a gamer with a loose grip on reality. She'd had her werewolf fantasies—what kid didn't want a touch of magic, a secretly powerful Other Self? She still mined those fantasies for gaming material. She'd almost told Bastian about them.

Almost. Why always "almost", Bastian? Maybe if she'd been less stubbornly independent, they could have worked something out. But what if she'd tied herself to him, and then found something unspeakably twisted inside that carefully groomed facade?

Surely by now, she would have seen anything that bad. Surely she would have seen it early on, in the 30-hour days they'd spent slurping cold pho and arguing the details of the game that would begin the WarDove series. She'd had the visions. He'd found the security contracts and other scutwork programming the two of them cranked out to pay the rent.

By the time her student ID expired, she'd had the contracts and income to obtain a second-tier taxpayer's ID. Now she could do pretty much what she wanted.

Or would if Bastian didn't keep her busy with marketing trips and seminars that didn't have any connection to her current markets. She shrugged off the irritation. *Old news.*

She could call Celie and re-route her passport, but she'd have to be an idiot to miss the short time between giving Celie her location and having men snap the door-chain of her room.

If Celie had deliberately set the Black Hats on her, the sun would set in the east. But Celie could not keep her mouth shut to save her life. *Or mine.* So, who to call?

Bastian? He says he loves me. But what I hear is that he wants me. Or wants HandPlus. His kisses, his soulful gaze, even his roaming hands felt preplanned. Choreographed. That impression had, time after time, made her catch his hands and step back.

He'd taken her rebuffs in good humor until that Denver seminar. There he'd moved in, pressing her against the wall and kissing hard. He'd bitten her in the mouth. She'd bitten him back.

His animal snarl had frozen them both in place.

"Bastian, we've worked together for years. Don't change everything."

"Everything changes." He pressed a key-card in her palm. *"We're already a team in everyone's eyes. My Family wants an announcement."* His voice deepened. *"Come to me willingly."*

"Don't wait up, Bastian."

The shuttle hissed to a stop. A line formed and moved through the door in lockstep, as if the people formed a single centipede-like entity. She made mental notes; her concept artist might be able to do something with that image.

The wind picked up, whistling sharply. On that signal the people shrank, like they were freeze-drying, and the image of the centipede broke apart. Tyler buried her chin in the loose cowl-neck of her sweater.

Bastian Truc spoke of his Family; the word always mentally appeared in capital letters. His mother, outwardly the epitome of Southern Grace, might be the creepiest Grande Dame in North Carolina. The Truc base of operations in Raleigh was reason enough to keep the Tyler domicile in Atlanta.

Bastian might not be behind all this kidnapping stuff, but the weirdness started with him. In games that meant it would, in some way, loop back to him.

So who can I turn to? A lawyer picked from the phone book? Too random. Gamers from the nearest arcade? They'd be cannon fodder. The "telephone actresses" who'd moaned and cooed through her breakout piece, the hardware/software package everyone called FuckWare? They were plenty tough-minded, but had the wrong skill sets.

The classic decision would be to hire a private eye. A large, rawboned man with scarred fists, who would take her to bed and make everything all right.

The man who'd brought that newspaper in Memphis could take her to bed and make everything all right.

How could she still see every line in his face? Details like his slightly uneven haircut and the clean, square nails on his big hands? She even remembered his salty, woodsy, smoky smell. Her nipples tightened with sharp little cramps.

Stop that! He's in Memphis, a thousand miles away. And his image should give her the creeps, not the hots.

Chapter 3

Esau paced through the cathedral Denver called a train station. These ceilings had to be sixty feet high, and the noise pawed unendingly at his sore ears. Saccharine diesel fumes and the stench of too many people sickened him. The woman could pass within yards and evade his nose.

He ran a thumb along his phone, but it remained quiet. Unless she hid in the crowd, Denver's young wolves would call the moment she entered the tunnel to the trains, or detrained at the Light Rail, or left a taxi or shuttle at the curb.

The Denver boys hadn't asked questions when he'd enlisted their help. All of them would remember the fishing expeditions he and Ben had led.

He staked out the ticket windows, leaning against the cool marble sill. A couple hundred pregnant women had come through here, some meeting his eyes, some avoiding him, some oblivious. The trail was cold. But the one woman he sought had shown a preference for rail travel and night travel, so here he waited.

The California Zephyr backed in at 7:20, a few minutes early. In the swarming crowd, with its overwhelming sounds and scents, he almost missed the vibration of his phone. On the second buzz, he cupped the unit close to his ear.

"Slightly pregnant blonde, age 25 or so, blue or gray eyes, no escort. Climbing out of shuttle now. Looks like—yeah, just one bag."

"Perfect." He moved to stand in one of the doorways to the street exit; from here he could see her whether she went to the ticket window or the information window.

The phone vibrated again. He opened it mechanically, his ears pricked for the sound of her voice.

"Busted. Mom's calling us home."

"Head home then, and tell all the guys I said thanks."

"We said you hadn't marked ground outside the facility, Memphis. Don't get caught. Really—don't get caught."

"I don't plan to." So long as he wasn't caught outside a transportation facility, he hadn't trespassed on Denver's turf, and wouldn't pay the penalty.

Here she came.

Her confident stride gave none of the lost-waif impression he'd seen before. She wore white slacks and a pink sweater that rolled loosely to frame her face.

Six feet short of the ticket window, three men intercepted her. She jumped back just before they could box her in. One of the men spoke to her while the others crowded her. She backed away, a question in her voice.

The speaking man flashed a badge and the others grabbed for her elbows.

She neatly evaded their grasp, scowling, her own hands chopping the air in negation. Her mouth moved, but the chaos of the crowd swallowed her words.

People turned to stare.

The men grabbed at her again. She dodged, planting her heel in one man's instep and slinging her shopping bag at another.

The men were amateurs. They stepped back, looked at one another, then gathered their mass for a collective attack.

She threw a narrow-eyed, assessing glance across the room, and screeched, *"Gun!"*

Screams broke out, echoed and re-echoed. People pushed to get out, pushed to get a better view, pushed to keep from being crushed against a wall—and some of them just pushed.

The woman lunged for the street exit.

Esau sidestepped to let her by.

Her gaze caught his, and her eyes widened.

One man, a human, grabbed her pink sweater at the shoulder. Esau caught the man's hand and snapped it.

The human's bones shattered. He shrieked.

Fear surged through the crowd in waves of noise and scent. From the jigsaw-pile of limbs and torsos and luggage, a uniform emerged.

Time to move out.

As he turned, another human swung openhanded at him. Esau ducked, guessing at more than seeing the slap-patch in the man's palm, and boosted the man just that extra bit off balance. The human fell against an avidly watching teenager.

The teenager crumpled, unconscious. A pair of girls behind him squealed, triggering another wave of noise that splashed off the ceiling and washed back among the people as pandemonium. Terrified people flooded through the exit, and Esau let them push him ahead.

Instinct and the press of the crowd pushed him across the street to an open area lined by small, aromatic shops.

He paused to filter out the farrago of jostling, shouting, perfumed humans, a nearby brewery, and several ethnic cuisines. A sense of being watched drew his attention. He pivoted to face her.

She stood with her back to a scrawny excuse for a tree, her shopping bag held like a shield in front of her. Despite the milling people between them, their gazes meshed.

According to the scraps of recovered data from the lab, she was Subject H-31-K, aged twenty-six, blood type O positive, slightly nearsighted, slightly anemic. He'd seen her blood scans and her bone density scans. She still had her tonsils, adenoids, appendix, and wisdom teeth. But he didn't know her name.

She watched him warily. Not an invitation. But, for the moment at least, she'd stopped running. He spread his palms in a gesture of peaceful intent, and walked slowly toward her.

The mob noises and the blaring horns and the cops' whistles receded before the reality of the tall man. She'd half-convinced herself he belonged in her dreams. But here he was, wearing an expensively tailored suit. As real as the shiny pink lines left on her arms after the scabs peeled off.

If he was the villain of this game, he certainly went to extremes to establish his cover. The crunch of bones and the fake-cop's scream had been convincing. But letting the man approach was like opening a lion's cage. He seemed to know that. When her courage wavered, he stopped in his tracks.

As soon as she caught her breath and scolded herself out of bolting, he came closer.

The third time he stopped at the right instant, she bristled. He was reading her, like a predator reads prey.

He took one step forward and settled in place, relaxed and alert. Like a gunslinger. Like a wolf. "I'm Esau Kirkland."

She wrestled down the impulse to respond politely. "Are you from Memphis or did you just happen to be there when I was?"

"Memphis is home."

She *had* to use that Ole Miss accent in the next game. He sauntered closer.

She put up a hand. "Stop there."

He stopped, just out of reach.

She said, "If you're a Paladin for hire, I'd love to hire you. But if you're for hire, you're already hired, aren't you?"

A guy didn't get as prosperous as he looked just by wandering through train stations in search of potential clients.

His nostrils flared, as if sniffing her. His gaze fell lower than her eyes, but not much lower.

Her skin heated. The cowl-necked sweater had covered all the marks earlier, but now it sagged out of shape, showing her throat to the collarbones. Her hands wanted to pull the cloth up to her chin. She made fists instead.

The man's voice deepened. "Which one of them bit you?"

More heat rushed under her skin, and buzzed in her ears. "Go away, Esau Kirkland."

"I can't go without you."

"Can't?"

"Won't."

"Are you stating an intent to kidnap me?"

His nose pinched and flared, and his pupils dilated. "No."

"Why do I hear a 'but' hiding inside that word?"

His smile softened his eyes without affecting his mouth all that much. Sadness lurked there. Lived there. Esau Kirkland had lost something or someone, and he wore the loss like a backpack of rocks. "Because no one can anticipate or avert all contingencies."

He looked toward the train station, where people pushed to get back in despite the uniforms blocking the door. "I dislike mass transport. What would persuade you to drive with me?"

"The steering wheel," she said promptly. His gaze snapped back to her. She added, "Your name on all the rental car paperwork. And answers to my questions."

Chapter 4

Tyler woke suddenly, the steering wheel jerking in her hands. Lights and a roaring noise zeroed her focus to the road ahead, and the blinding eyes of a dragon. She froze.

A big hand tugged gently at the wheel, easing the tiny rental car to the right as the dragon—a triple-trailer truck—blared its horn at her and on past her, doppler-ing off like a ghostly moan. *Those things do not belong on two-lane roads!*

The hand fell away.

Tyler pulled on over to the rough edge of the road and let the rental jounce to a stop. The dash clock said 4:07. Here in the leading edge of winter, four o'clock was the deepest part of the night.

She rested her head on the steering wheel, remembering the dragon rush-ing at her, reducing the image to fractal elements. She had to put that rush in a game. The guys would love it.

She deliberately did not look at her passenger. If it was Bastian Truc sitting there, this would be his chance to comment on her need to control versus his ability to control.

But instead the big man said, "I suggest a motel."

She peered at the empty and fake-looking road spread under her headlights, at the rocks and twiggy bushes on either side of it. "What motel?"

"We passed an exit three or four miles back."

"Okay." Her hands were sweating while the heater blasted stale air at her scorched ankles. She turned it off. "You want to drive, or you trust me to get us that far?"

His voice held a touch of amusement. "You have enough adrenaline in you to stay awake for the next few minutes."

Adrenaline. That was the aluminum-foil taste in her mouth, the sick sweat on her skin. She U-turned to follow the dragon's red tail-lights. The turn set her stomach on a spin it didn't want to stop. *Ugh. So much for the old iron stomach.*

She pushed the lever from 'off' to 'vent.' They wouldn't freeze to death in a few minutes, and the fresh cold air reduced the roiling sensation. "I don't feel good," she muttered.

"Is it an adrenaline reaction, or the baby?"

She stood on the brake. The car bucked sharply, but she let up before the wheels locked. Last thing she needed was to let the car spin out of control, roll over, and pin them to the map two miles east of the middle of nowhere.

No, the last thing I need is to be pregnant and on the run from some unknown entity. Actually, pregnant and on the run was better than pregnant and caught.

Caught and caught. She smothered a half-hysterical laugh, tightened her grip on the wheel and brought the little car back up to cruising speed.

How does he know? Might be too early to take a pregnancy test, but she knew what a test would show. She'd carried the idea like a hidden obscenity of a tattoo, something she couldn't look at too closely. And now he had to bring it out in the open. He touched the back of her hand lightly, inquiring without speaking.

She spoke to the windshield, to the road ahead. "I don't know which it is. I'm not used to being plural—or to being quite so frightened."

"I'll take care of you."

Who are you to make a statement like that? What makes you think I need— She bit her lip. *Be rational, Tyler.* Right now she needed muscle, would need him until she identified who was chasing her, and until she found a way to stop them.

She flicked the man a sideways glance. She had not asked any of the questions that swarmed and tangled in her mind. She'd waited for him to talk. But Mr. Mysterious remained silent.

He sat now with his back and broad shoulders against his door. The dashboard lights played Halloween on the right side of his face while the left remained entirely dark.

She shivered, and his big hand cut off the vent fan.

"Once we get inside," he said, "you should eat a little something. It's been two hours since you had that packet of crackers, and the scare with that truck burned all the sugar out of your bloodstream."

She opened her mouth to snap at him, and bit the remark off. He was right. Again. She concentrated on the green sign identifying the exit a mile ahead, and said, "Talk."

"About what? How do I answer questions you haven't asked?"

"How about you figure out my best question. Answer it and move on from there."

"Single room, king-sized bed is my choice. A motel would need name and ID for you if you got a separate room, and I could defend you better if we stay together."

Oh, man! How about reeeal close together? Waitaminnit— "King- sized beds usually come only one per room."

"That's right. My motives are, of course, purely selfish. I can stretch out, and you can keep me warm."

She resisted the urge to smack him. *When it's my idea, it's female initiative. When it's your idea, it's male arrogance.* Then she shook herself. *Balls, Tyler. Hold the hissy for a real problem.*

Two motels squatted alongside a pancake house. The one-story motel was dark; orange neon from the restaurant's sign illuminated its potholed and overgrown parking lot. The few cars hunched in patches of weeds, as if they'd been abandoned there long ago, as if a nuclear bomb or a disease-spreading comet had wiped out all the people for miles.

The two-story motel's lights glittered on the glass and metal of a couple dozen cars. The hour pretty well guaranteed they'd be waking up the night clerk. She hated waking people up. *But that's why motels have night clerks, right? To welcome the road-dazed traveler. And occasionally dial nine-one-one.*

Esau started to open his door. She hit the switch to lock it. "First explain. You need to defend me from whom?"

He looked away. "I don't know exactly who they are."

"How did you come to have an interest in defending me?"

"If I go in alone, no one will be able to look at a picture of you later and say, 'yes, she was here.' Unlock it."

She unlocked it.

He climbed out, stretching hugely, giving her a guilty twinge for the number of hours he had been folded up in a bucket seat. But he had rented the damned car. He'd chosen it. Why should she feel guilty?

She rolled down his window. "Esau! Agreeing to answer my questions carries an unspoken agreement to answer them when I ask, not a week or so later."

"Yes, I was just coming to that conclusion." He paused to button his blazer. "Maybe that's a sign we have great minds?"

"How did protecting me come to be your job?"

He turned toward the glass door of the motel.

I can drive off without you, Smartass!

He spun to face her. She stared back.

He turned again, slowly, and entered the lobby. A dark woman wearing a white blouse and a skewed tie came into view at the desk.

Tyler tilted her seat back a notch. The adrenaline had burned off, leaving her hungry and tired. Who the blazes was Esau Kirkland? He acted like a private cop, or a bodyguard, but he didn't dress like one. That suit, so blue it was nearly black, had a hand-tailored fit. Why had he stepped in as her white knight?

He'd asked *'which of them'* as if it made a difference. It could make a difference only if he knew 'them' or some of them. If he'd been part of it, though, he wouldn't have to ask.

What do you know, Esau Kirkland, and why are you here with me? Just exactly how much trouble am I in?

The lot's ragged hedge waved like an arena crowd. She was glad to be out of that wind. They were hours south of Denver, maybe an hour north of Amarillo, but November was November, and the wind would be cold.

Another movement caught her eye: Esau at the door. He unhurriedly surveyed the lot, left and right. Then he locked his eyes on her. A thrill tightened her skin. *That one's mine.*

You're deluding yourself, Tyler. Odds were, Esau Kirkland (if that was his real name) had been hired to bring her back to Memphis—or back to Bastian.

He looked at her from under his heavy brows, focused and intent. A predator.

Hungry, but not for money. He couldn't look at her that way and be thinking of money.

He wanted her. He meant to have her.

He crouched by her door. She lowered the window.

"I'll go through the building," he said. "You drive around that far end; park right at the laundry room entrance and wait. I told the clerk you'd turned your ankle, so she expects me to block the door open and carry you in."

"You don't want me to leave a scent trail."

He smiled his bare-hint of a smile.

"They came for me with a dog before. How did you know?"

"What faster way to search a motel, if your quarry might be using a false name or a disguise?"

"Do we need to go buy some black pepper or something?"

"I always carry a few packets with me."

"Oh." She studied his laugh lines, or crows-feet, or whatever. How much of her trust in him was based on those lines?

He reached as if to touch her, but hesitated, and dropped his hand on the car door. "You're too tired to think, sweetheart. You need to trust me until you get enough rest to think on your own again."

He was right. Again. She raised the window and turned on the heater, sighing when the warm air poured around her feet. *Denver would've been a good place to buy warm boots.*

She found the laundry room door easily; he was standing in it. She expected to climb on his back, but he scooped his arms under her and carried her like a bride. The thought moved her insides. She nuzzled his warm, warm neck, and he made a noise like a purr.

Yeah, this one's mine. He tasted as good as he smelled, evoking a driftwood campfire with the sound of waves and guitars in the night. Her tongue teased the sensitive pulse points that deepened his purr to a growl and tightened his arms about her.

At the door to the room, he paused. "If this is a game," he said, "stop. You don't play games with me."

He sounded like he spoke while holding his keys in his teeth. She twisted to see his face, but he looked away. She could say she played games for a living, but he might take that wrong. Besides, this was a different game entirely.

She kissed the triangular muscle under his jaw. He growled again. Suddenly reckless, she locked her mouth on his neck, suckling and rasping her tongue over his heated, salty skin.

He shouldered the door open and threw her on the bed, kicking the door shut in the same fluid motion. In mid-bounce, she met his weight, and it bore her down. He buried his face in her hair. His chest heaved with each rasping breath, sending hot eddies around her neck, while his pulse hammered between them.

And to judge from the bulge under his calfskin belt, Esau Kirkland had a big one.

He growled. "If you are playing, stop. I don't know enough about you, and you sure don't know enough about me. If you think you have to do this to buy my loyalty, stop." He breathed heavily a moment. "Hear me now; I will protect you to the death whether we mate or not."

Mate? Did this jargon signal some new game she needed to know the rules for? She couldn't see his face in the dark.

His hand brushed over her face. She nuzzled the tough skin of his palm. He stood suddenly, leaving her awkwardly spread and alone.

"I need to move the car before it's towed. Keep the heater off. It would create an overpressure in the room and push your scent out under the door. Don't turn on the light either."

Don't you dare say to stay inside and keep the door shut!

He cleared his throat. "When I come back, be in skin if you want me, or in clothes if you don't."

Chapter 5

When a choice arose, where the correct decision was so obvious that it seemed to obviate the point of making a decision, a prudent gamer backed up a step and reconsidered the situation.

Balls. She shucked her clothes and piled them on the chair.

Her foster mother's exasperated voice rang in her ears. *You have so many clothes you can afford to let them go to ruin?*

No, she didn't have so many clothes. Effectively, she owned only what she could reach right now. On the other hand, if she stood at the closet-nook to hang up her blouse, that would put her feet right in front of the crack under the door. She pictured a cartoon wolf padding along the hallway on hands and feet, nose elongating to sniff under each door, and couldn't suppress a grin.

In the dark, she draped her things over the chair.

Esau ought to bring her clothes bag when he came back. She'd forgotten it when being carried in, but it hadn't been in her line of sight. Esau, though, would have to move her bag to get to his. Surely even a guy could not overlook it.

She grinned again. *I make a pretty penny knowing what guys will see and what they won't.* But a game controller in his hands and a screen two feet from his nose made a guy a hundred times more attentive than real life ever could. The game encapsulated the world for him, giving him a way and a reason to truly focus.

Like Esau focuses on me.

Any female who worked in an overwhelmingly male world knew the feeling of eyes on her. On top of that, Tyler was known for the game-worlds she created. Gamers reading her nametag at cons tended to drop things and babble. Sometimes she put a WarDove pilot's name on her tag instead, to count the double-takes and the rapt stares of recognition.

Esau's eyes already had that focus, but was it real?

Never trust a man until you've puked on his feet. A cheerleader had confided that over the last beer of a long night. *Until that happens, he doesn't see you. He sees what he thinks of as you. It's all fantasy.*

She yanked loose the bedcovers and squirmed between the cold sheets. What did Esau Kirkland see when he looked at her with that intent gaze?

Feet made shadows under the door; he had approached with no sound. "It's me," he said before working the lock.

She huddled, naked, under the covers. She'd declared herself. He could crush her ego so easily, simply by not noticing, by undressing and getting in his side of the king-sized bed and turning his back on her and going to sleep.

He threw her a glance as he locked the door, and set down his gym bag and her shopping bag. He tucked something under the door, blotting out the bar of light from the hall.

For a moment she couldn't see past the little red lights on the hair-dryer and the coffee maker. When her eyes adjusted, she saw his muscled back. His bare muscled back. As he stripped, he methodically laid his clothes across the chair with hers.

His silence unnerved her. At the same time, it freed her to watch him. He moved as gracefully as a dancer, while the crimson light caressed his sculpted musculature. *Oh, man.* Was he a weightlifter? Or a model, to have a butt like that?

Just as he turned toward her, he stepped forward, silhouetted by the red light.

She blinked, setting that image in her mind forever, and then realized what she had missed.

"Step back, Esau."

He obediently retreated, raising one hand to throw shadow over his face. "Why?"

"I want to see you."

The hair on his chest arrowed down, and the shadowed outlines of his abdominal muscles flowed together just right to draw attention to his up-thrust and very thick cock.

Wow.

That unfamiliar contour was a foreskin. She'd heard that an uncut cock was more sensitive. She felt dazed and overly warm, and her insides melted in readiness.

"Let me tell you, Esau." Her voice was hoarse. "You are something fine to look at."

He growled something she couldn't make out. In silhouette again, he came to her and snatched the bedclothes down to her shins. He froze, his muscles bunching under his skin.

Was he looking at the marks left from Memphis? At the older scars from when she'd learned not to ride motorcycles? Her fingers found the edge of a sheet, and twitched it over her lap.

He stood up straight. "Are you withdrawing the invitation?"

"No," she croaked. She swallowed. "No, I'm not."

"You want me, now, as we are?"

She frowned. "Are you trying to get me to beg?"

"No." He fell to his knees beside the bed. "No, I'm not."

His big hands, hot and rough-skinned, brushed away the sheet. He stroked her shoulders and breasts, and down her flanks, pausing at the scars and moving on without comment.

Rough fingertips rested under her navel, and tickled down across the top layer of hair. He caught curls between his fingers and moved her skin in a circle.

Shivers of expectation raced through her, and delicious heat fought back the chill of the dark room.

Warm breath gusted across her shoulder, and a tongue flicked along her jaw line. The mattress dipped as he added his weight to hers. Her knees parted to accommodate his coarse-haired legs, and the bed moved as he did. Closing her eyes in the darkness, she basked in the living heat he radiated.

A hand passed over her side again, waist to shoulder, slowly pressing, leaving her skin more sensitive and more alive in its trail. She tasted his collarbone, the salt on his skin, as he adjusted his angle. Blunt pressure nudged her lower lips.

Panic exploded through her. *Nooo!* She wrenched sideways. *Let me go! Let me go!*

She gasped in enough air to scream, but a hand folded tightly across her mouth. Only a muffled grunt got past that big hand.

Let me go! She fought him. Blind, deaf, and mindlessly afraid, she strained against his arms, his legs, his heavy weight. She twisted and bucked, trying to throw off the weight. Her clawing hands ripped indiscriminately at the chest and arms that held her to the bed. *Let me go!*

She bit, hard. The hand did not relent.

An endless loop of sound became words. "Don't scream," he said urgently. "Don't scream; don't scream. We can't have the cops coming in. Don't scream."

Had he been saying that all along? For how long? She nodded tensely. Her breath rushed past his loosened grip. She lay on her side at the edge of the bed, with Esau Kirkland's rangy body wrapped around hers, immobilizing her.

"Can you hear me?" he asked. "Are you with me?"

"Let me up, Kirkland." Her voice was raw and wild and hardly human-sounding. "I got to sit up."

He whipped her upright, moving her so fast her teeth snapped together. She sat in the vee of his long legs, slowly relearning to breathe. One arm circled her loosely while his big, rough hand stroked her back.

She wanted to lean into him, let his strength surround her and his heat seep through her. She wanted away from him so she could breathe cold, free air instead of his salty, woodsy scent. She sucked in a breath, tasting his aroma and the blood on his skin, and burst into tears.

He held her, crooning wordlessly into her hair, stroking her arm or her back, patting her shoulder, and just letting her cry.

Eventually she hiccupped to a halt, and blew her nose on the t-shirt he held for her. "There were these three guys, Esau. Three guys plugged me and if one of them passed me on the street tomorrow I wouldn't know it was him."

"You won't see any of them."

"They could be people I know! People I work with, laughing at me, and I'll have to pretend nothing's wrong because I can't prove anything against anyone."

"It won't happen. They—died. The quake buried them all."

Good! With the thought came uncertainty. What did he know? What was the pain in his voice? Sympathy, or more?

He massaged the base of her skull.

"Talk to me, Esau. Who did this to me? And why?"

His fingers tangled in her hair, and moved from massage to a simple stroking.

She tried again. "If strangers grabbed me at random, they would have had their fun and dumped me nearby, in Atlanta, not at a Trucker's Delite on the Arkansas/Tennessee border."

He still didn't answer.

"Esau, talk to me."

"I hate giving partial answers, and I don't know the full ones." His fingers rested against the nape of her neck. He seemed to be choosing his words.

She lay against him, listening to his heartbeat, and waited.

"Someone," he said finally, "some male—I don't know who—was paid fifty thousand dollars to deliver you to a laboratory on the Arkansas border. The lab was to keep you sedated for five days. After five days, if a certain signal was received, the lab was to return you and receive one hundred troy ounces of 18-karat gold for their risk. Without that signal, they would keep you and place one thousand troy ounces of 18-karat gold in a New Orleans bank vault."

Alternative plans, both very well-funded. *Bastian.* He never took one step without planning contingencies for the next two steps.

With her gone, Bastian could take HandPlus as his own, and gut it before anyone noticed. If the Asian licensing agreements came through as expected, he could spin several millions out of FuckWare alone. She could also see him paying out the company's dollars for ransom, if one of his cross-schemes fell apart.

Even if Bastian lost out on HandPlus, over half a million dollars in gold would let him bust free of his mama's control. If anything ever could.

Aside from her handful of shareholders, though, who'd profit from buying her? Why would a lab pay out that kind of money? Where was the profit?

She looked at the mirror, at Esau's rough-hewn, sympathetic face. Blood streaked his neck, shoulders, upper arms. She'd scratched the hell out of him. *We won't quite match, though—you don't have bites on you.* Except on his hand. "What was the point of three guys banging my unconscious bod for five days?"

Please, Esau, don't say for the fun of it. Besides, the three young men had not acted for the fun of it—one had even tried to protect her. She frowned, trying to pin down that impression, but it crumbled like a dry sand-castle.

"They had you less than 30 hours."

Thirty hours? She probed her memory for any sense of time, and instead found a urine smell, heard an animal scream. *The other girl.* "Lucky me."

He flinched. "The recoverable data doesn't refer to fertility testing, but that obviously was part of the deal."

"Why?"

"While I can't disparage the power of pure curiosity, economic factors are in play."

Balls. "Why is my fertility anyone's business?"

"Because you are something more than human," he said in a low, slow voice, as if the words were dragged from him.

More than human... Her derisive snort didn't come out right. She blew her nose again. "What is there besides human?"

"Shapeshifters."

She tried to grin. "Shapeshifters? You mean like a werewolf? Hate to tell you, but I've never changed shape and I'm not allergic to silver."

He spread his hand in front of her face. His nails thickened and whitened, and grew to pointed claws extending an inch past his fingertips.

Claws.

She shrank away from him. It wasn't real. Couldn't be real.

"Don't scream," he said quietly.

She looked quickly into his shadowed face. Her ears had already told her his words weren't a threat, but believing it took seeing it. Whatever else he might be, Esau wasn't a threat. Not to her. Not tonight.

Claws. She touched one gingerly. "Can I do that?"

"If you could, you'd know by now."

Yeah, I'd know. And I can't. But if you want to think I'm something special, you just go right ahead.

One of the helicopter stunt pilots she liked to send to the gaming conventions had an extensive collection of were-creature stories. The winter wolves of Krakow, turning back an army of Tatars. Bear dancers luring hillbilly girls from their cabins at night. Mama Coyote and the lost children, *los niños perdidos.*

She turned his hand over in hers. His fingers seemed a little shorter. Her teeth had left a tattoo of blood-blisters in his palm. When she touched the mark apologetically, it faded.

She dropped his hand and rubbed the chill-bumps off her arms.

The bloody furrows she had raked across his skin healed and faded. She watched one line go pink and shorten. When it vanished, she searched for the others. All gone.

If someone was interested in her fertility, on the loopy notion she was not quite human, why use plain humans as the other half of the breeding equation? No reason, if werewolves could be used. "Tell me you weren't one of those three guys."

"I was not." His voice went very deep when he said that. The vibrations resonated all through her.

She rubbed her arms again. She was naked in bed with a werewolf. Her business partner/would-be fiancé had sold her to the faceless black hats, but at least she had a werewolf on her side. "I think I have enough information to process right now, Esau. I'll let you know when I can handle more."

"Rest, then." He shimmied down to lie on his side with her back nestled against his front, and pulled the covers up.

His cock prodded her butt, and she stopped herself from squirming against it. Esau combed her hair with his fingers as if nothing was going on below the waist. She caught herself squirming again.

"I ought not have the hots for you," she said abruptly, and bit her tongue hard.

"You can't help it," he said in that slow voice of his. *Cainnt heyelp eeit.* "The most primitive part of your brain knows you'll need someone to care for you soon, and has spent the last couple of weeks looking for a strong, dependable male. Now that same part of your brain wants to bind me to you. Sleep easy. I said I would take care of you, and I will."

"I haven't had the hots for anyone else in the past weeks."

"Good." He threw one leg over her and hooked her closer. "I've never been the jealous sort, but something about you wakes up a few primitive parts of my brain, too."

Brain? His thick cock pulsed against her butt. "Are you going to get any rest with that thing pumped up like it is?"

"I might if you held still."

His irritation silenced her. She breathed in time with him, watching their faint red shadows on the wall. Mostly his shadow. The curve of her hip showed; everything else was Esau's hard angles and lines.

She burrowed deeper in the covers. The curved swell of her hip still rose above Esau's silhouette.

His cock prodded her butt again. She could pretend she didn't notice it. She could pretend to sleep and maybe ease into real sleep.

Esau's arm draped over her waist. She ran her fingers over his perfectly ordinary square-cut nails. He held her fingertips lightly between his for a moment, then let go. She moved his hand to cup her breast. Against her back, his heartbeat sped up, and his cock throbbed in time.

"It's got to be awful to be a guy, and advertise your interest whether you want to or not."

"Did I mention the primitive part of the male brain, sweetheart?" His breath gusted in her hair, tickling her temple. "It's shooting out messages like 'Hey! Naked woman in reach! Beautiful! Fertile! *NEKKID.*'"

She laughed. He laughed with her, and the sound loosened her tension.

She had to want more out of a man than dibs on a protector. Since Memphis, she'd avoided speaking to men, or meeting their eyes. Some deep part of her trusted Esau, though.

And yet the emotional scars from Memphis wouldn't let her have him.

His big fingers covered a bite mark now, and she wondered if he could feel the pink lines. Those lines would fade from her skin, but she'd always see them. What happened in Memphis would rule her life—if she didn't take charge.

Right now.

She backed off that thought. Being aggressive in bed took a confidence she couldn't summon. She turned over. "Esau? Could we try that again?"

"That what?"

"I want you to turn back the clock a few minutes."

"*Woman?* Do you *specialize* in mixed signals?"

She flinched, and he pulled her closer.

"I'm sorry," they said together, her speaking into his chest as he spoke into her hair.

"I've never let my past run my present," she said. "I don't like the idea. Would it put you in too much—um, discomfort—to go as far as you can before I freak out?"

His big hand weighed her breast, then brushed up and down her arm. "You deserve hours of touching and tasting, sweetheart. Hours of exploring and teasing and warming. I wanted to wake you to sensations you've never dreamed of. I walked in here thinking I was man enough to do that."

"You are," she whispered.

He made a choked noise and hugged her tighter. "When I saw you, I knew if I tried, I'd go crazy—and then even if I didn't hurt you, you would freak."

"I freaked anyway," she said, and found the face-inviting corner where his neck met his shoulder.

"But not because I hurt you."

"I'm sorry."

He sighed. "If we got too far into it, I don't know if I could stop. The moon governs when a female is too wild to hold onto her senses, but the male is always ready to lose control."

She tasted his hot, salty skin. He should be steaming in the cold air. Under the covers, she traced the groove between two ribs, and down his hard-muscled abdomen. His breath hissed between his teeth. *Control.* "I'll take the chance."

"I'm not sure you should."

"Luckily, you're not the boss of me." She pushed one leg under him.

He hesitated, then rolled over top of her in a crawling position. His arms and legs caged her like iron pillars. His powerful shoulders blocked out the light. Not holding her in. Holding the world out. Narrowing the focus to just the two of them.

She looked up at him, dark and solid with red light tinting his left side. *This might work. It just might. I don't need fireworks, Esau. I just want—I don't know. I want right now.*

She opened her legs. He moved one knee between hers, then slowly lowered his chest until his hairs tickled her nipples.

She shivered, and he backed off. "No—it's okay. I'm okay."

"I'm an idiot—you need to be on top, in control."

"No!" She caught his arms and held them in place. "Too exposed. I want you between me and everything else."

"I can do that." He rolled unhurriedly to one side, though, and stroked all the shivers out of her skin. His big hand rested a moment at the hollow inside her hipbone, and turned to cup between her legs. "The spirit may be willing, but the flesh is dry. I'd hurt you bad."

You need to stop being right at the wrong time. She was relaxed enough. Horny enough. But not all her signals were in sync. She cast about for some image to bring the cream. *Esau's muscled form glowing in the red light.* She felt a hint of slip. Not enough. "You got anything in your bag that might help?"

"I'm thinking." He rolled off her and went to dig in his bag. The red light limned his muscles, and her mouth watered.

His head came up and he turned to her. With the light playing over him to maximum advantage, he slid one hand over his upward-straining cock. He went rigid, his muscles in sharp relief. *Oh, man.*

She cupped her breasts for him, using her fingers like little mouths to pinch her nipples, offering them to the naked man in the ruby light.

He pumped his hand up and down his cock. She passed one hand down her abdomen, remembering the living warmth of his hand, and used two fingers to part her lips.

She thought of his mouth on her, and gasped at the electric zing. And *yes*, that was wet. The sweet tang of it spiced the cold air. "Esau!"

He leaped for her, landing with hands and knees boxing her shoulders and hips. Just as quickly, he moved to the side. His hand cupped her breast in rough-textured warmth and his face moved over her shoulder, inhaling, testing her reaction by scent and touch. She looked at the ceiling, waiting for panic.

No panic.

"Okay," she whispered. "Bring it on."

He crawled over her, nuzzling her neck and shoulders as he moved. She lay back and opened to him, framing his flanks with her shins. He lowered his sculpted body, and this time the blunt pressure brought another electric zing. She arched to him, working her hips to get him all the way in at once. He slid in—hot and sleek and perfect.

He withdrew. "Is it good?"

Yes! Her answer came out a barely voiced keening noise.

He filled her again, with deliberate care. His lips touched hers with a reverent delicacy. By the time the third slow stroke eased in, her insides had stretched to take him without any question.

Now she wanted more than the fullness. She wanted the passion. She caught his rough-edged face in both hands.

"Esau, I'm not going to get anywhere if you stay in first gear."

"Then let's rev things up a bit." He slung his hips forward, driving her breath out in a gasp.

She gripped his shoulders to brace, just in time for the next hard stroke. *Yes!*

With every thrust, he pressed her clit and pumped more tension into her muscles.

Excitement tingled the soles of her feet, and with no more warning the glory burst across her vision, bringing her alive as she exploded from within.

Esau surged forward, and fell groaning across her.

Chapter 6

She woke to his hand stroking from her shoulder along her arm and across her flank. His erection again nudged at the small of her back. She turned to him.

He propped up on one elbow and smiled down at her. It was the gentlest, most real smile she had seen in days. Maybe in months. She couldn't help smiling back, however goofy and sleepy her smile must look. She rolled away from him to hide it.

His hand paused on her hip, and those long fingers massaged the bony plate at the base of her spine. Luscious warmth spread through her pelvis.

"If you want to," she told the pillow, "go ahead. If this is a dream, I don't want to wake up."

"A little less than enthusiastic? Should I stop?"

She searched for any hint of hurt ego in that voice, and found none. He kissed the back of her neck, his lips caressing there while his fingers carried on at her lower spine.

She squeezed her thighs together experimentally. *Tender.* The memory sent twinges of pleasure and a trickle of moisture where it counted. But as fun it might be to contemplate more of the same, she probably couldn't tolerate anything but slow, easy loving. If that.

"You need to sleep, don't you?"

"Don't stop," she said. "Unless you want conniptions and contortions, that is. If that's what you want, roll over and dream your own dream. I'm happy lying here and not doing anything."

His weight moved on the bed, and his arms slid around her, his hands clasping her lower abdomen. "Sleep, sweetheart."

⁂

Her smothered cry woke him, erecting his fangs and snapping his muscles rigidly alert. Daylight glowed around the edges of the curtains, giving plenty of light to see the chair, the dresser and TV, the cooking area and their bags to the left. His mate whimpered again, sleepily, in a room that held no threat.

He smoothed her fine hair away from her face and yawned until his fangs retracted.

"I have you," he murmured when he could. "You're safe."

"You're warm." She snuggled in, pressing her softness against him, and sighed in dreamy contentment. A man could get used to that. He made a mental note. *When we get our own bedroom, close off the heater vents.*

Her nose wrinkled, and her eyes opened. She whipped her head around, her mouth opening in an *Oh!* of alarm. He laid a finger across her lips. They were even softer than he'd expected.

She relaxed, sinking into the bed and pillow, and smiled.

"G'morning, mister tall, dark, and horny." She yawned, stretching languorously and with full attention to each tantalizingly curved muscle in turn. "Or is it afternoon?"

Before he could recover from that hypnotizing sight to say *morning*, she caught his hand and wrapped her mouth around the tip of his forefinger. She massaged it with lips and tongue, her eyes closed as if to better concentrate.

He sank into the hot, wet contrast between slick lips and pebbled tongue. A man could definitely get used to this.

From under the blankets, warm air brought her aroma, and his. Delicately questing fingers traced his dick up and down, tightening his skin from scalp to foot. She weighed his balls in one hand and shivered.

"Oh, man." She released his finger and brushed her face through his chest hair. "No wonder I'm sore."

Sore? Shit! "You're hurt? You need a healer—a doctor?"

Her eyes, a wolfish pale blue, opened wide. "No, no! I'm not hurt."

Confused images whirled in his mind. The aches he'd lived with while weightlifting as a kid, and the beating he'd taken when his liniment stank up the boys' dorm. Precisely how fragile was a human? A half-human? He felt her abdomen. "The baby?"

Her laughter jiggled under his hand. She caressed his balls, instantly riveting his attention there.

"Esau, if vigorous sex could end a pregnancy, how many teenagers would ever have a baby?"

He inhaled deeply, drinking in her scent mingled with his. So long as he kept his scent imbedded in her skin, only the best noses could tell at first whiff that she was not a full-shifter.

That uncertainty would soon work to her advantage; shifters did not officially recognize a pregnancy until it had survived the first full moon. But injuring a pregnant female past that moon was the only crime worse than publicly tearing up a human.

She brushed her lips over his left nipple and exhaled a wave of warmth across that sensitive skin. Even more of his blood supply rushed south. But he needed more than mating. He needed her trust, and her name.

"If I told you where the sorest spot was," she murmured, each lip movement a kiss, "would you rub it for me?"

He held his fangs in. "On one condition."

She leaned back and looked at him, teasing and wariness blending in her fascinatingly complex expression. "Being?"

"When the slamming thrusts of my magnificent manhood, the blatant evidence of my manly ardor, drive the love-lava to erupt from my core and I groan with a guttural outpouring of manly ardor—"

She slapped his shoulder. "You said 'manly ardor' twice!"

"Sorry. Replace the duplicate with 'soul-shattering intensity'—or maybe 'blinding pulsation of ecstasy'—and tell me what name to cry out."

She sat up. "What?"

"I want to know your name," he said patiently.

He wanted to know what she called herself, what her friends called her. The rest of her human life might be so much trash by the side of the road, but she could keep the name.

She bit her lip and stared at him.

She needs time to think. He extricated himself from the bed and zipped open his bag. "How about I heat you a packet of rice? Can you stomach anything stronger than chicken broth on it?"

"What are my options?"

Yesterday she'd gagged at chili. He set that aside. Best stick to chicken broth. "Smoked oysters, eggplant, jambalaya—"

She lurched for the wastebasket.

Shit. No jokes about food! He gathered her hair as she knotted up.

He blew across her sweating neck to soothe her, his stomach clenching in sympathy. When she slowly unknotted, he relaxed with her. *False alarm.*

She slumped sideways and looked up at him. "You, sir, are a sick bastard. Never mind the food. Not hungry."

"If I'm Sikh Bastard, who are you?"

"Tyler Randolph."

He'd expected a lie, but Randolph for shifters was like Johnson for humans. Had she been raised by a Family? Despite the lucrative organ market, some Families maintained a few of these conveniently sterile females to keep their young studs out of trouble. Then again, half-bloods might have adopted her to raise like any human child. "Where are you from, Tyler Randolph?" She sounded like she was from Georgia, or maybe South Carolina.

She wrapped the covers securely about her. "What am I supposed to think of you following me a thousand miles when you don't even know my name?"

"Probably that I'm a love-sick bastard."

She looked at him through her lashes. "Esau…" Under cover of that sultry look, her hand snapped out and captured his balls. "Having sex with a man who lies to me is against my religion. And a man who selectively withholds info is lying."

"Does your religion frown on holding a man's tender parts when you have steel in your voice?"

Her lips thinned with what he hoped was a suppressed giggle. If he could keep her laughing while she became accustomed to the Hidden World, she might miss her human world rather less.

"If I were to develop a religion," he mused, "I suspect that would be a basic tenet of it."

"Why did you follow me a thousand miles?"

"My religion would also preclude having to answer a question when I have neither a complete answer, nor an answer I think would be believed."

"Are the werewolves after me?"

"I don't know who is after you."

"Are the werewolves protecting me?"

"So far as I know, only I am protecting you right now. Once we get home, Lady Memphis will also protect you, with everyone we command."

She released him abruptly, and wrapped the blanket tighter around herself. "You are... Lord Memphis?"

"No. I'm called Memphis because my sister is Lady Memphis. If she had a bondmate, a husband, he would be Lord Memphis. He would have the right to speak for her, which I do not, and other rights I lack."

Her brows clenched, and her darting eyes followed thoughts that must be flying in all directions. In a tight voice, she asked, "Is Lady Raleigh named Truc?"

He thought. "Truc, yes. The tiger."

"Bastian Truc is a werewolf?" She said this slowly, perhaps not quite able to believe it.

"Lady Raleigh is a tiger, as is at least one of her daughters. I don't know about her sons, or any Truc named Bastian."

"You are not working for Truc, or his mother?"

"No."

"Then who *is* paying you to follow me?"

He answered, "No one. I followed you because from the moment we met, I had to see you safe."

Her face smoothed. "You're telling the truth."

Interesting that she could tell. He moved close enough to catch her scent without effort.

She stretched up and sniffed leisurely along his neck and collarbone. He froze, unwilling to make any movement or say any word to interrupt that intimate examination.

She smiled and snuggled down again, pressing all warm and soft and fragrant against him. He stroked her hair while her breath deepened to the peaceful rhythms of sleep. A man who got used to that would kill to keep it.

Chapter 7

Thin, rubbery cords snaked about her like so many nooses, and yanked taut. The lines radiated out like a spider's web.

Another noose darted at her and dropped over her head. She caught it on her chin to protect her throat. The cords dug in. What would break first—her aching ribs or her jaw?

She grabbed cords in each fist and fought for enough slack to wriggle loose. But where one cord stretched, the next would contract. Each gasping breath took all her strength.

The cords thrummed. All around, wolf-sized spiders fought one another. With every slash and leap, they jerked the lines. She sucked in a full breath and yelled, the ululating Golden Guardian warcry from WarDove.

The spiders turned as one to look at her. Human-faced and wolf-faced and tiger-faced, the spiders came toward her.

"Wake up, sweetheart! Wake up!"

She sat up and looked around. *A motel? Where?*

Esau was right beside her. "At least I know what you're dreaming about."

"What?"

"The Guardian Call. The kids at home love that game."

She looked down at her wrist, trying to figure out why he was holding it like that. Oh. Counting her pulse.

"Sweetheart? Tyler? You're scaring me."

Good. We can both be scared. She shook him off her wrist and swung her legs out of the warm bed.

He grasped her arm.

The air flashed white. *Hold her arms, stupid! She's coming to again. What kind of firecracker is this gal?*

She wrenched a hand free and raked at her blindfold, only to find it taped in place. She ripped one side loose, but tears smeared her vision so much she saw only the intense white light.

A hand grasped her hair and the blindfold came back over her eye.

I vote we forget the meds; let the males have at her. If she gelds one, the others will just have to work harder.

No, this one has to be under all the time. Hold still, gal—this will make you feel reeeal goood...

"Tyler!" Esau's commanding tone sliced through to her. "It's a bad movie;

you don't need to watch it right now."

"This is what changed everything." Why did her voice seem to come from farther away than his? "It has to be important." That was simple logic. What changed things was what was important.

"Not right now." His fingers traced her eyelids. "Look at me instead."

She opened her eyes to the cozy dimness of the motel room, and to Esau holding her upright. He wore a damp towel low about his hips, and he smelled of motel soap. "Listen to me," he said, "and believe me. I will take care of you."

She looked around stiffly, orienting herself to the motel room. Simple, safe, and anonymous. North of Amarillo. She tested her balance and found it good, but she still didn't want to let go of Esau. She ran a hand absently over the hair on his corded forearm, feeling the thin male skin and the hard muscle layered under it. "I guess it's time to move on?"

"Wash up, eat, and go. As soon as you're up to it."

"I'm not going to Memphis."

"Not tonight. We'll stop in Sooner City. No Man's Land."

"I'm not going to Memphis tomorrow, either."

He said soothingly, "You relax in the shower, sweetheart. I'll pack and take the bags out."

"You're not listening to me, are you?"

He slapped his bag on the dresser top, thumping the dresser against the wall. But his voice stayed calm. "I hear every word. I just don't intend to argue with you. I have to keep you safe, and I can guarantee your safety in only one place."

Memphis. She felt the cords constricting around her.

He crouched beside her and took her hands. "Sweetheart, I *can* protect you in Memphis. Please don't look like I'm a monster ready to eat you. We're all wolves there, and the power of a wolf is the power of his whole pack. No man can stand up against me once we're on my turf. You'll be *safe.*"

One-track minds don't see any room to negotiate. They were a long way from Memphis, though. She had time to find a way to convince him, or a way to dump him and get to her own turf alone. She had somewhere to be—very soon. "I'm driving."

"Then finish with a good blast of cold water." His voice smiled, but his face looked as serious as ever.

He escorted her to the exit by the laundry room, where he opened the door cautiously and sniffed the early-evening breeze.

"No one is close by. Go straight to the car. If someone stops you to ask the time or if you have a buck for an old man, scream and run. I'll deal with checkout."

"Do you think I'm competent to handle all that? Without you to guide every step, I might get lost on the way to the car, or stop to primp in front of a security camera!"

He gave her one of his almost-smiles and made a shooing motion.

A moment later, she pulled up to the front door and put the car in park. In the predawn darkness she'd been able to see in through the glass, but now in the slanting daylight she could barely see the mass of Esau's body as he stood at the desk.

She closed her eyes and pressed hard on her lower abdomen. What changes things is, by definition, important. *What am I going to do about you, you bean-sized cluster of cells?*

If I have to have a baby, why couldn't it be Esau's?

Someone touched her car door. She jumped so hard the car rocked.

Esau stood by her door. How had he come so close, and circled the car, without her noticing? He grinned broadly and pulled at her door handle. He had a question. She reached for the lock switch, but some inner reluctance slowed her hand.

Esau rapped the door impatiently with one knuckle. What did he have to ask, or tell her? Did he need money?

He grinned again, radiating reassurance and friendliness with a touch of impatience.

Her skin prickled all over. *Something's wrong.*

A long shadow leaped across the hood of the car. Esau! He thudded against the man at her door, who suddenly looked nothing like him. The two men fell together to the ground.

Three more men came out of the bushes. One piled on top of Esau and the first man, rolling on the ground. The other two lunged for the car itself.

Tyler groped the floorboard for the heavy flashlight that would be there if this car were hers. No flashlight. *Balls!* She turned the key and revved the engine.

"Go!" Esau roared.

A man jumped onto the hood and squatted there, spread-kneed, pumping his hips obscenely. His lips curled back to display costume-party fangs big enough to cut his mouth to hamburger if they were real.

Tyler threw the car into reverse, and the hood-surfer tumbled off, tangling with another man.

She popped the gear in drive. The little car knocked and shuddered, but the transmission held. She accelerated toward the clump of men and, remembering the airbag, turned at the last second to clip the men with her right fender.

The rear wheels bumped, throwing her against her seatbelt, and someone screamed. *Eww!* She gritted her teeth against the nausea and clenched her hands on the wheel and the gearshift. *It's them or me, and I didn't choose this game.*

As she passed Esau, he stood and shook off his attackers.

She shoved the gearstick up to reverse and plowed backward, hoping the guys would jump clear, jaw still clenched against the shock of speedbumps that screamed.

Esau grabbed the passenger-side door, opening it as she clicked the lock-switch. He hauled himself in.

At the same time, a man yanked her door open.

She accelerated, still in reverse, and crunched into a parked car. Alarms went off, horns blaring. Her seatbelt jerked tight across her shoulder and neck.

Oh, perfect. Kill the car, Tyler, so the bad guys can keep up with you!

But noise was good. The Black Hats did not like attention. They'd proved that in Denver. Better, the guy reaching through her door lost his hold and fell thudding against a parked car.

A robotic voice commanded, "Get *away* from the car! Get *away* from the car!"

She yanked the gearshift down to first gear for power. Momentum slammed her door shut as she revved past the motel's glass-walled entry and the open-mouthed clerk at the door. She'd done it right—the airbag didn't deploy. A face full of airbag might be a little much on top of everything else. She giggled helplessly.

A big hand cupped her neck. Her pet werewolf bracing her against whiplash. New emotions surged through her: excitement and confidence and a gut-deep joy at combat in any form. She frowned. Then the giggles overwhelmed her again.

None of the attackers was standing, but all of them were still moving. *I probably haven't killed anyone.*

She threw the gearshift forward, one gear at a time, to overdrive. Her tires squealed as she fought for control all the way back to the highway and around the onramp. A highway patrol car cruised in the opposite direction. The officer looked curiously at her and then away.

"Esau! Tell me you didn't give your real name."

"I gave them my old army name. They can trace me if they really want me."

"Do the car people have your real name? Or the army name?"

He nodded.

"So we need to change cars."

He nodded again, smiling his barely-there smile and settling into the seat. He brought up one fist and licked the cuts on his knuckles.

As she watched, a deep satisfaction warmed her, loosened all her muscles. When she examined the sensation, she found long-buried emotions about the true and good feel of a brawl. Shaking loose from restraint sweetened the air and opened the horizon.

Looking at Esau in the slanting light, she recognized the satisfaction: His.

His healed fist braced on the dashboard. He looked at her, recognition and surprise in every line of his face.

Oh, shit.

Chapter 8

They changed cars twice in Amarillo; Tyler knew how to get around the newest security systems, while Esau had the strength, the reach, and the fingernail tools to accomplish the job. He found working under her direction interesting; she gave precise instructions, but with the way she leaned her softness against him, those instructions needed lots of repeating.

He was ready to swear in frustration when he caught her quirky, teasing smile. He turned quickly and nipped her ear.

She yelped and jumped back, rubbing it.

"Woman, let me work."

She gave him a long, speculative look. "You don't expect to get away with that, do you?"

He caught her arm and pulled her close enough to kiss where he'd nipped. "Yes."

She smiled. "Wait and see."

She drove a rusty four-banger toward the heart of Tejas until the gas ran out, with him following in a pickup. They abandoned the car and laid a trail across a drift of yellow dirt to some randomly chosen car tracks. Then they topped off the pickup's tank and sprinted back to Amarillo, to the neutral turf of I-40, changing the pickup's tags again on the way.

As he tossed the latest license plate into the trash compactor behind a gas station, he asked why she was keeping track of the plate numbers.

She shrugged. "I can afford a new car. People who drive rusty shoeboxes can't. I'll find a way to pay them later."

Odds were at least one of these shoebox people would lose a job for lack of wheels, or get arrested for lack of a tag. The response to her impulse to pay for a new car would be demands for a luxury vehicle, a few years' lost wages, mental anguish, and anything else a lawyer could contemplate.

If she's comfortable enough to pay out all that, could she have been kidnapped for ransom? Or some kind of human politics? No, a human motive would not explain the lab, or the shifters jumping them at the motel.

Until puberty, neither sight nor smell could distinguish a human from a shifter from a halfie. A biologist, however, could probably identify each of them with blood or tissue samples. Had that lab known what they had in her? Were they covering contingencies, making sure?

He couldn't worry her with the implications right now. Her eyes had settled deeper into her head, ringed with bruises of exhaustion. Even after just a few hours, she needed sleep. Was that characteristic of a healthy human? Which of the healers who owed him was strong enough to treat someone who could not shift?

To the south, a combine with headlights chugged across a hidden field. Dust rose like smoke behind it, blotting out the stars. They needed to stay on the interstate to Sooner City, the Capital of No-Man's Land. With any luck, he'd find the Parkers at home at their fishing camp just outside city limits.

Snoring greeted him when he climbed back in the pickup. He adjusted her seatbelt and draped his jacket about her. For a moment he leaned over her, breathing deep. He'd kept a world-class boner for most of the past hour, no matter how he'd tried to avoid her scent. He was going to suffer no matter what; he might as well immerse himself in it.

He brushed her hair off her forehead, and an image splashed across his vision. Himself. A big man, standing naked in red light—then the image blinked out.

He needed a moment to catch his breath, to remember where he was. After another moment he tucked her in, as he'd tucked in the children when they were small.

Dream-sharing. She'd shared her dream when he touched her. Who would guess a half-human could bond like that?

⁂

The truck bounced in slow motion over a rutted road, or maybe across country. The headlights showed scraggly brush and rocks. Esau's blazer, a fine worsted wool, surrounded her with his scent. She snuggled into it, pretending she was naked under his blanket. The truck bucked, throwing her off-balance and tightening the seatbelt across the side of her neck. "Oof!"

"Sorry."

She pulled his coat tighter about her. Cold air blasted from the vents. "Do your secret fetishes include nude snowball fights?"

"No." His wide mouth did something that might be a tic or his version of a grin. "Do you need the heater?"

"I'd rather be cold than spread over the landscape by a sleepy driver. Have we been driving all that long?"

"Not really. I'm afraid your sleepiness is contagious."

She sighed a vapor cloud, and watched the vent blow it apart. "Should I talk to you to help you stay awake? Play guessing games?"

He gave her a quick glance. "Yeah. You can start with who's after you?"

Well, that certainly changed the subject. "Werewolves, I think we can say."

"We say shifters, shapeshifters, or fur-walkers. But from what you said, I think humans are involved, too."

"I wish you could find out which shifters and I could find out which humans. That would be a tidy division of labor."

"Have you any idea which humans?"

"By now maybe an insurance company. My company has three mil in key-man insurance on me, and my secretary says I'm thought to have croaked in the earthquake."

"What do you do, to be a key man?"

"I design software."

"Yeah? Any I might have heard of?"

"Some games. Some security apps. A personal health app."

"What games?"

"You into artificial mayhem for teenaged males?"

"I raised the boys of my pack. Girls too, for that matter. I guess I know most of the popular games now."

There was sorrow in his voice. Quietly she answered, "I did the aerial sequences, combat sequences, and puzzle mapping for most of the WarDove series." If he could selectively withhold information, she could, too. "I'm also in with the spinoff, a Golden Guardian series."

His eyebrows went up. "Guardian At The Gate is out now?"

"Not in the US. Not legally. The Japanese licensee demanded 60 days' lead time for their market. But 'used' copies are being auctioned on the Internet, and we handed out plenty of demos."

"The boys gave up study, dating and sleep to compete in WarDove VI and VIII." He took a deep breath, and the lines of his face deepened. Esau added finally, "They said VII didn't match up."

"It didn't. I was busy with another project then."

He made a visible effort to shake memory off. "Okay, I have to ask. What other project?"

"Ever hear of HandPlus?"

"HandPlus? FuckWare?" He turned to look at her, and she braced a knee against the dashboard. He returned his attention to the road. "The one where a kid hooks up a wristband to monitor his pulse and blood pressure and move-ment rate, and then jacks off, and the software uses that information to feed him sounds and images… um…"

"Designed to heighten the sensual experience, as tailored to the individual's arousal profile. But it's not for kids." She studied the desolate countryside. "Has somebody hidden a road somewhere around here?"

"More like a track."

He eased the truck to a stop by a fencepost with a boot inverted on the top. She frowned. That boot thing was common out west; she'd heard a dozen explanations. None of them made sense.

Esau opened the door of the truck and stood, balancing on the headrest and doorframe. He whistled sharply. She barely heard the faint return whistle. Esau responded with a complex series of tweets and trills, which was answered with what sounded like a flock of birds fighting.

Esau settled back into the cab. "Ben's heating food and clearing out a bedroom for us. His wife and kids are in town for the weekend, so we won't be disturbed."

Her face warmed.

The house was stone, and huge. A man in layers of denim and checked flannel leaned against one side of the door, smoking a massive pipe. He looked a lot like Esau, but darker-skinned and shaggier.

He strode toward the truck as Esau opened the door, then flung his arms around Esau and lifted him off the dusty ground.

Tyler quietly opened her own door, sliding her feet down to the frost-glittered ground, and stretched. Esau's jacket was plenty roomy enough to let her stretch all she wanted.

Esau and the other man—Ben—thumped fists against each other's backs and hooted. Clouds of steam surrounded their heads in the cold air.

Male greeting rituals. She could use a scene like that in her game.

She blocked them like models, setting her mind to remember them in terms of stick figures, wire frames and centers of gravity. And the shirt-wrinkles—her concept artist liked such details. She automatically put them in orange Guardian uniforms.

When the man turned to her, his grin vanished. He took a step back from Tyler, like she was some sort of threat. "I don't understand."

Esau tensed, and stepped around to insert his big frame between her and Ben. She peeked around his arm, not at all upset by the macho-guy maneuvering after that incident in the motel's parking lot.

"She is mine," Esau rumbled. "What is there to understand?"

"I have children, Esau. You bring a woman that my Family has acknowledged to be the property of Raleigh, and you ask shelter in my own house. You know we will pay forfeit!"

Esau spun and looked down at her. "Raleigh?"

She backed up against the cold truck. "*Property?*"

Esau's heavy brows knitted. "WarDove. Those games are put out by Truc's company."

"*My* company."

"You're Truc's," he said. "One of Raleigh's pet humans."

She wasn't going to let that pass. She replied hotly, "Bastian Truc owns thirty percent of HandGames Inc. His family owns another ten percent. Various employees split ten percent. I own fifty percent. Bastian runs the company, but you'd be more accurate to say he's my property than to call me his!"

Esau frowned at this, then looked over his shoulder at the other man. "The cabin I used to bring the pack's kids to—is it still registered as a vacation rental?"

"Yes." Ben's glower dropped away. He grinned. "It is at that. So is the smaller cabin, which happens to be vacant right now. Go on up. I'll send the bill like before. Firewood's already there, and I'll bring hot food directly."

Esau nodded back, as if that settled everything, and crowded her back to the door of the truck. He lifted her to the high bench seat, then scraped his shoes across the ground where she'd stood, obliterating her tracks.

When they passed the booted fencepost on the way out, she asked, "Why does renting this cabin make a difference?"

"It's registered as a rental, effectively a motel room. Neutral turf. Ben can't be accused of harboring someone who stays in it."

"Harboring. You make me sound like a criminal, or some animal escaped from a zoo." *Escaped property.*

He shut off the vents with an impatient gesture and slid her a glance that did not seem at all friendly.

"Esau?" *Have you put me into a different category just now? Do I need to be afraid of you?*

He took a deep breath and let it out. "You don't need to be afraid of me. I'm upset with myself. I should have followed up when you asked about Truc in Raleigh."

He drove in silence to a cabin in a copse of evergreens just below the crest of a rise.

She shed the jacket and climbed down while Esau was coming around the front end toward her. He rested a hand on her shoulder. "I would have helped you down."

"I'm not used to needing help." The ground here had less frost than Ben's driveway, and buffalo grass grew in scattered shin-high clumps. She missed the warmth of Esau's coat. "You said why you were mad at yourself. Why are you mad at me?"

"You have the damnedest habit of asking short questions that would take hours to answer."

"Then give me an outline now. You can fill in the details once we get inside. Why are you mad at me?"

He turned to the cabin and put an arm about her shoulder. "Come inside so I can lay the fire."

She dug her heels into the hard pale dirt. "Talk first."

"Inside." He propelled her two steps.

She dropped out from under his arm, and crouched by the pickup's front tire. "Talk now."

He stood over her; she felt his blood pressure hammer his temples and the back of his skull. Fury and frustration pounded in that pulse, along with things she could not readily identify.

Her skin shrank. This guy was dangerous. A lot more dangerous now than before he'd heard about the Trucs.

He reached down for her. She scrambled crabwise on her hands and feet along the side of the truck, until the rusty bumper snagged her sweater. She jerked free of the snag, and fell on the glittering ground.

He rubbed the back of his neck. "Stop, please. You really have nowhere to go, and I am no danger to you, here and now."

In theory, a man who could speak reasonably could be reasoned with. She rose hesitantly. "Here and now, Kirkland? What about inside that cabin? How far does 'here' stretch and when does 'now' end?"

"*I don't know!*" he roared, and she fell on her butt.

He lifted his face to the indigo sky, and cut off whatever flowed between them. Unidentifiable things creaked faintly, and he inhaled like it hurt.

Then he reached out a hand. "Tyler, please come inside? I'm cold. You're cold. It's bad enough we're mad. If we get sunlight on our skins, it'll be that much harder to get to sleep."

"You have the damnedest habit of making sense when I'm ready to fight."

He blinked, as if recognizing his own words coming back at him. "I hope you don't intend to fight anyway."

Not if I'm going to lose. She picked at the torn place on her sleeve. "I'm not going to win this one, am I?"

"Tyler, I'm afraid neither of us is."

She took his hand.

He pulled her to him, and for a moment held her close. She could not help snuggling in against his wrinkled dress shirt. He should be cold. Instead, he radiated heat and comfort.

"Thank you," he whispered. Then he carried her inside.

Chapter 9

Alone for a moment, she prowled the cabin. The downstairs was mostly one room, with a kitchen area and a bathroom opposite the fire. Three sets of bunk beds had been crammed into the upstairs room.

Esau brought in their bags and laid a fire in the miniature fireplace. He lit it using only one long-stemmed match and a bare handful of the strong-scented splinters of fat wood. The nose-pinching aroma drew her close.

When he spread a sheepskin rug on the hearth, she sat cross-legged on it, watching the fire flow like a living thing around the splinters and bits of wood. "I could never get tired of watching a fire."

"Never's a long time," he observed.

"When is your buddy coming with the food?"

"Any minute. But he won't come in, if that's your worry. He'll load the ice chest on the front porch. You can go ahead and change into your sleepwear. Wear socks. It'll be cold."

She poked the fire with a sticky splinter. Her splinter flared, sending up dense swirls of black smoke. Burning sap dripped freely from the burning end. She splashed a few drops of orange flame on the cut face of the all-nighter log, then wedged the splinter between logs. She glanced up at him. "What if I want to sleep in my skin? So much for that?"

He ran fingers through his dark hair, and rubbed hard along the back of his neck. "Tyler... Tyler, what is your intent? Are you bonded? Am I your second male?"

Sap-stained, her thumb and forefinger stuck together, and made smacking sounds when she pulled them apart. She considered saying: *No, I'm not bonded. My security bond expired years ago. Don't need one now.*

What in blazes is a second male? Step two in building a guy-harem? Or was he asking how many guys she'd ever slept with? Who knew what this jargon meant? Ask a biologist what a first mate is, then ask a sailor. *Circle back. 'Bonded' is probably a different word in his jargon than mine.*

Smack. Smack. She knew game theory. And in business, denying the enemy concrete information was a crucial layer of defense. But applying Bing Fa truisms within the family tends to turn a home into a war zone. He wasn't an enemy, she was sure. *But when did Esau Don't-Call-Me-Werewolf Kirkland become family?*

"Esau, I have no clue in the world what you're talking about."

The fire popped twice, and after a pause popped again. *Is it cherry wood that pops all the time?* She lit another sticky splinter to watch the drops of fire run out. The dripping fat sizzled, and the curling scent stung her nose.

He coughed. Or laughed. It was hard to tell. "Okay, my question probably did not make sense, out of context."

"Care to put it in context? Failing that, care to tell—" She abruptly made the connection. "Oh! That's why you're mad at me." *Balls.* She made a deliberate decision not to yell. "You think I did some sort of femme-fatale entrapment to get you to take a subordinate position to—ooh, let me take a really wild guess here—Bastian Truc or his creepy, stripey mommy?"

He watched her out of the corner of his eye. So he did think that. Or he wondered, which was almost as bad.

She threw her splinter to the back of the fireplace. The bit of wood stuck for an instant, then flared and dropped, burning, out of sight.

"Kirkland, I didn't do jack shit to entrap you. I've been on the run for a couple of weeks and—lo and behold!—every time the track takes an unexpected turn on me, Esau Kirkland shows up. Which one of us has reason to be suspicious?"

He watched her. Just watched her. She wanted to smack him. *But adults don't do that.* She got up and paced again, walking in and out of his shadow across the tile floor. Her thoughts bounced uselessly from Bastian to Esau to the guy with the fake fangs who'd perched on her car hood.

One wall was solid closet doors; when she opened them, she saw something like an enormous built-in ironing board. A Murphy bed, just like in the movies. Oh, man, how cool was that? Could someone really hide a body between the mattress and the wall? She pulled the bed down. No way. The pillows were squashed flat.

She found the thermostat for the electric blanket and turned it to medium. Then low. Snuggling would be more fun than stretching out in warm sheets. If Esau refused to snuggle, the blanket would be a really poor substitute anyway.

The opposite wall had heavily curtained windows and a wallpapering of photos: Kids and adults of various ages and races in outdoor shots, all grinning hugely and holding up fish.

She came up close to identify a shot of Esau Kirkland squatting, surrounded by grinning dark-haired tykes in shorts and t-shirts. Each tyke held up a tiny fish or two, while Esau held a sign: It Got Away.

She stared at the photo, looking for someone who wasn't there. Someone she hoped was never there. In a casual voice, she asked, "Where's Mrs. Kirkland?"

"My mom was nailed by a sniper just before Atlanta."

"Atlanta? You mean the Atlanta Riots?"

"We call it the Atlanta Massacre."

The hair raised up on her arms. She rubbed the sleeves of her sweater, exploring the hole at one elbow. "My folks died in that." So had a hundred other cops and four other paramedics. "What about your wife?" She knew he had to have been married. But he wasn't anymore. She knew that too. "Did she also die then?"

"No. Tiffany died in a challenge match a little over fifteen years ago. She was... ambitious."

Note to self: among these people, 'challenge matches' involve more than electronic attaboys and bragging rights. "So you raised your kids alone?"

"They were my... wife's daughters. The woman who killed Tiffy got them. As a prize."

She barely heard him. How can you be so calm? She opened her mouth to ask, and shut it. He wasn't calm. His hands moved in slow motion, hypergraceful, like an anime villain, his emotions packed like explosive in a cartridge. The fire crackled, and a rush of sparks swooshed up the chimney.

Her insides tightened. "The woman who killed your wife got to adopt your kids?"

"I'd like to think she raised them as her own."

"I'd make it my business to find out." *Balls, Tyler!* You don't goad a wild animal when the cage might fall apart!

"I don't doubt you would." His remote, polite voice might as well have been computer-generated. "But with their mother gone, I had no rights." He stirred the fire; it cracked like ice chips thrown in hot grease. "I believe the baby was half-human, so I tried to steal her back, but I screwed up. She was sent away, probably given a new name. I never found her again."

Tyler circled to the couch and leaned on the thick woolen blanket that draped the back of it. "So what difference does being 'half-human' make?"

His shoulders hunched. "It means she had neither the protection afforded to humans nor the deference afforded to a female shifter. It means that when she hit puberty, she did not shift. Instead she began smelling pretty much like a human. She could have been kept as a spare female, but more likely she was sold off in one of the January auctions. My niece—she would be the youngest in that picture—kept tabs on as many auctions as we could find, but we never found the right one."

Tyler drew in her breath. "She would be auctioned off as someone's property?"

"If a Family badly wanted an infertile play-pretty for their extra males, maybe. The real money's in the parts, though. She was probably sold as two corneas, or a pair of them. Two kidneys, or a pair of them. A heart and a pair of lungs." His hands clutched the fleece of the hearth rug, and in the wavering firelight his tendons were stark shadows. His voice continued, though, without inflection. "So many square centimeters of skin, so many liters of blood, and so many CCs of bone marrow. And so on. A human could spend forty years actively ruining his own liver, and if he had the money, he could start over with Suzu's."

"But if she's only half-human—"

Esau took a deep, slow breath. "A human body doesn't reject half-human organs. Some Families make a great deal of money at the auctions. My sister once picked up a dozen human runaways to breed for market, but her son threw such a fit she gave up the idea."

"You're talking about these kids in this picture? Which one is half-human?"

"Tiffy's girls never came here. You're looking at my nephew and his age-mates."

She breathed shallowly, holding back the waves of anguish and nausea. "Why did you stop tracking the auctions?"

"We didn't, or I guess we hadn't until now. Gabie, the one who could hack into the auction sites, is gone. In fact, everyone in that photo is gone, except me."

The fleece in his hands vibrated. He believed what he'd said, and it must tear him up. But that sort of thing couldn't happen. Even if the auctions were hidden or censored from the regular news, the tabloids couldn't be blindfolded or censored.

She picked a thorny bit of stem out of the blanket's coarse threads. Reflections danced around her hands as Esau adjusted the reflector to send more heat into the room.

When he finished, he turned to her. "Anyway, half-humans can't be members of a Family because they neither shift nor reproduce."

Yeah? What about me?

"You are so rare we have no laws for you. But for Truc's claim, I would announce our bond as if you were a shifter and dare anyone to challenge my rights or yours."

Are you reading my mind?

He stood and stretched. "Let's get some food in you and then catch a nap. If you crouch down right where you are, you won't be in the line of sight when I open the door."

"I wish I had an untraceable phone," she fretted, sitting on the cold tile floor behind the couch.

"Feel free." Something landed on the couch.

No blast of cold air had yet announced the opening of the door, so she got up to look. A phone, curiously bulky.

"What's this on the back of your phone?" she asked.

"Something to keep my calls from being traced. The phone bills don't show any calls I make, so it might work."

Something home-built in any case, and with exquisite craftsmanship. The chance was worth taking. She dialed the familiar number.

When Celie answered, her voice was thick with sleep. "I charge seventy-five bucks a minute to listen to unsolicited calls and you are being recorded. Talk."

"It's me."

Celie hesitated. "Prove it."

"You didn't like the pilot who had that piece of spinach between his front teeth." She held the phone at arm's length. A cold gust fluttered the curtains and made the shadows dance. In a cartoon, Celie's voice would have the same effect.

"*Tyler!* You are in *so much trouble!*"

"Yeah, I am. Lots of it is due to Bastian Truc."

"He *fired* me, Tyler! Just up and *fired* me!"

"Well, I'm hiring you. Me as me instead of me as Hand. That okay with you? Get back at Bastian?"

Celie laughed. "I can't wait to twist his ears. How we gonna do it?"

"First I need that Rolodex memory of yours. The stunt pilots for WarDove VIII. Remember that chopper pilot with the big—uh, feet—you were telling me about. Jimbo. Wasn't he from Sooner City?"

"No, from Kansas City. The Sooner was the other stunt pilot, Casey, the one who kept downloading pictures of his newborn twins. O'course, they're all there right now, for the Con this weekend."

This weekend? The Sooner City Con was this weekend? "I need a home phone number for Casey."

"I only remember his business number. Wait, I have the emergency contact list."

Impatiently, Tyler held the phone, waiting for Celie to find Casey's number. She heard a movement behind her and turned to see Esau standing over her, holding a picnic plate and a thermos. "Can you bring your conversation to a warmer spot?"

"Hang on."

Esau microwaved the plate while Tyler saved Casey's number in the phone and promised cross-her-heart and spit-on-Truc to call Celie tomorrow.

Then she settled on the fleece in front of the fire, and he sat beside her with steaming roast chicken and mashed potatoes. Hunger abruptly twisted her stomach.

"Slowly," he advised. "Take very small bites and keep some space between them."

She did not want to ask how he knew, but he was right.

When she'd eaten what she wanted, he cleaned up the rest of the food and then washed the dishes. She stared into the fire, wondering whether to call the pilot tonight and what to tell Esau.

Esau turned off the water and dried his hands. Turning from the sink, he said. "Have you figured out how much of your plan to reveal to me yet?"

Annoyed, she said, "I'm not sure I want to reveal anything. First, maybe you should tell me how much mind-reading you can do, and why I get these flashes from you." She glared at him. "Is it like you know how to broadcast? Or does everyone broadcast, and receiving is the trick, and you're teaching me to receive the broadcast?"

He crossed the floor silently and squatted beside her. She stared into his eyes, watching his pupils dilate. Her eyes closed on their own, but she still saw him, firelit and strong. His breath brushed her cheek like warm fingertips. He smelled faintly of smoke and the roast chicken they'd eaten.

"You keep asking questions I can't completely answer," he whispered. "When I am in my wolf shape, I can pick up emotions and sensory data from any wolf around me. I can sort of 'talk' to a few wolves and to most healers. But you are neither wolf nor healer. Nor were we bonded as children, when our minds were pliable." He hesitated, then said, "What we have is usually dismissed as myth, fantasy. Everyone hears of bonded couples who can share their minds, but who personally knows one?"

So where do we stand, you and me? Are you saying we're bonded? Does that mean I'm your property? She bit her lip. *Truc declared me property, and leased me out to that lab.*

Esau's lips brushed her cheek. "I don't know what ugly thing is in your head right now, but I will protect you as long as I live."

"What did you do to protect Tiffany?" It was a cruel thing to say, but he looked back levelly at her.

"Tiffany was not a bondmate. She was a breeder, selected for strength, intelligence and fertility; her children were her trophies and I was—I don't know. Not very important to her. I didn't even know she'd gone to challenge Cincinnati until I heard she'd lost, and that Cincinnati had taken the girls." He took her hand. "You, however, are a part of me now," he said simply, "and I will be part of you, as long as either of us lives. No one can lawfully separate us. If you were a shifter, I would leave my Family to join yours, unless my Family bought us both."

It sounded so foreign. She said, "But I'm not a shifter."

He shrugged. "Then as things stand, it looks like I will have to either follow you to Raleigh, or declare war, or spend my life running with you."

She pressed her cheek against his. He needed a shave. Normally that would be a turnoff, but right now his stubble felt incredibly sexy. He was declaring himself hers for life, and that—that was really sexy. "Can we buy off Truc, give him enough money to shut up and go away?"

His arm draped over her shoulder, heavy and warm. "In a word, no. I'll have to kill him." He said that so calmly. As calmly as he had mentioned his Tiffany dying. All the dying. His world was so brutal. "May we discuss this another time?"

Discussion could wait. Thinking could wait. She wanted Esau between her and the world again. Wanted him inside, above, all around her. Wanted to see his skin in the firelight, feel his heat and his strength.

His nostrils flared. Being a wolf, he probably could smell her desire. A pulse stirred in his throat, and she leaned her forehead into his shoulder.

Esau pushed her gently away.

Feeling dazed and off balance, she looked at his shaking arms, his hunched shoulders, his grim face.

"Esau?" She touched his sleeve, and he flinched.

"I could say something ugly enough to turn you off, sweetheart. But the truth is that we just can't do this now."

"Why not? I really want you to make love to me." She'd never begged before. Never needed or wanted to. But she wanted him.

He closed his eyes and took a deep breath. Then he undressed her, using mostly his lips and teeth, pushing her hands away with his face when she tried to help and resting his own hands on her hips. Here and there his teeth pinched lightly at her skin, sending rushes of heat through her. The process took a long time. The firelight toasted her left side before he stood and led her to the edge of the bed.

Esau knelt in front of her there and nuzzled her thighs apart. His hair was just long enough to grip with both hands, and the scrape of his stubble against her thighs brought another rush of heat. Her knees folded. She fell back on the bed, spreading her arms to bounce on the hard mattress.

He bit gently just above her knee and crawled up her body, kissing and licking and nibbling until he reached her left nipple. There, he kissed her thoroughly.

She gripped the bedclothes, her eyes shut, giving herself up to pure sensation. She was hot where he covered her, and cold where he didn't.

He blew across her wet nipple. It knotted tight, like a fist, and sent a pang straight down.

She wrapped her legs around his waist. He unwrapped them and worked his way down to her navel. He drew circles around it with his nose and with his bristled chin, and nipped just below it.

She came up off the bed with a strangled cry.

"Make all the noise you want," he invited, his lips moving against the skin below her navel. "No one will hear."

She shook her head violently, a lifetime of caution and circumspection muting her. He lightly scraped his teeth across the inside of her thigh, raising chill bumps all over.

A new thought opened her eyes and made her grab his night-dark hair. "Werewolf, right? Not vampire?"

"Shapeshifter. Wolf. Not vampire. I do not vant to drrringk yourrr blooood!"

She laughed, curling her body over his head.

"Your other juices are a different matter," he whispered, releasing her mouth and pulling her butt toward him until it rested on the edge of the bed. He sat back on his feet and shouldered up under her thighs.

The first lick along the edges of her inner labia tickled, and she laughed again. Then she gasped at a long, firm lick.

He held her by the hips and drew circles and lines and figure eights, quickly and slowly, tickling-light and hard. Through it all he kneaded her thighs and lower back with his strong hands, and held her down when she thrashed, and reached a long finger inside when she most needed it. His touch built the pressure inside her and his touch ignited the explosion.

She came up off the bed, gasping his name. "Esauuuu!"

He chuckled. "I'm right here, sweetheart."

Before she could respond, he lit the next fuse. The rasp of his teeth and tongue on her sensitized flesh pushed her harder, twisted her nerves tighter than before. Her vision darkened and her breathing stopped. The explosion took her, a lightning flash of searing pleasure.

Her back arched again, but he held her down, mercilessly prodding even further. He gave her no chance to catch her breath before his hands and his mouth pushed her into the next explosion. The climax rolled through her with tearing force, more thunder than lightning, and this time she did cry out, not caring who might hear.

Before her cry faded, he was pushing her again, bringing the thunder in stunning waves that rumbled in her bones and then crashed through her. She locked her hands in his thick short hair and shrieked. *Too much! Too much!*

He growled into her thigh, and turned back to lick places that could no longer bear any touch.

She howled at him to stop, drumming her heels on his back and yanking his hair.

He hesitated again, long enough for her to feel the quivering tension in his arms. Then he ran a trail of kisses down to the inside of her knee and pulled away. She lay sobbing, exhausted, saturated with pleasure.

When he climbed in bed beside her, she turned to snuggle with him and found buttons. "You're still dressed."

He didn't answer.

She hauled herself up on one elbow. "Aren't you going to..."

"Not this time."

"Why not?"

"I don't need a reason."

You're lying. "Why?"

"Sometimes a man just has to prove he can."

"That's not the whole answer." But she let him push her back on the bed.

"It's all you're getting right now. Sleep."

"If I'm bowlegged tomorrow, it'll be from beard burn."

"You liked my beard." He pulled the covers up and laid a cloth over her eyes. "And if beard burn is the only souvenir you keep, I will be most insulted. Now sleep."

"That's an order, isn't it?"

He sighed.

She lay tensely, waiting for something she couldn't identify. When he spooned up behind her and put his heavy arm over her, she knew that was it, and she slept.

Chapter 10

Tyler awoke when the door exploded inward. A lopsided ball tumbled across the floor toward her. Recognizing the grenade shape, she buried her head in the pillows. The flash-bang stunned her anyway, and pepper-gas smoke filled the room.

Men in ninja-SWAT suits and respirator masks flooded in through the door.

Tyler lunged for the nearest window. Her eyes and lungs burned, blinding her and suffocating her.

Esau yanked her off-balance and thrust her deep among the pillows and blankets. He roared a demand for personal combat.

Wheezing and barely able to see in the thinning gas, she scrambled for the Bowie knife hidden under the mattress. She flicked a glance at Esau's ember-rouged profile and gasped. Pepper-gas scoured her throat.

Fangs? Esau had *fangs*?

One of the ninja-SWAT-whatevers raised a large pistol to him and fired. The twin darts trailed wires, and a stream of glittering confetti. The darts plunged into Esau's bare chest.

She yelled a warning, and tried to yank out one of the darts to break the circuit, but the surge of voltage moved quicker.

Esau screamed and convulsed, falling back on the bed and then to the floor, writhing helplessly.

She snatched out one of the darts. Two more zipped past her and struck home, wracking him in waves of convulsions.

A third pair of darts bit into her shoulder. She clenched her teeth, waiting for the sizzling jolt to follow.

No jolt came.

She looked up slowly, over her shoulder at the intruders, knowing that her dread and anguish showed on her face.

A lithe Asian man pulled off his respirator and handed it to one of the other men. Then he approached her, a smile of cold triumph on his astonishingly handsome face.

"Don't!" Esau gasped from the floor.

"Orders from the powerless," the Asian said. "Incoherence from the incompetent. We shall have to teach him better. Won't we, my pet?"

"Bastian," her mouth said, although this was plainly not Bastian. *What the blazes?* Her arms rose toward him. *What kind of trick is this?*

Not a trick, she realized abruptly. A dream. Esau's.

She sat up in the dim, silent cabin. Outside, a hawk called "Keew, Keew!" The door stood shut, with a four-by-four bar across it. No silver darts burned in her shoulder. She shivered in the cold.

Esau moaned, and she turned to him. In the dream he'd been naked. Now his dress shirt clung in ripples to his undershirt and spiraled about his arms. He had his pants on, too. He had removed nothing but his shoes and belt.

Play power games with me, you son of a bitch, and you can find your own way out of your nightmares.

She picked up the phone and her bag of clothes, ignoring the repeated little twinges in her nether regions, and locked herself in the bathroom.

Property.

Balls!

The touch of toilet paper brought an unlikely rush of cream. *Damn Esau for making her think of him! I am not property. I will not be property.*

She shivered so hard in the unheated air that she could barely hit the three buttons needed to dial that one programmed number. A sleepy woman answered.

"Hi. This is Tyler. I'm looking for Casey to give me a ride to this weekend's con."

"Oh, goodness! He's a'rdy gone. Are you the new rappeller?"

"No, I hire Casey to fly stunts. How can I reach him now?"

The woman's tone cooled. "That Tyler? The dead one? Sorry, I left my Ouija board in my other purse."

Balls! "Don't hang up! I'm not dead. Look, I'm locked in a bathroom in a fish camp in the middle of nowhere and the bad guys have done everything but shoot at me!" *And the 'good' guy is a werewolf!*

"How do I even know if you're really her?"

"Ask me something about the WarDove filming."

The woman on the phone paused, and then demanded, "Okay. Tell me this then— when did you throw up?"

Tyler said defiantly, "Not on the chopper. At Six Flags. The choppers never could make me lose it."

"That could be part of the filklore. What's the yellow flash on level three?"

"If you're wearing the armlets, they become orientation devices. The spinners are 75% likely to leave you pointing in the same direction you were before the spin, and anyone trying a sneak attack on you has halved chances of achieving surprise."

"No shit?" Casey's wife made rustling noises. "Where did you say you were?" She still sounded skeptical, but willing to take a chance.

Tyler rifled through the pile of magazines in a basket beside the toilet and found a likely address. "I think it's Parker's Fish Camp, star route—"

"Just off the interstate? Hey, I know that one."

"I'm in the smaller cabin."

"Cabin? I guess he can find it. Can you run up a signal?"

"From *the can*?"

"Hey, for real? You're really locked in the bathroom? How do you plan to get to the bird?"

That's a good question. "I'll figure it out," Tyler said. "Tell me why you thought I was dead."

"It's all over the internet you are."

"Then I ought to make a grand entrance. Was Hand sending one helicopter or a full show?"

"You don't know?"

Tyler rubbed the knot between her eyebrows. "If people think I'm dead, they ought to believe I'm out of the loop, okay? How long will it take Casey to find me?"

"You sent three birds and tons of goodies. Casey'll be in your driveway in half an hour. Hey, Miss Tyler? No disrespect intended, but you plan on getting my man shot at?"

"No, but it's possible. I know he has you and the twins—"

"Yeah. So he won't take stupid chances. But if you're in trouble, this is your town and Casey's your man. We even have costumes for the Con—what size can you wear?"

The doorknob turned. "Twelve! Hurry! Please!"

She disconnected, stepped into the shower, and turned on the water. "*AAAAAAAAAAAHHH!*"

She slapped off the faucet and stood shivering, in shock.

"Yeah, the water's cold, Tyler." Esau's voice held humor of the driest sort. He opened a utilitarian blue towel. "Takes a while to warm up out here. What did you expect?"

She looked up at him. "Dh-th-uh-N-nothing *that* cold!"

"Step out and let it run a minute to warm the pipes."

She let him buff her skin, and then huddled against him, soaking up his warmth. He smelled salty and woodsy, and so very good.

How in blazes was she going to get past him to the bird if he decided not to let her go? He reached past her and turned the water on again.

"Esau?"

"Right here, sweetheart."

"You're going to Memphis today."

"Or tomorrow. Soon. It's home, Tyler. We belong there."

"It's not my home." A curling tendril of mist indicated that the water was warming. When she stepped in, the water sluiced over her breasts and belly, warmer every second.

She remembered not to wet her hair. If she planned to make a grand entrance at a Con in less than an hour, mussed hair would work, but wet snakes of hair dripping on her shoulders would not.

Esau undid his shirt buttons.

She eyed him warily. She didn't have time for another round of suck-and-seizure. "If you want to wash my back, I can do it myself. If you plan to get frisky, you need to go play with some other co-dependent sex-addict. I got no time for a man who wants to perform instead of share, and who thinks I can't even open a door or take a shower without help."

Esau undid another button. "More of your religious tenets?"

What the blazes? Oh. That. Her comment hadn't been that funny the first time. Why revisit it? Why even remember it? "Of course."

"What does your religion say about Capture Brides?"

That sounded like a game term. She soaped between her legs. *Ow!* She did have a raw spot. Not big enough or, honestly, raw enough to whine about, but it caught her attention. "What does the Esau religion say about them?"

"That they may be our defense against Truc."

She soaped her knees and on down. That last wax job was growing back, but the fuzz wasn't terribly thick or dark yet. She could ignore it. "Against Truc?"

"Yes. It might force him to release you. If I carried you against your will into my territory, then by law you would be torn from your family. Erased. Only the Lady of your city—and Atlanta doesn't have a Lady now—or the father of one of your children, or a bondmate would have the right to demand your return."

Contemplatively, she soaped her breasts. "So instead of Truc property, I'd be Kirkland property. Your sister would be my boss, my owner. You don't see a problem with that because you would not be subordinate in any way to the Trucs."

"Yes." He wriggled out of the form-fitting undershirt. Was it truly necessary to flex so many muscles, or was he making a point? "The simplest solutions often end up being the tidiest."

"I see the advantages, but I don't want to be Kirkland's property any more than I want to be Truc's. For all I know, your sister might make Bastian's mother look like Mrs. Santa."

"Rinse off and let me dry you."

"Balls! I am *not* Truc's property. I am not *your* property. Get that through your thick wolfy skull."

He looked sadly at her. "Rinse off. If I dry you with soap on your skin, it will chafe later."

Behind his head she saw a bottle of cheap aftershave. She instantly visualized the dragon on the road, rushing at her, and concentrated on how every detail would play out in a game.

"Tyler, if you want to hide something in your mind, you don't need to metaphorically hold both hands over your mouth."

"You need a shave, Esau."

He wiped his hand over his jaw, leaving bare skin, and showed her the beard-hair clinging to his fingers. "I'm a wolf, only better. I can shed. When is your helicopter coming?"

Of course he knew about the helicopter. He could read her mind. She touched his smooth, gleaming jaw. "You don't need to know."

"Tyler, I need to know you will trust me."

But I don't trust you. Dragons! Dragons! Wait. A dog can hear—balls! "You already know. Why ask?"

He stepped out of his slacks. His voice came rough and soft at the same time. "I wanted to hear that you trusted me."

I hurt his feelings. "Poor baby."

"Your life will be uncomfortable and disorienting for some time, Tyler. Alienating me will not help your situation."

"You want some of this water before it goes cold?"

"Please. Come let me dry you."

She stepped up against his chest, and felt that thick cock of his stir. She would be awfully cold in a minute, but right now the room steamed around her and she distracted herself, just for the moment, with the memory of that cock sliding into her, hot and insistent and perfect.

Esau buffed her dry a second time. She measured the distance to the aftershave bottle with her eyes. Couldn't reach it. Her temperature rose, her skin remembering the heat of his. When she reached down, his cock rose to meet her hand.

She could kneel, holding his buttocks as he had held hers, and take that padded head in her mouth. Heavy and soft at first, the shaft would swell and harden on her tongue. She could tease that little vee in the head until he went crazy.

Except this was Esau Kirkland, and although his breath came harsh and deep right now, she knew all the way to her bones that he would reject her. *Why?*

The answer came, simple and ugly. "You can't fuck me now because you think I belong to Truc and Bastian Truc hasn't said you could."

His face distorted, and went back to its usual lines before she could take a breath to ask.

"Making use of Truc's property would entail more sanctions than Memphis could pay," he said calmly.

"Never mind I'm already pregnant, or that we've already done the dirty? That sucks, Esau. What happened to this bond? What happened to being bondmates?" She shook her head. "Water's getting cold. I'll dress in the other room."

"No. Stay here where I can see you and don't dress. Don't make me throw your clothes in the water to keep you."

Whup!-whup!-whup!-whup!

He looked up, as if he could see the helicopter through the ceiling, and fangs sprang from his mouth.

Tyler lunged for the magazines, and he lunged for her. She scrolled a magazine in her hands and whapped him hard in the nose. "Down, boy!"

He snatched his head back, his fangs receding, his expression confused. Perfect! She scrambled free of his grasp and scrolled the magazine tighter. This was going to hurt. *But he can heal at will. He will heal before I'm even on that copter. And I have to get on that copter… or I won't ever be able to leave him.*

She sprang at him, stiff-armed, spearing the end of the rolled magazine into his face. Then she hopped over him and used the magazine to smack down the aftershave bottle. It exploded in the tub like a stinkbomb, glass shards tinkling everywhere as she snatched up her clothes bag and opened the bathroom door. She slammed the door behind her and used her hip to butt the couch up against it.

The helicopter roared overhead and swept back. Sand spattered like sleet against the window.

"Tyler! Don't go! *Tyler!*"

I have to.

She wrestled the bar out of its brackets while behind her the couch scraped across the tile floor.

She ran to the hovering chopper. The frosty ground burned her bare feet as the airborne sand stung her naked skin. She saw Esau's reflection in the chopper's side. He'd stopped to pull on his pants. That few seconds was her lead.

Throwing her bag in the open crew door, she scrambled after it. She slipped, and fell sprawling across the searing-cold metal floor. She screamed, *"Go! Go! Go!"*

Esau roared right behind her.

The chopper lifted. Then it jerked downward and tilted out from under her. She slid toward the open door and grabbed the icy Oh-Jesus bar. The chopper jerked. Her cold-stunned fingers couldn't hold their grip. She slid halfway out, naked legs dangling in space, at the last second twining a cable about her forearm and praying it would hold.

A big hand closed around her lower calf and shoved upward, propelling her onto the cargo floor just before the pilot corrected his tilt.

"Damn, Miss Tyler!" the pilot yelled over the sound of the rotors and the wind. He inclined his head towards the cargo door. "That your bad guy?"

She heaved herself up off the cold metal floor and found her bag. "Believe it or not, that's the good guy." She brushed sand off her front. The scrapes bled just a little, and they were beginning to sing to her. She'd always been tender-skinned, but then, like Esau, she healed fast too. "Please tell me you packed something warm for my costume."

"Yes'm." the pilot said over his shoulder. "Yes'm. Paper bag in the cargo net. Please tell me you won't tell nobody I saw you in your birthday suit. I'd lose both eyes and at least one nut by-time my wife slowed down."

I sure hope you don't mean that literally. "I don't plan on putting this in my press releases."

She pulled on her own socks and underpants before opening the paper sack. The fabric shimmered orange at one angle and deep brown at another. Soft cotton jersey lined the inside. A Golden Guardian flight-suit, straight out of WarDove VIII. *How perfect can you get?*

Well, perfect would have included the right size boots. These boots were a mile too big. She jammed her numb feet into her sneakers.

Only when suited up did she creep toward the door and look down. She somehow knew what she'd see. Sure enough, Esau crouched on the runner, arms locked in a death-grip about the strut. His skin shone white in the frigid wind, and dried blood streaked his chest.

Do werewolves catch cold?

No, but their bondmates occasionally catch hell.

He raised his face to her. Under a smear of blood, his skin was white, stretched tight over his bones. Snowflakes glimmered like stars in his whipping dark hair and in his eyelashes. He was angry, not afraid.

Relieved, Tyler retreated to the front seat and picked up the headset so she could talk instead of screaming at the pilot.

"Casey, play 'Enter the Guardian' on approach."

"No way to download it, ma'am. You'll have to pick a good one from the tapes in that box there."

At this angle, she could barely see Esau through her window. He looked miserable, but reasonably secure. She opened the tape box and held a tape up. "What's this one?"

He whistled between his teeth. "*Night on Bald Mountain.* A little ominous."

"Perfect! I'm using Bald Mountain for boss fights in GG."

"Ooh, yeah!" he grinned. "I mean, so I hear."

She laughed as two helicopters rose to flank them, and people poured out onto the roof of a hotel below.

The pilot played the opening measures twice, and called orders to clear the helipad. The people just cheered and waved. More pushed out to join them. She wondered what they thought when they saw the man gripping the runner.

"I'll rappel down," she said finally. "When I get the roof clear, set down gently. I kind of like the guy on your skid."

"Shhh! I don't think I should know I been flying with a half-naked man on the outside of my bird."

When he cut the music, a chant rose over the rotors' chop. "Tyler! Tyler! Tyler!"

She strapped on the 'biner belt, pulled on the smallest pair of leather gloves from the glove box, and climbed out the cargo door onto the skid beside Esau.

Woman! Are you crazy?

No more than usual. She grinned. In the bitter-cold wind, her lips stuck to her teeth. How cold must Esau be? Surely a werewolf could do funky things with his body temp. She exhaled slowly over her cold teeth.

From another chopper's speaker, belatedly, came the Call. "Guardian, Awake!"

The response roared up from the roof. "I am the Golden Guard-i-an!"

The speaker boomed the next line. "Who answers the call?"

"A hero arises to answer the call!"

"A hero arises—the Guardian!"

She dove face-first at the crowd, relying on the rope's friction to slow her descent and her people to break her fall.

They caught her, an eager mass of arms and shoulders. She yelled again, the ululating Guardian's cry that crowned each winning round in the games, and they roared it back to her.

"Inside!" she yelled. "Before we all freeze!"

Chapter 11

Numb and miserable, Esau clutched the burning-cold, heavily vibrating leg of the helicopter. He'd locked his joints in place; all he could do was hold on.

After a long time, the loudspeaker sounded again. "Hey, Good Guy. Stand up so I don't have to worry about landing on any body parts."

He struggled to his feet. Standing meant changing his grip, though, and his foot found ice. He fell, unable to close his hand on anything small enough to grip before the runner was snatched upward out of reach.

The fear of falling slammed through him just before he struck the roof, heavily, on his shoulder. The shoulder cracked.

He rolled, gracelessly but effectively, and scrambled to his feet. The icy wind pounded his back as he staggered away from the chopper. His numb feet found another slick patch, and skidded, but he stayed vertical.

Assess injuries. Hypothermia. Broken shoulder.

Hypothermia was a stranger. He'd always had proper clothing or fur to keep warm. Between the light snow and the wind of three choppers landing, his body temp was dropping more than he knew how to counter. The numbness that was replacing the cold was not his friend.

But the shoulder he could repair. He felt out the bone, found the break, and made the jagged edges flow together.

Something struck him. He turned, instinctively batting it away, and found that it was an orange jacket. He shrugged the jacket on but his fingers might as well be cold chunks of wood; he couldn't manipulate the zipper. Trusting the jacket to protect his core temperature, he increased the blood flow to his fingers until life returned with fierce kitten-bites.

The pilots triangulated on him as he worked the zippers up and adjusted the collar bands. All three pilots were human males, and all wore orange uniforms to match his jacket.

One man, a natural commander, looked Esau up and down before speaking. "Man, do you know how lucky you are we got permits to do stunts at this Con today?"

"My cup overfloweth," he responded grimly, his lips stiff with cold.

"You need a doctor? That looked like a hard fall."

"No doctor." He lifted his hands and clapped them to prove he could.

"So who are you?"

"I'm Esau. I'm with Tyler."

"The fuck you are."

"Cap'n, he's right," said another pilot, unexpectedly. "Miss Tyler said he was a good guy. I went to pick her up like I told you. Instead of her alone, they both come pelting out of this cabin like Satan was on their tails. I didn't wait on him a'cause I didn't want to see what they was running from. So it's my fault he got the cheap seat, Cap'n."

The captain's tone de-iced, but his face kept its wary, calculating look. "Well, sir, could I talk you into downing a hot drink or some battery acid in the con suite?"

Esau shivered violently, something he hadn't allowed himself to do before, and once he started he couldn't stop. He closed his eyes. *Tyler!*

She was chattering with a dozen people at once, but she stopped when she sensed him and reached out with her mind. *Why does your shoulder hurt so bad? Are you okay?*

He thought back, *Shoulder's better. The rest will get better. Come back to me, Tyler. We can't be separated!*

She smiled, and camera flashes dazzled their eyes together.

He blinked.

"I'll take that as a yes," the captain said."Come to my room first. You need a hot shower to warm you up. Then you can tell us who's after our Miss Tyler."

He forced himself to concentrate, to use terms a human would respect. The captain spoke in clipped Ohio accents, but he used the honorific 'miss' and he spoke with a soldier's inbred protectiveness. He would be an ally, if treated right. "It's not my story to tell. I'm just trying to keep her out of trouble."

The captain scowled, but motioned with his head. "Inside."

The pilots asked no more questions as they took him to a service elevator. His feet thawed slowly on the worn industrial carpet. He was glad he'd repaired his nose before leaving the cabin; by now it would have swollen enough to interfere with his vision as well as his sense of smell.

In the shower, he mentally reached for her again, just to assure himself she was close. She was laughing, babbling thanks, and hiding her dismay over a ribbon-infested six-pack of Tully. She loved Tully, but she couldn't drink it until she decided whether to keep the baby.

Whether? The shock threw Esau out of her mind. Whether? She didn't know whether to nurture or destroy the baby? A part of the pack? He leaned against the tiled wall and let the hot water sluice over him.

She wouldn't think in terms of pack. She would see a reminder of what had destroyed her former life. No matter how hard she fought to recover her old life, she had to see it was gone. Destroying the baby would not bring her back to where she'd been before. To much of the pack, her ability to produce a pack-member would determine whether she was seen as packmate or as property.

The baby would be Addie's salvation too. Once born, the baby would have to be DNA-tested, to prove Addie's bloodline. But in the intervening months, the possibility of a bloodline would shield her from the hungry young women who would otherwise challenge her, one after another, until she lost her city and her life.

He reached out of the shower, wiped his arm on the towel, pulled the telephone from his pants pocket, and stabbed the number in.

Addie answered in her clipped fashion. "Yes, I'm still here. No thanks to you."

"You've been challenged?"

"Twice." She sighed. "Good news travels *so* fast."

She thought he ought to be there. But if he were at the challenge, all he could do to help would be enforce the rules, protect the combatants from interference. Others could perform that function. Only he could protect Tyler.

Addie had chosen a cougar form over the wolf form she insisted on for everyone else. Although the added size, cat-reflexes and cat claws gave her multiple advantages, there were reasons a wolf headed nearly every Family in North America. A wolf had the power of all her pack, while a cat stood alone in the world.

"Two more weeks, Addie," he assured her. "Then her baby will be far enough along, and we'll proclaim everywhere that you have an heir. You'll be safe."

"Where *is* she?" Addie burst out. "Where are you?"

He wasn't about to tell her precisely where to send a snatch-crew. "We're in No Man's Land. We met up with Ben a little before dawn. He advised us of a complication. Do you know about the Raleigh claim?"

"You screwed that up too, did you?"

He frowned. Trust Addie to blame this on him. And to assume that casting blame was the most important task here. "I didn't know about the claim. If you did, you should have told me."

"A million and a half dollars in gold, Esau. That's what Raleigh demands for her. Do you know how much I'd have to liquidate? Families are entering unsolicited bids on all the children and most of the younger breeders. Very low bids."

He sighed and pressed the phone against his ear. "You can't sell off an entire generation."

"No, I can't." Her voice went low and vicious. "Come home now. I've pulled in three young females for you, two of them proven breeders and one of them the spitting image of your Tiff. You have two weeks to tease them up and make sure one of them catches on the full moon. This full, Esau. It has to be this one. I can't handle many more challenges."

Water ran down his elbow, tickling unmercifully. "No, Addie. I won't go with another breeder. I'm bonded to this woman. I'll bring my bondmate and her baby home. Trust me on that."

She laughed, and the laugh was a terrible thing. "Like I trusted you with my children, Esau? Like I trusted you on that? All you had to do was tell me what was happening! I could have picked up the phone and they'd've been on their way home. But no, you went tearing off like a one-wolf rescue mission and you got them killed."

She hung up on him.

When he came out of the shower, he found the youngest pilot sprawled across one bed, reading a magazine. The pilot looked up, grinning. "Hey, we got you an entire getup as a GG. The cap'n even found some jump boots for feet as big as yours."

These pilots were suspiciously helpful. "As big as mine?"

"Measured your footprints, man."

"Are you here to keep an eye on me?" Esau sat on the other bed and dressed, watching the pilot's reflection.

"'Fraid I am."

If he wanted to leave, this boy could not stop him. The problem was that this was a mighty big hotel, and Tyler could be anywhere in it. He closed his eyes and sought her.

Then, in his mind, he saw her. She sat about two-thirds of the way down a long table, minor actors between her and the end. Rapt fans—a good third of them in WarDove-inspired costumes—in front of her. A boy stood speaking to her. "Tony Edwards and I'm thirteen. How come the J'iai fighters freak when you maneuver them into spinning counterclockwise on the X axis?"

Tyler shimmered with triumph. *Yes!* She looked at the nearest security man, who wore the orange uniform but topped it with a silvery tabard. "Security? Would you please collect contact info on Mr. Edwards here? He gets the first US copy of Guardian At The Gate."

Jealousy, strong enough to taste, rippled through the room, filling it with variants on "He stole my question!" "I was just about to ask that!" "No fair!" "I really was!"

Tyler, Esau called. *Tyler. You're too far away from me.*

Tyler sat forward, and her foot struck the gift package. She rubbed her foot along one bottle, plinking it melodiously against the next, and wondered if he would like the taste.

Bring it, Tyler, and I will dribble it over your sweet skin, and I will lick it off, drop... by drop... by drop...

Her temperature spiked, her breath rasped in her throat, and no doubt the boys in the front row ate up the vision of her breasts pumping under that uniform top.

She looked beseechingly at the moderator, who was adjusting his notes. "I'm sorry," she said. "One last question."

The moderator said, "We're already over our time limit. This room has to be rearranged for the Anime Festival now. Thank you, ladies and gentlemen! A big round of applause, please, for all our honored guests!"

The Golden Guardian victory call echoed through the applause and the foot stamping. Tyler stood, the movement causing a slight sting in her labia. She clenched her teeth and saluted the audience, then bowed formally to the closest of the actors until the boys chanted his tag line, a roundelay that built a rousing crescendo of sound.

The vision of Tyler faded and Esau smelled coffee. Scorched, but hot. If these pilots were at all like the army's chopper pilots, it would also be strong enough to melt a spoon. "Mr. Esau? I said do you want it black or adulterated?"

"Sorry. My mind was elsewhere. Plenty of sugar, but no milk unless it's real milk."

"Dream on. I can weaken it with battery acid if you like."

"Pardon?"

"Eighty-proof. We call it battery acid for the taste."

"No, thank you."

Tyler eluded him now. He smiled. She would have to concentrate to keep him out now, and that concentration would itself keep some part of her mind on him.

Esau sipped, feeling his taste buds die as the coffee washed over them. Battery acid might have weakened it. He looked over the rim of the cup to the young pilot, who wore a holster, which held something that looked like a taser. The belt had buckle-creases two inches into the loose end. Whoever usually wore that holster belt had a substantially larger belly than the boy did.

"I take it we're here for a while," he said. "Did you bring a deck of cards?"

As if in answer, the phone rang. The boy picked it up, listened to a question, and handed the handset to him.

Tyler. She said, "Esau, I've been invited out to dinner in Bricktown with some of the guys. You want to come?"

The need to fill himself with her scent ate him alive. But neither his hungers nor hers could be satisfied in a restaurant. And she'd be safer with him here. His voice went deeper on its own. "How about room service?"

"Esau! That's not what Cons are for! People come here to *Con*gregate! *Con*fer! *Con*duct business! Experience *con*viviality!"

"Conjoin," he said quietly.

She coughed. "Esau, don't mess with me right now. I've been effectively off the planet for weeks. Now I have work to do. Fences to mend and bridges to build. You want to come with me, or sit there and eat alone?"

It was clear she hadn't given up on her human life—the acclaim, the challenge, the reporters. So Esau needed to be with her, to cover up anything too damaging that she might say about this other world she had just discovered. If she were quoted in the human media as talking about shapeshifters, giving accurate information, he would be forced to turn her in for punishment. And as her mate he'd have to watch from the suicide cage, forcing himself to survive so he could care for what was left of her afterward.

He ran his tongue over his fangs, blunting them bit by bit to the contour of human teeth. He wouldn't let that happen. Not with Tyler.

But if he didn't turn her in, they would both find themselves on the run, hunted at every turn and stop, forever.

Ordering her to come to him would be pointless until he could enforce the order. He could lure her, play with her hormones and her emotions until she had no choice but to come to him, and stay with him. But she might fight him for a long time, and in that time she might reveal too much.

No, it was time to appeal to her tactical sense. "Tyler, you've been out of the loop, right? So isn't making a deal on your first night back a sign of weakness, a sign you're too eager? They expect to either make or receive a pitch, right? So you've shown yourself. Why not back off now? Let them stew and speculate until breakfast. Preserve all the mystery you can. Tomorrow's deal might be a lot better."

She was silent a long time. Finally she spoke, briskly. "Meet me at room 314, as soon as you can."

"Your room?"

"Ours," she said softly.

He lay back on the bed, boneless with relief.

"I think we can skip the card games," he told the pilot, who had pulled out a pack of cards. "I've been invited to another room."

"Somebody besides you needs to tell me," the pilot said, blushing but firm in his tone.

Esau tossed him the phone.

Chapter 12

As Tyler turned the corner of the hallway, she saw him leaning against the wall by her door. Studying the carpet at his feet. Waiting.

His face lifted. When he looked at her from under those heavy brows, her skin buzzed all over. Dropping the Tully, she ran to him.

His mouth met hers, and he sucked her bottom lip between his sharp-edged fangs. She held very still—those things could cut. The fangs retreated, their edges changing shape against her lip. Now they were just teeth, lined up with the rest of his perfectly normal teeth, as if the sharp edges had never existed.

"Inside," he growled.

She handed him the card-key while she went back, feeling foolish, for the wooden six-pack holder and the half-dozen bottles of whisky.

Inside the room, his big hand cupped her chin, turned it toward him. His face might never be open and expressive, but in it she read a want and a need that would melt any woman.

But instead of any kind of sweet talk, he said, barely audibly, "You are not safe without me. You are not safe talking with humans until you know what to say and what to keep hidden."

She pitched her tone as low as his. "I can guess that a Family would be pissed if I talked about them. Don't worry. Babbling about a telepathic link with a mythological creature wouldn't do my credibility any good."

He pulled her close and nuzzled her hair. She stood on her tiptoes and sucked his bottom lip just far enough into her mouth to nip it. Not releasing his lip, she spoke around it. "Now, about this Capture-Bride tradition of yours. What are the essential requirements and what are the extras?"

He waited, silent. She released his lip to let him talk, and was rewarded with that softening around his eyes.

"I have to carry you onto my turf. You can take part of the trip voluntarily, but you have to be carried the last bit of the way. Then there's the greeting ceremony, which is not as bad as it used to be, and you are dressed in clothes my pack furnishes, and then you belong to my Family. After you provide one daughter or two sons, whether you bear them or steal them, you can negotiate a release price. But we won't need to discuss that."

We won't, will we? "Daughters are worth more?"

"They're rarer. About 6 out of 10 births are male, and because puberty hits girls two years younger than it hits boys, we lose more girls at the first shift."

"Lose them? How?"

"Shifting hurts," he said simply. "The first few times, the pain is overwhelming. Until a few generations ago, the first shift hit at 14 to 15, when girls were old enough to comprehend what was happening to them, and when they had studied enough anatomy and pain-disassociation techniques not to lose control. But now they start as young as eleven, when their minds are still little girls' minds."

His hands, locked at the small of her back, trembled. She wondered if they had sprouted claws.

"Sometimes they die," he said, so much anguish in his voice that her eyes stung with tears.

She laid her head against his chest, and listened to his heart go thub-bub, thub-bub in the dark room. People passing in the hallway outside argued vehemently about J'iai fighters.

"How long does the greeting ceremony last?"

"It ends when the captor says it ends."

"That tells me a whole lot!"

"It should," he said softly. "It should tell you that I believe hearing the details would upset you and that I am neither willing to upset you in that manner nor stupid enough to lie about it."

"Okay," she said, trying to be reasonable, "I hear what you're saying. Let me guess at the rest."

She stepped back from him and peeled out of her uniform. She never had found a bra to wear today, so her breasts were sore from bouncing around, but when she'd pulled off the under-tunic and stood there in her underpants, the look on Esau's face was worth it.

"The initial function of capturing a bride must've been to broaden the genetic base of the Family," she said in her best seminar voice. "The captor might soften up the bride with lots of teasing and heavy petting on the way home, but he holds off potential insemination so they can ah—conjoin—for the first time on Family turf, maybe with Family representatives standing there watching, right? With the passage of time that fertility-based ritual has probably evolved to some kind of symbolic or mock-boffing. What's left is still something I would find incredibly embarrassing, right?"

"You aren't too far off."

"So in what way am I wrong?"

"I don't intend to tell you. Just trust me."

He moved closer, and she wrapped her arms around his neck. He inhaled deeply, burying his nose in the hair behind her ear.

Heat pumped through her veins. She spread her legs slightly, letting her sweet-tart musk rise to his wolfy nose. "Take off your clothes and talk to me, Esau. How else will I know?"

"You'll find out when we get to Memphis," he said hoarsely. "Sufficient to each day is the evil thereof."

She had aphorisms of her own. "The wise commander is the one who knows where to expect surprise." She ran one hand over the rigid shaft under his uniform's fly, and dipped the other in her own underpants. She swiped her wet fingers over his mouth. "Can you—oof!"

He pinned her to the wall, his big hands holding her thighs up and spread. He leaned into her, hips forward, his uniform's belt buckle cold against her and his body spreading her legs wider.

That's more like it! She grabbed his shoulders and jerked his upper body closer. His hair was luxuriantly soft against her face as she nibbled his ear. He breathed hard, like a man in a fight, and rested his forehead on the wall beside her.

He tried to say something, which seemed silly, with his face pressed to the wall like that. She wanted to pull open his uniform collar and taste the base of his neck, but he hadn't left enough room for her hands to maneuver.

"Bed, Esau. Let's use the bed for this."

"In—a minute," he gasped. "I need—shower."

Balls! Your hair's barely dry from your last shower! She got a sudden vision of him jacking off in the shower, bleeding off the pressure so he could lie beside her all night without losing his self-control.

I'll show you a loss of control! Try to keep your distance through this! She hooked her legs about his waist so that she barely needed his hands under her butt to hold her up, and she undulated between him and the wall, grinding against him like a pole-dancer.

He moved one hand to cup her open flesh, so she rubbed her clit against his palm. That rough touch set her off immediately. She spasmed against his hand, and bit his collar to smother her cry.

He pressed her harder to the wall. When she fell limp, he pulled her gently so her head and one arm draped over his shoulder, and carried her to the bed.

Okay, that's a good start.

He arranged her on the sheet, and started to cover her with the blanket.

She kicked the covers out of his hand and gripped his uniform collar. "Some lovers would find so little interest insulting, Mr. Kirkland."

"How many lovers have you manipulated with so little effort, Miss Tyler?" His cold tone slapped her with stunning force. "You demand truth, but you won't tell it or listen to it. How long did you think it would take me to figure out you didn't even give me the right name?"

"I told you it was my first name. I came close," she mumbled, but he'd hit a sore spot.

"Not close enough. In our world, a male takes his mate's name. How foolish would I look if I announced I'd taken your name, Randolph, when a million or so gamers know your family name is Tyler?" He tried to stand up, but she tightened her grip on his collar.

"Have you made that announcement?"

"Not publicly. Tomorrow, in Memphis, I will." He sat beside her and disengaged her hand from his collar.

She took the opportunity to undo his belt buckle.

"Stop, Tyler. You have to know when you can't win."

"No, *you* have to know when I've won."

His surprise whispered through her. He must know she meant it, but didn't see how.

She grinned and used that surprise to open all his zippers at once. "You're on my turf, big guy. My bird and my pilot carried you onto my turf, and that was one hell of a greeting ceremony we had on the roof, even if it doesn't fit your Family's script. You're surrounded by my people. You're even wearing clothes I designed and my people provided. So take them off, and let's get to the fertility ritual."

He caught her hands. "This isn't a game, Tyler."

She glared at him. "Everything's a game, Esau. The fact that the stakes are high does not change the nature of the game, or the rules we play by. I won. You're mine."

They were arguing like any human couple, but he wasn't human and he insisted she wasn't. *So how do were-critters argue? Mind to mind, or skin to skin? Both?*

She closed her eyes and inhaled deeply, as he did. He smelled of soap. She'd showered less than an hour ago, but she smelled her own sharply aroused scent. What she could smell, he could. *Nothing is more arousing than someone who thinks you're the hottest bod on the planet.*

She pictured his long lines in loving detail, and his hands tightened on hers. His breath grew harsher, and she matched it.

"What are you scared of, Esau? Scared Bastian's going to show up, sniff me over, and ask who's been squatting in his catbox?"

His lips thinned. "You have the most inelegantly precise way of saying things."

"Are you scared of Bastian Truc?"

"No. I'm scared of Raleigh. Memphis can't afford to buy you and can't afford to fight a war over you."

"Memphis doesn't have to. You're my capture-bride. You no longer belong to Memphis, if I heard the rules right."

He stiffened. Finally, she was getting through.

"You're claiming me as your property? That doesn't change the fact that you're property of Raleigh. It removes Memphis—my allies—from the equation but leaves us in Truc's power."

"Not necessarily. I think Bastian Truc was the guy who sold me to that lab for half a million. If he thought me dead, he probably didn't spend a fortune to exercise his option to rescind that deal. If Bastian Truc sold me, where's the Truc Family claim? Whoever owned that lab has a stronger claim than Truc." She mused, "Maybe we can set those two powers off against each other."

Esau watched her. "Why would Truc sell you? Aren't you two in on a very lucrative business together?"

"We had a disagreement. I might have upset him enough to make it personal, but I suspect he wanted the gold, plus his share of the three mil from the insurance, plus my company as effectively his own." She bit her lip. "If shapeshifters owned that lab, we need to find out which Family, right?"

"Humans owned it."

"How do you know?"

"Any shifters that close would answer to my sister, and if they defied Addie they'd answer to me."

Addie Kirkland? The name came back to her. *The scary lady who gave those sensitivity lectures that Bastian made everybody attend?*

"Also," he said, pain aging his face with deep lines, "the human subjects were housed upstairs and wore pajamas. The guards were human. The shifters were kept underground and naked."

Yeah, naked versus clothed makes it pretty clear who had the power.

Addie Kirkland knows Bastian Truc. Does Esau know that?

She licked her lips. "If Truc sold me to humans, then I don't belong to Truc or any other shifter family, right?"

"That assumes Bastian Truc had the authority to sell you. He seems to be a very junior member of his Family. Even if I kill him, we have the rest of the family to deal with. The negotiations will be delicate, and risky."

"Risky in exactly what way?"

"Have you ever known a person who had a frontal lobotomy?"

"Tell me you just changed the subject." But the chills tickling her skin said he had not.

"Whipping, burning and rape are the common punishments for insubordination, but when a Family needs a face or a body, and the person inside is too much of a bother, the Family calls in a specialist to make the person amenable. It's not like the human surgery where the tissue is delicately sliced. Our surgeons burn away portions of the brain. The brain generates a new personality as it re-grows the missing tissue."

She shook her head. "When human brains are damaged, they stay damaged."

"Exactly. They might leave you the ability to sign your name, or maybe just enough to recognize it when called."

Nausea rose. "And this is the cozy little society you've been trying to drag me into?"

He jerked her to him, and those long arms wrapped tight about her. "In Memphis, I could protect you."

She shivered in his arms. "Like you protected your wife, or her kids? Or the kids in that picture? What happened to them?"

She felt something break inside him. The noise was indefinable, like a soap bubble popping, but the released pressure spun in her head and grayed her vision. Despair tore at her, and regret. And rage.

His memories sucked her under.

She crouched in the moon-shadow of a blooming dogwood, cramping and sweating under rigid control, remaining human until Tiff completed the agonizingly careful maneuvers needed to take wolf shape without triggering a premature labor. Then she released her own shift. Pain and relief flooded every vein, muscle, nerve, and bone like an orgasm.

She drowned in the scents of the living forest flowing past, as the pack ran for the sheer joy of running together.

Suzu struck her with golf-ball-sized fists and squalled with hunger. But Tiff came in wearing outrage like strong perfume. "She won't let up, Esau! I can't stand it any more! Can't stand! Can't stand! Can't stand!"

"No, Esau, I *won't* settle for some Podunk town in the middle of nowhere!

I'll have my own city! Own city! Own city!"

Davie rode one shoulder while Petey rode the other. They wrestled overhead as she ducked to enter the front door. "Swing, Uncle Esau! Swing us!" Danny leaped on for a boot ride, nearly tripping her. She hopped around in a circle and the boys shrieked with laughter.

"Where are the girls, Addie?"

A woman's flat voice. "Cincinnati came for them. Tiffy's dead."

Something struck her windshield, shooting out a spider web of white cracks, and ahead of her a cinderblock building crumbled, each floor collapsing onto the floor below it, and Davie's presence in her head cut off with a horrifying finality.

"David!" she gasped, unable to scream with Esau's weight on her.

She was back on the bed, flat on her back, with Esau atop her wriggling out of his pants.

"I won't lose you too," he said, the words coming from deep inside him. "Whatever it takes, I'll keep you safe."

His thick cock pressed against her, and a little way in, but she had no slip for him. His memories had dried her out. Shaking, gritting his teeth, he got up on his elbows. If he disconnected, lost his momentum here, she could lose whatever advantage she'd just gained. She locked her legs about his hips. "Don't go."

"Look at me, then," he growled. "Feel me."

She looked hard at him, the strong lines of his weathered face. The knotted muscles of his shoulders. He quivered with the strain of not ramming into her with all he had, right now. With the strain of not hurting her. *That one's mine.*

The slip came, barely enough. He pressed slowly in.

"Feel me, sweetheart."

She couldn't avoid feeling him, big as he was. She moved under him, undulating her hips, feeling her insides stretch to accommodate a cock that thick. They lay together a moment, his forearms under her shoulders and her ear pressed against his haired chest, listening to his pounding heart.

He withdrew, leaving her with a stinging, irrational sense of loss. But before she could speak he surged back in, hard, and what cream she had was plenty to slick the way. She raised her hips to meet the next hard thrust, and the next.

Without missing a stroke, Esau lifted her butt higher and stuffed a pillow under it. Then he caught her knees in the crooks of his elbows, opening her body more than she thought it could open.

Deep he went, bruising deep, though his clenched face testified to the effort of holding back. His heartbeat thundered against her, inside her.

She grasped her ankles and curled tighter against him. *Don't hold back, Esau.*

"You are *mine!*" he said through his fangs, thrusting deep. His pubic bone pressed against her clit, shooting a near-painful jolt of pleasure along every nerve. "I will *not* give you over. *Not* to anyone. *Not* for any reason."

Mine! Mine! Mine! Every thrust pounded the word through her, leaving no cell, no thought unbranded with his heat, his hunger, his possession.

Her own hunger swallowed every wet, hot thrust. *Mine!*

•

Chapter 13

The partying in the surrounding rooms lasted all night. At various times Tyler awakened to a barbershop quartet, arguing, drunken laughter. Around four a.m., people wrestling or dancing next door bounced the mirror against the wall. That brought Esau awake and snarling, his rangy body angled to shield hers.

She chuckled, her cheek pressed to his muscled forearm.

He folded down beside her. "When do these people sleep?"

"Mostly from right after breakfast to around lunchtime, especially when breakfast comes with the room. Not much is scheduled for the morning: shopping and swapping, round-table discussions, beta-testing new games." She yawned.

His thumb rubbed languorously over her bottom lip. "How soft you are."

She sucked the pad of his thumb into her mouth, and twirled her tongue around it. No part of Esau was soft.

He rubbed his wet thumb over her bottom lip again, and then stroked his hand along her side, barely touching the skin, and followed the motion with one a couple of inches above her skin.

"Can you see that?"

"Your hand? Sure. What's odd is that I feel the warmth, even that far off my skin."

"You don't see your aura, how it shimmers as I run my hand through it?" He stroked above her skin again.

"That tickles! And no, I don't see any shimmer."

"To me it looks like the Northern Lights, but flowing toward my hand and pulsating with my heartbeat."

She listened. "Our heartbeats. They're in sync."

"So they are." His cock pulsed against her. "Want to feel something else?"

Oh, yeah.

⁂

If everyone else hadn't looked so ragged at breakfast, she probably would have collected more curious looks than she did. Esau followed her through the buffet line, nodding and making approving noises as she slathered peanut butter over her waffle but blocking her fork with a banana when she reached for the sausage. "Hey! I like sausage!"

"Sorry," he said, edging her away from the food bar and ushering her to an empty table, "I'd get so sick watching you eat it that you'll get sick in sympathy, and once the two of us barf, everyone else here will barf right along in chorus."

She laughed. "If you want me sick, you need to try harder."

"Have sympathy on the cleaning crew, and eat your fruit."

"You don't like how laws and sausages are made?"

"Regardless of how they're made, they're pork. Someone who gets a taste for pork will eat human meat, when he's in no position to think through his actions."

"Whoa!" She closed her eyes and swallowed a few times, and the nausea abated. "I wasn't daring you to try harder."

"Sounded like it to me. Sounded almost like an order."

"Tyler likes giving orders," put in a smooth voice. Bastian. Of course. He would attend the con, especially if he thought she'd be there. He set a grapefruit half on the table and slid into the seat across the table from her, right next to Esau. Both men wore the same golden uniform, down to the pilot first-class insignia.

Unlike the motley, rough-edged WarDove uniform, the Guardian uniform had been designed to highlight Bastian's super-curly black hair and chocolate eyes. Next to Esau he looked like a model, too young and too smooth to have earned his medals.

As if Bastian didn't exist, Esau glared at someone hovering behind Tyler. Her back itched. What kind of muscle had Bastian brought? He loved dressing up an escort or two in uniforms as photogenic as his, even when the meeting was a seminar and the uniforms were silk business suits. Here, he could go wild.

"You must be Esau," Bastian said.

"Get them off her back," Esau growled, still not looking at him. She resisted the urge to turn and look. If Esau felt that threatened, he would tell her when to duck, or run.

Bastian smiled. "I hate to be the first to tell you, but I don't like taking orders."

Balls! Bastian was really enjoying this. She forced herself to peel her banana.

Bastian looked up over her head. "Tyler, Have you ever met my uncle Richard and my cousin Johnny-Ray? Richard is the new CFO for HandPlus, and Johnny-Ray is our new security consultant."

They hovered behind her like thugs. But Richard Truc was known as a high-level knight errant, a CPA who sometimes salvaged companies in distress.

"They're fired," she said. "So are you."

"Not without a vote of the shareholders, I'm not, and you can't get rid of my appointees while I'm still president." He sprinkled a precise half-teaspoon of sugar over his grapefruit. "Not that I intend to let you call a vote."

"How you plan to stop me?"

Bastian smiled.

From two tables away, a quartet of men and boys stared at her. She rounded her eyes a little, to suggest distress, and as one they scowled. Dozens of people in this room knew who she was. She couldn't be taken out of here without her agreement or a scene, and Bastian loathed any scene he hadn't personally staged.

The quartet broke up. Maybe she should have thrown them more of a soft, beseeching look. Bastian worked his way clockwise through his grapefruit, ignoring her.

Esau, in guard-wolf mode, ignored his food.

She nibbled her banana. *Esau? Ease down. We're in public. In the public eye. He can't do a thing here.* But she got no impression he heard her. This mental bonding thing worked a whole lot more often when he wanted it to. *What a pisser.*

As tense as Esau was, as much as she disliked people standing behind her, the objective threat during a crowded breakfast buffet was not all that extreme. *I need to break up this tableau before the situation deteriorates.*

"Hey, Uncle Richard?" she asked. "What do you say about Bastian here screwing the rest of the Family out of half million in gold? Doesn't income derived from the sale of a Family asset belong to the Family as a unit?"

One of the presences left her back. A distinguished-looking gentleman in the shimmering deluxe Golden Guardian uniform dropped into the chair beside her. He had Bastian's curly hair, but it was all salt and pepper. "Miss Tyler, you have my ears."

Just then, orange Guardian uniforms and tan Hotel Security uniforms converged on them. A big, dark man in muscle-hugging orange stepped forward. "Miss Tyler, I'm Andrew Black Horse, chairman of the Con Committee. I missed my chance to welcome you yesterday evening."

She smiled at him. "Delighted to meet you, Mr. Black Horse. I met Miss Barnes and Mr. Kaufman yesterday, and of course I know the McGregors." She nodded to the Con Committee members ranged behind him. "Thank you for comping us such a nice room. Most kind of you all. Have you met Richard Truc, Bastian Truc, Johnny-Ray behind me, and—" she took a breath, for she'd never said this before— "my husband Esau Tyler?"

Esau's eyes gleamed as he rose and stuck out his hand, both he and Black Horse moving to stand over Richard.

A stranger's hand settled on Tyler's neck, and something sharp prickled in warning against her skin.

She froze. *Esau?*

Esau's gaze met hers and moved up behind her. He spoke quietly, but with death in his tone. "Get your hand off my wife's neck."

Black Horse nodded. "That would be a good idea, sir. I don't want to step into a Family dispute, but we need to discuss the day's schedule with Ms. Tyler right now, before things get moving for the day."

Esau, did I hear Family in capital letters?

I don't know. He's not a shifter, but he might be a Friend.

The hand lifted from her neck. She took the opportunity to rise from her chair, and turn to take a look at this Johnny-Ray. He was the only Truc she'd ever met who actually looked Asian.

She forced a brittle smile and turned to the Con Committee. Only one of them seemed hung over, but they all had the uneasy look of people who know more is up than they can follow. "Who has some ideas of how I can pay for my keep today?"

They laughed. Nervous laughter. Then they swarmed around her as they had upon her arrival, chattering on top of each other, verbally wrestling and pushing for attention.

The warmth at her back was Esau. When she reached back, his rough hand engulfed hers.

❦

When they escaped the breakfast room with its reek of fried pork, Esau breathed deeply to clear his nose. The Con Committee's youngest member, a plump black-haired girl with "Cherokee National" on her t-shirt and kanji-painted blue tattoos at the outer corners of her eyes, bounced along beside him, flaunting the structural inadequacies of her bra.

The girl bubbled over about how she'd issued an invitation, but never expected Miz Tyler to actually, like, appear. She'd just, you know, daydreamed a little. Daydreamed to the point she'd planned out a complete alternative schedule for the con, based on Tyler dropping out of the sky.

Tyler ribbed her about the 'dropping out of the sky' part and someone said one could never over-prepare for contingencies. Tyler and Bastian Truc traded off outrageous contingencies that would bankrupt anyone planning for them. Everyone laughed.

He didn't like Tyler and Bastian laughing together.

Bastian laid an affectionate hand on Tyler's shoulder, and she went cold, her hand tightening on Esau's.

Bastian looked into Esau's eyes and gave Tyler's shoulder a quick squeeze before dropping his hand. Tyler's hand relaxed. So long as they stayed with the Con Committee, Tyler felt safe. That would have to be enough for him, too.

The bouncy girl tugged at Esau's sleeve. "So you're, like, her hubby? Where'd you come from? How come nobody knew Miz Tyler was married? How long ya'll been together?"

"I'm from Memphis."

"Oh, *turrble* about the quake. My church sent two trailers of food and clothes. I hope you didn't lose anyone close?"

He clenched his jaw as the fangs erupted, letting them stab into his own mouth rather than show them. Tyler's hand tightened on his.

Bastian Truc was the one who answered. "Esau lost his nephew, and other Family members. We don't like to talk about it."

Tyler's surprise and suspicion rivaled his own. So she hadn't told Bastian. Who had?

The plump girl put a hand to her mouth, fingernail kanji spelling out verses on her skin. Did she even know what those words were? She babbled apologies until someone hushed her.

Tyler looked at him with soft eyes. *The quake? All those kids?*

Every one.

Esau. Her sympathy rolled through him. He had to say one thing before Bastian Truc said it, or before it occurred to her. *My nephew was in the lab with you.*

A child—there? Her fury spiked, sharp and hot.

No longer a child, he told her.

The spike of fury abruptly wilted. She withdrew, putting her skin like a veil between them, shutting him out of her mind. That wasn't enough. She let go his hand and walked quickly to catch up with Black Horse. He didn't need telepathy to know she'd suddenly remembered fifteen years having passed since Ben photographed the pack's children. Even if she did not want to think through the implications, she would. Sooner or later. Before or after Truc slapped her—and him—in the face with that information.

Esau pressed his aura into hers. Her step faltered. He barely paused to acknowledge her dismay. She had to hear it from him, not from anyone else. *They'd grown up, Tyler. My nephew and his mate were caged in that lab as breeders.* She stopped. She turned and stared at him, her eyes stark in her pale face.

Truc caught her arm. "Ty? You okay?"

"She's not going to faint," Esau growled. "She doesn't need your support." *How it started is less important than what we have, Tyler.*

She stared at him. Then she looked down, as composed and as distant as a marble statue in a cemetery.

"Do you three need a room to play out this drama," Black Horse asked, "or is the audience a necessary part of it?" As he spoke, he pushed open the heavy door to a small meeting room.

A woman snored on the long table, cuddled up to a vodka bottle. By the rankness of her smell, she'd been there a few hours. Black Horse pinched her earlobe to bring her upright and escorted her to the corridor with a tersely worded order to find her room right now or lose her con badge.

Esau pulled Tyler close. Her erratically jumping pulse settled to a steady rhythm as her skin warmed against his. "How it started is less important than what we have," she murmured to his chest.

"How sweet," Bastian murmured in the same tone. "And what precisely do we have?"

"A bond," Esau said, hoping Tyler would let him decide how much was safe to say in front of the humans here.

Tyler shivered and turned to the bouncy girl. "Let's see your contingency plan."

"Um, yes." She pulled a mini-CD from a knee pocket. "I need to go use the printer in the business suite. How many copies?"

"Half a dozen, to start." Black Horse handed her a copy-card. "Use this. We prepaid plenty more pages than we've used."

While they waited, a waitress rolled in a cart with an urn of coffee and baskets of fixings. Tyler doctored hers with plenty of milk, Esau noticed. He leaned against the wall to watch the interactions. Tyler and Bastian both courted and charmed the committee members, who actively courted them in return.

None of the committee members was a shifter, although the woman with long silver braids was half; the oldest human male hovered by her, managing to stay between her and any of the shifters. They wore the gold finger-rings of married humans, scratched and battered-looking rings that must have seen decades of wear. Tyler stole glances at those gnarled hands with their matching rings, and the sadness in her face pinched things inside him.

She looked up at him, then she blinked and assured Black Horse that nothing would thrill her more than the honor of helping judge the costume contests. The man grimaced, and they laughed together.

As she laughed, Tyler reached for Esau's hand. He moved close enough to mingle their auras. A certain tenseness left her. She ate up the smiles and the flattery and the joking, but all the time she sought his solidity at her back.

There were worse ways for a woman to think of her mate.

After the meeting, they rejoined the carnival atmosphere of the con. Tyler pored through the wares at the book swap, glanced over the figurines and the cards, and finally sat on the corner of a table to debate the merits of old 8-bit and 16-bit games.

Esau leaned against a nearby wall, watching the comings and goings and keeping only general tabs on the conversation. The debate segued to a discussion of online RPGs, which had taken up so much bandwidth at home that the family budget had always included this year's upgrades. The debate wandered over to movie tie-ins and whether Tyler had pulled her vanishing act to privately negotiate movie rights.

She laughed, and he wondered why that laugh didn't make all these people know the truth. "Wait and see."

Someone in a passing group asked if they knew the radio play was being taped now.

Tyler jumped up. "Oh! I want to see that! Um, hear it!"

Esau followed her down a corridor packed with aliens, elves, vampires, mystics, and paramilitary types. More than a few of them needed to familiarize themselves with the wonderful human invention called deodorant.

Beside Tyler, a door suddenly opened. She recoiled.

An older boy darted out of the crowd and shoved Tyler mightily toward the door.

Esau lunged for her, but a third boy—a shifter—tripped him. Johnny-Ray Truc reached through the doorway and yanked Tyler to him. The door snicked shut.

Chapter 14

"Tyler!" He wrenched open the door, just in time to see a gurney speed through the door at the far end of the room. Another door slammed shut. *Scream, Tyler. Raise hell!*

No response. A tidy snatch—only he understood what had happened. He and those two boys, who had vanished in the crowd.

He covered the ground to the other door. This corridor was empty, but on the floor lay a scrap of paper smelling of freshly burned ink and bearing the stylized face of a tiger. He inhaled deeply. Johnny-Ray and another male shifter had been here. They'd left scent trails in both directions, wholly masking Tyler's subtler aroma.

Tyler! No answer. She had to be unconscious.

Truc had taken her.

But Truc had erred. As Memphis, the rules of engagement would now bind Esau's actions until he stood helpless outside his turf, away from his pack. But after last night, he was no longer Memphis; nothing could stop him from recovering his mate except his duty to keep the killing out of human sight.

He picked up the paper. Ornate script invited him to an impromptu Family meeting, in Conference Suite 17a, immediately.

The invitation could be a trick; they could be heading for the roof or out the back exit right now. But he was only one person. He could go in only one direction at a time.

Two young girls eyed him from the corner. When he looked up, they squeaked and ran, their fear pinching his nose. He closed his eyes. *Wolves! Wolves! Come to me!*

The power of a tiger is in himself. The power of a wolf is in his pack. *Wolves!*

He'd never Summoned a pack before. Maybe he should've. Maybe he should have spent less time in the city, using the ubiquitous electric lighting to keep his wolf-self under control. Maybe he should have spent more time on all fours in the unadulterated moonlight, fighting something besides the moon in his blood.

Wolves! Come to me!

Faint, startled presences responded. No words—that would take abilities he didn't have. He repeated the Summons. He'd have to keep repeating it until they understood, until the force of his will compelled them to obey.

Here in the hotel, no one would accuse him of defiling another wolf's turf. No one would demand greater compensation than he could pay.

Wolves!

One of them objected. Esau mentally snarled; to master a pack, he could allow no challenge. The protesting wolf hunkered, too weak to fight. Too weak to be of much use, but Esau needed every wolf he could get. *Come to me!*

A youngster, barely old enough to shift, came close, with two younger siblings. Their mother awakened in an upper floor, her astonishment like limes on his tongue. *Memphis?*

Ben's mate. *Esau yes. Memphis no.*

She understood, and she didn't like it.

Come!

A male boomed in his head. *Who Calls?*

A healer? Could he be so lucky? *I am Esau Tyler. My mate is taken. Come to me!*

He couldn't focus long on one without losing his nebulous contact with the others. *Wolves! Come to me!*

He walked slowly toward the south end of the building and the conference suites, gathering in the lines that connected him to his new pack.

A pair of teenagers joined him within the minute, sweating a nervous stink. The shorter one pulled out a phone and speed-dialed. "It's that tall guy who came with FuckWare Tyler. We're at the elevators on the first floor, heading into the south wing."

Esau mentally crushed another sub-verbal protest. "Suite 17a. Tell all wolves to come immediately."

"Yes, sir." The boy saluted, a Golden Guardian salute, reminding Esau he was in uniform, and relayed that information into his phone. "Sir? My sister is a bear, but she loves the game. Should she come?"

"Yes. Tyler needs all the Family support she can get."

"There's about a dozen of us here today, you know."

Twelve? He squelched the immediate thought of Tyler as a Lady in her own right. These people had come to this place in search of a party, not a Family. She wouldn't be able to hold them together. But for today... "Call them all. Every one of them. Call the Friends, too."

The boy made call after call after call, and Esau drew in the lines.

If the Trucs were smart, they'd bring no wolves to this meeting. They could. They might think they had a wolf who could dominate him, but such overconfidence on their part would be too much of a stroke of luck to even pray for.

Her shoulders and upper arms ached. Her neck hurt too, but not as bad, and she felt nothing below her elbows. She smelled Esau's salty, smoky, comforting scent. She moaned, pressing her face to his muscled abdomen.

And came upright, reeling. The scent was wrong. *Whose bod am I nuzzling?*

Bastian Truc cuddled her closer and nipped playfully along her neck. "Don't stop, Ty. Come back and do some more of that."

She staggered to her feet and pulled away from him, though she felt off-balance. Her arms had been fastened behind her. The sharp angle suggested it was wrists to elbows instead of wrist to wrist.

"Where's Esau?" Was he hurt? Killed? *Esau!*

"Ooh, Tyler. You're going to be so much fun to break in."

Balls! Bastian and his games. "He told you that he and I bonded. You're poaching."

The laughter vanished from his face. His brown eyes heated. "Halfies don't bond."

"Halfies don't get pregnant either, do they? If I followed the rules, you and I would still be assistant programmers working as contract labor in Denver. Why am I trussed up like a rotisserie chicken?"

He smiled again, slowly, but the heat remained in his eyes. In Esau's eyes that heat was a promise. Bastian made it a threat. Fear ate at her anger. She scowled. She couldn't afford fear.

"I'm treating you as a shifter," he said. "That's pure flattery, and you should take it as such. When a shifter brings home a captured bride, the pretzel-arms keep her from shifting until they mate."

"Shift? Make up your mind. Am I a shifter who can bond and breed and all that good stuff, or a halfie who can't?" *Esau!*

Sulfurous rage—Esau's rage—tightened her muscles. Her shoulders stretched until she screamed.

A hand clamped over her mouth. She bit down, and tasted blood as hard fingers squeezed her lips against her teeth. She kicked back, raking her boot down the shin of the man who held her. But he wore boots too. *Esau!*

An eerie calm, smelling of wet clay in the winter, replaced the rage. *Don't fight, sweetheart. Anyone who helps hold you for him has the right to take a turn.*

A turn? Her knees folded. Cool mist swirled about her, momentarily hiding the floor. *What the blazes?*

A man—Johnny-Ray—stooped over her, lifted her easily from the mist, and carried her back to Bastian. She didn't fight him. Most carefully didn't fight.

Bastian used one arm to steady her in his lap and with the other reached over her to catch Johnny-Ray by the wrist. "Biting, Ty? There are rules for biting, and penalties when you break them."

Her heart pounded while Johnny-Ray studied her. She still tasted blood. She'd split her lip, at the very least.

Johnny-Ray drew back his bruised hand and wiped it on his hip. "The blood is hers and the fault is mine," he said. "I forgot the filming story and hurried to quiet her."

Filming? Behind him three other men stood in ankle-deep mist, working out the wiring and lighting for a video set-up. A camera on a tripod stared straight at her with its hooded purple lens and tiny blinking lights. On a table beside it, two more cameras sat amid a tangle of wires. Mist spilled from a squat gray machine on another table.

Several spotlights flared, their beams converging on the doorway of the room. The light reflected off the wallpaper around it with painful intensity. *They can make any kind of noise they want. They might get away with growing fur and tails.*

Esau, they're talking about filming. They have lights set up to blind you as you come in the door.

Bastian moved her to straddle his lap, and probably not too coincidentally to straddle his cock. She tried to move away from it, but he held her effortlessly.

She frowned. She was nobody's idea of an Amazon, but she'd never been this weak. "What did you drug me with, Bastian?"

"Don't worry about it. The narcotic component has been neutralized and the other components are wearing off." He pulled one of her zippers halfway down and groped under it, flipping his knuckle over her nipple. "No reaction, Ty? That'll change."

"Bastian, you should seriously consider taking a class in Basic Foreplay."

He pinched, hard. *Ow!*

"You have no idea, Ty, how long I have anticipated tutoring you in the exquisite arts of obedience."

"I always wanted a tiger-skin rug."

"Settle for wolf-skin." He turned her to face the door. "Places, everyone. Aaaand—showtime!"

The door burst open. Instead of Esau, the lights caught a burly, bearded man in a monk's robe, brandishing a thick staff, the upper half of his face hidden in his deep hood. He strode in, the staff in his right hand striking the floor in time with his left heel. A slender young man and a teenaged girl, both in Golden Guardian uniforms, marched behind him.

Bears. She identified them without thinking. *Esau?*

Here. Be patient, sweetheart.

The lights abandoned the attack on the door to focus on the approaching monk. He centered himself in front of the main camera, shin-deep in mist.

The light men assume he's the target, she realized, and her bruised mouth reminded her not to grin.

The monk turned to Bastian with a crisp military right face that stirred the mist, a thump of his staff emphasizing the thud of his left heel striking the floor.

"I am *Bear!*" he roared. "I have no master. I have no Lady. What I say of this dispute, all Families shall hear!"

Bastian's uncle Richard projected a trained baritone. "I am Tiger, and first male of Truc. I know your scent, Bear, but with all due respect this dispute is private. A rogue male has trespassed on Truc."

"Truc is the trespasser," Esau said, his quiet rough voice carrying just as clearly. On the other side of the light he stood, his uniform shimmering like molten bronze. Half a dozen guys, a couple of women, and some teens clustered behind him. Most of them wore home-made or cheaply run-up orange variants on the Guardian uniform.

"I am Wolf," Esau went on, his harsh voice raising shivers on Tyler's skin and taking some starch out of the cock pressed against her inner thigh. "Truc has taken my bondmate by force and by deceit. Took her from my side, from under my arm."

Johnny-Ray leaned forward.

Esau stopped him with a glare. "She carries my child. By these facts, she and I demand forfeit."

"Truc denies your facts," Richard replied smoothly.

Balls! "What—"

Don't speak, Tyler! Esau warned. She frowned at him, but before she could speak again, Bastian's chuckle silenced her.

Bastian twined his fingers in her hair and snatched her head back. A new spotlight glared hot and white on her face and throat.

For a moment, everything stood still. Then Esau's scent seeped into her, past Bastian's too-similar scent.

She didn't have to see past the light. What Esau saw, she saw. The living force at his back was hers to draw on and command. If only she knew what to do with it.

She relaxed in Bastian's grip, and felt Richard Truc's gaze travel curiously over her. From her angle, his head was a curly-edged silhouette, the light glinting red through individual swirling hairs. With Esau's eyes, she saw his intelligent face and implacable will, and behind it a tiger's hunger. The throat show was for him. To whet his appetite and egg him on.

"Look at him," Bastian whispered to her neck, and licked the vein under her ear. "You might as well want him. He's first."

"She is my bondmate!" Esau's rage burned through his calm.

Maybe the bared-throat display was for Esau after all, to knock him off balance. Or, like most of Bastian's tactics, maybe it was aimed at more than one result. *Steady, Esau. If you lose it, who's going to stop all hell from busting loose?*

Chapter 15

The Bear-monk's staff hammered the floor. "The wolf asserts a fact. Does the tiger contest or accept it?"

Esau stared at her. She glowed in his vision, like the spotlight was inside her.

Steady, Esau. The bear's playing like he's in control, but he's just playing a role. If you lose your cool, and the tigers do too, he'll switch roles. Then they might as well set up a sausage factory in here.

Esau nodded, shortly. A mental screen dropped between her and everyone else in the room, dimming the lights and muffling Richard's voice. Only scents remained at full force.

Tyler sorted through the scents: the faint chemical scent of the equipment and the mist. The musk of the bears in front of Esau. The mixed scents from the Guardians clustered behind him. A faint whiff of gun oil, which alarmed him no less because it came from his rear. They couldn't afford gunplay.

One of the Guardians was fully human. Esau carried an extra level of anxiety for him, but the boy eagerly anticipated a fight.

A fight? Surely not a free-for-all. That would make more mess than any "movie" explanation could possibly cover.

One on one, man against man, she would bet on Esau against any of the Trucs. Except maybe Johnny Ray. Logically, then, Johnny Ray had come to do any fighting that needed doing. She measured him with Esau's eye. Not a walkover, but he didn't want to win bad enough to beat Esau.

A shapeshifter one-on-one would just as likely be tiger against wolf, though. That sounded like a bad idea. A wolf ran what, a hundred twenty, hundred forty pounds for a really big one? And a tiger had to run at least three times that. So if—

The power of a wolf is in his pack.

But he worried about his pack. He wasn't sure of victory, and she caught tendrils of uncertainty in whether he had the right to risk these people in this personal combat.

Uncertainty is the surest way to lose a fight, Esau.

Then again, he had reason to worry. If it came to her being a live-action inflatable doll for a while or a dozen strangers getting maimed or killed, what kind of choice was that?

It won't come to that.

Then what? This wasn't like a testosterone display in the wild. Most of those were just grandstanding displays, without much real harm done.

It can be the same here. When one side has overwhelming force, the other will back down.

If you need overwhelming force, Esau, use the power of my 'pack.' I have hundreds of WarDoves and Guardian wannabes in this building.

Only wolves generate group energy.

What desert island did you grow up on? Ever attend a football game? Ever get caught in a riot, or a rave? What do you call that, but human group energy? The question is how to tap it.

He withdrew from her to take his turn talking, offering some kind of negotiation she couldn't really follow. The monk pounded the floor again, and Richard Truc answered him. The few words she could catch might as well be in another language. Bastian protested, and she used that distraction to ease out of the strained, chin-up position he'd held her in.

Something about Esau's emotional filter had left her unable to translate sound into meaning. Why? She could blow apart a misguided macho need to protect her delicate sensibilities, but there might be something more dangerous at play.

Maybe something to keep any listening human from following along, which affected her too? No, that was too far outside reality, even the expanded reality she was coming to recognize.

More likely, she could be expected to react to something being said, and he could not afford for her to say anything at all.

She knew from Esau's reaction that the dickering—it plainly was dickering—led to a test. A display of strength. How could she get the Guardians in on it?

The equipment table wasn't visible from her angle. *Esau, do you see a sound system? A karaoke rig? Can you link it into the hotel's intercom?*

Esau said something else and turned on his heel, a military about-face that stirred curls of mist to waist level. He spoke briefly, and the human boy erupted with excitement.

The boy had almost succeeded in doing it at school. He was currently on suspension for it, a fact his mother did not know. He knew what had gone wrong and was sure he could do it right.

The kid had to be psychic as hell, to broadcast so much information. Did psychics have secret societies like the shapeshifters?

The boy clung to Esau's arm, nodding like a spring-headed toy and spitting out cryptic words that wouldn't convey too much to any listener.

The monk listened to a Truc oration and pounded on the floor.

Tyler, the answer is yes. But the hotel can cut us off as soon as they hear it. One line. Just a few words.

The Guardian Call.

Lost somewhere in the glaring lights, the monk pounded on the floor again. Bastian stood, holding her in front of him like a shield, and walked forward with her.

The lights kept her blinded until she realized they were focused on Esau's face. He was the blinded one. She let go of him, settling back inside her own skin, and then she could see.

Bastian snarled and lifted her bound arms behind her. Molten pain seared from mid-skull on down, folding her forward at the waist to ease the pressure.

Don't scream! You can't be prey. Not now. Aloud, Esau said, "Stop playing, kitty-boy. You haven't earned the right."

She'd closed her eyes against the pain, leaving Esau blind in the spotlight. She stood up straight and opened her eyes, determinedly.

I don't need to see. Let go, sweetheart. You can pass out if you need to.

No. She wouldn't be some inert piece of meat for these predators to fight over.

He gave some signal, and his pack's strength flowed into him, and through him into her. They all remembered the pain of shifting, before the body learns how. They knew the twisting and tearing at every joint and in bones that didn't have moveable joints. Their combination of stoicism and sympathy locked her failing knees.

She pulled the expression from her face, as she would for a tense contract negotiation. She smelled Esau, and then he was close enough she could press her face against his collarbone, feel his belt buckle above hers.

The downside was Bastian, pressed just as firmly to her back. Esau and Bastian reached around her, warily, like arm-wrestlers trying for the best leverage in an opening grip.

One on one. That's what he'd negotiated. No, not quite. A wolf was only alone if he chose to be. It was tiger against pack. So why was Bastian the tiger in this? Why not Richard, who glowed with power, or Johnny-Ray the fighter?

Because Bastian has the most to lose, Esau supplied grimly. *He set up a dangerous game, treating you even partly as a shifter. Now he can win his own Family, with a breeding pair as his subs, or he can lose everything.*

Why would his Family—

Later!

Power surged through her, an electric current that vibrated her teeth and brought her straining against the wall of Esau. Bastian, all fur and teeth and ruthless sharp edges, sliced through her mind—and swirled there, as disoriented and as baffled as she was. *Ty?*

Wolf-Esau tore into him, lunging straight for the throat, using his smaller wolf-shape to elbow in too close to allow those tiger claws to rake his belly open.

Where am I? Tyler asked, bewildered, surrounded by wolf and tiger and yet not there—not anywhere at all. *Where's the me in this?*

Later!

The tiger wrapped paws about the wolf and sank his claws in deep, trying to tear Esau free and get that massive tiger maw into action. Esau hung on, his pack feeding him strength to match the tiger.

"Guardian, Awake!" The Call, straight from her game, blared from every speaker on the wall, and echoed through the building.

"I am the Golden Guard-i-an!" Thousands of voices reverberated in the walls, the ceiling, the floor. The wolves' power flared.

The tiger, blinded and stunned, fell away.

Wolf-Esau leaped in close again, too smart to give the tiger time to recover or room to fight.

"Who answers—" the speakers cut off. The voices carried on, distant but still powerful "—the call?"

"A hero arises to answer the call!" The voices thundered through her. She fed that energy to Esau. The tiger shook himself and tried to feed on her power as Esau did. The tiger burned. The wolf was an arc-light, too brilliant to look at, and the fire that ate at the tiger fed him.

She found her own voice. "A hero arises—the Guardian!"

"I am the Golden Guardian!"

A raw scream rang in her ears, and Bastian sagged behind her. She staggered under his weight. Esau held her up.

"Cut off those lights," he said, and someone did.

She blinked a long time before she felt ready to look around, though, and then she found the world lopsided and blue and dizzying. "What happened to my eyes?"

"Wolf vision."

"Don't tell me my eyeballs shape-shifted."

"No, mine did. We'll be fine in a moment."

She closed her eyes to wait out the moment, and felt tugs on her arms. Esau, cutting her loose. Returning circulation burned up and down her arms. She bit into his uniform sleeve to muffle any cry.

"You're safe now," he murmured, holding her against him, rubbing shoulder to hand and back.

Her vision cleared, and the first thing she saw was Bastian Truc lying at her feet, shuddering, his face slack.

How are we safe with tigers all around? How did you cut his Family out of the fight?

"I don't feel any separation in the joints," Esau said, "but you probably have torn muscles. We'll get you to a human doctor now."

The bear-monk snorted. "I am a doctor. She needs a sling for each arm. Keep her from lifting anything heavier than an apple for a few weeks and she'll be fine."

"What about the Trucs?" she asked. She met Richard Truc's interested gaze. "What about you-all?"

He smiled, a tiger's smile. "The flippant answer is that 'FuckWare' has just become 'TrucWare.' HandPlus was partially dismantled already, and having to pay back the key-man insurance proceeds that my nephew made disappear will finish off the company. I suggest you move quickly to form a new company and consolidate your licenses on the games. We won't fight you more than necessary, if you hold to the bargains your bondmate made."

He gave a little bow to her, and to Esau.

"Tyler?"

Moving her head made the world spin.

"Adrenaline reaction," he said matter-of-factly, scooping her off her feet. "It hits hard when you're breeding."

Chapter 16

Esau stepped into the shower before she finished. "Let me wash your hair."

She sighed. "Would you believe I tried to do it, and I couldn't hold my arms up?"

"I'd believe it."

She leaned against his chest, feeling his heart thump against her cheek and temple. The warm water beat down on them both. She could stand there with him, time without end. Good thing this was a hotel. Her water heater at home would have given out long ago.

She struggled to recover the sense of injustice that had sent her to the shower, disgusted and alone. "I am not helpless and I'm not brainless, you know. I'm just tired."

"I know."

She pushed away from him. "This is the guy who sat down with a bunch of were-whatevers to decide about my life and how I'll live it?"

He draped his arms over her shoulders. "Am I there now?"

"All that means is you've made the decisions."

"No, it means we've come to a point where we can't make any more decisions without your input." He pulled her back against him. Sensuous fingers manipulated her scalp.

She leaned into him for a little while.

"What kind of input?" she asked at last, and yawned.

"Where do you want to live? Do you want your own city to run and defend? If you'd rather serve another Lady, and let her carry the responsibilities of the Family, we've received invitations from Raleigh, Denver, Austin and New Orleans so far. We can expect more. Everyone wants in on the ground floor of the new HandPlus, or whatever you come up with next."

"No gilt-edged invitation from Memphis?"

His fingers paused, but he answered steadily enough. "You cut my ties there. I have not chosen to renew them."

She wiped water from her eyes. He radiated a depth of hurt she couldn't begin to measure; they'd have to work through that sometime.

But not right now. He dropped a hand to her lower abdomen. Under his touch, she could feel the new life there. She leaned quietly against him, absorbing his strength.

"Is it still you and me, Esau? Are you with me for keeps? Even when I'm bloated and bad-tempered and puking on your feet?"

Soap stung her eye. Esau blotted her lashes with a towel corner. He hadn't answered. She caught his wrist and scrubbed her face against the towel, so she could squint at him.

His face softened in that almost-smile. "Forever and ever. Even if you keep asking questions you ought not have to ask."

She leaned into him, hearing his heart. *You're telling the truth.*

"Get used to it."

"If I had a city of my own, my first step would be to hire an administrator. I don't like the daily grind of management."

"So we'll negotiate a situation with some other Lady."

"What's wrong with us living in Atlanta?"

"Too much is going on there right now. You can stay in hotels a while, if you want to put off the decision, but where you incorporate will affect your tax status and—"

"I've had classes on corporate entities and taxation." She yawned again, leaning into the strong soapy hands kneading her back and neck. "I need to call Celie, my secretary."

"The one who doesn't need a loudspeaker? She's here now, giving Black Horse up-the-country about this hotel's inadequate wheelchair accommodation. He was gentleman enough to distract her when she tried following me down the hall, chewing my butt."

That's Celie, all right. "Be glad she didn't latch onto you. I don't share."

He held her close. "Good."

About the Author:

Amber Green is a professional paper-pusher who keeps submerging herself in fiction in an attempt to find a reality that makes sense. Really. Visit her at www.ShapeshiftersInLust.com.

Surrender

by Dominique Sinclair

To My Reader:

What woman hasn't fantasized about an Italian man? A man who is as handsome as he is dark and dangerous? To be the woman claimed and brought into a life of old world traditions and family honor?

I brought this man for my heroine, Madeline Carter. Ah, if only happily ever after didn't come with a price...

Chapter 1

Ten stories below, New York was little more than a distant humm. The balcony doors opened, spilling out the tinkling of champagne glasses and gay laughter, then closed, returning the quiet she came outside to seek. His footsteps moved toward her, his form blocked the lone light glowing in a lantern by the door.

She dared not move.

Dared not, for as much as she feared, she craved.

Her fingers wrapped tightly around the wrought iron rail. A breeze, scented with the promise of rain, lifted the ends of her hair. He stopped behind her, the tips of his fingers lightly skimming her shoulders, down her arms, up again, sending a feverish chill, warming her from the surface deep into her core. He moved one hand beneath her hair to the diamond clasp at her nape, the gold band on his pinky brushing against her skin as he released the latch.

Releasing her grip on the rail, she held the draping ivory halter dress in place with her forearm over one traitorous nipple, her palm cupping the other and tilted her head to the side as he lowered his mouth to kiss the dip in her neck where it met her shoulder.

His hand slid around her throat, fingers wrapping to press against her pulse, just enough pressure to remind her he could take her life if he so chose. She swallowed as his hand moved upward, pressed beneath her chin and tipped her head into the hollow of his shoulder. He cupped her jaw, angled her head to the side.

Slowly she lifted her lashes, met his penetrating gaze, his eyes onyx in the night. His mouth inched toward hers, slowly spanning time. Her mouth parted in anticipation, and the back of her throat went dry. His kiss began a languid exploration, slowly built with teases and strokes. Then his mouth demanded, bruised. He delved deep into her mouth, sought her hollows, learned her textures, the pad of his fingers pressing into her jaw, holding her there to receive.

For a moment in her mind, she tried to separate herself from the kiss, only she could find no line between the moist heat of his mouth, the tingle in her body with each sweep of his tongue, and the stirring in her womb with each nip of teeth. His kiss fused each point of pleasure to another, and another, until all of her burned with undeniable want. Unforgivable want.

She whimpered, his name resounding deep in her throat.

Rough, strong, his hand smoothed up her rib cage, fingers over warm silk to the underside of her breast, slipping beneath her hand to test the point of her desire, clenching his thumb and forefinger on her nipple.

A fierce jolt of trembling need pulsed against her lace panties, images of his erection pushing into her walls, filling her, stretching her, pleasuring her, sent her teeth sinking into his bottom lip on a orgiastic cry of want. Want that had been building for tortuous weeks, bringing this moment she couldn't deny.

Want, she told herself, she could handle when she started this dangerous game.

She lifted her hand, ran it through his wavy dark strands, fisting a handful at his nape as she turned, changing angles of the kiss without breaking contact. The halter-top of her three thousand dollar dress fell to her waist. Pressing upward, her breasts gliding up his chest, nipples against the soft fabric of his black shirt, she swept her tongue into his mouth. Her other hand clenched around his bicep, steadying herself.

He backed her into the rail, cool metal against the small of her spine. He drew his hand up the ankle-to-hip slit in her dress, lifted her knee and wrapped it around his thigh. His fingers moved just below her bottom, forcing her hips forward to meet the strain of his erection beneath his tailored slacks.

Greedily she aided him, working small circles with her hips, moving along him. Her short polished nails scratched down his back to his waist and she locked a finger through his belt loop, securing him against her. Pressure built, damp, pulsing. She wanted, *needed,* him inside her.

Then a cell phone rang, a specific ring tone she knew meant business.

She gazed up at him, knowing she should be grateful for the interruption, instead finding words on the tip of her tongue to ask him to ignore it. Before she had the chance, he swept his finger along her moist lower lip then lifted the dress to cover her breasts. She held the fabric in place, watched him step away, her body whimpering. He answered the phone in a hushed voice, speaking in Italian.

Standing alone to face unearthed passions, she turned around to the night, faced the moon hidden behind a scud of thick, black clouds, and slowly exhaled a shuddered breath.

As she clipped her dress into place, a raindrop fell on her sensitized skin. She allowed it to trail down her shoulder, hearing only enough of his conversation to know they wouldn't finish what they started.

She should have been grateful.

He snapped the phone closed, came to her, kissed the damp drop on her shoulder, then walked away without saying a word.

Dressed in a smart black blazer, fitted slacks with a slight flare at the ankle, hair twisted into a messy ponytail bun, Agent Madeline Carter's low heels clicked on the marbled floor as she hurried down the long corridor.

Madeline stopped in front of a door. Etched in gold lettering on pebbled glass read THE DEPARTMENT OF PUBLIC SAFETY. It made her smile every time. Nothing but a ruse for the Department of International Crime, D.I.C., a small division of The Department of Homeland Security.

A smile failed her this time however, as she turned the door handle and entered. "I know, I know," she said. "I'm late." For the meeting *she* requested.

Mrs. B glanced over the rims of her red, outdated Sally Jesse Raphael glasses and gave a disapproving look, lifted the phone off the desk and pressed a button with an orange polished press-on inch-long nail. The earpiece flattened her permed gray hair as she spoke. "She's here." Mrs. B hung up, swiveled to her manual typewriter, began hen-pecking keys while a brand new Macintosh with an aquarium screensaver sat unused.

Madeline knew she was being given the silent treatment for being late.

Mrs. B ruled her roost by making her displeasure known by saying nothing at all. If only the woman knew what a pleasure it was to have her quiet, she'd change her tactic.

Giving Whittaker's door several light raps, Madeline let herself in before she changed her mind. She sat in the chair before his big oak desk, feeling like a high school student before the principal. "Good morning, sir."

Whittaker grumbled, scooped pills off his desk, dumped them in his mouth, drank them down with a bottle of Evian. "Ginko, vitamin E, lycopene..." He twisted the cap on the empty water bottle, tossed it into the trashcan at the side of his desk. "Four of those a day. Keep telling my daughter the vitamins won't do any good long as I'm pissing them out every hour."

Madeline tried to smile, wishing she still had her father around to fuss over, to make sure he was taking his vitamins, eating healthy, exercising.

"Between her and Mrs. B, I can't get a moment's peace. Now tell me, Carter, what brings you in?"

She shifted in her seat, drew in a deep breath and said, "Sir, I need to be pulled from the assignment."

Whittaker leaned back, chair squeaking. "Any particular reason?"

The entire train ride into D.C. she tried to figure what to say, but couldn't come up with anything other than the truth. The agency invested manpower and money into creating a cover for her. She'd made progress getting into Sebastian Maiocco's inner circle.

Flashes of the night before swept through her mind.

Sebastian's fingers wrapping her throat.

His mouth delving hers.

Hands upon her breast.

Memories of the truth that would ruin everything.

Shame burned hot through her body, scorching everything she believed in. She swallowed, turned her head to the side and closed her eyes as if she could erase what she allowed to happen. *What she wanted to happen.*

It was only two weeks since she'd "accidentally" bumped into Sebastian at a gallery showing in SoHo and the game of seduction began.

Only it was supposed to be a job, the means to gain his trust, an invitation into his life where she could analyze, listen, observe his every movement, every action.

She wasn't supposed to be attracted to him.

Wasn't supposed to forget every time he looked at her with those dark eyes he was a criminal.

"Carter?"

"I'm in too deep," she said, forcing herself to listen to her own words, knowing if Sebastian hadn't gotten the call when he did last night, she would have woken in his bed. It would have been too late then to stop herself from making a mistake that would haunt her for the rest of her career.

The rest of her life.

No matter how much she craved, how taut her body with desire, she couldn't share pleasures with the man she would ultimately send to prison. Which meant she needed off the case. One more moment like last night and she knew she would surrender completely, totally.

Whittaker twisted open another water, handed it to her. "You're coming up on five years with the agency, Carter; you know the deeper in the better."

She took the bottle, wrapped her fingers around it. "It's different this time."

"Ah, it's like that." Whittaker pulled open a drawer, took out a file, opened it and tossed it in front of her. "Go ahead, take a look. It has yet to hit the American news."

She glanced at the glossy 8x10 picture of a sidewalk café in Italy, blown apart by a car bomb, bodies lying scorched, blackened. Dead. Raymond Agueci's trademark for handling those who resisted him.

"Who was the target?" Madeline asked, her stomach knotting. So many dead. Innocent bystanders. Everyday people living everyday lives.

"The Director of the Bank of Sicily, Albert DeBarge. He was having coffee with his niece."

"Christ." It shouldn't have been a shock. Raymond was also believed to have put the fatal bullet in his aging father's heart. A clear message to the other Sicilian families Raymond was taking over the Agueci branch. The knot in Madeline's stomach spread to a wave of nausea.

She'd seen pictures of the eighteen-year-old niece. Beautiful. Young. Vibrant. Now she was dead because her uncle uncovered embezzlement and political corruption in the bank's operations. Albert had gone to the authorities, informed them he'd been threatened by Agueci's *bravi*—hired thugs—of retaliation should he not *overlook* the incriminating findings.

There should have been round the clock protection on Albert and his family.

Perhaps there had been and the protector's bodies were smoldering in the café along with Albert and his niece.

Madeline closed the file, slid it back to Whittaker.

He came around the desk to sit in the chair beside her. "We've all been where you are now, Maddy," he said, using the nickname he gave her as a kid. Back then, he spent every Sunday night at her parents' house for dinner. "The agents on drug enforcement battle that line when they're looking at a smoking bowl of meth a dealer passes their way. You." He touched her hand lightly, squeezed. "You pretend to fall in love with powerful, dangerous men. It's understandable if the line between the job and reality begins to blur a little. I won't ask you to go over the line. You know that. But I need you on this case. Three years we've been looking for a way in and haven't come close to the progress you've made. That said, if you want out, say the word. I'll understand."

She swallowed hard, staring at his aging hand. He'd been her mentor since she joined the agency, following in her dad's footsteps. Her father lived long enough to see her take her oath to serve and protect her country, tears swimming in his eyes. As she tossed rose petals on his coffin six feet down, she'd vowed to serve the agency he dedicated his life to with just as much pride and devotion.

She swiped a tear away with the back of her knuckle. "I can handle it," she said, knowing her dad would have made the same decision if he were alive.

Whittaker patted her hand, stood. "Good. But if you think even for a moment you're in over your head, I want you out. Get to the safe house."

Madeline knew she was already in over her head. She just needed to surface long enough to drink in a big gulp of air; then she'd be able to handle the tumultuous emotions Sebastian Maiocco made her feel.

Madeline spent the day in her little house in a quiet suburb of D.C. catching up on bills, watering plants, returning phone messages weeks old. While in New York she severed all ties to her life in D.C. Now the routine of everyday activities, being far away from the glam of her undercover life, the expensive clothes, the elegant parties, helped give her the breathing room she needed to refocus her mind on the job she just promised to complete.

She'd already conquered the hard part, gaining Sebastian's trust to invite her into his life. Now that she was there, she could pull back a little, cool things off. Focus on gathering intel, names, dates, anything that would tie him to Agueci's organization by more than association. The agency knew Agueci had an American associate, someone he trusted to revive the dying New York clan, someone like his cousin, Sebastian Maiocco.

No, there was no doubt Sebastian was involved, even though they had no evidence Sebastian had been in contact with his cousin. It was just a matter of finding the knot in the rope that bound the loyalties. Only when Sebastian touched her with his strong hands, spoke to her with his Italian accent seducing every word, looked at her with dark, smoldering eyes holding her captive, leaving her breathless, the search slipped away, leaving only a woman where a trained agent should have stood.

But find the connection, Madeline would. The break away was what she needed. She would go back to New York on the six o'clock train with a clear head and resume her assignment while her counterparts worked to stop the spread of new-age Mafia crime that included all the shticks of the old regime—racketeering, gambling, money-laundering—and moved up to ladder to computer crimes.

If Sebastian was involved, she would expose him, and put him away. For life.

Chapter 2

Madeline stepped off the train at Penn Station and followed the early night crowd to the street. Cars sloshed through the rain splattering down in big drops, kicking up exhaust-tainted water, horns blaring, wipers swooshing. Drenched head to toe before she made it to the corner, Madeline stood on tiptoes and waved to hail a cab coming her way. The taxi sped by, swerved into a slot to pickup a group of four, clearly anticipating a heavier tip.

Pushing her limp bangs off her forehead, she hiked her purse strap up her shoulder, tried again. A limousine slid up to the curb. Her stomach heaved into her throat.

Sebastian's driver stepped out of the car, came around and opened the door for her. She forced a smile while her instincts told her to run.

How did Sebastian know she'd be getting off the six o'clock train?

She coolly slid into the back seat, thanking the driver. If Sebastian had someone follow her to D.C., if he somehow found out she was working under-cover, she needed to know what else he'd learned. Needed to know if the entire case was jeopardized. That she could be walking into a life or death situation was simply part of the job.

⁂

Two of Sebastian's men were waiting outside his building when the lim-ousine pulled up. They were dressed like b-rated Hollywood FBI agents, three-piece suits, shiny shoes, sunglasses despite the night, arms crossed over thick, barrel chests. Damn if they didn't stick out like black sheep in a pasture of pure white lambs.

Sebastian once told Madeline it was exactly the look he wanted. He wanted it clear to anyone looking he had twenty-four hour protection.

When she'd inquired why he needed such protection, he merely ran his hand down her cheek, told her there were things about him she didn't need to know.

As one of the guards opened the door, she wondered if Sebastian knew that she'd been planted in his life to find out his secrets. "Thank you", she said politely, determined to keep her inner turbulence hidden. There was still a chance Sebastian knew no more than she'd left New York for the day.

The guards flanking her a step behind, she entered the old warehouse, stepped inside the freight elevator, jumping when the barred gate slammed behind her. Caged. Exhaling a long breath, she pushed the big red button, glancing up at the surveillance monitor positioned in the corner, feeling Sebastian watching her.

Too late now to run even if she wanted to.

The elevator rose with a clang. Madeline pulled the elastic band out of her hair, drug her fingers through her wet, tangled hair, knowing Sebastian preferred it down. Her long, blonde hair pleased him. He often toyed with the ends as they sat drinking wine, watched the theater, stood studying exhibits. Sebastian loved the arts, from music to literature to obscure paintings.

The elevator jerked to a stop. Madeline pulled open the gate and steel door beyond, taking in one last calming breath.

Play it cool, keep calm, she told herself, taking a step into the converted top warehouse floor which created a penthouse that would make anyone on Fifth Avenue envious.

The lights were out. Silence filled the large, expansive room where only the night before elegantly dressed guests mingled, sipped wine, danced. Shadows cast along the walls from pieces of art displayed on pedestals and freestanding sculptures. Beneath the light of the overhead track lighting, the art was beautiful. In the dark the pieces twined, elongated. Menacing, as if she were to take a step inside she would walk through a child's nightmare.

Madeline slowly closed the door, feeling as if she were shutting herself into the lion's den. Which, perhaps, she was.

"Lock it," came his voice, low, commanding from somewhere in the room.

Her hand trembled slightly as she pushed the inch thick deadbolt across the door, sliding the rod into the iron eye. A single track light above her suddenly flicked on, disorienting her with a flood of bright white light. She whirled, searching the darkness of the room, unable to see beyond the halo of light into the black veil.

"Remove your clothes."

Madeline looked in the direction his voice came from. She saw only darkness, but felt the heat of his gaze on her, watching. *Testing.*

Whittaker's words came back to her, *I won't ask you to go over the line.* To do anything but obey Sebastian would risk the entire operation, could put agents in jeopardy, their lives at stake. *Her* life at stake. If there was a chance she'd been made, if there was a chance Sebastian knew who she was, she needed to find out for sure.

Which meant she had to continue forward in this dangerous game. She had to proceed as if nothing were wrong, pray she'd find a way out before the stakes got too high.

Biting the corner of her lower lip, pulling her teeth slowly over the lobe, Madeline stepped into the role of seductress, temptress, her hand going to the top button of her damp blouse, fingers slipping the nubbin through the hole, moving down to the next until her shirt parted, revealing a slice of her from her throat to the waistband of her low riding jeans she'd changed into before boarding the train.

"Where are you," she asked, her voice as low as his had been, nearly a whisper lost in the blackness.

"*Shhh.* Your clothes."

She slipped a foot out of her high-heeled sandal, stepped onto the cool concrete floor and removed the other, all the while searching for him. Taking her time, she unsnapped her jeans, slid down the zipper and pushed the denim to the floor, hands trailing her legs, over her calves, one foot, then the other. Folding the jeans, she turned and set them on the table beside the door, the scoop hem of her shirt brushing the elastic band of her French cut panties.

She sensed him moving toward her before she heard the padding of his feet. She didn't turn. Couldn't. Her breath caught in her throat, expanding deep in her diaphragm. Would he wrap his hands around her throat again, this time choosing to take her life?

"I missed you today," he said, his voice still low, his accent soft. He lifted her wet hair, settled it over her shoulder, slid his hands beneath the collar of her shirt, lowering it down her arms until it fell away. Lowering his head, he kissed the back of her neck, soft, gentle.

A shiver vibrated down her spine, nipples erecting beneath her lace bra. Madeline was unable to stop her body's traitorous response, heightened by relief he meant her no harm. She'd worried for nothing, his driver just happened by as she waited for a taxi.

Sebastian linked his hand with hers. "Come, let's get you dry."

Following him out of the light, wearing nothing but her panties and bra, bare feet leaving the concrete floor to step on a thick, soft area rug, Madeline once again found herself being led into Sebastian's sensual world where every word, every touch seemed a slow seduction.

Deep into the room he paused at the bar to light a votive and pour a glass of fragrant red wine, holding it out to her until her fingers wrapped around the stem, then held it still. She lifted her gaze to look at his face, the glow of candlelight accenting the hard set of his jaw, his assessing eyes.

Before she could determine his mood, he released his hold on the wine goblet, walked around her to disappear behind a room sized oriental screen and returned moments later with a thick terry robe, draping it over her shoulders. She took a sip of wine and inhaled the spice of his cologne lingering on the fabric of his wrap.

"Perhaps now that you are warm and dry, you care to tell me where you went today."

Surely if he knew she was an undercover agent he would have called her out the moment she stepped into the room. Which meant the most he knew was she took a trip to D.C. The least, that she was outside the train station on a rainy night. Madeline would provide him no more and no less than necessary.

Cocking a brow, she drew her finger around the crystal rim of her glass. "After the way you left last night, I didn't think you cared."

He slanted his dark eyes. "Don't try my patience."

"Excuse me?" She feigned dignified disgust, slamming her glass on the bar top. "I'm the one you ran out on, *again*. Your phone rings and off you go, to heaven knows where. You won't tell me a thing about yourself, won't tell me where you go, who you see."

Afraid to push him too far, to become a nagging lover he'd want to rid himself of, Madeline stopped animating her hands through the air, and stepped toward him, softening her expression as she ran her palm along the hard plane of his jaw, the tips of her fingers reaching into his soft wavy hair dusting his collarbone. Rising up on her tiptoes, she pressed her mouth to his. "I can handle it, Sebastian," she whispered. "I can handle it because I want to be near you. But I don't have to like it."

Sebastian stared down at her, his body rigid, unyielding. Madeline wondered as the moment stretched on if she laid it on too thick, not thick enough, or if he saw straight through her lies, her deceit.

"I do not allow people near me I can not trust," he finally said, clasping her wrist and pulling her hand away.

The band of his fingers increased pressure, his thumb deep into her pulse. "You're hurting me." Madeline twisted her hand to free herself.

He spun her around, robe falling to the floor, and craned her arm behind her back like a beat cop would a punk kid selling dope on a street corner. "The thing about pain, it will eventually go away. Providing the answers are satisfactory." With a jerk he lifted her onto her tiptoes. Her arm burned in its socket as he hauled her forward, ramming her into wall, her forearm going up just in time to cushion her head.

Sebastian kicked apart her feet, widening her stance, the length of his jeans brushing against her bare legs. "Tell me now. Where were you today?"

Madeline clenched her molars, controlled her breathing, ignored the pain searing from her shoulder to hand. He was right about the pain, it would eventually go away, whether the answers were good or not. She'd been trained to take a beating, to survive even the worst interrogations. She also could have released herself from his hold at any given moment, had him flat on his back, dead even, if she so chose. But to defend herself with the swift precision of her training would give her instantly away, and while thoughts of him dead at that moment seemed mildly satisfying, he was no good to the agency in the morgue.

So she remained pinned against the wall in the darkened room, the man who inflicted pain as easy as pleasure visible in her peripheral vision. "I went to visit a friend in D.C.," she said, sticking to the truth. Director Whittaker had been a family friend her whole life.

"For what purpose?"

"I needed someone to talk to, clear my head." Again. *The truth.* "Help me understand why I'm falling for a man who scares the hell out of me and excites me at the same time."

Sebastian loosened his hold on her arm, just a fraction. "And what did this friend tell you?"

"To stay away from you. Run like hell."

Pressing his body flush against hers, her bent arm the only barrier between them, he sunk his teeth gently in her earlobe, then kissed just behind her ear, sending a shiver of unwanted pleasure down her nape. "Then why are you here?" The breath of his question was warm and tingling.

"Because I can't stay away." She closed her eyes, fearing the reply was also the truth, that being with Sebastian was more than an assignment, more than a job.

She wanted and craved and knew it was dangerous. And wrong. So wrong. Still, she couldn't help herself any more than a feral kitten could resist a saucer of warm milk set inside a trap.

Easing away from her, Sebastian unbent her arm, raised it above her head, his fingers locking with hers, tightening into a fist against the wall. He trailed his other hand down her spine, stopping to release the clasp of her bra before trailing into the hollow of her lower back, further to dip under the elastic band of her panties. He pushed the lace over the arch of her bottom, his fingers probing between her legs, slipping forward into her valley of dampness, the tip of his middle finger unhooding her nubbin, pressing upward.

A whimper escaped her throat. To stifle it, Madeline sank her teeth into her raised arm, her breath damp, warm, against her skin. She couldn't allow him to do this, couldn't allow herself to want this. And yet, her hips tilted back, and she rotated against his hand, pressure building, coiling. Heat engorged her nubbin, became an inferno deep within her contracting walls. She wanted him inside her, wanted him to cure the ache, spill his seed deep in her core.

His mouth lowered to her shoulder, suckled, nipped as he slipped into her center, just far enough to slick the pad of his finger stroking once... twice... slowly, barely penetrating her before easing back to her nubbin, working small circles with just enough pressure against the point of want. Her fist tightened, nails nipping into the palm of her hand. Somewhere in the distance of her mind she heard words to make him stop. They melted away as he once again moved to her center, this time pushing his fingers deep into her core, her soft walls stretching for him.

Her knees weakened, her breasts filled with a heavy sensation, her center cried with heat and pulses, needing release. As if to torture her, he stilled his finger deep inside her, pushing upward, his thumb parting the seam of her bottom.

"Please," she said, bearing her hips down on his hand, forcing him deeper still. "Please, Sebastian."

He slanted his lips over the corner of her mouth, drawing his tongue under her upper lobe, his chest against her shoulder, his hand squeezing her tiny bones beneath his palm. Slowly he slid his finger from inside her, followed the path he'd taken, slipping her panties back over her bottom.

Achy, needy, she whimpered. He couldn't stop his sweet torture, not now.

Sebastian turned her around, bra straps falling down her shoulders, the lacey cups loose against her budded nipples. He pressed between her legs, his erection thick and hard beneath his jeans bearing into the apex of her damp panties. He stared down at her, his dark hair messy over his brow, his eyes penetrating her as much as his touch had. He pulled her bottom lip down with his finger scented and moist with her desire, suckled the flavor off her lip with his mouth.

Sebastian stepped away from her then, ran his hand through his hair, the muscles in his arms flexing, his black t-shirt stretching across the breadth of his chest. "*Permesso. Ora.*"

Confused, the heat that flowed hot and pulsing moments ago withering, Madeline shook her head. "I don't understand." She reached up to touch his face.

He blocked her hand, wreathing his fingers around her wrist and hauled her forward, pushing her toward the door. "Leave. Now. My driver will take you home."

Something dark and dangerous curled in Sebastian's tone, telling her not to hesitate. Madeline didn't. Thrusting on the robe, she grabbed her clothes and ran.

༠ᘓᗢᘔ༄

When the door slid closed and the elevator hummed, Sebastian slammed his fist against the wall, knocking a painting to the floor. Curling and uncurling his fist, he jerked open his pants, released his jutting erection, took it in his hand still damp and fragrant with Madeline's sex. He stroked. Fast, hard. His stomach tightened, visualizing his dark shaft slipping between her milky white legs, thrusting deep into her molten core. She'd been so hot, tight, wet. Ready.

A light film of sweat beaded his brow as he fought against release. His hand pumped, buttocks clenched, wanting another moment of fantasy where he took her. Hard. Deep. Bruising her with each thrust. Her small, creamy tits with pink, erect buds bouncing, cries pouring from the smooth column of her throat, head thrashing.

On a deep, guttural growl his release slashed the wall where he'd pinned her, could have taken her. She'd all but begged for it, her body primed, ready. But he would not sink himself into one of Agueci's *baldraccas* sent to spy on him. His brief fantasy was all he'd have of her.

Porca l'oca. Sebastian half-fastened his jeans, walked to the bar and lifted her glass of wine, drinking it down in one swallow. She played her part well. For the first time in many years he found himself wanting more than a one-night stand and a firm good-bye.

Not only was Madeline beautiful, she was intriguing, vibrantly alive, a contrast of vixen and sweetness. She made him want to draw out each and every exploration of her body, to reach deep into her soul to know her secrets, desires, fears and dreams. He wanted to be near her, smell her scent, hear her laugh. See her smile.

His gut furled, crawled anger. Raymond chose well. Sebastian would not have suspected if he hadn't ordered Madeline followed when she left the party last night. He wanted her safely home. Instead she went straight for the train.

What a fool for worrying about her, caring about her.

Sebastian almost believed her story of visiting a friend for the day. Perhaps, even, would have believed her, if one of Raymond's *bravi* hadn't gotten off the train as well.

"*Diavola bella,*" he whispered, snapping the crystal stem beneath the pressure of his hand. "We could have been good together."

Chapter 3

Madeline shoved her rain damp clothes in the hamper, jerked Sebastian's robe off her abased body and twisted on the shower, stepping inside before the water even warmed, washing away the residual feel of Sebastian's hands, mouth, scent. She scrubbed hard, vigorously, trying to erase the memory of what she'd done as well as the lingering sensations still humming through her body that had been taken to the edge of desire and left unsatisfied.

She turned her face into the spray of now steaming water, closed her eyes against a swelling of fat tears. She would not cry, would not allow herself the weakness. She shouldn't have come back to New York. At least not so soon. She should have given herself a couple of days to strengthen her resolve, to calm her body's need and make her duty priority. Instead she'd jumped right back into a smoldering volcano, knowing it was still about to explode.

She tried to tell herself she would not have had sex with Sebastian, that she would have stopped him, only her traitorous body contracted low and deep. She could not deny the truth. She would have lain for him. Not as means to burrow further into his life so she could investigate him. Rather because she felt as if she didn't have him inside her, she would die from crazed want. She would have surrendered body and soul to him. Completely, totally.

Would have, had he not pushed her away and demanded she leave.

Madeline knew she was being tested the moment she got into the back seat of the limousine at the train station. Tested and failed. And still, she didn't know how much Sebastian knew.

Turning off the water, Madeline stepped out of the shower, feeling her sins had been washed away, at least on the surface. A towel wrapped around her body, hair soaking wet down her back, she went to her bedroom to dress. One glance at the clock on the bedside table and her heart skipped a beat. The LED displayed blinking zeros.

She dropped the towel and thrust on a pair of jeans, sweatshirt, shoes, no socks and hurried from her apartment. Hair still wet and uncombed, she walked briskly through the rain to an all night drugstore four blocks up, watching for anyone following her.

The clock was Madeline's only line of communication with Whittaker. When working this deep undercover he wouldn't risk contacting her directly by phone, fax or email. To do so could expose her. So he'd wired the clock to respond by remote. A set of all zeros meant he needed contact with her, *immediately.*

Satisfied no one shadowed her, Madeline entered the drugstore, lifted a handcart and made her way down an aisle, selecting items to drop into her basket. Items a woman might need suddenly at this hour. Midol, tampons. Chocolate bars. Still no sign of anyone watching her, she paid at the pharmacy counter at the back of the store, asking to use the restroom as she took the brown sack from the clerk.

He pointed to a set of swinging double doors. "Through there, down the hall to the left."

"Thank you." Madeline pushed through the doors marked *Employees Only*, and into the ladies room. Locking the door behind her, she set her bag next to the sink and climbed up on the counter, stretching to push the ceiling tile aside.

She padded her hand until she felt the smooth duct tape, peeled it back and removed the credit card slim phone from beneath it. Quietly getting down, she turned on the water, and punched in the routing number to Whittaker's secure line. After a series of beeps, the phone rang once before he answered.

"Sir, it's me."

"About time," Whittaker said. "I tripped your clock hours ago."

"Sorry, I... I didn't go straight to the apartment. What's happened?"

"Raymond Agueci is on his way to New York."

She rubbed a piercing pain shooting through her temple with two fingers. If Raymond was coming to New York, it meant he planned to meet with his associate. Planned to meet with Sebastian. Still, not important enough to warrant Whittaker's alert. "What else?"

There was a stretch of silence permeated only by Whittaker's breathing over the line. "The bodies of Lou Mendoza, Harold Trapone and Freddie Aster were found earlier this evening upstate. Appeared they'd gathered for a meeting at Mendoza's ranch. Coroner is reporting deaths sometime between midnight and three a.m. this morning."

The tiled floor undulated beneath Madeline's feet. She gripped the edge of the counter to steady herself. Lou, Harold and Freddie were the *cupola*—board of directors—of the New York Sicilian Mafiosi. Madeline had no doubt who ordered the hit. Raymond Agueci. Clearly he was ready to begin his expansion into New York. A bold move, but one that would leave no doubt he would meet any and all resistance. The Department feared and also suspected this very scenario. But that wasn't what caused Madeline to stagger.

It was the phone call Sebastian received on the balcony while his mouth and hands were upon her body. The phone call that was received just after midnight and important enough for him to leave her in what promised to be the coming throes of ecstasy.

The phone call that contained an order to assassinate.

Any doubt of Sebastian's involvement with Raymond, doubt she knew she created to justify her actions, had just been obliterated. The hands of a killer hand intimately touched her body, had stroked and probed, flamed desire and molten need so great she thought she'd die of want.

"I need you to watch Maiocco's every step, want you to be there when Agueci arrives," Whittaker said.

Madeline drew in a shuddering breath. "Sir, my cover's been blown."

A muttered curse followed by a long pause. "Are you sure?"

She stared at herself in the mirror over the sink, taking in the sight of her wet hair, pale face, swollen lips… How did she allow this to happen? "He had me picked up from the train station when I arrived." She closed her eyes against the woman staring back at her, mocking her, reflecting failure and shame. "I thought I had him convinced I met a friend in D.C., but then suddenly he was throwing me out. He knows something."

"You're not being followed now are you?"

She shook her head. "I don't think so."

"Do you want me to send someone to pick you up?"

"No." God, the last thing she needed, one of the guys to see her all shook up, tore apart from the inside out. "I'm not far from the safe house. I'll go there. A couple days maybe, then call for extraction. I think it's best if I lay low." Maybe she hadn't completely blown the investigation, another OP could take over.

"Call me the moment you're locked down."

"I will. And sir. I'm sorry. Sorry I failed you."

"Don't do that, Maddy. Don't beat yourself up. There's no way to predict how these things go. You don't hold the cards, just play what's dealt the best you can. Get to the safe house now, rest up."

Madeline disconnected the call, broke the slim phone into small pieces, dropped them in the toilet and flushed, hand trembling slightly. Once she got to the safe house she would be able to breath, calm down, put perspective on everything.

Whittaker was right.

She did the best she could.

So why did it feel like her best wasn't good enough?

"*Sì*. I will be there. *Bueno*." Sebastian flipped his cell phone closed, fisted his hand around the cool metal and took in a deep breath. His stomach hardened, his jaw ticked. Soon he would seek payment for what was done to his family.

Opening his safe, he made a final call. "I am going away for a couple days. I will need my boat stocked and ready. See to it immediately. I will be ready to go within the hour." Sebastian removed a wad of bills, his .45 ACP. Ramming in a jungle clip and six strippers he once again vowed revenge.

Madeline stood damp and cold on the dark stoop of an innocuous looking brownstone. She removed the rusty letter style mailbox hanging next to the door and ran the tip of her finger over the keypad, finding the numbers in the dark that would unlock the door. Once inside she would be completely safe. The doors were steel. The windows shatter and bulletproof, walls insulated with fireproof foam.

And should that not be enough, the basement held a large holding container that would remain intact even under the pressure of explosives or worst of natural disaster. She could enclose herself inside and have enough oxygen tanks, bottled water, freeze-dried and canned food to last at least a month, more if supplies were rationed. There were homes just like this one in all major cities across America, even around the world.

One hell of an expense to The Department of International Crime, but the money was well spent to ensure a safe place for its agents to go in any sort of catastrophe or, as in Madeline's case, the need to lay low, disappear until it was safe to return to headquarters.

Entering in the last digit, a green light blinked twice agreeing with the code. Now to insert the key and she would be inside.

A gloved hand clamped over her mouth and nose.

Reflectively she sucked down a breath and realized instantly her mistake. The slight burning of chloroform on the glove hit her lungs and seeped through her blood stream. Knowing she had mere seconds before she lost consciousness, she rammed her elbow and head back, making contact with both, staggering her attacker away several steps, momentarily loosening the hold on her. Knowing she couldn't run, couldn't fight, she lunged for the door, fumbling the key into the lock.

Her attacker barreled his weight into her back, flattening her against the door, pinning her in place with his hulking weight. The key dropped to the ground with a resounding clink against stone, the sound magnified. She felt warm blood from his nose drip down her neck, his heavy breathing hot against her cheek. The side of her head throbbed where it bashed against the door and white tracers of light flitted around her vision.

Eyelids suddenly leaded, Madeline stared myopically at three red blinks above the keypad, telling her she would have to enter the code all over again to get inside the safe house.

"Be a good girl now," her attacker's voice rasped from a distant tunnel, echoing in the wooziness and ache in her head. "*A tutto c'è rimedio, fourchè alla morte.*"

There is a cure for everything except death, Madeline translated before blacking out.

Chapter 4

The sky merged with the sea in a blanket of dark blue velvet, endlessly spanning in all directions. Above, stars dotted the night, the moon, a sliver slipping toward dawn. Sebastian should have been exhausted, commanding his yacht from the harbor in New York, crossing the dark ocean in the deepest part of night. He felt no exhaustion seeping into his bones, only the salty, damp air of the sea.

Sebastian cut the boat's engine, dropped anchor, killed the lights. He arrived early for the rendezvous. Nothing now to do but wait. Raymond played him like a puppet, again. Sebastian was fucking tired of the games. He wanted his sister returned to him. *Now.*

And then, to get Raymond Agueci dead. *Now.*

In the most satisfying way possible.

Slowly. Painfully. Begging for mercy.

Sebastian would draw out the end, wouldn't give the bastard the satisfaction of a swift death. When the moment came, and the devil's claws were ready to claim, Sebastian would look into Raymond's eyes and remind him what family loyalty meant.

Love.

Honor.

Trust.

And revenge on those who harmed any one of them.

His right hand flexed and unflexed as he watched the yacht approaching in the distance. Raymond, too, chose to be early. Just about the only quality Sebastian could find to admire about his cousin.

Boarded on Raymond's yacht, Sebastian slid the .45 from his waistband.

A man stepped out of the wheelhouse, lit a cigarette with a Zippo lighter, inhaled deeply and exhaled slowly, a wisp of smoke curling into the night. He slapped the lighter shut, slipped it into his trouser pocket. "Cousin, it is good to see you," he said, taking a second drag. "It has been a long time, no?"

Sebastian nodded slightly, taking note of the guard standing at the back of the boat, another at the head. "Can't say I've missed you too much, Bordo. Where's Tessa?" He knew the chances of Tessa being here were slim before he even came, still his heart refused any opportunity to get Tessa back.

Bordo pinched a piece of tobacco off his tongue, flicked it away. "Change of plans."

"Ray?"

"You'll be dealing with me. The package?"

Sebastian's upper lip twitched as he tossed the briefcase across the deck. It landed with a few feet from Bardo. "You and I both know it's empty. Why bother playing the game?"

"On the off chance you have decided to be cooperative." Bardo motioned to one of his thugs, who stepped out of the shadows like a trained dog. He hurled the case into the ocean.

Sebastian's cool gaze never left Bardo. "Tell Ray to give me a call when he's ready to do business." He took a step backward, never letting his anger show. He should have known Ray would play games. He enjoyed toying with situations like a child at Christmas with a new toy train.

Bardo flicked his cigarette butt in the direction of the briefcase, slipped his hands in his white trouser pockets. "Where is the disk?"

"I will only deal with Ray."

"Ray has given his permission to me to handle this transaction."

"I find no reason to repeat myself. *Buenos noches.*"

"I find no use to keep you alive, as my brother does. Let there be no doubt, Sebastian, I would prefer you dead along with the rest of your family."

Sebastian's hand clenched around the handle of his gun, the pad of his finger pressing along the cool barrel, wanting to slip into the trigger well and pull back. Unlike this unsavory branch of his *familia*, Sebastian would not kill for pleasure, no matter how satisfying it tempted to be. "Then shoot me," Sebastian said, tone void of emotion. "I will watch from hell with laughter spilling from my dead soul as you try and explain to Ray why you put a bullet into the one man who can deliver what Ray so desires." Sebastian slipped his .45 into his pant holster, turned, satisfied his back to the enemy at this point posed no danger. He stepped onto the ladder, ready to descend onto his boat. An entire night wasted.

"I am afraid, cousin," Bardo said, "you will not be returning to your boat so soon."

Sebastian laughed, turned around. "And what, *cousin*, could possibly stop me?" It killed him to be so nonchalant, to cause even a small risk to Tessa. But he knew how to play the game, no matter how he despised it.

Bardo slipped his hand out of his pocket, tossed his cell phone the distance between them. "See for yourself."

Sebastian caught the phone, which rang nearly upon impact in his palm. He flipped it open, glanced at the small video screen. His stomach clenched before he fully absorbed the image feeding live before him.

"Ah, Ray thought that may get your attention." Bardo leaned against the wheelhouse. "She is beautiful. Tell me, Sebastian, is she as pleasurable in bed as I imagine her to be? Or shall I ask Ray?"

Sebastian had since slammed his eyelids closed. The ocean, which only minutes before undulated softly beneath the boat, now seemed turbulent. The image on the screen played before his blackened vision. He may have believed her one of Raymond's whores. He may have believed she was sent to seduce him, spy on him. But there was no way he could believe the fear on her bruised face in the video, the writhe of her partially stripped body trying to free herself, was anything but real.

Raymond held Madeline against her will.

Sebastian's hand fisted around the phone, his other hand pulled the .45. He should have known Ray would up the ante. His finger went to the gun's trigger without hesitation. The bullet met his mark directly between Bardo's inset eyes. The force of the bullet knocked his cousin's head against the round wheelhouse window, a sickening spray of blood and brain washing the fisheye glass before his body collapsed to the floor.

Sebastian adjusted his sight to Bardo's guard, gaze focused down the barrel of the gun. Aware of the second thug in his peripheral vision, he spoke with an even voice. "Unless you want me to blow your brains as well, I suggest you take me to Ray. Now."

The first thug merely nodded, as if he anticipated this very scenario. The man stepped over Bardo's body and into the wheelhouse, starting the yacht's engine.

Sebastian possessed no doubt this scenario was exactly what Raymond planned—Ray had a way of getting his dirty work done without soiling his manicured hands. Bardo apparently lived past his usefulness to Raymond Agueci.

"We do not have far to go," the man said, nodding forward to another yacht anchored in the near distance.

The sound of a distant gunshot roused Madeline from the semi-conscious state she'd been hovering in for countless minutes, hours, days? The first thing she became aware of after the echo of the shot was the sound of footsteps moving toward her. She held perfectly still, though her body seemed to slowly rise and sink in a dizzying rhythm.

She hoped she would be as invisible to the person approaching as her surroundings were beneath her blindfold.

Apparently not. Moments later a hand fisted the back of her hair, yanked, pulling her chin upward.

She gave no resistance. Made not even a whimper.

"Are you ready to make this easy on yourself now, *Bella*?"

A piece of fabric tight into the bite of her mouth and knotted behind her head, she couldn't have answered if she wanted to. Breathing was difficult. Her lips dry and cracked. She'd give anything to be untied, for a deep breath of unrestrained air, a sip of water. A chance to orient herself in time and place. Anything, of course, but give Raymond Agueci the pleasure of thinking she was scared, beaten, willing to cooperate.

Fighting away nausea spreading from her stomach throughout her body, Madeline thought it ironic she knew none of the answers the bastard who'd beaten her demanded from her periodically throughout the night. Even if she had answers to Raymond's questions, she would have continued to remain silent.

The sluice of Raymond's breath steamed at her temple, his hand fisted tighter in her hair. "You think you are strong and brave, no?"

Untie me, you pig, Madeline cursed silently, her numb hands bound together fisting, *and I'll show you just how strong I am.*

As if he'd heard her thoughts, or perhaps the firming of her body spoke for her, Raymond laughed. "Sebastian has always surrounded himself with beautiful things. If you are thinking you are anything more than an addition to his collection of art, more valuable than a rare book of poetry think again, *Bella.*" She sensed a smile upon his face. "Ah, do not worry. He is coming for you. It is one of Sebastian's many weaknesses. He thinks with his sense of duty and loyalty. A man of honor. Admirable qualities, to be sure, but ones that ensure a short life span. Like his father."

Throughout the night Madeline listened to Raymond Agueci and his men talking quietly in Italian, moving about. She was fairly certain Sebastian was not in the room. She would have sensed him, felt him, recognized his movements if he were anywhere near. But she hadn't trusted the instinct. Not completely. For all she truly knew, Sebastian ordered her to be picked up. Ordered she be beaten, tied and gagged.

But Raymond revealed more with his words than he probably intended. *He is coming for you.*

Madeline was being used as a pawn. Used to bring Sebastian onto Agueci's turf, on his terms. Sebastian was not a willing participant in Agueci's plans.

Madeline should have felt relief, should have felt reprieve for the tangled emotions she'd been sparring with whenever Sebastian touched her, kissed her. Instead, she wondered how she could have been so wrong about Sebastian's involvement with the Agueci clan.

Raymond suddenly shoved her head aside, releasing her, then moved away. Madeline listened to his footsteps until she was certain he had left her alone, gone back to his business. Only then did Madeline's shoulders slump and she exhaled a long breath. After a moment of calm, she used her bare feet to push her body backward, firming her sitting position against the wall, doing little to restore her equilibrium.

Despite her fatigue, the blindfold, her bound hands. Despite her swollen left eye, tender jaw, bruised ribs, Madeline needed to find a way to stay alert this time. If Sebastian was coming for her, she needed to be prepared. Needed to be able to help him.

Or perhaps she had the situation figured out entirely wrong.

Perhaps things would only get worse for her when Sebastian arrived.

Perhaps... She was simply too exhausted to try and think any longer. Blackness crept back in, settling over her, taking her to an easier place where the pain and confusion seemed distant.

Sebastian leapt over the rail of the second yacht, slammed through the door and took the flight of stairs below deck two at a time, only to come to an immediate stop. The sight of Madeline slumped over on the floor, her hair tangled, gag in her mouth, another around her eyes, made hatred boil deeper in his veins.

He'd dealt with the similar emotions when he found his family slain. Only then he'd been helpless to do anything. Nothing more than drop to his knees and cry out loud. To swear if it was the last thing on this earth he did, would kill the man responsible for his family's death. Put an end to the clan that destroyed others with a blood thirst for power.

He renewed the same vow when he learned Tessa was alive, and now once more as he fought outward reaction to seeing the woman who'd made him feel life was possible lying on the floor in a disheveled heap.

Raymond, hands deep in his pockets, came casually down the stairs, a satisfied look upon his face. It took every ounce of willpower for Sebastian not to wrap his hands around his cousin's throat, watch him gasp for air, slump to his knees and die before him.

The time would come for such satisfaction, Sebastian reminded himself. Once Tessa was safe. Then he would take such great pleasure in the moment.

"You were supposed to bring my sister."

Raymond rocked back on his heels a moment. "Ah, but there is more work to be done."

"And Madeline is what? More collateral?"

"On occasion, it is important to be reminded of the goals one's work is being done for. I've found certain… *motivations*, shall we say, work better for you than others."

Despite the continual rise of anger and rage, Sebastian forced his blood to keep flowing smoothly and flawlessly through his body.

His father had also been a man in control over his emotions and reactions when the time called for it. Few people outside the immediate family ever witnessed the passionate man who lived beneath the surface. Sebastian had been fortunate to be raised within the shell that kept the world at bay.

It is a gift, his father once told him, *to make others believe they know you from what they see. Only allow those you love to feel you.*

But, *goddamn,* to stand there, pretending the sight of Madeline didn't affect him. Flames licked inside Sebastian. Burning hatred. Singing restraint. "Why her?" He had to know, couldn't help but ask. Raymond had taken so much already.

"Ah, I think you will find her much more useful than you could have imagined. You have had a long night, cousin. Rest. There is much work to be done. Your computer has been delivered for your convenience."

Sebastian didn't bother to ask how Raymond was able to extract the computer from his studio so quickly as to have it aboard. Raymond's endless pit of money no doubt meant Sebastian's guards could no longer be trusted. A reminder that anyone who ever had even the briefest contact with Ray was corrupt.

"There is everything you need aboard. When I return, you shall have the information ready for me. Twenty-four hours. No more. No less." Raymond glanced at Madeline, shrugged. "It must be difficult, to have another life on your shoulders, *si?*"

Raymond headed up the stairs, pausing before the third step, turning around to add, "If you think to try anything... shall we say as an American? Stupid. There is a wonderful device implanted on the yacht. Do, say, think even, and *boom*. Ah, go ahead. Search for it all you'd like, you will not find it. This I assure you." He tossed an envelope. "Your assignment. *Buenos noches.*"

Sebastian forced his feet to remain anchored, settled his weight into his feet and resisted the urge to lunge as he caught the manila envelope. Rooted in place, taking slow, deep breaths to try and calm himself, he listened to Raymond's steps above, then the other yacht's motor start.

Only after he was certain Raymond and his goons were gone, leaving him and Madeline alone in a rigged boat, did he move.

In a heartbeat he had Madeline scooped into his arms. He stared down at her as he adjusted her limp weight. "I am sorry," he whispered, crossing the cabin into the bedroom, laying her down on the bed. He smoothed a strand of hair off her bruised cheek, tucked it behind her delicate ear. Nearly as much as it pained him to see her like this, his personal betrayal of her trust ate at him. She didn't deserve his accusations. She didn't deserve to be a part of Raymond's sick reign.

"It is okay now," he whispered, once again vowing to kill his cousin.

One way or another.

Chapter 5

For a long time Madeline thought the warm, silk sensation engulfing her body was merely a dream. She didn't force open her heavy eyes for fear the heavenly place she seemed to be floating in would disappear and the nightmare she escaped would return. When something soft and soothing touched her sore cheek, she finally lifted her eyelids, braced herself for continued blackness. Instead she adjusted her vision to soft, near vanilla light, vaguely aware she was in a tub of warm water.

"Sebastian?" she whispered, moving her mouth to the inside of the wrist resting against her jaw. She knew it was he before she even lifted her eyes to gaze myopically at his handsome face.

"Shhh," he sounded, pressing the cloth to her cheek gently. "I'm here. Rest, you have been through much. I am sorry. So sorry I did not protect you."

Witness to the pain in his face, in his eyes, when he spoke the words, pain she sensed wove deeper than the moment for which he spoke, Madeline wanted nothing more than to comfort him. Pressing her lips to the pulse at his wrist, she closed her eyes. "You're not the one who hurt me."

Sebastian moved his hand from her face, dipped the washcloth in the bath water and up again to her shoulder, fisting his hand, squeezing water from the terry fabric. "Everyone who comes close to me is hurt, there is no reason you should be any different."

But I am different, Madeline wanted to say. She held the thought to herself, knowing even as she lay naked beneath scented water, glorying even as she pained in the protectiveness of Sebastian's presence, she must not forget why she was there.

Raymond Agueci.

The man who had beat her with his own hand. Ordered her beaten more by his thugs while he watched with a bemused smile upon his devilish face before blindfolding her.

But Sebastian rescued her. She owed him her life. "Thank you... for saving me."

"You do not understand." He turned his face away. "You have not been saved."

Madeline shook her head slightly as his words sunk into her muddled understanding. "I don't... what do you mean?"

Sebastian stood, turned from her, thrust a hand through his hair. The moisture in the room dampened the white t-shirt stretching across his back, nearly transparent over the muscle bunching beneath his shoulder blades. He cupped his neck, massaged. "It is complicated." He took a thick white towel off the warming rack, came to sit next to her on the edge of the tub.

She scooted up in the tub, a slight dizziness overcoming her. "Sebastian, please, tell me what's going on."

Offering his hand for assistance, he helped her to rise, eased her onto the lip of the garden tub, wrapped the towel around her shoulders. "Raymond will not let you go until I have done what he asks."

It took a long moment to catch her breath, the pain radiating from her ribs threatening to make her cry out. She inhaled slowly, shallow, trying to keep from expanding her lower lungs. Trying to understand what Sebastian was telling her. "What is he asking?"

Sebastian said nothing, merely walked out of the bathroom. Why wouldn't he tell her what was going on? She wanted so desperately to believe Sebastian was not involved in Raymond Agueci's operations. But until he gave her reason to think otherwise, she had no choice but suspect him a willing participant.

Only the emotions she'd read on his face minutes before, his tender touch... it was difficult to make her heart believe him the monster she set out investigating.

Easing herself to her feet, Madeline stepped out of the tub, a little unsteady on her feet. One hand on the wall for support, she followed Sebastian's path, determined to find out what the hell was going on.

※⟨⟩⁂

Sebastian glanced through the bottom of the crystal tumbler of Scotch he tossed back. Madeline stepped barefoot, still wrapped only in the towel, out of the bedroom and braced her hand on the edge of the counter, swaying with the gentle rocking of the boat. He shouldn't have left her alone in the bathroom, but damn it to hell, something had twisted inside him. Twisted so hard he'd felt his entire insides rip.

He was responsible for Raymond beating her.

Responsible for her pain.

Responsible for the look she gave him, like he was some goddamn saint.

But he knew he was anything but a saint. He was a man who killed mere hours before. A man's who was fueled by revenge and hatred.

A woman like Madeline had no place in his life.

Refilling his tumbler, he poured one for Madeline, ordered her to sit, then crossed the small quarters to hand the drink to her. The overstuffed leather sofa seemed to devour her, making her look small and vulnerable, when he knew she was quite the opposite.

No other woman would have survived what Raymond put her through without hysterics and tears.

She'd remained strong.

Hurt, but strong. He'd sensed that strength about her from the moment he met her. She was like no other woman. And still, he had been wrong to allow her into his life. Put her in danger. He had thought she worked for Raymond. His wrong call could have gotten her dead.

"We're on a boat?"

He nodded. Without looking at her, he laid the Tylenol tablets on the coffee table. "Take these."

"Where are we going?"

"Anchored."

"How far from New York?"

"Too far."

"I think I deserve answers, Sebastian. As a matter of fact, I think I deserve a whole lot of answers. Start by telling me why I've been drugged and kidnapped. Why Raymond used me as a punching bag. Why I'm on a boat, God only knows where." She inhaled a breath, her hand trembled just slightly.

Damn if Sebastian wanted to go to her, wrap his arms around her, comfort her. Offer her things he had not to give.

"It's Raymond's way of getting what he wants."

So tired of playing games with Sebastian, tired of fending off emotions she couldn't deal with, Madeline looked at the man who made her want with her entire body and soul one moment and made her fear the very next.

"What does Raymond want you to do?"

"It does not concern you." He set his untouched drink down and went above deck.

Madeline's attention instantly moved to the computer set up across the room. A blue screen saver glowed in the dim lit cabin. She glanced to the stairwell Sebastian ascended. Did she dare? Was there time to access the files on the computer, find some kind of lead to Raymond's next move?

Hoping, she stood, still unsteady on her feet. Quietly she walked to the computer, moved the mouse, sending away the screen saver and displaying a password protected login panel. "Damn," she whispered, not having believed she'd get so lucky as to find an open file. A wave of dizziness threatened to overcome her, she braced her hands on either side of the keyboard and sucked in a deep breath, paining her ribs.

She stood, willing the hurt to ease, demanding her body toughen up. A light film of sweat beaded her forehead. Madeline stayed that way until she sensed Sebastian's coming before even hearing the first footfall at the top of the stairs. Knowing the screen saver wouldn't flash back on quick enough, she powered off the monitor, stepped away from the computer. By the time he appeared, she'd almost made it back to the sofa. Turning half way around, she braced herself on the coffee table, pretending to lever herself up from where she'd been sitting.

Her gasp from the pressure on her rib cage was no lie.

"Sit. You'll hurt yourself."

"I-I'm fine."

Despite her protest, his large hands circled her waist, steadying her. She straightened, one weak hand holding the edges of the towel together above her breasts.

"I don't want you hurt," he said in a near pained whisper, his words warm and moist on her nape.

A shiver coursed from the spot of his words, spreading like a waft of sauna steam. What was it about his man that made her crave, made her weak?

He leaned her back against his front, a brace of power, security. And still it took all her strength to remain upright. Suddenly she needed to absorb as much of his presence as she could, wanted to accept the fact she wasn't made of steel, that she had needs. Womanly needs. To give in to a moment where she could abandon everything that made her strong and tough as her father raised her to be.

Sebastian's strong hands smoothed up her sides, pressing with care over her sore muscles and battered bones. Around her shoulders to feather over her collarbone, down the back of her arms, spreading awareness and heat throughout her body. Slowly he turned her in his arms, his hands crossed like butterfly wings spread from her spine.

Leaning in closer, her nose pressed to his throat, she closed her eyes and inhaled deeply the scent of sea and salt and man. Her lips pressed against his skin, a sigh floated from deep in her throat. How much she wished for this sense of rightness to be real, not an assignment that would come to an end.

His face tipped downward, his mouth pressing to her forehead in a lingering, soft kiss. "Madeline…"

She raised her chin ever so slowly, time spanning, the hurt in her body dissipating, until her lips hovered in the long exhale of his breath. "Make love to me," she said, the words barely spoken. A plea. A want. A need she hadn't meant to voice.

His mouth came to hers, touching softly, sweeping gently over the cut on her lower lobe. She lifted on her toes, straining to deepen his kiss, to open for him fully. His hand pulled under her wet tangled hair at her nape, cupped the back of her head, pads of his fingers pressing.

Madeline met his dark gaze for a long moment, then reached up and cupped his nape, lowered his head to her breast, holding him there.

She would surrender everything to have this man, she realized. Her body. Her heart.

His head bowed against her chest a long moment, the chords in his neck tensing, jaw flexing. On a long, slow exhale, his hand came to lift her breast, his mouth took her nipple in a heated, damp suckle.

God help her. She wanted his body, his heart, his soul. He lowered to his knees, the rough palm of his hand skimming down her side, around to cup the arch of her bottom. Madeline's head dropped back as his kisses moved over her ribcage, below her naval. *Help her*, such a soft tease of his tongue down the softly covered V of her body… Her breath hitched in the back of her throat, her hand slipped up his nape to clench strands of his hair. Probing apart her folds, he pressed the tip of his warm tongue to the tender nubbin engorging with heat. Her knees warbled. Her mouth began to dry.

Heat. Dampness. Sprays of pleasure. Madeline fell back against the cabin wall, holding Sebastian's mouth to her most intimate place, begging him with tiny cries to never stop touching her. She spread her legs to make better room for him, one knee going over his shoulder, the heel of her foot pressing in the center of his back. Closer. *Please.*

"Sebastian…" His name, no more, as he suckled her nubbin, slipped his finger into the sheer heat of her center. Her free hand plastered against the wall, fingertips pressing, knuckles aching.

He pushed his finger further inside her, pressing upward, moving in slow, deep circles, farther, harder still. His teeth anchored around her nubbin, just hard enough to jolt, sear, swell her point of pleasure, keeping her shy of pain, taking her beyond the ability to think, breathe. He flicked the tip of his tongue, drove deeper into her. Every stroke, lick, nibble she felt more intensity than the last. Sensation upon sensation. Pleasure upon pleasure. Until she could take no more. A fierce contraction gripped him, holding him deep inside her as another cry, part sob, tore through her. He pushed upward with one hard thrust, pushed the pad of his thumb over her nubbin. Before her eyes slammed closed, she saw him ease back to watch her orgasm.

It wasn't until she felt him rise, wrapping her legs around his hips and slip the tip of his erection into her molten core, did she open her eyes. She draped her arms over his shoulders, found strength to lean forward and kiss her flavor upon his mouth.

He pushed inside her, stretching her still trembling walls, and entered her so deep she felt him throughout her entire body. "Madeline," he whispered. "Madeline. Sweet Madeline."

She slipped her tongue under the upper lining of his mouth, circling her hips against him, bringing him somehow deeper still. "I need to feel you come inside me. Please Sebastian. Now."

Slowly he pulled back the length of him, his hips thrust forward, lifting her body upward, pounding his desire again and again, never once breaking eye contact until she came again, her contraction milking hot semen from him, sating her, filling her.

Chapter 6

Sebastian cursed himself as Madeline stood staring out the small round window in the yacht's bedroom. She seemed lost in thought as she stared into the dark blue blackness of the ocean water in the deep of night. Her arms were wrapped around her middle as if holding herself together, as if she released herself the damn of her thoughts she would break. And he knew just what she must have been thinking, as he thought it as well.

Selfish bastard.

That he handled her so roughly when she deserved tenderness tore at Sebastian's gut each moment he looked at her. He should have been soothing her battered body, not ramming himself inside her, taking more than her body. But damn it, he'd wanted her from the first moment he saw her. Couldn't have denied her tonight when she asked him to come inside her. The mere words from her temptress mouth drove him beyond control, already so lost from the feel of his body buried inside hers.

"You should rest," he found himself saying again, moving toward her despite himself like a moth to a summer's garden lantern.

She nodded slowly, her gaze unwavering from the window. "I'm afraid if I fall asleep..." Her words trailed off and Sebastian sensed whatever she was about to say she thought better of.

He wanted to hear it, though. Wanted to know what she feared, wanted to know how to make it better, though he knew he was not the man to make it so. "Tell me, Madeline. Tell me what you're afraid of." Lightly, he traced the tips of his fingers over her shoulders, down her arms.

She leaned into him, inhaled a long, slow breath. Sebastian pressed his face to the side of her head, kissed her temple. "That I'll wake up to find you have been merely a dream."

"Would that not be a good thing?" This was no dream after all. She'd been cast in his private nightmare.

She turned in his arms, looked up at him, watercolors of blue shimmering in her eyes. "What my heart feels and what I know are two different things."

He pulled her against his chest, smoothed the back of her damp hair, absorbing her tears into his skin. A little bit of the twist in his gut unfurled despite his attempt to remain otherwise. "It's terrifying. Holding you like this."

Her arms tightened around him, tighter still, and yet he felt the weakness in her body. "Why, Sebastian?"

"Everything I have loved has been taken from me." A knot thickened in his throat. He knew he should not continue to speak, should not share with her what hardened his heart so, but once he began…

"Share it with me."

His eyes closed on the resurrection of memory.

Her soft hand touched his cheek, cupping her palm against the set of his jaw. "Let me care about you."

The warmth of her touch seeped through him.

Despite himself, Sebastian held Madeline, her head on his chest, until her knees slowly gave way, the slight weight of her dependant on his hold, reminding him once again of his selfishness. Gently he lifted her into his arms and laid her on the bed and kissed her forehead. "Sleep, Madeline. Tomorrow you will be strong again." Rest would once again make her wise. Make her realize the mistake she made in thinking she cared about him.

Lifting the blanket over her, Sebastian returned to the cabin and sat in front of the computer, knowing he had to complete what Raymond demanded of him. If nothing else, he would make sure Madeline left this yacht alive and no more harmed than she'd already been.

❧⟨✖⟩❧

Madeline woke to a halo of light shimmering through the small fisheye window, illuminating the bedroom in a haze of golden morning, the same room where Sebastian held her in his arms. There, she'd felt the shift deep within him.

If nothing else came of this assignment, she would forever take with her the feel of him inside her, the feel of his body so right with hers.

After using the bathroom, washing her face and teeth, Madeline found a large t-shirt in one of the dressers, slipped it on, then entered the living quarters.

Sebastian sat at the computer, his shirt stretched between his broad shoulders, hair brushing past the banded collar. A spray of warmth tipped her breasts, shimmered down her belly to coil deep inside her where she could still feel him buried. Her tender walls so sweetly stretched, her opening slightly sore from his thrusts, her nubbin engorged still from the stroke of the pad of his finger. Her breath caught in her throat, the want of him inside her again begging throughout her body. Yet even as her body reacted, her duty called.

Silently she walked toward him, unable to see the computer screen for his height and the width of his back. When she approached, she slipped her hands over his shoulders, down his chest to cover his pecks, her breasts flattening against his back, nipples beading to the sinew of his muscle.

His shoulders tensed, jaw line hardened. Her mouth went low on his throat, the point of his pulse as her eyes moved to the monitor just as he moved the mouse to minimize the screen. *Damn*, her mind said, even as her body pressed harder against him, the feel of her nipples against fabric and warmth softening the curse. With the tip of her tongue she circled his slow and steady pulse, exhaling a long, heated breath. "You're up early," she murmured, nose lifting to scrape the underside of his stubble jaw.

"I have not yet slept." He moved forward, easing away from her, pretending what they shared the night before meant nothing.

She'd made too much progress in gaining his trust to allow him retreat. No matter how foolishly hard she fell for him, she couldn't forget she was on a case. To forget would take away everything she'd worked her life for. She may have surrendered her body, possibly her heart.

Madeline would not surrender the promise she'd made to her father.

She pushed on the back of his chair, turning Sebastian around. "Don't," he said, even as she bent her knees on the black leather chair on either side of him, lowered herself atop his lap. Her ribs cried out in pain, she bit back a wince.

As she nestled her crotch over the fly of his jeans, an arm going around his neck, the other gripping the edge of the desk beyond, she rested her face against his cheek, drew in a deep, shuddering breath. The heat between them was instant, his erection coming hard and hot. "Don't, what, Sebastian?" she asked coyly, hips rotating just slightly, soft jeans against damp panties. She lifted her gaze to look into his dark eyes, her breath stilling as she absorbed a steely look. It was not one of passion or desire, want or need.

Murderous came to mind, the same moment his hand clasped her neck, fisting hair and pulling backward. "Don't play games with me."

She swallowed, fought the urge to free herself. All it would take was a lift of her hips, a repositioning of her knee to stun him a moment, just long enough to get free. *And then what?* She was on a yacht in the middle of the ocean. He could feed her to the sharks and no one would be the wiser.

Even as she contemplated escape routes, feared her life, her crotch throbbed, pulsed, begged to have the fullness beneath her enter her, sate the mounting tension. Her back arched, lessening the pain of his hold. Her breasts rose, her hips slid the length of him, stroking his cock with her dampness and heat. "You're hurting me," she said, closing her eyes, riding him in slow, tortuous motions.

His hold lessened the tightness at her nape, his hips rose to push against her. Madeline reached between them, slipped her panties to the side, spread her lips over the fly of his jeans, stroked her finger over her slick nubbin, moistening her finger with the scent of her sex. Her knees clenched Sebastian's hips, the length of her finger pressing upward against a crying need.

Moving her trembling hand from beneath her, she gripped the button of his pants. Suddenly the chair spun and Sebastian pushed her off his lap, gripped her at the hips and turned her, shoved her over the desk. Her forearms slammed down, palms stinging on the desktop. He stood between her legs, lifting her onto her toes, one hand between her shoulders holding her down, the other she felt go between her bottom and his crotch, the slide of his zipper echoing in her dazed mind.

"Tell me what you want." He pressed the hard length of his freed erection against her bottom.

Breath caught in her throat on part cry of desire and a shimmer of fear. "I—"

He slipped his hand beneath her shirt, fisted his hand at the edge of her panties and tore the seam. His other hand shoved her down harder, her head inches from the computer monitor. "Do you want me to fuck you?"

"No," she whimpered, wanting to hate the sound of his raw use of words, only to find herself lifting her bottom, rotating her hips, wanting him to do exactly that.

"No?" He shoved away her torn panties, spread her legs further open with his thighs, bending slightly to slip his erection beneath her and pressing upward.

"No," she echoed, biting her bottom lip, fingertips digging into the grains of wood.

Standing, his bare length eased into her folds, throbbing hardness nestling into her silky heat, the tip of his erection jutting against her nubbin, circling, teasing. Escalating.

"Yes," she breathed. "Damn you, yes. I want you to fuck me. Now."

His hips moved backward, then thrust inside her, lifting her off her feet, burying himself so far inside her everything hurt and pleasured at once. He reached over her shoulder, placing his hand over the computer mouse. His other hand fisted her hair, pulled her head up until she was near nose to nose with the computer screen. "Are you sure about that, *Agent Carter*?"

Chapter 7

Madeline stared at a picture of herself dressed in blues on the monitor.

Never before had she felt so abased. She wanted nothing more than to lock herself in the bedroom, avoid the slant of Sebastian's gaze, the hatred seeping from his every pore.

Instead of fleeing, she stood, keeping her back as straight as she could, demanding her body relax, forcing herself to breathe. Her tattered panties lay on the floor across the room, her body still pulsed from abandonment of fulfillment she shouldn't still wish would come. Words completely left her. She had no idea what to say, where to begin. Denial was out of the question. The picture taken of her when she graduated from the police academy was still displayed on the computer screen a few feet away.

Sebastian flexed his hand as if tempering the need to strike something. Possibly her.

She swallowed, opened her mouth to speak, thought better of it. Let him get around to airing the fury he clearly felt when he was ready. Madeline didn't have to wait long. The vein at Sebastian's temple throbbed twice before he said, "You may not be one of Raymond's *baldraccas*. But clearly you are a whore all the same, *si*?"

It shouldn't have hurt so deeply, his insult. Right to the core of her. A direct hit to everything she'd been battling with herself. "No," she whispered. "I chose to be with you, it had nothing to do with the assignment."

Sebastian's laugh came out dry. "Yes, the assignment. Tell me about this, Madeline."

She averted her gaze. "I can't."

Suddenly he was across the room, shoving her against the wall, lifting her off her feet by the shoulders. "That is the wrong answer."

Training demanded she react, but Madeline couldn't make herself fight back against Sebastian's hold. She deserved this. She betrayed him. Lied to him. That it was her job mattered none. Maybe if she'd never touched him, kissed him, allowed him so deep inside her she'd remember the feel of him until she died, maybe then she could distance herself, do what she had to do without hesitation. "It's the only answer I can give you, no matter what you do to me. Now please, release me. I don't want to hurt you."

"You seem certain I will not hurt you first. Why is this, *diavola bella*?"

Madeline closed her eyes, knew the words she was about to speak were risky. Perhaps deadly. "Because you care about me. Because you need my help. My agency's help."

Sebastian pushed away from her, paced several steps, dragged his hand through his hair. "I don't need anyone's help."

Madeline hesitated only a moment before moving toward him, lifted her hands and hovered them over his shoulders, wanting to touch him, to force him to feel her, to know she was there, that somehow, somewhere along the line she fell in love with him and wanted desperately to find away out for him.

These very same thoughts, she knew, were reasons his coffin would be nailed as tightly as Raymond's. If anyone found out she'd slept with Sebastian the case would become a circus, he'd be convicted just to make a statement of her public servant sins.

What a mess she made. Her hands dropped away, her head bowed. "It's time you tell me what's going on. I can help."

He rolled his neck, shrugged his shoulders like a fighter preparing for the ring.

"I know about Lou Mendoza, Harold Trapone and Freddie Aster. Did you kill them?" Madeline braced herself for the answer, needing to know, fearing the reply.

After a long pause Sebastian shook his head once. "I tried to save them. I arrived at the ranch too late."

Madeline's heart wrenched, knowing it was not the only time Sebastian had been the first on the scene to one of Raymond's blood baths. "What's your involvement with Raymond's operations, outside of old family ties? Why do you work for him? What did he bring you here for?"

Sebastian turned around, stared down at her, emotions dark and deep clouding his eyes. "Have you not figured it out?" He motioned to the computer. "I am as guilty as you believe me to be. I do Raymond's bidding. I seek out agents such as yourself, expose them, mark them for death."

The admission did not surprise her. Sickened her, yes. Made her want to strike out, punish him for confirming involvement with Ray. The image of her father before the coffin closed flashed in her mind and suddenly she thrust forward, hands shoving Sebastian's chest, then pummeling wildly, out of control. Blind rage. "Damn you! Damn you to hell!" Tears stung her eyes, her throat burned.

Sebastian took it all, his eyes closed until her anger and fury gave way to tears. "Damn you," she cursed once again, collapsing against his chest, heaving from the gut outward. "Damn you."

The last thing she expected were for his arms to wrap around her, for him to hold her, comfort her. Madeline knew she should push away, hate him. Instead she remained in his arms, sick and hurt and exhausted. All she wanted was for him to be there until the ugliness went away. "Why? Why would you do this Sebastian?"

"Because if I do not... my sister will be killed."

"But your sister is dead, she was murdered along with your family."

"No. She was taken. The young woman who was buried beside my *familia* was not my sister."

Rubbing two fingers to her temple, Madeline tried to absorb what Sebastian said, tried to find justification in exchanging many lives for one. "So you allow innocent men and women to be killed. If nothing else, haven't you ever thought about their families, children, loved ones left behind? How could you do that? How can you live with yourself? You, of all people, should understand what it's like to lose."

"Hah." He threw his hands in the air. "Innocent men and women? No. The men I uncovered are anything but. They are just as corrupt as Raymond, perhaps more so. At least Raymond does not hide behind a shield and pretend to be just. The undercover agents I rooted out work for the New York clan, just as their fathers before. They spend your Americans' hard earned money to ensure the prosperity of the mob."

Madeline shook her head. *Yes*, of course she knew there were dirty cops, always had been, always would be. But Raymond spoke of deeper mob connections than turning a blind eye or falsifying a witness. "So Raymond wants these agents wiped out. Why?"

"It will be impossible to fully take over the New York operations with such a system of protection in place. Raymond wants a clean slate. He needs to build relationships with people he can trust. New blood, if you will."

Suddenly it became clear why Raymond brought her here. "People like me?"

"Yes."

"I need to know who you've uncovered. I need—"

"No."

"I'm not going to allow Raymond to kill people, guilty or not. That is for the system to decide, not you or Raymond Agueci."

"*I* will not allow my thirteen year old sister to be murdered."

"You don't know for sure Raymond—"

"He killed my *familia*. Tessa." He raked a hand through his hair. "*Madre de Dios*. Tessa is pregnant with Raymond's child. She will give birth in less than a month's time. She will be delivering a son."

The knot in Madeline's gut sucked her breath away, the twisting of her insides nearly making her sick. A thirteen-year-old child pregnant with a monster's baby. A son, no less. Madeline knew the value a boy child would be to Raymond. His protégé. To be groomed to take over the family business. To be as ruthless as he. Priceless, this child. No way would Raymond give that child up.

She sunk onto the edge of the coffee table, held her stomach. "There must be some way to get to your sister. To put Raymond behind bars."

Sebastian picked up a vase, hurled it against the wall. Madeline shielded her face with her forearms as glass shattered. Shards flew through the air, plinking down like crystal raindrops. After a long moment of silence, as if the symphony just played its last note, he closed his eyes. "Do you not think I've spent every waking moment trying to find a way? Tessa is all I have left. Can you possibly understand?"

Madeline thought of her father, knew she would have done anything for one more day, hour, minute with him. If there had been a way to save him, she would have done so without question or hesitation. "What do we do?"

"Ah, that is a very good question, Agent Carter," Raymond Agueci said, stepping into the room, his gun making a slow sweep from Sebastian to Madeline.

The hardening inside Madeline, the want to attack, disarm Raymond, was nothing compared to the seething hatred emanating from Sebastian. It was clear he wanted to bring Raymond down, barely held himself back. And the restraint was eating him alive. His eyes shone dark and as menacing as the devil, his body rigid, tense, yet predatory, ready to move in an instant, the thirst for blood thick in the air.

Raymond must have sensed it as well. Without hesitation, he fired a single shot. Sebastian's leg jerked, his eyes widened. Stunned, knee buckling, he dropped to the floor.

Madeline grabbed Sebastian by the shoulders, eased him onto his side, noting his eyes already cloudy, heavy. A moment later he was out, his hand dropping off the bullet wound.

"Don't worry, *bella*. Sebastian will have a nice little rest, perhaps suffer a headache when he wakes. You do not think I would permanently harm my best computer man, do you? The next bullet in the chamber is quite deadly, however. Do not force me to use it."

Madeline pressed her hand to the trickle of blood soaking the hole in Sebastian's jeans. The wound wasn't deep, she could feel the pellet just beneath the broken skin. She glared at Raymond. "No, not until he's completed his work." Knowing she could do nothing for Sebastian until he woke, she stood, lifted her shoulders, drew up her spine, enlarging herself as she mentally prepared to spar with a man who disposed of lives as easily as throwing away a piece of trash. "Then he'll be as dead as everyone else who works for you. You're a bastard."

"This," Raymond shrugged, "I do not deny. But I am a bastard who gets what he desires."

And right now Raymond desired her services. "Okay, so you got me here. You've sucked me into your game. Now what? You think because you're threatening to kill Sebastian's sister I'm going to go on your payroll? Think again. The girl means nothing to me."

Raymond winked. "Ah, but you care about Sebastian."

It proved difficult to steel herself against the truth of his statement. "You're wrong. Sebastian is a case. A number in a file. I'll put him behind bars and wipe my hands clean, just like I will you."

"Tough words." Raymond lifted a picture off the wall, revealing the eye of a camera peeking through a drilled hole. "Yes, there is one in every room. It has been… hmm, interesting, the way you perform an investigation, Agent Carter."

Her blood drained, pooled in her gut, lower, anchoring in her toes, immobilizing her.

Knowing she couldn't allow the fact Raymond had watched, heard everything that passed between her and Sebastian since arriving on the yacht throw her off balance, she mentally distanced herself, drew in a deep breath, regained her equilibrium. She unfurled her fingers that had closed so tightly into her palms half moons of broken skin stung like tiny thorn cuts. "Duty called," she said flatly, hating the words spoken aloud that made her sound like a slut.

"Perhaps I shall bury my seed inside you as well. You would like that, hmmm? To have a child growing inside you. To not know who the father is. When you look in the little bastard's face everyday, you will think of your so-called duty."

"Don't you dare."

Raymond smiled, moved to the bar and poured himself a drink. "Or what? You'll fight me? I will only become more aroused. Making love is overrated."

"For a man like you, I'm sure it is. Raping young girls is more your style."

"Tessa has been a joy. If you mean to try and make me feel guilt for pleasuring her, I assure you this will not happen. Though I admit, I would have been disappointed had you not tried, but I am not interested in playing mind games with you. Drink? No, of course not, you want to keep your wits, keep a clear head. Figure me out. Let me tell you this, I am as twisted as you believe, and knowing this gives me the advantage you will not be able to obtain. You won't find a weakness, a button to push. I simply do not feel. Do not care. I take what I want and when I am done with it, I throw it away. Life remains simple this way."

"I don't want to play games either. Tell me the terms to have the girl released."

"There will be no negotiations until I know I can trust you."

"You have plenty on those videotapes to ensure my loyalty."

Raymond rocked back on his heels. "This is true. But it is not enough. I have watched you very carefully. You have great loyalty, sense of honor and duty, like my cousin. I admire this."

"You also know my face, my identity. Do you think I'm naïve enough to believe you'll just let me walk out of here? If I don't turn for you, I'll be six feet under. I understand how you work, Raymond."

"You could only begin to imagine, Madeline. Only to begin." A wicked smile splayed across his face as he moved toward her. She backed up a step, another, even as he reached out and snagged her by the hair, yanking her head back and staring down at her with eyes illuminated with sheer menace. He forced his thigh between her legs, pressed his knee upward into the apex of her sex. "Open your legs for me willingly. Now, and whenever I desire. Then I will be satisfied of your loyalty."

Madeline reached up her hands, cupped his bony cheeks in her palms. "Never." She spat in his face.

"Bitch." Raymond forced her by the hair to her knees, drug her across the room to shove her face first across the sofa, burying her face in the cushion as he reached his free hand between her legs.

At the sickening touch to the place she allowed Sebastian to love her, nausea welled inside Madeline. She wanted to vomit. She reacted without thought, her elbow swung back, ramming into Raymond's erection, her head followed, bashing his nose, flailing him backward. She clambered to her feet, spun and kicked him flatfooted beneath his chin, catching his head at an angle, twisting his neck as his body lifted to a ripping of spinal cord and bone as he flew backward, sprawling him onto his back.

Madeline stood over his body. Raymond's hand lay limp over his crotch. Blood was splattered over his face and still trickled from his nose. His head was angled grotesquely, his eyes blank, lifeless. She began to shake from the inside out. The vomit that threatened earlier rose to lump in her throat. She swallowed sickly, turned away from Raymond's soulless body.

She felt nothing for killing Raymond Agueci.

He deserved to die.

Without looking, she reached for the cell phone clipped to Raymond's waistband, flipped it open with shaky fingers and punched in the number to Whittaker's line.

"Sir, it's me." A cry punched up from her stomach. "Can you arrange for pickup?"

Sebastian's mouth tasted faintly metallic and felt full of cotton as he slowly woke. He groaned, hand going to his leg to a radius of pain. Slowly he rolled to his side, pushed himself up to his hands and knees, brain banging against the insides of his skull. He forced open his heavy lidded eyes, the room a haze of white cloud and blurry focus for a long moment. At first unsure if he was waking from a terrible dream, his memory came back to him.

"Madeline?" he whispered, then louder as his vision cleared and he saw her through a long tunnel, seemingly miles away. Her knees were drawn to her chest, arms wrapped around tightly. She rocked back and forth, back and forth, her hair tangled over her face. He reached a heavy hand toward her. "Madeline."

Slowly she lifted her head and looked at him, tears wet on her face. "I'm sorry, Sebastian."

It was then the tunnel in which he'd focused expanded. Raymond lay several feet away from Madeline. "No! *Madre de Dios.*" His arms gave out. He fell onto his chest, a cry heaving up from the depths of him as if the hounds of hell were released.

Raymond was dead.

And now, with Raymond gone and unable to tell him where Tessa was being held, his sister and unborn child were as good as dead as well. "No…"

Chapter 8

Sebastian wouldn't even look at her, not that Madeline blamed him. The moment she heard Raymond's neck snap she knew she harmed everything Sebastian had tried to protect, what was left of his family. "I hear the helicopter," she said, fingers releasing the tense hold on the deck railing. For the sake of keeping a clean crime scene, Madeline insisted Sebastian go above deck until Whittaker arrived.

Sebastian sat in the wheelhouse, head tossed back, eyes closed. As she had for the past three hours while they waited for Whittaker to get a locale and send pickup, Madeline wanted to go to Sebastian, tell him how sorry she was, beg for his forgiveness, offer comfort. Anything but endure his strained, agony filled silence. The blades of the helicopter sounded closer by the moment and with each whir, her chance of last words with Sebastian closed in.

She stepped into the wheelhouse, knelt before him, placed a hand on his knee. Sebastian angled is head away, opened his heavily red-rimmed eyes and stared out the side window. "I'm sorry," she whispered.

After a long moment he knuckled away a tear. "This is no more your fault than mine."

And yet Madeline knew that he would never be able to look at her again without seeing all that was taken from him. "I know this is probably the last thing you want to talk about right now, but I need you to listen carefully. Can you do that? You have information that is extremely valuable to my agency. My boss will deal with you in exchange for the data you have on the corruption you've uncovered. Let me be there with you to get the best deal. I'll negotiate for you."

Sebastian slammed his hand on the yacht's steering wheel, slanted her a glare. "I don't give a damn about making goddamn deals, or what happens to me. Tessa," he closed his eyes again, scrubbed his face with his palm, "I just want Tessa."

She couldn't help cupping Sebastian's nape, massaging the knotted cords. "I'll make sure my agency uses every possible resource available to find your sister. Until we know for sure otherwise, there's still a chance. Someone must know where Raymond has been keeping her."

"No. Raymond has too many enemies. He moves around, never letting anyone know where his home base is at, not even his right hand man."

"Don't do this, don't give up. You've been through too much to try and save your sister." She had to yell over the sound of the helicopter hovering overhead. She could see a boat approaching, probably the closest coast guard craft in the area alerted to the situation. Only a few more moments with Sebastian. "Think, damn it. There must be a connection somewhere that we can find, some link—" Madeline's words broke off, the camera in the wall Raymond revealed to her flashing in her mind. Raymond told her he'd been watching.

Madeline's hand fell to Sebastian's shoulder, she forced him to turn and look at her. "Raymond was monitoring us on a camera. Sebastian, do you hear me?" She shook him until his glazed eyes focused. "Raymond was watching us, the video was being fed. We can trace the connection." It might not lead them to Raymond's lair, but it was the best shot they had.

Sebastian's gaze slowly moved forward as he watched the Coast Guard boat pull up beside the yacht. "Are you sure, *Agent Carter*, you want that video traced?"

Madeline knew what Sebastian was asking. Was she ready for her boss, and everyone else, to know she made love to a suspect, for her career to end? No, she didn't want that, didn't want everything that was her life to end in humiliation and shame, but for Sebastian, his sister and unborn child, she would endure anything, sacrifice everything. But her thoughts must have seemed hesitation.

Sebastian shrugged off her touch, stood and glowered down at her. "I did not think so, little *baldraccas*. I did not think so."

Before Madeline could correct him, the Coast Guard rushed the yacht, agents rappelled from the helicopter overhead. Orders were shouted, guns aimed. Within minutes Sebastian was in handcuffs and taken away. Whittaker was suddenly there, draping a blanket around her, holding her beneath his big, heavy arm, drawing her to his chest and kissing the crown of her head.

"It's over, Maddy. It's over."

Her entire body felt numb, cold, distant as she watched the boat carrying Sebastian slice through the water. Slowly she shook her head. "No. It's not. I went over the line."

Whittaker stood stone a long moment, then drew her closer. "No one needs to know, my girl. Put it out of your head. We'll finish up here, get you on a new assignment. You'll put all this behind you. You did good, your dad would be proud."

Madeline tamped down a sob, knowing otherwise. She'd sacrificed every principal her father raised her on, she shamed the uniform he gave his life for. "You don't understand. I love him."

"Do you think, my dear Maddy, your father wouldn't understand? He loved, just like the rest of us. He had his faults, just like the rest of us."

Somehow she couldn't fathom the man who'd been her hero ever making a mistake, nor did she want to imagine. "I have two things I need to ask of you. Two things, before the agency lets me go."

"Stop talking nonsense, Maddy."

"There's a video feed, I need its source. Immediately. And I need to be allowed to accompany the team there."

"If you're worried about what's on the tape, I can make it go away—"

"Tessa Maiocco is alive. The tape is the only possible lead to her."

"If you're sure—"

"I'm sure. Second, Sebastian is not to be prosecuted."

Whittaker shook his head. "I can only help you so far. There's no way I can let him get off, especially if whatever's on those tapes goes public."

"Sebastian has been uncovering blue corruption for Raymond. Everyone who has been on the mafia payroll in the states, Italy and beyond. It goes deep, deeper than you could ever imagine. He'll give you names. Enough to keep the agency busy for years."

Whittaker absorbed this information in silence, the boat rocking gently, agents securing the murder scene below deck. "If he doesn't turn evidence, hard evidence, I can't make promises."

Madeline leaned her head on Whittaker's shoulder, closed her eyes. "He will. Just get him released from custody, take him the computer that's below deck, and no I don't give a rat's ass if it's evidence, take it to him. Let him work, he'll deliver. And when you see Sebastian, tell him," Madeline swallowed hard, wanting so much to finish the sentence with, *tell him I love him*, "tell him I'll bring Tessa home."

⁂

Madeline silenced her ringing cell phone, leaned forward and paid the taxi-cab driver. "*Graci*," she said, sucking in a deep breath, staring at the Italian villa once beautiful. Just looking at the huge *hacienda* nestled in valleys of dying grape vines and weeded flower gardens she felt the love that had once flourished in this great home, felt the *familia* pride, the people that once lived here.

Now, all barren from years of neglect. Still, she could see Sebastian as a young boy riding a pony, chasing chickens, sitting on the patio with his *padre*.

Before she lost the courage, she opened the door and stepped onto the cobblestone driveway, wondering for the hundredth time if she had a right to be here on this day Tessa was brought home. She hadn't spoken to Sebastian since he was taken from the yacht, though she'd tried to contact him when she located Tessa. He refused to see her, refused her calls. He shut her out of his heart, where her betrayal assured her she didn't belong.

But on this day, Madeline refused to allow Sebastian to force her away.

As the taxi driver unloaded her bags and set them on the porch, Madeline walked the path to the back of the house, sensing where to find Sebastian. She opened a partly unhinged white picket fence trellised in grown-wild pink roses and continued on until she saw him standing ahead.

Her heart stilled.

She nearly turned to leave, instead forced herself to go to him, wrap her arms around his waist and rest her head between his shoulder blades.

They stood silently for a long time, Sebastian's shoulders shaking gently, his head bowed. A soft, grape scented breeze lifted the ends of his hair, played the hem of Madeline's skirt. "You should not have come," he finally said.

"I wanted…" she began, her breath against Sebastian's back. What could she say? What could she offer?

"Thank you, for sending Tessa home."

She nodded, her arms loosening around his waist until they fell away. "I wish…"

"Thank you, but I do not want you here. Go."

Madeline stepped back, swiped a tear from the corner of her eye. She turned and walked away. What a fool to have come, to think Sebastian would need her, want her here with him. He'd made it clear in his refusal to see her. Yet, she'd hoped. Steps quickening, vines and branches slapping at her as she navigated the path, her vision blurry, she ran to the gate, fumbled her hands at the rusty latch, unable to open it on the first try. Finally she pushed it open, turned to take one last look at the man whom she would always carry in her heart.

Sebastian sank to his knees onto the fresh turned earth, reached out a trembling hand and traced Tessa's name on the headstone. All that remained of Sebastian's family had been brought home in a casket. Madeline would live forever with the vision of finding Tessa's body, so young, so beautiful, the beginnings of life taken away.

Madeline turned, realizing she had no right to intrude upon Sebastian's grief, his pain, his sorrow. She'd been a but a mere fraction of time in his life, a life she knew nothing of, a life once filled with love and now veiled in pain. A fool to believe she could offer him love again, she betrayed him. Lied to him.

Fishing the cell phone from her purse, noting three more missed calls from Whittaker, Madeline called for the taxi to return. Where she would go, she didn't know. Not home to her little house in D.C., she no longer had a life there, no family, no career. She was as alone as Sebastian in this world.

Sitting down on the steps beside her bags, she drew her knees up to her chest, rested her head on her knees and willed her tears to dry. When she heard the sound of the taxi coming up the drive, she drew in a deep breath, stood and lifted her suitcase. A hand wrapped around her's, taking the bag from her grip.

"It is selfish of me, Madeline, and I am sorry for this, but I need you to stay. Just for tonight." Sebastian's words were spoken just behind the shell of her ear, words so deeply etched with pain, Madeline's heart fractured at the tone.

But to stay just for one night. To endure another goodbye tomorrow? He turned her to face him, lifted her chin with his hand until she stared into his pain filled eyes. "Please do not tell me no." He lowered his mouth to whisper across her lips. "I do not wish to be alone tonight."

Madeline knew she should refuse, only she couldn't. If she could give him one night of love, give herself one last memory to take with her… "I'll stay." *For however long you want me, need me.*

Sebastian twined his hand through Madeline's, led her into his ancestral home. The demons inside him needed to be stilled. Despite knowing how wrong it was to use Madeline, he needed to find solace. *Madre de Dios,* he needed to feel something other than the pain eating him alive.

He led her up the half moon stairway, feeling the tentativeness to her steps. He would not lie to her, would not allow her to believe he needed more than her body tonight.

And even as he told himself this, he led her past his own living quarters, down the hallway and opened the heavy door to the room where his parents had laid, and their parents before, and their's… It was the room meant for the newly wed, blessed and cherished. It was the room the Maiocco children were conceived for generations.

As he closed the door and stripped off his shirt, he looked at Madeline standing in a haze of sunlight pouring through the gauze drapes and damned himself for wanting to make love to her, to bring her body to culmination with his, to bring life to this *hacienda* again.

He was exhausted. He needed her body, nothing more of this woman who wormed her way into his life with betrayal and lie. But when she turned to stare at him with her jeweled eyes somehow knowing, sharing his pain, the weeks he'd tried to hate her for the secrets she kept from him faded away. He understood her duty, her loyalty.

Despite being an American, his *papa* would have loved her, his *mama* would have cherished her. Tessa would have made Madeline her best friend, the sister she'd always wanted.

Walking to her, he lifted his hand around to unclasp her hair, watched her golden mane fall around her shoulders. He splayed his fingers through her hair at the temples, pushed through the strands to cup the back of her head, fisted and pulled until her face tipped, her mouth parted. He stared down at her for a long time, savoring how beautiful, how angelic, knowing her passion, knowing she would allow him to take what he needed, that she would give herself completely.

A tremble coursed from his hand through his body, he released her hair, dropped his hand to her shoulder. He closed his eyes a moment, angled his head away.

Madeline slid her hand across his cheek, soft, butterfly wings over the roughness of his stubble. "I understand, Sebastian. I understand you need me for tonight. That I will leave tomorrow. You don't need to tell me you can never trust me again. Never love me. I'm not asking for your heart. Allow me to give you the peace you need tonight."

He heard Madeline's heart breaking in the tone of her voice, though she tried to sound brave. "I do not want to hurt—"

Her hand covered his mouth. "Just as you have been honest with me about your intentions, I will be honest with you. It'll kill me to leave you tomorrow. My heart is already feeling the pain just thinking about it." She tried to smile. Her beautiful mouth trembled. A tear pooled in the corner of her eye. "But I promise you I will go. Before you even wake, I'll go. But know this, Sebastian. I love you. I love you, and if you ever can find a way to forgive me, if you ever allow yourself to love, I'll come back." She leaned up, replaced her hand with her mouth, pressing firm against him while demons played against his want to return her love.

He breathed in her breath as he slanted his mouth over hers, delved his tongue into the silkiness of her, swept his tongue along the tip of hers, losing himself, forgetting all but the need to feel.

Madeline wrapped her arms around his shoulders, her body arched along his, offering him sweet solace with her touch, her kiss, her heart. How Sebastian wanted to lay her down on the bed with the portrait of Mother Theresa hanging overhead, giving her blessing for the marriage beginning, the children to be conceived. Ah, but he was the end of the Maiocco *familia*.

"Sebastian?"

Unaware he had released Madeline, Sebastian snapped himself out of the dark, dangerous place his thoughts took him. Moving around her, he stalked to the window, thrust back the thin curtains and planted his palms on the panes, stared down at the vineyards, the gardens. Fitting, how everything had withered and died.

Moments later Madeline's hands lay on his bare shoulder blades, whispered up the his arms, her sweet mouth pressing to the center of his back.

"I think you should go."

Her tongue flicked out to circle his skin, trailing ever so slowly up his spine, her fingers splaying the length of his against the glass. As she rose on tiptoe, her breasts flattened against his back, her breath hot, moist. She nipped her teeth into his nape, her hands dropped in front of his, crisscrossing to palm his pecks, his nipples hardening against her palms.

"No," she breathed, nipping again, squeezing her hands before beginning a slow descent, trailing his chest hair until it dipped below his waistband. She worked open his belt buckle, button, slid down his zipper. "If you won't use me tonight, allow me to use you."

His body tensed, his erection mocked. Once again he warred with what he wanted to take with what he knew his heart could not handle.

"Stop thinking, Sebastian. Just feel me. Let me love you, just for tonight." Madeline slipped her hand to palm his erection, pressing down the length of him. She wrapped her fingers around the base and pulled upward, skimming her thumb over the moistened tip before plunging downward again, hardening him further, surging hot blood through his body, winning the battle. He jerked her hand away, turned and shoved her head downward until she kneeled before him.

Fisting her hair he brought her mouth the jutting tip of him, watched as she flicked her tongue over his sensitive head before opening to suck him, working the base of his cock with her hand. His head banged against the window, his jaw locked. A shudder ripped through him as he watched, eyes fighting to stay open. He wanted to succumb, wanted to release in her mouth, watch as she drank in the hot come boiling inside him.

Instead he stilled her, drew in a gulp of air. If this night was all he would have of Madeline, he wanted it to be all he was undeserving of. He wanted to forget her lie. Wanted to make love to her. Wanted her love.

Loosening his fingers in her hair, he brought her to stand, kissed her, his tongue soft beneath her upper lip, nipping gently at the corner of her mouth, sweeping delicately inside her mouth as he undressed her.

Scooping Madeline into his arms, he carried her across the room, lay her on the white duvet, her hair fanning the lush pile of pillows. He stood over her, admiring her beauty, memorizing the blue of her eyes, the tip of her nose, the flush in her cheeks as he removed the rest of his clothing. "You are so beautiful, Madeline."

She smiled up at him and reached her hand for his as he knelt beside her. He brought her hand to his mouth, kissed the inside of her wrist. "You make me feel beautiful. Come to me, Sebastian."

Kneeling between her legs, he scooped his hands beneath her bottom and massaged her firm cheeks. Slowly he pushed his length into the milky heat of her with excruciating slowness, feeling her walls mold around him, welcoming him deep into her core.

Madre de Dios. He fought to keep from closing his eyes, losing himself in the feeling of being buried to her hilt. Instead he focused on her face, found solace deep in her eyes. Lifting her hips as he withdrew, he found himself pushing back into her, squeezing her ass, keeping her mounted against him.

"Sebastian…" She splayed her hands across his chest, her fingers pressing deep, palms hard against his nipples.

"Madeline," he echoed, finding the strength to push into her further, loving the way she watched him, gave herself completely. When she clenched her inner walls, drawing him deeper, tightening around him like a virgin, he lost all control. His orgasm came fast, hot, slickening her, readying her for his touch, which she responded to with a culmination, if possible, even more forceful than his. And it was only the beginning of the pleasure he showed her body. Only the beginning of the pleasure he sought time and again.

Chapter 9

Madeline traced the tip of her finger over the fan of Sebastian's closed eyes to the bridge of his nose, down the length, dropped lightly on his mouth. For the first time since she met him he seemed truly at peace, she only prayed the calm would stay with him. That when he woke in the morning, he would be at least partially free of the pain he'd endured, that tonight offered the beginnings of healing.

Pressing her mouth lightly to his, she kissed him a long, long moment, before carefully sliding from beneath the covers. More than anything she wanted to stay the night in his arms, be there for him to seek in the darkness, offer her body time and again until the sun rose.

If she stayed, she knew leaving would be all the harder.

By the light of the moon shimmering through the gauze curtains, she gathered her clothing, found her bag and headed to the bathroom to dress. Digging out her cell phone to call for the taxi she noted the display informing her of more missed calls. Whittaker.

No matter how much her former boss tried to convince her otherwise, Madeline had no place at D.I.C. Hefting her bag over her shoulder, she turned out the bathroom light before opening the door, stood for a long moment watching Sebastian sleep, then drew in the strength to leave. Tears pooling in her eyes, she left the bedroom, padded quietly down the stairs and slipped out the front door. She stopped dead in her tracks at the black sedan parked in the circular driveway.

The back window slid down. "It's about goddamn time you came out."

"What are you doing here?"

"I've been calling you all day. Get in."

Madeline rounded the car, opened the door and slid inside, shoving her bags to the floorboard. May as well go now, she'd call and cancel the taxi. "I'm not coming back to the agency." She glanced at Whittaker, what he held. *My God.* "Is that?"

"Yes, Madeline, it is. Do you want to make the delivery, or shall I?"

Hand over her mouth she took in a shaky breath, knowing she was about to change Sebastian's life. She carefully reached out and took the bundle from Whittaker and blew out a long breath. "I'll handle it. Wait for me?"

He touched her arm. "I'll be here if you need me, Maddy." But as she climbed the steps and opened the door, the black sedan pulled out of the drive.

"Damn you, Whittaker," she whispered, opening the door and finding her way back to Sebastian's room.

✳⁓(ᴗᴗ)ᵔ⁓

The sleeping baby in Madeline's arms opened his big brown eyes and fisted a lock of her hair as she laid him down on the bed beside Sebastian. "Shhh, little guy," she cooed, untangling her hair from his cherub hand. "You're home now. You'll be safe here." She tucked his arm back in his swaddling blanket, securing him tightly.

She knew so little about babies, suspected Sebastian would know even less. They'd figure it out though, together, Sebastian and this tiny child.

The baby smelled so sweet and perfect when she leaned down and kissed his forehead. "You'll be loved here," Madeline whispered, an ache welling in her throat. Despite Sebastian's determination to close his heart, she knew the power of his love, the comfort of his touch. Knew this child would fill some of the emptiness of Sebastian's life.

Lying down beside the baby she reached over and touched Sebastian's shoulder, gently shaking him. "Sebastian, wake up. There's somebody here you'll want to meet."

The expression on Sebastian's face was one of confusion when he opened his eyes. He looked a long time down at the baby in the low light of the room. Hesitantly he lifted a hand and placed it on the infant's heart as if needing confirmation of life. "I do not understand."

Madeline placed her hand over Sebastian's, feeling the beat of the baby's heart. "Your nephew, Sebastian. He's been waiting to meet you."

Sebastian's dark eyes moved to look long and hard at Madeline. He slid his hand from beneath her's, rolled over and grabbed his jeans, shucking them on before standing. "You allowed me to believe there was no child."

The baby made little sucking noises, his mouth working as if searching for a nipple. "I'm sorry, I didn't want to give you hope. There was no sign of him when I found Tessa. We thought perhaps he'd been stillborn. Until I knew something for sure, I wanted to save you the pain."

The baby suddenly let out a cry, his face squishing up and turning red.

Sebastian's face skewered. "My cousin fathered that child. I do not want him."

Madeline sat, reached into the diaper bag and found a pacifier. Scooping the crying baby into her arms, she slipped the nipple into his mouth, held it in place until he latched on, momentarily appeasing him. Taking the baby to Sebastian, she held the bundle to his chest. "Your sister carried this child, birthed this child. He is your nephew. You are all he has left in this world. And right now he is hungry. Take him, I'm going to warm a bottle, then *you'll* feed him." She tried to temper the disgust at Sebastian's reaction to the child, assured herself she had no right to judge him given the circumstance.

Sebastian cradled the infant while slanting Madeline a glare. "I do not know how—"

"You'll learn." Madeline stalked from the room, jerking the diaper bag over her shoulder as she went. Sebastian may wish to force her out of his heart, but there was no way in hell she would allow him to turn against this child.

When she returned a few minutes later with a bottle of warm formula, her anger dissipated.

Sebastian sat in a rocking chair by the window, the baby in the nook of his arm. The infant's fist was clasped around one of Sebastian's fingers while he let out cries between forceful sucks on the pacifier. Madeline carefully exchanged the binky for the bottle, smiled as the baby's cries gave way to tiny coos of happiness.

Sebastian took over holding the bottle, his gaze locked on the infant's big trusting brown eyes. "He has my father's nose."

"Of course he does, he's a Maiocco. When he starts to get agitated, you'll need to burp him. Don't give me that look. It's easy. Place him on your shoulder and swat him until he releases air, then feed him the rest of the bottle." Madeline turned and walked toward the door.

"Where are you going?"

Swiping a tear from her eye, she turned and watched the sun rising out the window for a moment. "It's dawn." Hurrying her steps, she made it into the hall before the first sob escaped. *Dammit*, she didn't want to tell him goodbye, it would have been much easier if she could have left in the night.

At the front door, she looked up the stairs to the door where Sebastian and his nephew were beginning a new life together. "Goodbye," she whispered. "May your family once again grow strong."

☙❀❧

Sebastian turned the page in the book he read from, adjusted the baby perched on his thigh, tightening his hold around his belly. Amazing how learning to crawl changed Tessaro's from cherub to *diablo* in a few week's time.

Tessaro reached out and touched the page of his favorite story, *Jennifer's Rabbit*.

"The rabbit is going on an adventure." While Sebastian spent many hours reading from classic tales to enrich his nephew's life, the lyrical verses of childhood favorites charmed Tessaro time and again. Reading provided few precious moments of stillness in his nephew, otherwise he was a little troublemaker, crawling around, getting into mischief at every opportunity.

The entire day had been spent in the park, Tessaro soaking up one grand adventure after another. Jugglers, dancers, paddleboat ride, cotton candy. The day before had been a tour of the White House. Sebastian wanted his nephew to experience a little bit of all he loved about the States in their brief visit. He'd bring Tessaro again when he was older, of course, it was important to Sebastian his nephew be raised exposed to all the riches of the world.

Only Sebastian didn't realize coming back would haunt him so deeply. Those early weeks when he'd first met her had been full of laughter, amazement. He couldn't help glancing around every corner, every crowd hoping to see her.

Not that she'd be there.

He didn't even know if Madeline was her real name. Didn't know where she called home. Didn't know anything beyond the look in her eye when he touched her, the flavor of her kiss, the feel of her body. He woke many nights, tangled in his sheets, calling out to her since she left.

Letting her go had been for the best, he told himself once again. He had Tessaro to think of, to care for, to love. And he loved his nephew more than he could ever imagine when Madeline thrust the crying baby into his arms. At first he tried to hate the child, tried to find evidence of Raymond, only to see his sister, father and mother in the tiny child who trusted Sebastian with all his needs.

Kissing the top of Tessaro's head, he smiled, wondrous of the fierce stab of love in his heart. *How is it possible to love you so very much?*

Chapter 10

How is it possible to still love him so very much? Madeline's heart punched against her chest, her feet came to a sudden halt. Anchored in place she could barely breathe, couldn't take her sight off Sebastian sitting on the park bench ahead of her, a beautiful little boy on his lap.

She'd never seen him so relaxed, unguarded. So loving and gentle and kind. How many nights she'd wished she could have provided him what he clearly found in his sister's child.

Love.

Making a sharp u-turn, she forced herself to walk away, not too quickly as to call attention to her flee. She placed her hand over the knot in her stomach, closed her eyes a moment, commanding herself to do what she knew was right. What she'd known was right since the last night she saw Sebastian at his villa.

Leave.

Until he decided he needed her, wanted her, couldn't live without her. Months passed since the night she left in tears, the hardest thing she'd ever endured in her life. Leaving the man she loved. It was even harder now, walking away without so much as a hello, harder would be another goodbye.

Coming to a jarring halt, her eyes flew open.

"Christ, lady, watch where you're going," a young man said, dropping his feet to the ground to balance the bike she walked into.

Madeline's hands went to her abdomen. "Oh, I'm so sorry." Ignoring the man on the bike glaring at her, she padded her stomach with her palms. "I apologize," she said, looking up at the man. "I wasn't watching where I was going."

"Obviously," he snarled, peddling off.

Madeline took a quick glance up the path to where Sebastian had sat. The bench was empty. "We got to go, little fella," she whispered.

"Tell me, where is it you need to go in such a hurry?"

Madeline started. Once again her eyes closed, pinching as her heart skipped. Inhaling a deep breath, she stood, dropping her hands to her sides, pulling at the hem of her oversized shirt. "Home." She angled away, hoping to compose herself for the encounter she wished to avoid and dreamed of for so very long.

"I shall walk with you."

"No. I'm fine." But her hand trembled. Her heart broke. *We're fine*, she whispered silently.

"It should not be a surprise, Madeline, to find you running from me. Again."

Tears pooled in her eyes. "What did you expect, Sebastian, for me to come running to you?" Despite herself, anger audibly tainted her words. Damn him. For the lonely nights. The endless days. The excruciating want for him to come for her.

"For you not to have left. To not have walked out when I needed you."

If possible, her broken heart splintered. What she wouldn't do to simply turn around and find her way into Sebastian's arms. "Needed me, for what? To care for your sister's child? You've learned how on your own."

"*Si.* Tessaro and I have learned how to get along just fine. It has not been the same as it would have been had you stayed."

"You didn't ask."

She felt the warmth of his exhale on her nape. "It does not matter now, does it? It was good to see you, Madeline. I think about you often. I wish you and your new *familia* the best."

A lump clogged her throat as she heard him walk away. Part of her wanted to let him go, to allow him to believe she'd begun a family with someone else. Another part of her, the part that yearned for Sebastian to be part of this child's life spoke louder. She battled with the right and wrongs of keeping his child a secret for so long, now opportunity to tell him presented itself.

"Sebastian," she whispered. Turning, she swiped a hand at the tears streaming her checks. "Sebastian. Wait, please."

The cherub on his hip blew a raspberry her way and grinned a one-tooth smile. Sebastian kept walking.

"Sebastian. Please. I have something I need to tell you."

Sebastian stopped, his feet rooting on the paved path. "I do not care to hear what you have to say."

Madeline drew in a deep breath of courage, knowing it was now or never. He may never love her, but she couldn't deny him the chance to love his child. She began to slowly walk toward him. "I'm pregnant." Bracing herself for a plethora of reactions, anger to hatred, she prayed for love.

Nothing could have prepared her for Sebastian's cool glare. "This, I can see. Tell your husband congratulations. I wish you nothing but happiness."

Her hand smoothed over the roundness growing bigger everyday. "This is your child, Sebastian."

An icing of pain crystallized deep his eyes. "I can not have children."

Stunned, Madeline watched him walk away. She didn't blame him for not believing her, she'd done nothing but betray him from the beginning. Lie to him. Mislead him.

She thought about running after him.

Making him stop. Listen to her. Believe her.

The reasons she'd had for keeping their child a secret crept in. Maybe it was for the best. Maybe this child was to be hers and hers alone. Maybe their life was destined to be just the two of them. She loved her child enough on her own, didn't she?

Tears blurring her vision whispered to her unborn son, "We'll be fine. Mommy promises."

Whittaker closed the file and leaned back in his chair. "The department thanks you once again, Sebastian. The work you have done for us, to say the least, is impressive. The depths of the Agueci reach into both the Italian and American police departments shames those of us who have dedicated our lives to putting criminals behind bars."

Sebastian nodded. Though he knew his work uncovering his cousin's counterparts was important, all he wanted to do was get on a plane, return home with Tessoro. Get as far away from the memory of Madeline standing in the park, claiming he the father of her child.

Madre de Dios.

Nothing could have hurt worse than her lie. To use some other man's child to—

Even as he damned her, Sebastian could not quite make himself believe she would do such a thing. He knew of her loyalty to her job. Knew of her heart. Had been touched by her love.

Realizing Whittaker asked something of him, Sebastian forced away Madeline from his thoughts. "If there is nothing else you need of me, I will return home."

Whittaker stood, handed him a check for his services and shook his hand. "I'll look forward to your next report."

"I do not think I will find much else."

"No, probably not. You've been thorough. If you change your mind about coming aboard, I've got the work."

"I just want to go home, restore my vineyard, raise Tessoro."

"That, I can understand. Going to buy myself a little cabin in the woods when I retire, spend my days fishing, lovin' my wife and grandkids."

"This is a good plan. Goodbye, then. My train will be arriving soon."

"Before you go."

Sebastian paused, his hand on the doorknob, knowing what Whittaker was going to ask. The same question he asked every time he came to the states to deliver his report. "*Si*, I saw her this time, quite by accident."

"So you know."

"About her child, *si*. I wish her well."

"You may not know this, but Madeline has been like a daughter to me. Her father and I were partners before he was killed."

"No, I did not know."

"She's a woman of honor and love. I'd trust her with my life. Hell, I have trusted her with my life on more than one occasion."

Sebastian nodded, turned the doorknob.

"It's not my place to say so, but she loves you."

Sebastian let out a sardonic laugh. "Not so much, she carries another man's child."

"Is that what she told you?"

"It is what I know."

"Even if that were true, would it make you love her any less?"

No, it did not make him love Madeline less. It was her lie, her attempt to pass the child off as his that made him angry, furious. She had no right to be so cruel.

Sebastian walked out, slamming the door behind him. He needed to be home, to forget Madeline, to numb himself of the pain knowing no matter a claim of her love, a child bound her to another.

And still, beneath the hurt...

❀❁❀

Madeline unlocked the door to her little house she hadn't returned to since her trip to D.C. to report to Whittaker all those months before. It felt a lifetime. She never thought she'd return. But nesting instincts were kicking in. The baby needed a place to call home.

Turning on the lights, she shivered, the damp spring air had settled in the house neglected for too long. She longed for the feeling of coming home, instead she felt a vast loneliness echoing off the walls. She forced away a frown, picked up her bucket of cleaning supplies and mentally commanded herself to forget the things she couldn't have and be thankful for everything she did. A healthy baby on the way. A house. A job, should she decide to return.

The bucket dropped from her hand. A bottle of cleaner broke open, spilling amber liquid across the floor, wafting up the strong scent of pine. Slowly she sank to the floor. Sitting criss-cross, she stared at the mess through thick tears pooling in her eyes.

How was she supposed to be strong enough to endure this? How was she supposed to go on, loving Sebastian so much she physically ached from it? How was she to welcome this child into the world, look into his eyes, eyes she already knew would mirror Sebastian's?

Like an image through a thick fog, a hand suddenly appeared before her. She stared at it a long moment before her gaze traveled up the arm to stare myopically into dark eyes. She blinked once, twice, before she reached a shaky hand, laid her palm against his. Not until his strong fingers wrapped around hers did she believe Sebastian stood in her living room.

Allowing herself to be pulled to her feet, a sob hitched in her throat, a thousand questions played through her mind, a trillion hopes danced through her heart. She tipped her chin to look up at him, a part of her not wanting him to speak, to break the spell of anticipation, of want so deep it cut through her like a knife. If he came to burn his goodbye into her, she couldn't bear it. She simply could not.

Sebastian swept a strand of hair off her brow, tucked it behind her ear. "I hoped to find you here, Madeline. I did not know where else to look."

"Why? Why, Sebastian? Why are you here?"

"Because no matter how I try otherwise, I love you. I want you. I need you. But, if you are in love with your child's father..."

She looked him deep in the eyes, an unwavering *Yes, I am*, whispering from her lips.

He closed his eyes a long moment. "Then I should not have come. I will do the honorable thing. I will go home. I will pray for your happiness. Yours and your child's."

Madeline took her hand, still twined in Sebastian's and placed it over her heart. "Look at me, Sebastian. Feel what is in my heart." She lowered their combined hands to press against her belly, the child within choosing that moment to move, a butterfly of activity against their palms. "Feel your child, Sebastian. Know that I love his father. Know that I love you. You *are* this child's father."

Sebastian's hand left her's to circle her stomach, such a light, loving touch over the swell of their child. "I was not supposed to be able to conceive a child."

Madeline slid her arms around his neck, drew up on tiptoes and pressed her mouth to his. "If you have any doubt, Sebastian—" She was about to say, if he had any doubt, they could get tests, whatever it took to prove to him what she had absolutely no doubt of.

He placed his hand over her mouth, smothering her words softly. "I have no doubt, Madeline. I love you. Come home with me. With Tessoro. Bring our child to my home so that we may make it ours."

She nearly cried out against his palm. Her eyes filled with tears anew as she nodded her head. He moved his hand to swipe away her tears, his dark, loving eyes looking deep in hers. "Please, Sebastain, take me now."

Sebastian merely took her hand and led her from the tiny house and didn't stop holding her hand until he scooped her in his arms at the foot of the spiral staircase in his villa and carried her to the room where generations of Maiocco couples laid beside each other, loving each other, watching through the thin gauze curtains billowing over the windows the vineyards, the life of the *familia* flourishing.

About the Author:

Maybe it was receiving a young author award in the fifth grade for her story about a boy and his wayward adventures. Perhaps it was her notebooks filled with poetry, ink blotted by a young girl's tears as she made way through difficult teen years. Possibly the journals and letters written as a young woman, telling what words spoken aloud could never quite say. Or the hours spent reading, browsing bookstores, curled on an overstuffed chair in the library, making friends with characters and places so real they lived and breathed and filled her dreams.

Whatever moment, whatever love of word and story, one thing Dominique Sinclair is sure of, writing is a consuming passion, an escape, a need that must be fulfilled.

Dominique hopes you fall in love, share the tears, thrill in the dangers, coil in desire and sigh along with her when the last page is turned. And of course, eagerly anticipate the next adventure.

Visit Dominique Sinclair at her website http://dominiquesinclair.com *for contact information, Myspace link, book excerpts and to enter her free monthly gift drawing!*

Stasis

by Leigh Wyndfield

To My Reader:

What would you do if a man you've secretly desired turns into a living, breathing statue, all yours to do with as you will? As days drag on and he silently begs you to touch him, would you do it? Or would you hold firm, even though you know it will be your only chance to have him?

Prologue

A drop of sweat cut through the thin sheen of dust on Osborn Welty's face, tracking lazily down his cheek to hang for an annoying moment, before plopping onto his Gatgun near his left hand. He ignored it, concentrating instead on the movement of a spindly shrub a klick away. The hot, close air on this desert planet was stagnant and dead, not a cooling breeze in sight, but the plant swayed and Oz felt the prickle on the back of his neck which told him they were about to have company.

He and the men who made up the 12th Division of Troopers were crouched in a trench, facing off with a group of Rebels so well organized, they never seemed to grow weaker, even after months of fighting. This planet, Triad, was one of their strongest outposts, and the Inter-world Council had deployed a whole regiment of Troopers to rout them out.

"If we don't move now, we'll be pinned here," Morgann Right, his Second in Command, growled into his ear through his exchange unit, using the channel which allowed just the two of them to communicate.

He glanced to his left, easily spotting her down the row of men from the peak of blond hair that had escaped her helmet. "Easy," he murmured, trying to calm her before she lost her cool. His SecCom needed tending or her emotions would spiral out of control at the drop of a hat. She wouldn't panic and run. She wasn't a coward. The problem was he never knew if he would get brilliance or catastrophe when she went into action.

His sanity had been sorely tested during the six months Morgann had been his SecCom. He was a master at understanding his Troopers' strengths and weaknesses, and above all else Morgann needed someone to help her gain the skills to be promoted. She would be an excellent strategist and teacher someday, but not if she never made it past SecCom.

A scraping sound filled his head as Morgann ground her teeth. Words like "easy" and "calm" tended to have the opposite effect on her, but she had to learn to think before she acted or, one of these days, she'd get into a scrape he couldn't get her out of.

She said something that sounded suspiciously like, "Stick it in your ear, Welty."

Inappropriate amusement welled up, but he quickly buried it. "Did you say something, SecCom?"

"No, sir."

"Glad to hear that." He should have chewed her a new one, should have reined her in, but when it came to Morgann, he just couldn't bring himself to do it. "Give me a plan," he said to distract her, trying to focus on the gently swaying shrub and not his fascination with his SecCom.

After the first two days spent in her presence, he'd realized his natural attraction to Morgann had to be dealt with or he wouldn't be able to command her effectively. So he'd crushed his desire into a little ball and stuffed it into a corner of his body where it didn't interfere with the job he had to do.

To say she was beautiful was a drastic understatement. His SecCom left men's mouths hanging open wherever she went. Straight blond hair streaked with orange highlights framed a heart-shaped, delicate face with enormous jade green eyes. But that wasn't what attracted Oz to her. What totally fascinated him was not the beautiful package so much as the juxtaposition of her personality against it. She was hotheaded and impulsive, making decisions at about three times the speed he did...some of which were drastically off-kilter. Although to give her credit, she didn't make the same mistakes twice.

And she disliked, no *loathed*, when a man made comments about her appearance. Oz had the distinct impression her looks annoyed her. She was a brain, destined for the halls of the Military Academy on Borrus, where she'd probably make full Captain in no time, if he could keep her from doing something that would blow her chances of promotion. Keeping her out of trouble was harder work than it should have been.

She blew out a long breath that Oz could swear he felt run along the side of his sweat-soaked neck, straight down to his balls. "They're working their way along our left flank. We should pull back or move right." She paused, and hummed. "Or we could—"

Two pops cut her off.

Without thinking, Oz flicked the channel so he could communicate with all his troopers. "Rebreathers on. Stasis incoming," he ordered, keeping his tone even, almost bored. The canisters bounced somewhere behind him with metallic clings.

His troopers were terrified of the new chemical warfare that, if inhaled, would leave them little better than living statues. A victim could breathe on his own, but that was about it. When the warning had come down from Command a few days ago to inform them that the supplies of antidote had run critically low on the planet, some of his less seasoned troopers had gone into hysterics.

With steady, practiced hands, Oz slipped the mask over his helmet as the gas began to fill the trench around him, hugging to the low lying areas like the blood-sucking slugs on Lak-Sui had attached to his flesh when he was stationed there.

"Crap Daddy," Morgann growled in his ears. "We have a situation. One of the Greenies just broke the valve off his rebreather."

"Everyone hold the line," he murmured on the shared exchange, lengthening his drawl to show his men just how unconcerned he was. Then he switched to the Command Channel. "This is Com12, requesting airlift and support. We are pinned and have a man down in Stasis."

"Air support is on its way, twenty minutes out, Com12," a computerized voice responded.

"Received." Oz dropped into the bottom of the trench and crawled on his belly to assess the situation. The fog of Stasis thickened, covering everything in a haze, the trench keeping the gas trapped with them.

He reached his SecCom just in time to see her struggling for her rebreather with a trooper named Melfry.

Knowing Morgann as he did, he immediately knew she'd shared hers with the trooper, knew Melfry had panicked and tried to keep the rebreather for himself, and knew without a shadow of a doubt he had about three seconds to act, or his SecCom would have to take a breath of the tainted air.

Against his training, against everything he'd ever been taught, against everything he believed, Osborn Welty took off his own rebreather, giving it to the trooper so Morgann could have hers. His hand shook as he tried to stop his action, but while he'd ignored his attraction to her, it was still there, wearing on him, intertwining with the growing friendship between them.

The trooper grabbed the mask like the lifeline it was.

Morgann's beautiful face filled with shock, then panic, then anger. "What the fuck did you just do?"

He winced at her language, even as he felt the first breath of gas fill his lungs.

What had he just done? He never acted impulsively. Never went against protocol.

His SecCom caught him as he fell, quickly straightening out his limbs before they became so rigid no one could move them. Orders rushed from her in rapid fire precision, but she pulled his head onto her lap with shaking hands.

"Don't panic. You're in command here," he said to her, before his vocal cords seized and any further speech became impossible.

Chapter 1

Morgann winced as she met the brown-eyed gaze of her Commanding Officer. Oz lay motionless on a cold metal exam table, only his eyes and the movement of his breath through his chest revealing he was still alive. He'd been this way for two days.

"What I'm saying, SecCom12," the orderly rasped, his tone telling her he'd long since had enough of this conversation. "Is that the last supply ship with the antidote crashed on its way here. Doc's trying to get them to send a shipment early, but the next transport doesn't arrive for another ten days."

She'd known that, but her heart still jumped. Ten days of lying in Stasis. She wouldn't wish it on her worst enemy. Even though she and her CO got along worse than two rabid dogs locked in a cage, she stepped closer to shield him from the words. He could hear, he could move his eyes, and his body could use its internal organs—heart, lungs, stomach, brain—but other than reflex actions, he was a statue, limbs held rigidly in position and locked tight.

The Medtech disconnected the Riostat, a machine that recycled his blood and cleaned his body of waste material. Hooking up once a day would keep his body healthy. It was Oz's mind Morgann worried about. She'd go insane trapped like he was. But if there was one person in the universes who had the patience for an extended stay in Stasis, Osborn Welty was it.

"Listen, this is the Com12, not one of the grunts. We need him functional, so if you have even one dose left, I suggest you scramble it up." She tried to keep the irritation from her voice because it wasn't the exhausted Medtech's fault, but it was there despite her efforts. How many times had Oz told her to remain calm, to take it easy? A million. She just couldn't seem to do it.

The Medtech rubbed his red-rimmed eyes. "He'll be the first in line when the transport comes in, SecCom."

Obviously she couldn't intimidate the Techie into giving up something he didn't have. Glancing down at Oz, she shrugged.

He blinked and she could almost hear him saying, "What can you do?" in that lazy drawl of his that never stopped infuriating her. He was always so, so—she struggled for the words that could adequately vent her main irritation with him—*in control*. Sometimes she just wanted to see him fly off the handle, just once, so she wouldn't feel so inadequate.

The Medtech crossed to the door. "We've run out of beds. His rank at least got him off the floor." The Techie shook his head. "Maybe he'll learn not to take off his rebreather so quickly next time." He disappeared into the corridor.

She sighed and vented her irritation at the object that constantly caused it. He was their CO, not a fucking knuckleheaded idiot. They needed him up and walking, not lying there like a rock. "May I compliment you again on the use of your brains two days ago?" she whispered, but spoiled the sting by curling her hand around his. Why would he give up his rebreather for a recruit he barely knew, anyway? It made no sense at all. For his friends, he might do something so courageously stupid, but for a Greenie? She shook her head, still puzzled but unable to ask for an explanation.

His brown, gold-flecked eyes narrowed, but he couldn't give her one of his calm, controlled retorts. Proving this wasn't so bad, after all. Although she didn't like these one-sided conversations they'd had for the past two days. She'd come to rely on Oz more than she'd realized, and she found the strong swirl of emotions she saw deep in his eyes confusing. She'd thought Oz didn't have feelings. Seeing that he did creeped her out. She wanted him up on his feet and back to normal as soon as possible.

On top of it all, she had a big problem that had started right after Oz went down for the count. It had never occurred to her just how much his presence had kept the men in line—specifically one man—Terrel McBain, the bane of her existence.

She didn't want to worry Oz by admitting to him that she'd just about lost control of the unit. She wasn't about to highlight her failure when he wasn't in a position to help her do anything about it. That wouldn't be fair to him.

She opened her mouth to tell him she'd be back later when she noticed the dirt on his face. Dropping his hand, she ran a finger down his cheek, coming away with a smudge of grit.

Flicking open the top catch to his shirt, she stared at the caked sand on his neck. They'd been ass-deep in a trench when they'd been attacked, and he'd lain in the sandy soil for hours while air support bombed the rebels into the Sweet Hereafter. She realized he was still dressed in the same uniform he'd worn two days ago.

"You've got to be kidding me," she growled, her eyes meeting his again.

He blinked at her but otherwise met her gaze calmly, in control as usual, except for that odd swirl of *something* in the golden depths of his eyes. She would have imploded if she'd been stuck here for days like this, the very lack of movement causing spontaneous combustion inside her.

The white track left by her finger stood out on his cheek, spiking her anger again. This was her commanding officer, not some pulse-rifle jockey. Even if he was an ass, he deserved better than this.

"I'll be back," she told him and spun on her heel.

Circling around the bed, she stalked into the hall to find the Medtech, feeling irritation come back tenfold. "He's filthy! Still wearing the same clothes I brought him here in!"

The Techie raised his hands. "We're short staffed." He pointed to the closet-size room in which they'd stashed Oz. "He's got a room and a bed. You did notice all the people lining the halls, SecCom?"

She had.

"You're welcome to clean him if you'd like." The look on the Medtech's face told her he didn't expect her to take him up on it. "Otherwise, you'll just have to be patient while we try to deal with this."

His attitude made Morgann fume. She understood his position, but she wasn't leaving even a self-controlled robot like Oz lying in a pool of dirt.

As she slammed out of the MedCommand, she contemplated her constant urge to do exactly the opposite of every order and piece of advice she'd ever been given. That tendency to go against the grain hadn't served her well in the Troopers. She made poor decisions, then complicated them by refusing to reconsider.

How many times had Oz told her she was just *wrong*? A hundred. When she and her CO were in sync, they made a fantastic team. They just weren't often in sync. And she knew he'd tell her she was wrong right now, that she should leave well enough alone and run the unit.

Well, fuck the Medtech and fuck Oz. She would do *exactly* what she wanted to in this case.

Forcing her brain to work, she went to search out the long list of people who owed her favors.

It had been hours, brutal, terrible hours since his SecCom had left in a heat of passion, and Oz would have bellowed in frustration if he'd been able to use his vocal cords. His skin crawled with filth, although the genius of modern science had at least made it possible for him avoid lying in a pool of his own excrement. The MedCommand was so short-staffed, he had no doubt he would be here for quite awhile more before someone came to help him.

There was no excuse for taking off his rebreather, no excuse at all. It was a moment of protectiveness on his part, because his deeply buried feelings for his SecCom had snuck out. It wouldn't happen again. He'd make sure of it.

His muscles ached from being held so rigidly by the Stasis drug. He could blink and breathe and oddly, he could raise and lower his eyebrows. Otherwise, his body only moved reflexively, like when the Medtech hit his knee, his foot had kicked out. For some reason, he clung to that, the presence of his reflexes keeping him sane.

But his obsessive need to know what Morgann was doing at all times fed on him here like never before. The look she'd had on her face when she left usually meant trouble was on the way.

As if he'd summoned her, she barreled through the door to his closet so fast, the portal slammed against the wall with a crash.

"Every person on this planet fucking sucks."

He winced at her language. She had a gutter mouth that worsened with every passing day, yet another of her many tactics to distance herself from those around her.

Her eyes widened and he realized she caught his reaction. "Don't even start on me again about my language, *Osborn*." She sneered his name, showing her annoyance.

She'd never called him that before, and he had to admit yet again that watching Morgann was better than watching a good movie on the Vidscreen. He raised an eyebrow, knowing that was all he needed to do to hear exactly what was in that head of hers.

She paced a circle around him. "I tried to call in every favor I have." She spun towards him to meet his gaze. "And you *know* I have a million."

He did. People either loved her or hated her guts. Those that loved her usually did because she'd helped them in some way. Morgann could solve any problem—or make it ten times worse. She had no middle ground.

Pacing again, she flung out a hand. "I've spent the last six hours trying to get you out of here, but I can't get a single person to pony up. They all have these pathetic excuses." Her face twisted and she snorted in a totally non-delicate way. "I'm asking for a ten-day commitment, not a year of their sorry lives." She sighed, dropping her hands on her waist.

Oz watched her with his usual fascination and debated one of his secret obsessions. Did Morgann act like this because she was lacking a key filter to her emotions on some level or did she just feel things more than normal people? He flip-flopped regularly on this issue. Right now, he could see the swirl of anger and determination in the air around her, flushing her face red and making her gorgeous chest heave for air. He'd bet this time she felt more strongly, more passionately, than most. She was in a spectacular frenzy, but this was the first time one of her frenzies had been over *him*. It brought a strange warmth to his body, one he didn't want to examine too closely.

"I hate it when you stare at me like that. I can't tell what you're thinking." She shook her head. "If I didn't know better, I'd think you're amused—"

He blinked, widening his eyes to watch her better. For someone who never seemed to understand the political undercurrents of any situation, she was abnormally good at reading his emotions. Sometimes he had the feeling she watched him as closely as he watched her. The thought pleased him, even though he knew it shouldn't.

"Oh, too late to look innocent now." She stalked towards him. "The gold in your eyes gets all glittery when you're about to laugh, so don't bother pretend-ing." Bracing a hand on the wheeled stretcher they'd left him on for two straight days, she leaned down. "I have half a mind to let you rot here, but damn, just looking at the dirt from one end of you to the other, I can't do it." Her eyebrows lowered and her bow-shaped mouth pulled down. Morgann couldn't stop feeling badly for people in need, even if helping them meant she'd end up in hot water herself. It was, he thought, her greatest strength *and* her greatest weakness.

She pulled back. "So here's the deal…"

He waited to hear what she'd come up with, unable to vent the strangled laugh that welled up inside him. It would be brilliant or outrageous or just plain insane. Her ideas always were. The ball of desire he'd stuffed down shifted and tried to break free. He clamped down on it, holding tight to his emotions.

"I'm moving you to my quarters."

That made him blink, his surprise immobilizing his brain for a few moments.

"I talked to Trooper12 and they've agreed that while the rest of us are on night patrol, we'll rotate someone to stay with you and anyone else who ends up in Stasis. During the day, I'll bunk down with you. Since I'm the only person with my own room, we'll turn my quarters into an impromptu infirmary for you until the antidote is re-supplied. The Doc has agreed to check on you once each evening." She flipped her arm up and peeled back her sleeve to view her exchange screen. "Since I've just eaten my whole day jacking around with these arrangements, I'm going to get you set up and crash out."

She stopped to meet his gaze. "Blink once if you agree, twice if you have concerns."

He carefully blinked twice. There was no way he would let her pull another body off night patrol to baby-sit him. That would weaken the unit even more.

A slow, outrageous smile spread across her face, making his gut twist. "I can see that there are going to be small joys during the next ten days." The smile turned into a full-fledged grin that showed every one of her straight, white teeth. Still holding his gaze, she yelled, "Jimmy, Mick! He's ready."

Oz would have strangled her if he'd been able to move. He pictured hands that lay rigidly at his side around her neck instead. He wanted to curse and yell, but all he could do was narrow his eyes. Hell, he couldn't even grind his teeth.

As Jimmy and Mick wheeled him by her, he silently promised retribution. He wouldn't be like this in two weeks and then...

Under her breath, Morgann tsked him. "Your eyes have turned such a dark brown, they almost look black. I haven't seen that since the whole unit showed up late four months ago to roll call." Her grin flashed again. "Don't tell me you're actually about to lose your cool, Osborn?"

Chapter 2

Morgann had tried to beg, bully and force anyone else to take Oz in. Gods, goddesses, and any other higher being! She did *not* want to bathe him. It was going to embarrass the crap out of them both, but she'd moved him specifically so he would be taken care of, which meant that someone—her—would have to clean him off.

She forced herself to meet his gaze, feeling the heat flood her face. Damn the peaches-and-cream complexion her mother had passed on to her. "This is going to suck for both of us, so get ready."

Brown and gold eyes asked a question.

"We need to get you clean and I'm the only person who'll do it. I know you can't wait."

An odd flicker passed through his gaze, before he raised one eyebrow at her in that "What can you do?" way of his that usually made her want to punch his lights out.

This time she nodded. "Yeah, what can you do?" She gathered supplies to give him a sponge bath, silently arguing with herself, turning the problem around, wishing there was an escape.

Nothing came to her, not even one of her crazy ideas.

"Time's wasting and I need at least a few hours of shut-eye to deal with McBain," she said, then realized her error when his eyes flashed wide.

He'd caught the slip and she could hear his deep, rich voice saying, "McBain? What's going on with McBain, SecCom?" in that deadly calm voice of his that he used when he was pissed with her.

She purposely started undressing him to avoid the subject. "This is so embarrassing, but I'm not going to think about it. Just think of me as your nurse." Her voice held a breathy quality she'd never heard before. "I stopped by your room earlier to get new clothes for you."

Her hands slipped button after button through their holes, until finally she could rotate him onto his side to slide one of his arms out. "My gods, you're heavy as hell," she groused, struggling hard to turn his massive body, ignoring almost completely the weird shiver that came from undressing her Commanding Officer.

It made sense that he'd be heavy. He was over a foot taller than she was and one big walking slab of muscles. She managed to balance him on his side, but his rigid arms made sliding his shirt off impossible. Returning him gently onto his back, she rubbed the bridge of her nose. She could modify his shirts and pants so she could get them on and off easier. It wouldn't take much to sew Velcro into them or buttons along the arms. But not today. She needed sleep too bad.

"Okay, I'm cutting you out of this shirt. We'll bathe half of you today and I'll work on something tomorrow to make this easier on both of us." She dropped her hand and met his gaze. "We need some basic communication here. So how about we stick with blinking once for yes, twice for no?"

He blinked once.

"You okay with what I'm about to do?"

He blinked once.

"Fantastic." She flicked her right wrist, releasing her knife from the sheath hidden in the sleeve of her shirt. It slid into her hand in a move so practiced, she didn't even think about it anymore.

Oz's eyes widened at the display.

"You don't think you know all my tricks, do you?" Over the course of working with Osborn Welty for the last six months, she'd figured out one thing and that was that she would never have to surprise Oz with her knife. He was the one male on this planet she wouldn't need to defend herself against. His lack of attraction to her had been a welcome relief.

Sliding the blade along the seams, she tried to salvage the shirt as much as she could. Cloth was expensive as hell. She slipped the fabric from under his body.

She hesitated to actually wash him. Morgann had dealt with men all her life by ignoring them or fighting them off. Once or twice she'd let one get close to her, but it had always been a mistake.

This is just Oz, Morgann. He's your friend, as much as you have one. Don't leave him here like this because you're a coward.

The pep talk helped. She squeezed out the sponge and ignored the tightening in her stomach.

Starting at his wrist, she began washing his right hand. It shouldn't have been hard, but it was. His fingers were strong and scarred from setting up the Gatgun that was his specialty. He could have the large pulse-rifle up and running in seconds, but she'd noticed his hands bleeding more than once, the skin pinched in the process of assembling the seven heavy parts so quickly.

His hands were, she realized, the only part of him that had ever touched her, brief pats to get her attention on patrol when they couldn't communicate out loud, and that had been infrequent at best. His skin was dark, streaked with white scars, and she had the oddest vision of his hand resting on her bare stomach.

Shivering, she scrubbed up his arm, blocking out the strange thoughts. Who would have known she was turned on by something so silly? Not her.

Wringing out her sponge, she went to work on his forearm, ignoring the developed muscle.

Pick up the pace or you'll be here all day, Morgann! You idiot!

She cleaned his bulging bicep, blinking at the odd design tattooed there.

Unlike the rest of the men, he never took off his shirt when they were on patrol, yet he appeared tan, the olive sheen of his skin part of his genetic makeup, to match the black hair on his head.

To break the tension, she asked him a question. "What's the tattoo of?" She leaned over to read the words, but the writing turned out to be in a language she didn't know. "It almost looks like a family crest of some sort." A shield with a lion-like creature on it, with words above and below. It was well done, but certainly not beautiful. In fact, it was downright ugly, the creature too fierce, the black ink too harsh for a man's body.

She met his gaze. He stared calmly back at her, no expression at all in his eyes.

"Guess you can't tell me even if you wanted to."

He blinked once.

The distraction had been good for something. She hadn't felt that ache in her stomach for at least as long as it took to try to read the writing on his arm.

The minute she bathed his chest, it was back again.

His flat stomach rippled with muscles. He constantly pushed his unit to keep in top physical shape. Hell, she had gotten in the best shape of her life serving under him. It had only been since he went into Stasis that she'd stopped working out.

Dropping the sponge into the bowl of water, she grabbed a washcloth and ran it down his skin, over dark, flat areolas that tightened in reflex when her hand, separated only by a thin piece of cloth, passed over them. She hadn't expected that and it made her pause to stare.

His body had reacted to her touch even though he couldn't control his responses, reminding her he could feel everything she did to him. Had it turned him on? Her gaze dipped to his pants. The bulge there told her she wasn't the only one having these feelings. He had an erection, yet he was trapped in a body that couldn't move. She struggled to catch her breath, then realized he could see her staring at him, her very stillness giving her desire away.

She rushed to cover her blunder. "I need to flip you onto your side again." She didn't mean to, but she met his gaze and it snared her like a fish on a hook. His eyes had turned more gold than brown, but she didn't think he was laughing at her. It took her two tries to say, "If that's okay."

He blinked once.

The struggle to lift him onto his side was a relief. *Holy moly*, this had gotten totally out of control. Without him watching her she felt much better, scrubbing his back quickly, only getting distracted a little bit by another tattoo she could barely see peeking from the top of his pants.

When she returned him to his back, she almost moaned. She still had a million miles of skin left to clean. Rinsing her washcloth, she moved to his other side to bathe his left arm. Glancing up from his fingers, trying to distract herself from what she finally admitted was a massive turn-on, she caught him staring not at her face, but her chest.

She looked down and realized the way she held his arm, she only had to move his hand a fraction, and he'd be touching her right breast.

Both her nipples hardened so tightly, she gasped in painful pleasure. Her breasts felt heavy and her body screamed with desire, wetness pooling between her legs in anticipation of something he shouldn't, and couldn't, give her.

Keep it together, you nitwit. Do something to cover this now, while you still can. There can be nothing between you. McBain is watching, waiting for you to make a stumble, so even a single indiscretion will land you in trouble. And if you put in for a transfer, they'll send you somewhere that makes this hellhole look like a palace.

Fraternizing destroyed careers. If they were caught, they were both so screwed, she couldn't even comprehend the consequences.

Do something!!

She lowered his arm gently and rubbed the washcloth over the last of the unwashed skin. Then she turned, picked up the bowl with slow, deliberate actions. "I need clean water," she said, surprised that only a small amount of panic threaded through the words. Then she walked into her bathroom and managed to bolt the door before she lost it.

Oz focused on his breathing. The ball of desire he'd tried to stuff away had broken free and exploded inside him, the bath taking it from simple attraction to something much more serious. He had no idea what had just happened between him and his SecCom, except that he didn't find her amusing, or irritating, or frustrating. He'd found her sexy as hell and if he'd been a whole man, instead of this pathetic shell, he would have ripped her clothes off and thrust himself so far inside her, she'd feel him for the rest of her life.

He shut his eyes to try to blot out the way her nipples had peaked from only a brush of his gaze. Who would have thought the woman most people joked had no sex drive at all would be responsive just to the thought of him watching her?

Breathing, breathing was good. Besides studying what went on around him, it was all he could control right now. Gods above, he was in serious trouble. Because even if they tried to ignore it, even if he and Morgann tried to pretend it never happened, it had and now he had to lay here with the biggest hard-on he'd ever had in his life. He couldn't even jack himself off to get some relief.

The moment she'd started bathing him, he'd known he was in trouble. She'd told him to think of her as his nurse, but no nurse had ever run her fingers along the scars on his hands, or followed the curve of the muscle in his arm, or sent her breath across his skin while trying to read the words in his tattoo.

And that had happened in the first minute. He'd had to endure nine others that were way worse. It had been the most pleasure-filled torture he'd ever experienced in his life.

Water ran in the sink in the bathroom.

She'd left scared, he knew. He was sorry about it, but she wasn't the only person who was shaken.

If he'd been able to move, he'd have chased her. Her emotions needed careful tending or she got out of control. He'd become an expert in redirecting her, since she'd caused trouble from the first moment she'd arrived on the planet.

The first night together on patrol, he'd reached the decision that she was worth his extra attention when her quick thinking had them ambushing the enemy instead of ending up as blaster-fodder. Her amazing mind held a million different tactical scenarios, half of which were her own special concoctions. He rarely made a move in the field without her input.

But on a personal level, she was a mess. Her pretty face, no matter how much she tried to down play it, had men practically humping her leg when she got near them, much to his extreme irritation. It didn't matter that she wore absolutely no makeup and never had on a uniform that wasn't at least half a size too big, they were on her like white on rice. And she would rather bust their heads than back down. Granted, if she showed weakness, she'd be in bigger trouble.

The knife appearing from under her sleeve had him reconsidering. He'd thought she had no restraint when dealing with the men who hit on her, but he now realized she wasn't as out of control as she'd appeared. Studying the white, plast-board ceiling, he suddenly realized she had used the fury and her insane responses as a tactic. Most of the men gave her a wide berth because they thought she might not be shooting with all her energy capsules in place.

The line of thought brought him to McBain and he remembered her earlier slip. She was having trouble with him again. Fuck and damn. He should have transferred the asshole out long ago, but he'd been trying to help her gain the skills she needed to deal with the horndog.

The bathroom door clicked open and he watched her stride to him, her face showing a mixture of anger and reluctance plainly in the narrowed eyes and frowning mouth. Well, he knew the feeling, but for some reason she amused him again. Gods, she was just so melodramatic.

"Shut your eyes. I'm going to wash your face and we can be done with it."

He raised his eyebrows to ask if she was okay.

"If I don't get to sleep now, I'm going to be in trouble on patrol tonight."

He waited, studying her face, noting the dark bruises under her eyes. He knew her well enough to know she wouldn't be able to leave him without finishing what she'd started. The very fact she was still trying to complete his bath proved that he could persuade her to talk to him.

Blowing out a breath, she closed her eyes in defeat. "You win, as always." She met his gaze. "I'm fine." She held up the blue facecloth. "Now close 'em."

He blinked twice.

She hummed her annoyance. "Okay, I'm not fine, but I'm not talking about it, got it?" She leaned down so close he could smell the teeth cleanser she'd used. "Not. Talking. About. It."

Oz calculated that he could push one more round and get a concession from her, so he did. He lowered an eyebrow, calling bullshit.

She threw out a hand. "You are such a jerk. A self-controlled jerk." She continued her tirade through clenched teeth. "If you are going to be such an asshole, we can talk about it tomorrow when I get off patrol."

He blinked once and closed his eyes, even though he would have asked her a million questions if he could.

With a touch as light as a kiss, she cleaned his face all the way to the hairline, then lifted up his head to wash the back of his neck.

It felt like heaven and ended too quickly. With a heavy heart, he watched her toss back a halcien sleep tab. He would have told her she'd feel like walking death tomorrow from taking it, but as her eyes flickered closed where she slept in the bed beside his, he figured she already knew.

Chapter 3

The next morning, Morgann woke up feeling like she'd been beaten repeatedly with a large club. Which is what she deserved for taking the halcien, knowing she'd only get three hours of sleep. Rolling from the bed, she caught herself on the edge, so out of it and dizzy that she wondered why she was completely dressed for a few moments. Then she remembered. *Everything.*

Raising her head from her bunk, she turned to meet the brown-eyed gaze watching her.

He has that angry glare thing going on at the moment, she thought, feeling remarkably detached about it. Reviewing the last twelve hours, she realized he must be pissed about the halcien, about her poor decision to take it knowing she wouldn't get the full sleep required. Well, either she took the drug or stared at the ceiling thinking about his body under her hands. Feeling like crap was better than three hours of that hell.

Straightening slowly, to make sure she didn't fall flat on her face, she reminded herself the effect would wear off throughout the day. The dizziness would be gone if she could just make it to the shower. She shut her eyes and opened them again to make the two doors to the head go back to one. Then she set off, reaching the bathroom with less effort then she'd thought would be required.

She turned back to Oz and said, "Ha!" then staggered through the door to the shower, stripping, then jumping in without waiting for the water to warm. "Oh shit," she moaned, but felt instantly better.

Hopping out as soon as she could, she dried off and stared at her face. She'd need makeup today. Whatever she did, she couldn't let McBain see her weakness. If he even guessed, he'd go in for the kill, then she'd have to defend herself and everything would blow to shit.

Hair and teeth brushed, she turned and almost walked out naked before she caught herself. "Mother humper. I forgot my clothes. You flipping idiot!" Grabbing her towel and winding it back around herself, she marched out, grasped a clean uniform, then marched back in without meeting Oz's gaze.

And she knew he was watching. He was *always* watching. The asshole.

Of course he's watching, you evil witch. He's in Stasis. He can do nothing but watch. What do you expect him to do? The thought made her ashamed of herself.

Suitably chastised, she carefully applied coverup under her eyes to conceal the circles, but then realized her face had tanned from being outside in the harsh, desert clime of Triad. She'd have to blend base across her whole face or the coverup would stick out as much as the circles. Which then meant she had to put blush on to balance her complexion or she'd look like she needed a one-way ticket to the MedCommand. She stroked on a little mascara to bring out her eyes, loathing the whole process, but afterwards admitted that she would pass muster this way.

She strode out to check on Oz before Jimmy arrived. "Do you need anything before I leave?" Bending over him, she pursed her lips, adjusting the blanket up over his chest, ignoring the sharp sizzle the sight of his bare flesh brought her. "I'll need to do something about your shirt tonight, but you'll be okay for today, won't you?" She met his eyes.

Except he didn't meet hers in return. He was running his gaze across her face in much the way she'd run her finger down his to see what was on it. She realized he saw the makeup and didn't like it. Or maybe it wasn't that he didn't like it. His narrowed gaze might mean he was puzzled.

"Hey," she said, drawing his attention. "I had to cover up the circles under my eyes, which threw everything off. It's a woman thing." Then something occurred to her. "You think it's too much? I should take it off?"

He blinked twice.

"No, don't take it off or no, don't leave it on?" He blinked but she held out both hands. "Wait. Let me ask just one question."

He raised his eyebrows and gold flecks sparkled.

"Take it off?"

He blinked twice.

"Okay." She straightened at the buzzer. "Gods, that was a bit of a mess." With Jimmy only feet away, she could safely toss him a smile as she bolstered him up into a seated position. "I'll see you tonight. Try not to get in any trouble while I'm gone." Then she giggled at her corny quip, staggering across the room. Her punchy attitude was probably a side-effect of the halcien. "Sorry. Bad joke."

He may have winked at her, but it was hard to see from across the room.

She slipped out, pushing Jimmy back into the hall. "I need to talk to you."

Jimmy was all right. Better than most and she generally thought he was an okay guy. Not a ringing endorsement, but really as good as it got with her these last few years. Oz was the only person she halfway liked, and he was an asshole.

Jimmy shoved his blond hair out of baby blue eyes and flashed her a grin complete with dimples. "What's up, SecCom?"

"I need your help." No way she could make this an order. That would push old Jimmy straight to someone up the command chain with tales of her un-orthodox behavior. With Oz unable to speak to defend her, she'd be in trouble again.

"Watcha need, darling'?"

"Cut the crap," she snapped, nipping his bull in the bud, before he stepped out of line and she had to hurt him. "Oz needs a bath, and I was wondering if you'd give him one."

Jimmy laughed until he grabbed his knees. "Not on your life," he managed to work out between guffaws.

"Look, Jimmy, he's my CO," she started.

Jimmy cut her off. "He's my CO *and* he's a guy." He spread his hands. "No way am I touching a guy under his shorts, got it? Not for all the money in the thirty-two universes that make up the Inter-worlds." He shook his head. "Don't bother asking any of the other guys, either, cause if they want to touch him, Oz will have your stripes when he can move again, if you get my drift."

"Shit." She closed her eyes and groaned. "I can't ask the women. That would be sexual harassment or something."

"Why can't you just do it?"

When she opened her eyes, she could see Jimmy really meant the question. She wasn't about to tell him why. "Forget it." She turned on her heel and went to go meet the unit.

⁂

Oz counted the seconds until his SecCom returned, watching the clock while Jimmy dozed in a nearby chair.

Jimmy had babbled for the first couple of hours, telling all about Morgann's current problems with McBain and the unit's growing apprehension with her inability to control him. "Wish you were up and about to handle it, Sir," he'd said, tipping his chair onto its back legs to rest against the wall. "It's getting ugly. I pulled McBain aside myself and told him to cool it, but he's so pissed she turned him down, he can't see straight."

If Oz could move, he would've had McBain's head on a pike. But he couldn't move, couldn't do anything at all but watch by the sidelines.

When Morgann finally came in, she was dragging tail so bad, weariness dripped off her.

Jimmy popped up, grinning like a dope. "Hey, SecCom. See any action tonight?"

Morgann threw her pulse-rifle onto the table, the smell of energy charge telling him the story before she nodded.

"Sweet." Jimmy bounced on his feet with excitement. "What happened?"

"Out." She pointed to the door. "You have five seconds before I shoot you."

Jimmy stopped bouncing and studied her. Coming to the right conclusion, he hit the door at a run.

Morgann shrugged out of her jacket in slow motion, dropping it onto the floor. "I know I promised we'd talk when I got in." She met his gaze. The makeup was gone, leaving her green eyes impossibly large in her sunken face.

He blinked twice, unwilling to drag her into a discussion when she was obviously exhausted.

"Thanks. Later, I promise." She pulled the uniform shirt over her head, leaving the tight white undershirt hugging her upper body.

His erection raged back in full force at the sight of the first form fitting clothing he'd ever seen on her. He almost missed the burn mark on her left arm. Almost.

He made the only sound he could, a huff of breath that shouldn't have attracted her attention, but did anyway. Big green eyes met his. He deliberately stared at her arm, then met her gaze.

"Just a burn. Tell you later." Then she toed off her boots, dropped her pants and climbed into her bed, effectively distracting him by the sight of her tight ass clad in only a pair of thin, white panties. She hauled herself under the covers with obvious effort and rolled towards the wall, forgetting to take him out of the seated position he'd been propped in all day.

Six long, painful hours later, he'd memorized every one of her possessions that he could see from his vantage point, trying to ignore the delicate curve of her back. Her hair appeared more orange than blond against her white pillow, the long strands slowly working their way out of the knot at her neck as she slept. The sheet had fallen away to reveal the burn on her arm and he could tell it wasn't that big a deal. He had similar scars all over his own body, he just didn't want her to have them, too.

When she woke, he knew it. He could tell the exact moment her breathing changed, could hear the soft hitch of her breath. From where he sat propped up on a set of pillows, he had a perfect view of her.

She turned onto her back, blinking herself awake and pulling the covers up to her neck.

Rolling her head, she met his gaze. "Are you as miserable as I would be in the same position?"

The question wasn't one he'd anticipated, but he'd start the dialogue between them any way she wanted. He blinked twice, quite sure she'd feel ten times more of any emotion than he ever would.

"But you're miserable?"

He blinked once. Half his body was still covered in filth and he hadn't left the stretcher in three days. Hell, yes, this sucked, to use her favorite word.

She ran a hand over her eyes, which still had huge black circles under them. "Oz, I just wish you were up and functioning again. It would make everything so much easier."

As much as he hated to leave her unprotected, part of him knew she needed the experience of leading without him there to clear the way. He waited for her to come out of hiding and stop feeling sorry for herself.

She dropped her hand. "I'm having trouble with McBain."

So, she chose to discuss that, rather than what had happened yesterday between them. He raised an eyebrow.

She read the look as he intended. "Let's take the problems one at a time, please. I'll self-destruct if we don't."

He blinked once.

"McBain. I need your advice. He's pushing me hard, and I can't seem to scare him off." Her frown and the nervous tapping of her fingers on the covers told him just how worried she'd become. "So here are the options as I see them. I can report him to General White. I can try to keep ignoring him. I can sit him down and ask him to stop. Or I can beat the crap out of him."

He would have smiled if he could have. She wasn't falling apart so badly she couldn't see her options.

"Correct me if I'm wrong, but going to White over something like this would completely ruin my chances for promotion. If I can't handle McBain, White will think I can't handle a command."

She had that right. White would tank her career in a heartbeat if she came to him with something this petty. He blinked once.

"Okay. That's out then. I've been ignoring him and he's just escalating. So that's out."

He blinked once.

"Which leaves the last two options, neither of which are good."

Blinking twice, he tried to correct her. This method of communication was about to drive him insane, but in this case, she needed to figure out the right answer for herself.

Her mouth dropped open, and she turned onto her side facing him, then hissed when her burn came into contact with the sheets. Rolling onto her back again, she held her arm. "You think I should sit him down and talk to him?"

He blinked twice.

She didn't see him. "Because that won't work. He'll see it as weakness and everything will escalate."

He blinked once, feeling frustration rise. Yelling would have gotten her attention. Too bad he didn't have that outlet.

She continued her rant. "He'll put his slimy, disgusting hands on me again, and then I'll lose it and knife him in the guts."

He shut his eyes, refusing to participate if she was going to ignore him. Slowly, he repeated to himself a calming mantra his father had taught him from childhood, something that never failed to give him back his control when it slipped.

Morgann went silent.

Good. Finally. She was the most frustrating human in all the universes.

His temper rose again at the thought.

He repeated his mantra again. *Right. Honor. Family. Soul.*

The same words tattooed on his arm.

When he opened his eyes, he had himself under control again.

"Sorry."

He blinked once.

"Let me try again. You think I should talk to him?" She shut her mouth, pressing her lips together in a tight line.

He would have laughed if he could. How like Morgann to take him from emotion to emotion like a raging river during a flood.

Very slowly, with exaggeration so she'd hear him loud and clear, he blinked twice.

Her eyes went comically wide. "You think I should kick his ass?" she breathed, totally shocked.

He blinked once, counting to three with his eyes shut, before opening them and raising an eyebrow at her.

Her mouth dropped open and a half laugh escaped, then a torrent of amusement bubbled over, making her grab her stomach and roll into a ball. "Oh gods, oh gods."

Taking deep, calming breaths, Oz waited her out. She'd tell him what was in that insane head of hers when she could get the words out. He had no doubt about it.

Finally, she gasped out, "I've spent six months side-stepping him because I thought you'd hammer me for kicking his butt."

He blinked twice. McBain needed a swift, well executed set down. Fast.

"No," she repeated, then shook her head. "Gods above, you're classic." She grinned up at the ceiling for a moment, and he got the strange impression she was reliving their exchange. Then she turned her head back to face him. "So how should I do it? What's my strategy?" She hummed. "Knowing you, you want me to be perfectly in control."

He blinked once.

"Of course." She rolled her eyes. "That would scare him worse. Being unpredictable with him hasn't seemed to make an impression." Biting her bottom lip, he watched as her fantastic mind flipped through the possibilities. "Hits to the body, to minimize the external damage." She met his gaze. "Blink if I go wrong. Hit him fast and out of the blue, take him down. In front of the unit?"

He blinked twice. She shouldn't push McBain into a corner where he'd have to defend his manly honor.

"Okay, so one-on-one then." Her gaze never left his, as if she pulled the answers from his own brain. "Do I threaten him? No. Just tell him why I'm doing what I'm doing and that he'll get more every single time I can give it to him if he doesn't back off?"

He blinked yes. They had a moment of complete accord. He wished he could be there as her back up, but she needed to do this on her own.

She rolled out of bed, crossed to her clothespress and tugged on a fresh pair of pants. "I'd better go see if I can catch him now."

Her turn caught him checking out her rear end, still imagining her plain white underwear between his teeth as he pulled them down her legs.

"We'll talk about that when I return." Blowing out a breath, she finished dressing, then readjusted his position on the bed as if she read his mind and knew he wanted her to do so. "One step at a time, Morgann, one step at a time," she whispered to herself.

Morgann came back from her successful mission feeling like she'd just single-handedly blown up a rebel base. Her surprise attack on McBain had accomplished her goal. She was quite sure he wouldn't pull his crap with her again. Or maybe he would, but he'd think long and hard before he did it.

"You are such a bitch, SecCom," he'd spat, his words slightly muffled because she'd pinned him to the wall, one arm twisted behind his back.

"Yeah, I am, McBain." She'd gone up on her tiptoes to whisper in his ear. "But know this. If you try to touch me or question my authority again, you better never, ever let yourself be alone, because I'll find you."

"I'm not scared of a five foot girl." His breath huffed and she knew the blows she'd given his chest and stomach had hurt him.

"Then you're dumber than you look, McBain, because this five foot girl can kick your ass any day she wants." Her training was better than his. Period. He had the weight over her, but not the skill.

"The CO isn't going to like this."

She'd laughed, unable to stop herself. "Oz has given his blessing. In fact, he suggested this." At McBain's open-mouthed disbelief, she'd added, "Ask him when he's out of Stasis."

"I will," McBain had said, his words a threat.

"I hope I'm there when you do." And she meant it. Oz would eat him for lunch and spit out the bones.

A grin still on her face, she pushed through her door to find the Doc taking a needle from Oz's arm.

"Something wrong, Doc?"

"I'm completing the routine that allows his cells to rid themselves of waste and get the fluid they need." He pulled out more tubes and needles as she came closer. "I'm just finishing up here."

Morgann's protective instincts suddenly flared to life. She met Oz's gaze, then flicked her eyes to the Doc and back. "You all right?"

He blinked once, his eyes clear of any hidden meaning, and she relaxed. What was her problem, anyway? Oz needed no one to protect him. He was an island, a land unto himself. It was only a matter of time before he'd be in charge of an outpost like this, instead of just a CO. He'd been born to lead and with that came the ability to take care of himself.

"Things went well. Thanks for the advice," she told him. Oz searched her face, and she shrugged one shoulder. "He's still green. Even his greater weight can't compensate for his lack of training."

The Doc leaned back in his chair and Oz raised an eyebrow.

"Once he learns to fight, I might be in trouble, but for now, not an issue." She allowed herself a small grin. "He's going to tell on me when you're up and walking again."

Gold sparks flashed in Oz's eyes.

"That's what I thought, too. I hope I'm there for that one." She took down her falling bun and twisted it back up again. "I should have done it forever ago."

Oz blinked his agreement and Morgann got the definite impression he was humoring her until the Doc left, so he could grill her on what happened yesterday.

"You two are actually having a conversation, aren't you?" The Doc leaned closer to study them.

"Sure, he's still in there." She considered keeping the Doc around to see if Oz lost his cool with her, but she couldn't put this conversation off forever. "Thanks for checking in." Picking up the doctor's case, she escorted him to the door. "No chance of more antidote arriving sometime soon, is there?"

"There's a transport coming in tomorrow with replacement troops. There might be a shipment on that, but no one can guarantee it."

Morgann tried not to get her hopes up as she thanked the Doc and shoved him out the door. It was time to face the devil.

Oz narrowed his eyes so Morgann could see he was done waiting.

"Okay, we've got a problem on our hands." She shoved a hand through her hair, messing the twist she'd just made. "Something weird happened between us yesterday." She paused. "Agreed?"

He blinked yes.

"And you need a bath, bad, all over, not just your chest." Blowing out a breath, she glanced away, then seemed to force herself to look back, raising her chin a bit. "I'm the only person who will do it."

He knew. Jimmy told him and he'd spent some time while Jimmy slept, contemplating how he'd keep his desire in check when it seemed to be something he couldn't control. At least not the erection part. He *could* control where his mind wandered, although he wasn't sure that was so easy when she had her hands all over him.

"You know that everyone else turned me down." She pursed her lips. "How?" Then she snorted. "Jimmy, that jerk. He told you."

He wanted to tell her to stop changing the subject. They needed to figure out how to deal with this.

To get her attention back, he dipped his gaze to her chest. That had been the problem, not Jimmy's big mouth.

He heard her gasp, but couldn't believe it when her nipples hardened again without the foreplay of the day before. Oz inhaled deeply, picking up her desire in the air.

He met her gaze, cursing himself for taking off his rebreather three nights ago, which made him unable to touch her now. Of course, if he hadn't given up his rebreather, he wouldn't be in her quarters, which made his present state the only one that would allow him to see her tightly beaded nipples.

"Oh, gods." She covered her face with her hands. "We are so doomed." Resting her head on the exam table, she groaned.

The noise didn't help Oz's erection, which seemed to have a mind of its own. His cock went from warming up, to fully ready. When Morgann looked up, she would get an eyeful. He wasn't small and the tenting sheet didn't help, although his pants were trying their best to do their job.

If he could use his vocal chords, he'd beg her to unzip him, just to stop the metal from biting into his shaft, but instead he lay in complete and utter hell, striving for his famous control.

He only hoped Morgann looked at his face and not his crotch.

She didn't. For two long seconds, her gaze roamed his groin. "Oh, gods," she repeated, dropping her head back down again.

Oz stared at the ceiling and waited for her to get her panic attack under control. They were adults, they could deal with this. She wanted him, that much was clear, and the thought doubled his own desire.

Unfortunately, they couldn't fraternize. That didn't mean they couldn't have a discrete one night stand.

But damn, it would need to be way on the QT. People watched Morgann. They couldn't help themselves. He knew they could get one round of love-making in and probably survive anything that came their way with only a slap on the wrist.

The issue for him was…what happened after he had her? Maybe nothing. Maybe once would rid her from his system. But if it didn't and he had to work with her every day, gods help them both.

A real relationship was out of the question. They would have to marry to stay together. The Trooper policy was to move dating people to different universes, adding pain to something already painful by sending the two offending parties to bottom of the barrel assignments. He had worked too hard to risk that.

And marriage. Hell. Marriage was an automatic sentence to a complete pit of an assignment. Very few married couples made it off the frontier and back onto a prime location like Borrus.

So it was one night or nothing.

He wanted one night, but he wouldn't get it until he was out of Stasis. It was time to start praying for deliverance.

Morgann stood up, having gotten herself together, although her hair was down now, brushing her shoulders, the strands catching the light and framing her beautiful face. "Okay, this is totally out of control, but we're soldiers, right?"

He blinked, loving her courage. She was going to master her fear and bathe him and he couldn't wait. He would have her the moment his body worked again and this was just elaborate foreplay.

"You're as turned on as I am, aren't you?"

He blinked yes, but thought about saying no. He was about twenty times more turned on than she was, for once beating her out on an emotion. He would have laughed at the irony if he could.

"But we're professionals. We can do this."

He told her yes, but he wanted less talk, more touching.

It surprised him to realize that he and Morgann had this one thing in common. Once they made up their minds, they both went for it, guns primed, cocked and loaded.

She marched to the bathroom, came back with a bowl of hot water and some towels. "I'm washing the bottom half of you first, to get the scary part over with as fast as possible."

Fine. Get going, he thought.

"What were you just thinking?" She paused, the sponge and washcloth from the day before in her hands. "I couldn't tell."

He met her gaze and tried to look innocent, which got him a hum of irritation.

She tossed down the sponge, flipped off the covers, then unbuttoned his pants. "I can do this. I really can. Seriously."

Her chatter insulted him and wasn't much of a turn on. He told himself that was good, since this wasn't about satisfaction.

Then she peeled off his uniform pants, taking his underwear with them. All his good intentions were replaced by the rush of blood to his cock as her hands skimmed down his backside.

She kept the chatter going. "He's your commanding officer. He's like your father." Dipping the sponge into the water, she grimaced. "Ewww. That's disgusting. You're washing your father." She scrubbed his legs, but even her insane prattle wasn't deflating his desire, although he would have laughed if he could. This little peek she gave him to the inner working of her mind had him enthralled almost as much as the feel of her sponge on his skin.

"He has nice thighs, though," she murmured, washing them. Which bought her up short, turning her gaze to his. "As much as I'm fighting it, the fact is, you have a fantastic body that I really wish I'd never seen, let alone gotten to know this intimately."

He raised his eyebrows. Unlike her, he hoarded memories for later replay and this one would be on his favorites list. If he could speak, he'd have tried to convince her to take off her shirt and run those fantastic breasts of hers over his bare skin, but instead he tried to deal with the flood of desire running in his veins.

"I'm going to wash between your legs, but you've got to close your eyes, or I'll lose my nerve."

He had to rip his gaze from hers and pry his eyelids down. Instantly, he knew it was a tactical error. Without his sight, her hands separating his thighs had him gasping for air. The feelings didn't lessen, they intensified. A lot. She used the warm washcloth to scrub under his balls first, pressing by accident onto one of his biggest hotspots. The skin between his scrotum and his anus had always been extra sensitive. A secret place no lover had ever discovered but, of course, Morgann went straight to it. She always did the unexpected. He wanted to open his eyes and see her touching him, but he was afraid she'd stop.

Then she gently rolled his balls in the cloth, pulling on the skin lightly, with just that right amount of pressure.

She rinsed the cloth, then worked from the base of his shaft up. And up. And, oh gods, she was going to cup his head any second. In that moment, he pictured her mouth sliding down over him just as her hand closed over the tip of his cock.

The flashfire in his body zapped through every one of his nerve endings. There wasn't a damn thing he could do about it, except keep his eyes closed and try to breathe.

As he came in her hand.

Chapter 4

Morgann closed her fist over his pulsing cock, her instinct telling her to grab him tight.

Oh, shit. Oh, shit, I've made him come!

She held until she felt him finish, her own body shuddering in sympathetic desire.

"I—I didn't mean to."

His eyes popped open and she could tell he was mad.

"I'm sorry. Look, Oz, I—" she searched for words, aware that her panties were soaking wet and she still held his cock in her hand. "Are you mad at me?" she finished lamely.

He blinked twice.

"You look mad," she whispered. Her breasts throbbed with the lack of his touch and she wasn't quite sure how to clean him up without making a bigger mess of things.

He rolled his eyes, blinked twice and stared at her hand.

"You're not mad at yourself, are you?" He'd better not be. She knew exactly who to blame. She'd done it on purpose. Not *on purpose* on purpose, but she'd made it sexual because she'd been so damn turned on by his body.

He blinked once.

"Well, don't be." Taking a deep breath, she wiped him off, then grabbed his clean clothes. "Because that was more my fault than yours." She worked on his briefs.

Braving a look at his face, she realized her words had annoyed him. "I'll argue with you in a second. Let me get you at least half dressed before something crazy happens again." She struggled to get his pants on, then closed the fly, thanking the gods his fantastically huge, gorgeous cock stayed quietly under his underwear. In a way it was his fault she'd lost control. If he hadn't been so damn hot and had such lovely body parts, she wouldn't have had to touch them so reverently.

She forced socks over his feet, then met his gaze. "Let's just agree we're both at fault and leave it at that."

He blinked twice to let her know he wouldn't. She geared up for a nice argument that would take the edge off her desire.

Instead, Oz did something strange that threw her off balance. He stared behind her at her bunk, then met her gaze again and raised one brow.

"You want something?"

He blinked yes, and repeated the eye motion.

"My bunk?" she guessed.

He blinked yes.

Her first instinct was to tell him to stuff it. Sleeping on his exam table or on a chair would suck and she wanted to get another couple hours in before the night patrol left. Then she reconsidered. The table had to be hurting him after three days on it. "Fine. You can have my bunk for the night."

He made the eye movement again, from her to her bunk, to her, and back again, until she could see some of his precious control slip as he became frustrated.

"You want me to stay there?" She was confused. Hadn't he just said he wanted her bunk?

He blinked yes.

Then it hit her. "With you? At the same time? You have got to be kidding."

Nope, he wasn't.

"Why?"

He raised his eyebrows, but couldn't answer.

She shoved his table over, raised it, then secured it so it wouldn't move at the wrong moment. "Get ready," she said.

Giving him a shove, she dumped him onto her bunk, then rolled him onto his back.

"I'm not sleeping with you, Oz. That would be completely stupid."

He gave her a murderous look.

"Tough." She stomped to the door, threw the lock, then crossed to her dresser. Grabbing a new pair of panties, she then marched into the bathroom to take off her soaking wet underwear.

Stomping back, she curled into a chair and growled, "Lights," plunging them into darkness.

She lasted all of ten minutes, before she'd turned herself from definitely no to maybe. The fact was, she would like to touch him again. She'd just had a form of sex with him and it would be nice to sleep next to him for a few hours. Tomorrow the antidote might be here and they would go back to CO and SecCom. It would be the last time she'd have to enjoy his touch. What finally swayed her was the realization that no one would ever know.

The word, "Lights," left her lips before she'd finished that last thought.

"Move over," she said, shoving his hips, ignoring the gold glittering in his eyes. "I can't sleep in that chair."

She pushed his shoulders, then his feet, then repeated the process until she had him against the wall. "You're huge. This isn't going to work without me sleeping half on you. Are you okay with that?"

He blinked yes.

"I don't know how in the hell married couples sleep in one of these bunks. I know they end up with quarters that are exactly like this." She met his gaze and realized what she'd just babbled. "Lights," she said, trying to cover her slip.

Lying on her side facing him, she anchored her body by sliding a leg in between his and putting an arm over his chest.

For the first time in a long while, she considered her Life Plan. As much as Oz told her she never thought things through, the fact was she did. She'd already passed every exam needed to qualify for Military Instructor Grade in the top one percent. All she needed was to be promoted, then she could apply to TroopEd. With her exam scores, they would take her hands down and she could then transfer to Borrus. From there, she planned to meet another instructor, get married and have a few kids, while teaching classes and completing research. It had sounded like heaven. The only hard part was being promoted. She knew she wasn't cut out to actually lead in the field. Her specialty was tactics, not dealing with idiots.

Lightly, she ran her hand through the dusting of hair Oz had on his chest.

Her plan would effectively work her around the restrictions the Military put on the Troopers in terms of relationships. It made a lot of sense, except that she had secret doubts about finding that special someone. She just didn't do well with men.

A weird, niggly little voice in the back of her mind asked her, *what about Oz?* They certainly had chemistry, if the last couple days were anything to go on. He was one of the few men she completely respected and even his annoying control made him better than other men in her eyes.

She sighed and kissed him on the arm, right where the tattoo would be. He was destined for great things and would no sooner want to tank his career for her than she wanted to give up her dreams. In fact, it wouldn't be fair to take him from his destiny. He would be an excellent field commander, running a whole outpost like this one on the edge of the Inter-worlds.

Unlike her, he could put her tactical ideas into play, executing them brilliantly. They did make a good team when it came to that.

For a few moments, she let herself play with the idea of how good a team they really could be, running her hands down his chest, down his flat, amazing abs. He was awake, she could tell. Stroking him wasn't very nice of her, but for some reason, she liked the feel of soft warm skin over hard muscles. And if she was honest, she liked that he couldn't do anything but lie there. She had absolute control.

Gathering her courage, she propped herself up on one arm, and found his face in the dark. Then she leaned down. "I think I like you better, Commander Welty, when you aren't constantly telling me everything I'm doing wrong," she whispered against his lips. Then she ran her tongue across his bottom lip in a slow sweep.

His lips were warm and full. She pressed her own to his in a kiss. Nothing wild, just a press of her mouth against his. Desire spread across her body in a hot wash.

She pulled back in surprise, blinking down at him in the dark. "Go to sleep, Morgann," she told herself, barely understanding the strangled words.

Snuggling down beside him, she thought she wouldn't be able to get any rest with him beside her. She turned out to be wrong.

Morgann was asleep, cuddled up to him, her breathing slow and even. It amazed him. Here they were, entwined in her bed. He would never have guessed it would happen in a million millenniums. His SecCom had a side to her he'd never seen. She was so brash, so over-confident and in your face, he hadn't been prepared for the almost hesitant, unpracticed feel of her hands when she touched him. As if she had very little experience with men's bodies.

The thought had everything inside him tightening curiously, and he shut his eyes so he could feel the press of her against him. Her arm crossed his chest, her leg was tucked between his, her head snuggled into his neck. It was so sweet, so wonderful, and so new to him. He'd never had a woman in bed like this. Beyond sexual, it was the most intimate thing he'd ever experienced. He suspected it was Morgann herself that made him feel this way and not the specifics of what they were doing. After all, he'd never wanted to cuddle with another woman.

She shifted, sighing in her sleep.

Her breath filtered across his skin like a caress and her leg brushed his groin. His whole body lit on fire in a single heartbeat and suddenly he wanted, more than anything else he'd ever wanted before, to run his hands across her bare skin.

Wake up and touch me so I can feel you. He wanted to scream the words, but his throat muscles wouldn't move. Instead he stared at the ceiling in the dark.

The memory of her hands running along his body with the cloth had his cock so hard, it would have hit his belly if his pants hadn't been in the way. He shouldn't have dragged up the memories, because now the burn turned into a raging inferno.

He was almost delirious, he was so damn turned on. *Please help me, Morgann. I need you like I've never needed anyone in my life.*

She shifted, lowering her leg across his cock, the action pushing a harsh breath through his lungs.

"Oz?" she asked, her voice sleepy and lost. "What's wrong?" She half sat, propped up on one arm above him. "Lights." Something scared her, because her voice held a thread of panic.

Oz closed his eyes as tightly as he could, unwilling to let her see the naked lust he knew swam there.

"Are you okay? Can you breathe?" She checked his pulse, leaning her head to his chest as if she listened to his heart. Then she shook him. "Open your eyes, dammit. I need to know you're okay."

Bossy. She was so bossy. He flicked open his eyes and let her have the full brunt of his need.

Hissing a breath, she drew away, but ended up scraping her body across his erection again.

He shut his eyes, so in pain he couldn't take it another second. If he had his GatGun, he'd have turned it on himself and pulled the trigger, just to end the misery.

"Oz," she whispered, as if lowering her voice would make it go away.

He opened his eyes, unable to keep from looking at her.

"Is it bad?"

He blinked once. Help me, he wanted to beg, his control so completely gone, he wasn't sure it would ever return.

She dropped her head, then blew out a breath, as if she gathered her courage. "Okay, this isn't anything to freak out about." Raising her head, she met his gaze. "There are things we can do to help you."

His eyes grew so wide, he was surprised they didn't pop out of their sockets. Morgann wasn't suggesting what he thought she was. She just couldn't be.

She brushed a hand down his chest. "I don't think you need any foreplay, do you?"

So close to having his desires fulfilled, his mind shut down and he couldn't respond. The thought of her fulfilling his silent request had his pulse raging and his body burning from the inside out.

"I take it that's a yes." She laughed and it wasn't a Morgann laugh. It was the sound a woman made when she was sure of her power over her man. The sound one lover made to another.

It was beautiful to him, and he prayed this wouldn't be the only time he'd ever hear it.

She sat back to open the fastener at his waist. He sprang free so fast, she gasped, then hummed in pleasure.

The need for her to use her mouth had him shutting his eyes. He selfishly didn't want her hands again, but she'd probably use them. He wasn't exactly in a position to complain either way.

Instead of the brush of skin on skin, wet warmth covered the head of his cock. If he could have screamed in pleasure, he would have. He met her gaze as she pulled back, hoping she'd see how much this meant to him.

"You taste like the air on Lack Sui." She shrugged, a rosy blush spreading up her face. "Like the air of an ocean world, salty and rich." Her face turned redder and she ducked her head as if she was so embarrassed, she'd rather lick him than meet his eyes.

And lick him she did. The feel of her tongue started out as only an exploration, a slow caress of every inch of the skin on his cock. She nuzzled his balls, then sucked one into her mouth. He would have twisted the bedding with his hands, grabbed the back of her head to show her what he wanted, but all he could so was lie there at her mercy.

It only took a few strokes before he came, the orgasm jerking from his body so powerfully, he bowed off the bed in reflex.

If he could have returned the favor, it would have been perfect, but as she curled into him and called for the lights, he was left with a feeling of half fulfillment.

Confusion had his mind reeling in circles. Since when had sex become just as much about his partner's pleasure as his own?

When they injected him with the antidote, he didn't care how he'd make it happen, but she'd be screaming his name as she orgasmed twice for every time she'd made him come.

With that promise, sleep finally took him.

≈⟅(ʊ̈)⟆≈

Coming back from night patrol, Morgann congratulated herself on actually running the unit through a single evening without something going wrong. She'd pretended the whole night that she was Oz, thinking through every decision and being calm, cool, and collected.

It had been hell. She didn't know how he did it or why he'd even want to. Thinking before she spoke gave her a massive headache.

Jimmy caught her at the door to her quarters. "You aren't going to believe this, SecCom." He held up his hand, a box resting on his palm. "Mick got a doctor from one of the freighter ships to cough up a dose of their Stasis antidote."

"You're kidding me." She took the box, reading the packaging.

"I stopped by the MedCommand on the way here, but the Doc can't come by for another six hours."

Morgann stepped inside her room, meeting Oz's gaze from across the room. "You owe Mick big. He's tracked down a dose of the antidote." She had to force a smile on her face. As much as she hated to admit it, she'd spent the day thinking about the coming night with him. She planned to ask him if he'd let her do a few things that shocked her for even thinking them—things that involved her body riding his. Now that was blown to hell.

A shiver crossed her skin as she remembered what she'd done to him the night before. It had been the most wonderful thing she'd ever experienced, having this man, this amazing, powerful man, under her control. And he'd loved it, she knew. It only would have been better if he'd held so still on his own, without the drug chaining him.

Oz's eyes narrowed, then he raised an eyebrow. He could feel her odd mood and wanted to know what was up.

She shrugged a shoulder.

Pete stood from his post in the chair by the exam table. "You don't mind if I go now, do you, SecCom?"

She shook her head no. "Thanks for staying with him. Get out of here, Pete, while you still can. You, too, Jimmy. I'll wait here for the Doc."

"You think we could give him the dose now?" Jimmy asked.

"I'll talk it over with Oz and see what he wants to do." She turned but caught Jimmy's surprised blink from the corner of her eye. "Beat it, Jimmy," she ordered.

He popped to attention, giving her a halfhearted salute. "Come get me if you need help."

"Thanks." She locked the door to her quarters behind them, then turned to Oz. "We've got six hours before the Doc can be here. I'm going to grab a shower.

While I'm gone, you can decide if you want me to go ahead and administer the antidote or if you want to wait for him."

Oz tried to hold her gaze and give her the fifth degree, but she didn't feel like dealing with him or her feelings. Instead, she grabbed new clothes and ducked into her bathroom.

When she finally returned, she had herself under control. He wasn't her personal sex toy, for gods' sake! She owed him an explanation, she knew, but didn't want to give him one. Soon, he'd be cured and they'd go back to the way it had always been between them. The thought depressed the crap out of her.

"Okay, you want to wait for the Doc?" she asked.

His eyes were narrowed and she knew he was pissed about her not telling him what was going on. He blinked twice.

"You want me to do it? Are you sure?"

He blinked once.

She picked up the antidote and turned the box in her hand. "I need to inject this into a vein." She met his gaze. "You realize it's been a long, long time since I've had field trauma training, don't you?"

He blinked once, and she got the feeling he was really annoyed with her.

"You just want me to get on with it, huh?"

He closed his eyes for the count of three, then stared at her, his right eyelid beginning to tick.

She grinned, then on impulse pressed her lips to his. "I'm going to miss you, Silent Oz."

Something unreadable passed through his gaze, but she pulled the pillows from under his head so he could lie flat.

"Okay, here we go." She took the needle from the package and unclipped the safety snap which protected it from accidental deployment. Then she rolled his arm over and located a vein. "Last chance to wait for the Doc," she warned.

He blinked twice.

"So be it," she said, and injected him with the antidote.

Chapter 5

Oz could feel the antidote burning up his arm, and he couldn't wait to be free. Urgency the likes of which he'd never known gathered in the pit of his stomach. His body shook and trembled, the drug that had held him immobile pushing from his very pores, scalding every inch of his skin.

As he waited, he kept Morgann's gaze locked with his and made a list of what he'd do to her. First, he'd kiss her, he decided.

He couldn't stand being trapped for a moment longer. Frustration filtered through him, sharp and bitter.

Too sharp, he realized, too intense. He closed his eyes and tried to calm himself by repeating his mantra, but the drug seethed through his veins, burning him up, churning his blood.

"What's wrong?" Morgann whispered, her hands grabbing onto his arm.

He opened his eyes, and she recoiled from what she saw there. Her eyes widened, and he knew the exact moment her worry went over the line to fear.

"Oh shit. I need to get the Doc." She turned and would have run out, but he caught her wrist. "Oz!" She said his name with the edge of pain.

His hand had tightened into a vise, crushing her beneath strong fingers. He tried to loosen his grip, but one part of his brain screamed not to let her go.

"Oz, please, you're hurting me." Her voice calmed, but her green eyes were wide and pleading and scared.

He took a breath, his whole body on fire with emotions he'd never had before. "Don't." He swallowed. "Leave me."

"No." Her gaze softened, and she brushed her other hand down his cheek. "I won't. I promise."

Struggling, he tried to relax his hand. She'd be bruised for sure if he didn't. So much for kissing her first thing, but something was wrong inside his mind. He turned over the problem, feeling anger, frustration and desire churning in his stomach. With a start, he realized he wanted Morgann violently.

"What's wrong?" she whispered, and he knew his internal struggle showed on his face.

Trying to calm himself, he turned his head from side to side and shrugged his shoulders to release the tension four days in Stasis had built. Another rush of anger and sheer aggression whipped through him, making him hiss.

"Oz?"

Using his hold on her, he pulled himself up until he was sitting. Breathe through it, he told himself, fighting the need to smash his fists through the walls, the uncontrollable urge to throw the furniture and break it into little pieces, the compulsion to pull her down and drive himself into her until she was senseless.

What the hell was going on here? He breathed in and out. *Calm down, find your control.*

Whatever was in the antidote, it had impacted his personality and made him want to destroy everything in his path.

Get her out of here. Get her out now *before you hurt her.*

He raised his head to meet her gaze, inch by inch, the rage swimming in his body giving him almost superhuman strength. He could take on a hundred Rebels by himself, run forty miles without stopping, rip this whole building down around their heads.

The sane part of his brain fought to rise above it. Under no circumstances could he hurt Morgann. She was his SecCom, his friend, his lover, and he wouldn't hurt her. She had to get out, fast, before he lost total control and turned into the animal lurking inside his body.

Finally able to meet her gaze, he watched her breath catch at what she saw in his eyes, her heaving chest distracting him for a moment. He realized her fear turned him on and he inhaled deeply, taking in the scent of her shampoo, the scent of soap and clean woman. It was almost his undoing.

Jerking her a step closer, he didn't let himself trap her with his legs, but part of him wanted to so badly, the muscles in his thighs quivered. Instead, he said, "The drug is causing a strange reaction." His voice was a hoarse shadow of its usual self, rough and strained. "You have to get the fuck out of here *now.*"

Her mouth dropped open at his cuss word.

"And Morgann."

"Yes," she whispered, her voice traveling up his skin like a physical touch.

"Whatever you do—don't run."

Morgann stared at the person sitting on the edge of the exam table, wondering who this was before her. Because it wasn't Osborn Welty, that was for sure. Taking a deep breath, she watched the internal battle he fought play out in his eyes as he tried to bring himself to release her wrist from his crushing grip.

One by one, he peeled his fingers from her arm, until she was free.

Slow, she thought. He'd told her not to run and so she wouldn't, but every instinct in her body told her to sprint for safety.

Not wanting to let him out of her sight, she backed to the door. Step by step.

She was halfway there when she saw him lose the battle for his restraint. Saw it in his eyes as surely as if he'd said the words aloud.

Spinning around, she dashed for freedom.

Behind her, he actually howled in rage, scaring the crap out of her. Even though he'd been in Stasis for four days, a glance over her shoulder showed he was on his feet, staggering towards her.

She grabbed the door lever, but it didn't turn. "Shit," she gasped, and remembered she'd locked them in.

Her hand made it almost to the lock before he was on her. He braced their fall, keeping her from slamming violently onto the hard tile, rolling her away from escape, back beside her bed.

Instinct said to fight, but she lay absolutely still. He'd kept from hurting her when he'd taken her down. Oz was still in there.

"Damn, damn," he panted. "I can't stop it. I can't stop."

She expected him to beat her, for the rage she'd seen boiling in his brown eyes to spill out all over her body, but instead, he ground his rock hard erection into her buttocks.

"I have to have you, or I swear to the gods, Morgann, I'll tear this whole building down on top of us." He had an ironclad grip on both her wrists, and he stretched her out beneath him. "Don't hurt her, don't hurt her," he growled.

Morgann shut her eyes tight, fighting fear. They should have waited for the Doc, should have understood the ramifications of giving him the antidote before they'd done it, but they'd rushed. Rushed because the strange attraction between them had clouded their judgments. It had taken two people to get here. She might not be the best leader, but she was woman enough to admit when she'd made poor choices.

She realized how ironic it was that they were in this position. She had been preparing herself all day to ask if she could make love to him when he was in Stasis. She'd had a vision of straddling him, sliding his erection inside her body, touching him any way she wanted. Of course, knowing her, she wouldn't have had the courage to ask him. It was her fantasy and one she wasn't sure she had the guts to share.

So why was this different? Besides that he was moving, able to participate in the sex between them. It wasn't different, except for the fact that he had gone insane. The thought made her laugh, slightly hysterically, but laugh still.

He breathed deeply, pressing his chest down on her, burying his face into her shoulder. "Why are you laughing?" he murmured, in Oz's voice, instead of the one the crazed maniac inside him used.

"Because we've fallen completely apart." She relaxed, not really scared anymore, her mind accepting the hand she'd been dealt. "I'm acting like a scared mouse and you're acting like a crazed lunatic. A week ago, you'd never lost your control and I'd never let a man touch me without breaking his hand."

He sighed, his breath running down her neck, making her shiver. "It's the antidote. Something's gone wrong."

"What's it feel like?"

"Like I'm trapped in a nightmare. I'm panicking badly, Morgann. If there was a hell made special for each of us, this would be it for me."

For the first time, she understood how much his control meant to him. She'd thought it came naturally, but it didn't. He had to work for it and here she'd been pushing at him every chance she got.

"I'm afraid of what I might do. Some of the thoughts going through my mind right now scare the hell out of me." He breathed deeply again, his erection pressing between the cheeks of her buttocks, but she knew he didn't mean to do that. He was still fighting the drug, still searching for his control.

"I want to tear this room to shreds, smash holes in the walls. This isn't me." Desperation crept into his voice.

In a secret place in her heart, she was oddly relieved to have an excuse to do exactly what she wanted with him. It gave her courage to suggest what she knew they both wanted. "We can turn the rage into desire." Her voice purred out, the words sexual, although she hadn't intended to make them that way. "I know you want me, Oz. Instead of letting the aggression you're feeling free, why not turn it to something else?"

He let out a low growl, his hands convulsing on her wrists painfully. "Yes."

His easy acquiescence had her blinking in surprise. She'd been ready to give him another round of reasons. "Let me turn over," she whispered.

He rose off her only a scant inch, as if he had no intention of letting her get away. That was fine with her. She wasn't going anywhere.

Rolling to her back, she brushed her whole body against his. He still pinned her wrists, but transferred them to one hand. Keeping his gaze locked to hers, he fingered the top of her uniform blouse.

His eyes were so gold, she could only see a ring of brown around the outside of his pupils. She knew what he was going to do and relaxed into it when he ripped her shirt in two.

"You're paying for that," she said as calmly as she could.

His full lips stretched into a grin that was more like a leer. "Remind me later."

"Don't worry. I will."

He dropped his head so fast, she flinched. Capturing a nipple through the fabric of her undershirt, he sucked it almost brutally into a painful peek. She moaned and arched into him. "Oz. *Oz.*"

His assault on first one breast then the other continued, until she was writhing beneath him, unable to stop struggling for a free hand to touch him in return.

"So frustrating," he murmured. "Isn't it? To be trapped, unable to move, unable to touch when someone you desire is touching you. Unable to do anything but come." He jerked her undershirt up to trap her arms above her head, baring her breasts.

"I'm sorry," she whispered, feeling terrible for him, even as heat pooled between her legs, desire soaking her underwear and pants.

He went still and she followed his gaze to her wrist sheath peeking out beneath her shirtsleeve. Brushing the fabric away, he studied the catch, then met her gaze. "Thank you for not bringing this out."

She didn't bother to tell him she hadn't even though of it. In her mind, she'd decided he was safe. As she lay there, her wrists pinned above her head, she wondered if she had dismissed as harmless the one man who could actually seriously hurt her.

"The appearance of a knife would have escalated everything." He reached up to unsnap the release mechanism, then ran the flat of the blade down her chest. Cold metal and danger made her shiver, chill bumps rising on her arms. "Don't fight me. Whatever you do, don't fight me," he warned her.

His body blazed with heat, his whole chest, neck and face flushed red, sweat bathing his body. She could literally see the drug burning him from the inside out.

When the knife reached the waist of her pants, he suddenly whipped it up and sliced off her shirt, freeing her hands completely, then he threw the blade across the room, where it bounced off the wall, skittering beneath the chair she'd tried to sleep in the night before.

While she watched it spin to a halt, he stripped them both of their pants, rising up on his knees to drag hers off and toss them away, before ripping her underwear from her body.

She blinked up at him. Now was the choice. Fight him or love him?

Narrowing her eyes, she put first one leg, then the other, on either side of his body, opening her sex to his view. "I'm all yours, Oz," she whispered.

He settled himself on top of her like a blanket, keeping his golden gaze locked with hers.

"Yes," he agreed and entered her with a slow glide until he hit the top of her passage.

❦

Sweat dripped in rivers down his face, chest, legs, and arms. He was literally on fire, the drug eating his control like a flamethrower to a wooden house.

Sanity struggled for supremacy, winning now that he was inside her. He let go, giving himself up to her body, morphing all the rage into desire so strong, he could only drive himself as deep as he could again and again into her body.

She moaned, the sound sexual, shuddering from her lungs, and he knew she liked it. The power of owning her roared through his veins.

Her green eyes opened and she met his gaze, her face filled with pleasure. He kept his strokes deep and hard, watching her pupils grow larger, her eyelashes flutter, her lips part. Everything appeared sharp and clear, too clear, but he couldn't do anything but ride her to completion.

"I," she said, and then her body went rigid.

Knowing she was peaking, he kept himself deep, rubbing his body across hers, purposely shifting so he could pin her clitoris at the top of every stroke.

Her scream when it came was unexpected, passion clear in the sound. It tripped him over the edge, slamming him down the slope of desire, crashing him into an orgasm so sharp, he couldn't breathe.

Chapter 6

Oz didn't know how long they'd been on the floor, but his body had cooled somewhat, telling him time had passed. He'd shifted at some point to one side, so he wouldn't crush Morgann beneath his large body.

The peace didn't last. Like a groundswell, heat crawled up his skin, the drug once again rearing its head. Aggression and anger came on its heels, the feelings just as intense as when he'd first been injected with the antidote.

"Damn," he growled, grinding his teeth.

Morgann blinked open her green eyes, raising a shaking hand to push her hair away from her face. Then she surprised him by putting cool fingers on his hot chest. "Lay back."

Immediately he was on guard, paranoia sweeping through him. She was going to try to leave. She was going to run. *No.* He wouldn't let that happen.

"Oz," she said, her voice soothing and sure. "Lay on your back. There's something I want to do for you."

"Don't run," he warned, his voice a growl.

"I won't." She stared him down, daring him to trust her.

He took a deep breath. *Right. Honor. Family. Soul.* Every drug-induced molecule of his body told him not to give up control to her. Not to trust. To hoard the small amount of control that remained for himself.

Beating away the crazy tide of feelings, he rolled onto his back, watching her for any hint of betrayal.

She sat up and he almost grabbed her, he was so sure she would try to run.

"Shhh," she soothed. "This is me, Oz. I always do what I say I'm going to do, even if it lands me in trouble." She smiled, brushing a hand down his chest.

He wanted to smile back, but he could only watch her.

She slid closer, her hip against his, until she could lean over him. "I've been wanting a real kiss from you." As she spoke, she brought her lips closer, until they pressed against his.

The kiss started innocently, but like a key in a lock, his aggression turned to desire and he grabbed the back of her head, working his tongue into her mouth.

She let the kiss go on for a long moment, exploring his mouth with her own, softening him when he tried to make things harsh.

"Hey." She tried to sit up, but he held her down. "Osborn. Let me go so I can kiss your chest." Out of nowhere, she grinned. "I love when your eyes go gold like this."

He was so confused, he did as she asked, then immediately wished he hadn't. Circling one wrist with his hand, he felt instantly better.

She straddled his upper thighs, then bent over him. "Roll your head to one side."

Why? What was she doing?

Her unshackled hand pushed gently at his chin. "Trust me. It will feel good."

He allowed her to turn his head, then moaned when she ran her tongue from his lips to the lobe of his ear. She bit him softly and he trembled, the drugs making his skin supersensitive. From somewhere under all the sensation, he realized that only Morgann could have defused him. Insane, unpredictable Morgann, with her creamy skin and huge green eyes framed by perfect long lashes. Lashes that fluttered against his neck as she kissed along his throat.

He wanted to possess her again, but she had sacrificed a lot for him in the last few days and he would honor her by letting her do what she wanted. As long as what she wanted had to do with touching his body.

She slid further down his torso, nibbling at his shoulder.

With a supreme effort, Oz released her wrist and dragged his arms above his head where he could grab onto the side of her bed.

Green eyes danced with delight, rewarding him for his effort. "Gods above, Oz, you have the most beautiful body I've ever seen." She sat up and wiggled her fingers like a child about to plunge her hands into a barrel of candy, before running them along his arms, down his chest, and onto his stomach.

He laughed. How could he not? She was just so outrageous. "Morgann—" He would have said more, but was cut short when she licked his right nipple.

He took his hands off the bed.

She sat up. "No. You got your turn, now it's mine."

Narrowing his eyes, he slowly replaced his hands.

"Rush, rush, rush," she murmured into his neck.

Then she shocked him by reaching between them to hold his cock still while she slipped him inside her, working herself down his shaft in small, glorious pulses. He hissed in pleasure. Gods, this woman had courage and life.

"I was going to lick you, but you misbehaved."

It turned out she had further punishments in mind. Instead of moving, she stayed firmly seated, kissing him until the effort to keep still made his arm muscles bulge and the heavy bed creak from the strain as he pulled against its legs.

"Morgann, please," he said when she let him up for air.

"Okay." Her breathy voice and flushed face told him he wasn't the only one on the edge. "Punishment's over."

She rose halfway up his cock and pushed down, the motion clumsy. He wanted it smooth and fast.

"You're so big," she murmured, grabbing the bottom of the bed frame with one hand. "I need leverage."

He moaned and tossed his head as she struggled to set a rhythm. "Morgann, dammit."

"I'm trying." She rose up slowly, but came down too fast.

His hands released the bed and caught her hips. "Balance on my chest," he ordered. Then he moved her by sheer physical force alone, his arms and chest bulging with muscles he hadn't used in days. The joy of using them increased his pleasure.

He set the rhythm fast and smooth, letting her weight bring her down to the base of his cock. Her gaze caught his and he could read her pleasure as surely as he knew she could read his. Something had happened, something both disturbing and wonderful, during the last few days. They had connected and he could swear in that moment, he could read her mind.

Watching her eyes glaze, fierce satisfaction bloomed inside him. He could make her come, just from adjusting his depth. He knew it.

So he did, plunging deeper by forcing her hips into a different angle. What he didn't count on was that the moment she came, she dragged him over the edge, and there wasn't a damn thing he could do about it.

✳≈⟨☯⟩≈✳

Morgann stirred enough to look at the clock. It had been hours since they'd injected him with the antidote and her body felt used up and worn out. All at once, memories flooded back. Her mind stuttered, unable to process what had happened. Turning her head, she buried her face into Oz's neck, smelling the musky warm scent of him. The arm draped across her body tightened and pulled her closer.

It felt nice, she realized, to lie on the floor with him holding her like he didn't plan to let her go.

She'd always been terrified of being possessed. Possession smacked of ownership, as if she was just a beautiful object to be taken out of its box and displayed. Like her mother had been with her father. Her mother's only power had been to use her good looks to get what she wanted in life. Morgann had often thought that beneath her mother's beautiful package was a seething nest of mindless scorpions. No one saw past the beautiful exterior to the danger inside.

On her eighteenth birthday, Morgan had known with every particle of her being she wasn't going to become her mother. She wanted to use her brain to create a life of her choosing, a life where her mind was showcased, instead of her looks.

That night, when her mother instructed her to change her clothes so she could attract the eye of a wealthy senator her father had invited for dinner, Morgann made a decision. Instead of donning the lovely dress her mother had chosen for her, she walked straight out her parents' house and signed on with the Troopers.

She would not be owned.

Yet here she lay in Oz's arms and he certainly had put his mark on her...inside her at least.

But it didn't feel ugly or wrong. Feathering a hand along his biceps, she smiled when he hummed in pleasure. It felt, well, glorious.

From the corner of her vision, she saw the clock again. The Doc would be here soon and if they weren't careful, he'd find them in a sweaty heap on the floor.

With a shaking arm, she pushed herself up. "Shower," she said, her voice hoarse.

Oz's eyes narrowed and he caught her wrist in a shackling grip.

"Gods, we aren't starting this again, are we?" She straddled him, even though her inner thighs protested harshly.

Brown eyes watched every movement, suspicion filling them.

She couldn't help but snort. "Don't worry, you're coming with me. Up, up." Waving at him with her free hand, she tried to look encouraging, rather than annoyed. Under her, his body still burned with heat. Until the drug wore off, he would be hers and she his. She planned to enjoy it instead of fighting him.

He sat and she rewarded him with a hug and chaste kiss on the cheek. Then she relaxed against his shoulder for a moment. "I'm so tired and weak. Hold on while I gather my energy to stand."

She thought she felt his lips brush her hair, then he released her wrist to cradle her under her buttocks. "Put your arms around my neck," he said, his voice hard and only slightly resembling the one Oz usually used.

When she did, he stood easily, every muscle bunching under her body like a machine. It was amazing. "I'm surprised after all those days in Stasis you're this strong."

He carried her into the bathroom, sliding through the tight doorway sideways. "It's the antidote. I feel like I could lift a starfreighter right now." Ducking partially into the small shower, he held her while she turned on the water.

"You realize when you come down from this, you're going to crash hard?"

Instead of commenting, he asked a question of his own. "Why were you looking at the clock?"

She wiggled to be put down, but he simply stepped into the shower with her. "The Doc will be here soon." His gaze met hers with a snap and she sighed. "We need to figure this out, Oz. We need someone to tell us just how long you'll be this way."

He let her slide down his body and she was momentarily distracted by his chest. Olive skin turned shimmering as the water hit it, highlighting all the definition of his amazing abs and muscled arms. His legs were shoulder width apart, showing off thighs that were almost as big as his trim waist. He leaned against the back of the shower stall, letting her drink in her fill, the muscles in his arms tightening in a sensual roll.

That made her blink and meet his gaze. He'd been posing on purpose. Oz. Her cool, calm Commanding Officer, posing. And she'd loved it. She let her face drop onto his chest, the water slapping her back, bringing sore muscles to her attention. They'd lost their minds.

She didn't want to analyze it, she didn't want to come to the conclusion this was wrong. She just wanted to feel for awhile.

A big, scarred hand smoothed back the hair from her face. "Your hair looks red when it's wet."

She stiffened, unable to stop the natural reaction to compliments from anyone on her appearance. Her mother had given her this hair and the eyes and the perfect, heart-shaped face. A lying face, a deceiving face. She'd sworn she'd never use it to get her way as her mother had always done.

Oz leaned down, wrapping his body around her. "Don't go all militant on me. I didn't say I liked it, or that it was beautiful, SecCom, just that it was *red*." He laughed, a low chuckle that rumbled in his chest. "Touchy, that's what you are."

She relaxed, realizing for the first time that in her quest to not become her mother, she'd lost a part of herself that made her a woman. That part that enjoyed a gift of words, spoken from a man's heart.

Picking her up, he traded positions with her, then pulled her hands under the dispenser and covered them with soap. "Wash my back, Red."

She huffed as if she was outraged, but really she wasn't. He hadn't been like the others, hadn't waxed poetic about her mother's face. As he turned, presenting his back, she closed her eyes in relief. "Thank you," she said, the words escaping from her mouth completely on their own.

He grinned over his shoulder, building a lather on his chest. "I think you're pretty, Morgann. I'd be lying if I said I didn't." Reaching back, he brushed his hand down her belly, and his brown eyes turned deadly serious. "But I think you know that's not why I want you."

In slow motion, he turned and leaned down, sealing his lips to hers in a kiss that blew all thoughts from her mind. His body slid across hers, spreading soap across her chest. He picked her up and pinned her to the back of the shower.

"I might be too sore for this," she whispered.

Gold sparked in his eyes. "Not for this," he told her, the heat of his body turning the water hotter as it hit his skin.

He let her down onto her feet, then began to wash her, every section of her felt the brush of his hands, every inch of her skin was cleaned. He turned to let the water rinse the soap away. Then he dropped to his knees before her.

Spreading the folds of her sex, he met her gaze. The tick in his right eye told her just how intent he was on her pleasure. Then he widened her legs and buried his tongue into her channel. He forced his way up through her folds to circle her clitoris.

Morgann was sore, the rough sex between them had taken its toll, but this, this didn't hurt. Her breasts ached so badly, she cradled them in her palms. He moaned at her action, spurring her on to roll her nipples between her thumb and forefinger for his enjoyment. But it tipped her into a small orgasm that had her crumpling forward.

Oz caught her, but she'd surprised him too, and they ended up in a tangled heap on the floor. Huge arms circled her, holding her tight to his too-hot body.

When she could speak again, she said the first stupid thing that popped into her mind. "I need to wash your hair." She tried to stand, toddling on her exhausted legs.

He steadied her, then knelt, making her blink with the sudden flash of desire that spun through her at the sight of this gorgeous man at her feet.

Chapter 7

Oz sat watching Morgann brush her hair, feeling better now that he was dressed. His body was still too hot, but he'd stopped sweating uncontrollably and had been chugging down water as fast as he could to keep himself hydrated.

The knock on the door surprised him, even though he'd been waiting for it. Morgann opened the portal and Oz felt the aggression come back full force when the doctor entered the room.

"Morgann," he said, needing her to back away from the other man. Now. Before he went insane.

She met his gaze, her own going wide, and she stepped towards him.

"You gave him the antidote?" The Doc's voice was pure panic, but nothing like the panic Oz felt at Morgann being so far away.

He stood, fighting the need to rush the other man.

"Don't go near him," the Doc warned her. And made a mistake. He reached for her arm.

Morgann evaded him, crossing towards Oz, both hands held in front of her. "Oz," she said, her voice filled with warning. Of course, she knew what he was feeling. They had that crazy connection that made his emotions an open book for her to read. "Stop," she hissed.

"Stay clear of him, SecCom." The Doc's voice came out as an order.

Morgann turned to the doctor, but continued to back towards Oz. He grabbed her the moment she stepped within range, then pulled her behind him, the action causing the Doc to jump in surprise.

Everyone went motionless for two heartbeats. Oz attempted to rein his emotions under control.

When Morgann tried to step around him, he blocked her with an arm, eyeing the doctor. The Doc wanted to take her away from him, and he wasn't going to let that happen.

"Let's all take a deep breath here," Morgann said, her voice calm and rational.

That had Oz meeting her gaze with a raised eyebrow.

"I'm trying to be you," she whispered.

A hoot of laugher escaped him, but he wrapped his hand around her right wrist just in case.

The Doc shook his head. "Morgann, no one is supposed to give the antidote outside a controlled environment. It causes extreme aggression and personality shifts. We strap down patients before we administer it or they'll come out of Stasis tearing apart anyone and everything near them." He glanced around the room, looking puzzled. "Your quarters should have been demolished." He turned his gaze to Oz. The Doc's brown hair had a ragged appearance, as if he'd cut it himself, and his clothing hung from his thin frame slightly askew, but Oz had always liked and respected the doctor. "I don't understand."

"Commander Welty has a firm grasp on his control, Doc, he just needs," she paused, narrowing her eyes as she chose her words carefully, "he needs me to ground him, I guess that's the best way to put it." A blush crept up her face.

Oz stepped before her so the Doc's sharp eyes wouldn't see the flush for what it was. "Can you give me something for the side effects?"

The doctor shook his head. "Nothing that won't have an even worse reaction. I need you to come to the MedCommand and let me lock you down."

Oz's hand tightened on Morgann's wrist and he heard her gasp of pain. Immediately, he loosened his hold. "I'm not coming in, Doc." He said the words as calmly as he could but they still came out as a dangerous threat.

"How long will he be like this?" Morgann asked, stepping to the side of him again.

"When did you give him the antidote?"

Morgann glanced at the clock. "Six hours ago."

"Six *hours*? You're lucky to be alive, SecCom." The horrified look on the Doc's face made Oz's gut twist.

"I won't hurt her," he said, the force in the words convincing even himself.

"He won't harm me, Doc." Morgann slashed the air with her left hand. "How much longer?"

"Another twelve to twenty-four hours." The Doc crossed to the chair that still had Morgann's knife under it from the night before. "I can check his blood and give you a more accurate picture." He put his bag onto the seat. "That's *if* he'll let me near him without breaking my neck in two."

Oz knew a test when he heard one. The Doc would have a squad of Troopers in here to take him down if he couldn't prove he could keep it under control. The fact was, he didn't want to be close to the other man. He wasn't sure he wouldn't slip up and smash his face in. He met Morgann's gaze. He'd need her help, although what she could do, he wasn't sure. He just knew he needed her like he needed food and water.

Morgann gave him a small nod. She knew what he was asking and would do what she could.

"I can stay under control," he said, not liking the rough quality of his voice.

"Then sit on the exam table and I'll take some blood." The Doc drew out the small machine that would collect and analyze the sample.

Carefully keeping his body between Morgann and the other man, Oz crossed to the bed he'd been confined to for four straight days. The flash of irritation he felt blossomed into something darker almost immediately with the memory of being trapped in Stasis for so long.

"Oz," Morgann hissed. "Stop. Now."

He met her green eyes, feeling the anger in his veins heating his body until he began to sweat. He had to do something fast, or he would be swept away by it. Morgann was the only person in the universes that could shift his emotions in the blink of an eye. He needed her to do that for him now. Fast.

Scrambling, he did something he'd secretly wanted to do for the last six months. It took him two tries to say, "You have really gorgeous eyes."

"You bastard," she growled, instantly furious just like he'd known she'd be.

The anger on her face and the pain from her ripping back his pinky finger from her wrist had him so tickled, he started laughing. "Ouch! Dammit, Morgann. That hurts."

"You are such a jerk, Oswald."

He winced as she started on another finger, but the dangerous feelings had morphed into amusement. "Come on, that was funny. Stop or you'll break one of them, then you'll have to apologize to me and we both know that would burn you up."

She exhaled through clenched teeth, but ceased tugging on his fingers.

"Interesting," the Doc said from beside him. "You're turning the aggression into other things." The doctor peered at him like he was a new strain of bacterium.

Oz felt a tick start below one of his eyes. He didn't want anyone near him for any reason. Except Morgann.

She immediately pushed him until he climbed onto the table, then sat beside him. "Hey, Doc, mind if I take the blood?" She held out her hand for the box. "If that's alright? I need to recertify my Field MedTech training and this will help me get in shape for it."

The Doc wasn't buying her excuse, Oz could tell, but he handed the analyzer over.

Oz swallowed down the growl that rose up inside him at the doctor being too close to her. Morgann waited patiently for him to master his emotions again, lifting an eyebrow in challenge.

He accepted it, rolling up the sleeve of his shirt with crisp motions. The odd desire to flex for her flashed through his mind, but he fought it off. Her reaction to his body in the shower had surprised and pleased him. He'd never seen her look at any man the way she'd stared at him, and he wanted to see her face like that again as soon as possible. Lips parted, eyes wide, her hand reaching to touch him without a single filter in her brain trying to stop it. She'd touched him because she *had* to. And he'd loved every second of it.

Morgann put the box against his skin over a vein and pressed the deploy button. A sharp pain made him tense, then it was gone. The whole time, he ignored the anger that came from the pain, remembering their love play in the shower. The feel of her hands on his body, the taste of her as she came. He understood now what was happening to him. Any feeling that came from the darker end of the emotional spectrum could set him off. Only his desire and need for Morgann could trump it.

She handed him the box, letting him pass it to the doctor.

"Interesting," the Doc said again. "She's covering your weaknesses."

Morgann shrugged. "Why bait the tiger? In another day, this will be behind us and things will be back to normal."

The Doc glanced up from the small screen that showed the results. "I wonder." He stared at them for a moment, before tapping the screen to scroll down. "Okay, the results show him metabolizing the antidote just fine. He should only have another eighteen hours or less left to go." He sighed and put the box back into his bag. "Morgann, I understand that he seems okay with you now, but he's not okay. He could very well hurt you when he goes into one of the rages associated with the drug in his system."

The doctor was going to take her from him, then cage him like an animal. Oz felt heat building between his shoulder blades. He knew the thoughts were unreasonable, but he couldn't control them.

Morgann shifted beside him and placed her hand on his wrist, curling her fingers around his pulse point. She did it to calm him, somehow understanding he felt better touching her. "I understand your concerns, Doc."

Oz almost laughed at her mimicking him, it was so unexpected, but then covered with a cough, raising an eyebrow at her. How many times had he said that exact same thing to her? A hundred?

She blinked once at him, the look faintly haughty, her eyes lazy and in exaggerated control, and he knew she gave him the expression that would normally be on his own face when he said the words.

He pinched the bridge of his nose to cover the smile twisting his lips. Gods, the woman just plain cracked him up. How could she tease him at a time like this?

"But he's doing just fine. He hasn't run amok and he won't." She shrugged one shoulder. "It's the unit's night off. By the time we're on, he'll be back to normal."

"He's not doing fine, Morgann."

"I am sitting here, Doc, in case you've forgotten." Oz rolled his wrist out of Morgann's grip so he could cover her hand with his. It made him feel more in control.

"You're sitting here, all right." The doctor placed his equipment into his bag. "With a chemical stew inside your veins." He sighed and seemed to debate with himself. "I'll release him into your care, Morgann, mainly because I'm afraid pulling him away from you might cause more problems than leaving him put. But the moment he gets out of control, I expect you to inform me and we'll neutralize him."

Oz took a deep breath and let it out. *Right. Honor. Family. Soul.* The mantra helped him, but not as much as he wished it would.

With that warning, the Doc left them.

Morgann rested her head in her free hand. "Now we just have to sit tight for another eighteen hours and it will be over."

Chapter 8

The words came back to haunt her less than two hours later.

Jimmy knocked on the door, yelling, "Hey, SecCom, is the CO there?"

Oz glanced at her, his eyes appearing normal and completely Oz-like. "I'll talk to him."

"You want me with you?" she offered, keeping her voice completely neutral. Now wasn't the time to set him off.

"No." He went to the door and opened it, leaning his body against the frame. "What's up, Jimmy?"

His casual stance had Jimmy stumbling. Oz was a formal guy, big on following rules and protocols. "I, um, Sir…"

"I've been half dead for four days. Spit it out."

Morgann felt amusement trickling up her throat. He sounded more like her than himself. She sat on her bunk so she could see Jimmy's shocked face.

"The Commander said they have intel on the lab that makes Stasis," Jimmy said in a rush.

Oz straightened and Morgann's stomach tightened.

Jimmy went on, oblivious to the rising tension in the room. "They had an informant give up the location. We've been tasked to blow up the building and any storerooms on site."

"We'll meet in the briefing room. Gather the men." The order was served and the door closed before Morgann had chance to shut her mouth from the surprised gape it had fallen into.

Oz turned to her, his eyes glowing with determination.

"No way." She stood and crossed her arms over her chest. "You aren't going, Oz."

He crossed the small space separating them to loom above her. "I'm going."

"I'm acting CO of Trooper12 and I say you're not." She said it just the same way she thought he would have.

"I'm the CO of Trooper12." Anger swirled around him and she watched the skin of his neck and face visibly heat.

"Actually, you're on Med Leave." She kept her cool, not backing down. He would only pounce on her if she tried to run. "I'm acting CO and there is no way I'm taking you on this mission."

"Understand one thing, Morgann, you aren't going one step from this room without me."

"Want to bet?" The words slipped free before she could stop them. Morgann words. She needed Oz's control right now. "Wait!" She held up her hands to stop him before he could reply, sitting on the bed to cool the conversation. "That isn't what I meant. What I meant is that if you try to force your way onto this team, you'll be hauled off to MedCommand where you'll spend days chained to a bed."

Some of the heat went out of his eyes, proving Oz was in there somewhere.

She pushed her point. "Even if it won't be your fault, they'll still hold it against you and it will impact your promotion."

He pivoted on a heel and stalked to her bathroom door and back. "So we'll put off the raid until tomorrow night."

That pissed *her* off. "I can lead this without you, Oz."

He spun so quickly toward her, she fought the urge to scramble off the bed. "I'm quite sure you can, SecCom, but I'm unable to let you leave without me. Period." He grabbed her chin, tipping her face. "I can't let you out of my sight, Morgann. I know it's crazy, but you can't go without me."

She realized he was being serious. He couldn't let her go, for whatever reason. Instead of panic, she had the overwhelming urge to throw herself into his arms and hold him tight. It was as if she, too, had been infected with the drug and had to have him close to her just to breathe. While it scared her, she also had a tingling feeling of rightness in her stomach.

"Come up with a plan to make it happen, SecCom," he said and the words were an order. "Reach into that exceptional brain of yours and pull out something brilliant."

A smile at his praise bloomed inside her heart and snuck out onto her face. "I am brilliant, aren't I?" She couldn't resist asking for another round of compliments.

He didn't smile back at her, the harsh plains of his face showing his internal struggle. "Yes."

"Okay." She bit her bottom lip and started thinking. "Our objectives are to run the raid successfully, while covering up our inability to be apart, buying us twenty-four hours until you're normal again." She hummed in irritation. "Without making it look like you don't want me running the raid because I'm incompetent."

Then another problem hit her like a ton of bricks, making her glad she was still sitting down. "Oz, how do you feel?"

He raised an eyebrow and she knew he wanted her to be more specific.

"You still feel powerful? Charged? Abnormally strong?"

He searched her gaze, as if he peered into her mind. Morgann had the oddest feeling they had somehow created a mind-meld, something that before she would have thought was a total legend. But she could swear he was reading her thoughts, at least to some extent.

"You're thinking it will wear off and I'll crash." He came to the right conclusion.

"I think in eighteen hours, you're going to be a puddle of slack muscles on the floor." She held up her hands to stop him before he reacted. "Think, Oz. There is no way you can keep this up. You've been flat on your back for four days. The amount of strength you've displayed shouldn't be happening."

For a moment, she thought he'd fight her, but then he blew out a breath and dropped his hands on his hips. "You're right."

"It would be best if I went without you."

"Not an option." His knuckles went white as he gripped his own body, rather than grab her.

"How about sending Mick in as leader?"

He shook his head. "He's not ready, no matter how much we prep him. The minute something goes wrong, he'll be lost."

"I can wait until this wears off tomorrow and go without you after you've crashed, since I'm assuming sanity will have returned and we won't need to be tied at the hip."

Oz sat beside her and leaned back against the wall. "You could but I'd rather you didn't."

"If you can't handle the Doc, how are you going to handle the twenty-two men on the team?" She tried to make her voice as reasonable as possible.

"Figure out a way, Morgann." Oz's brown eyes showed his faith in her.

She kicked an idea around in her head, slowly nodding. "Okay, here's what we're going to do. We'll take a small team. You, me, Pete, Mick, and Jimmy. Tonight we'll recon and take out the lab if it looks like we can. Otherwise we'll go back tomorrow. To be honest, I need to know all the information the informant gave to us to come up with anything more concrete." She leaned closer to him. "But Oz, you've got to find that control you're famous for or you're off this mission. I'm not endangering any of the team because you've got this problem."

"Okay. You're acting CO."

❧⟨♥⟩❧

When they entered the briefing room, all thirty of the soldiers who made up the bulk of Trooper12 went silent. Oz led the way down the center aisle to the front room, his huge body dwarfing the small space, the tan uniform shirt pulling tight across the muscles on his back. She'd never noticed just how good he looked from this view before.

Ripping her attention away from the image of his backside without the shirt, Morgann went straight to the map hanging on the far wall. Someone, most likely Mick, had circled the reported location of the lab.

She studied the layout for a moment with practiced eyes. They'd nestled the lab against a set of mountains that had sharp walls that would expose them if they tried to rappel down. Morgann pulled up a picture of the peaks in her mind. She'd seen them from a distance, the sheer, light brown walls rising up from the desert plain. It was a phenomenon seen only on Triad. The volcanic activity to the west had slammed one tectonic plate up against the land mass of another, forcing a set of cliffs made of compressed sand.

An interesting position.

She traced a small depression in the ground that would take them straight to the marked location.

Then she realized the room was still silent. She turned, looking a question at Oz.

He leaned up against a heavy table, arms and ankles crossed, staring at her with a raised eyebrow. Morgann didn't miss the fact that he stood carefully between her and the rest of the people in the room. Nor did she miss the emotion swirling around him. They were walking a tightrope here.

It hit her that he planned to let her do all the talking. She was, after all, the acting CO of Trooper12.

Turning to the unit, she dropped into her false-calm persona. "So here's the deal." She widened her stance, centering her upper body on her hips. "Oz hasn't been cleared to resume his command yet, so I'm still acting CO." She didn't open the room up for questions. She'd learned from Oz that this wasn't about everyone being happy. This was about following orders. "Jimmy, what intel do we have?"

Jimmy stood, all business. "A location. That's it."

She made a give-it-up motion with her hands.

"The intel came from a spy we have somewhere in the rebel structure. He went there only briefly. Other than the exact location, we have nothing."

In the back of the room, the door opened and General White stepped through. Everyone came to attention. "At ease," the general said, serious as always. "Proceed," he said to Morgann.

"If our intel only includes a location, we'll need to scout the building to develop a plan of attack, with an option to complete the mission if the opportunity presents itself. Jimmy, Mick and Pete, prepare to leave tonight an hour before dark. The rest of you plan to reconvene three hours before regular shift tomorrow night for an early departure."

"You think that's wise?" General White asked, no inflection in his tone.

She let her gaze touch Oz's, suddenly unsure.

He blinked once.

"I do, yes, Sir." She kept her voice Oz-calm. "With respect, Sir, I can't come up with a tactical plan until I have more than a red ring in the middle of a map."

"Why don't you bring your whole team, instead of a smaller contingent, SecCom?"

Oz rolled his shoulders just the slightest bit, and that strange connection between them buzzed with warning. White tested her in some way.

But she knew how to answer this question. "With a smaller team, the possibility of discovery goes down drastically. We need to understand the situation before going in guns blazing, Sir."

"Yet you go not just to scout, but to possibly complete your mission?"

"If we get there and an opportunity presents itself, I want to be prepared to take it. But otherwise, it's just a scouting trip. Tomorrow night, we'll return for the full assault." Morgann congratulated herself. She wasn't messing this up. She'd kept her cool, given all the right answers.

General White turned to Oz. "What do you think about this plan, Commander Welty?"

"I think this is the SecCom's mission. She'll run it the way she sees fit." Oz's face was blank, but Morgann knew underneath he didn't like that White had questioned her in front of the unit.

"You have that much confidence in her?" White's voice implied that he wasn't convinced that was a good idea.

"I do." Oz's voice was so sure, Morgann's heart flipped over. This wasn't about what had happened between them sexually. This was about his respect for her as a soldier and a tactician. In that moment, she knew he valued her skills, valued her mind, and she loved him for it.

White nodded, his eyes assessing her worth. "Let's hope you live up to your CO's confidence in you, SecCom. Report to me when you return in the morning." He marched out the door, and Morgann realized that if she didn't perform this task perfectly, she could kiss a promotion on this tour of duty goodbye.

Well, when it came to planning, she could stand on her own. "Pete, Mick, and Jimmy, stay behind. The rest of you are dismissed."

Everyone rose and beat a hasty retreat and Morgann breathed a sigh of relief. They'd gotten through this with Oz acting not normal, but not strange, either.

She started to turn back to the map, but then caught a movement from the corner of her eye. McBain approached her, the smile on his face telling Morgann he'd just picked the worst possible time to have one of his episodes.

Chapter 9

The expression on McBain's face as he stared at Morgann made Oz's guts curl in on themselves.

He knew he had to let Morgann handle this. Sheltering her hadn't done her any good. But the heat of his anger warmed the drug to a slow burn and the aggression he'd kept barely leashed through the short briefing came raging to life.

"I said dismissed, McBain. That means leave." Morgann's voice held a distinct warning and no fear.

Oz held onto his arms with his hands, repeating his mantra with every fiber of his being. *Right. Honor. Family. Soul.* He could make it through a confrontation without punching anyone. Really.

"CO," McBain said to him, clearly about to start telling tales.

"Tim," Oz said, and the name came out as a rasp. "If you get near me, I'll tear your arms off." He'd meant to say something controlled and wise.

Morgann coughed and he met her dancing gaze. He didn't feel her humor, but his aggression lightened anyway.

Nodding to McBain, she warned him. "The antidote to Stasis causes aggressive behavior. I would wait twenty-four hours to talk to him."

Oz held his breath. If McBain touched her, he'd have to take him down and it would be ugly. There just wasn't any other option.

McBain tried again. "I want to talk to you, CO."

"And I want to see your ass hang for insubordination. I suggest you leave while you're still breathing." Oz could feel his muscles bulge, feel his eyesight go crystal clear, power swelling in his blood.

Morgann took three steps forward, putting her body between them. "We can fight another day," she said, and her voice was almost gentle.

Tim McBain thought about being dumb, Oz could see it in his face, but something told him to leave, and for once, he took the right path.

Morgann turned to where Oz still lounged against the table, a clear warning in her green eyes.

He knew he was saved only because an idiot had made the right decision. He just didn't care. Not right then. Maybe not ever.

Morgann got the message and sighed. "All things considered, that actually went well." She returned to the map. "Everyone's limbs are in place and all," she mumbled, tracing something with her finger.

"You okay, CO?" Jimmy said, his voice careful.

"As okay as I can get right now." Oz shrugged a shoulder. "Take my word when I say don't give up your rebreather. The cure is almost as bad as being in Stasis." Although it hadn't really been that bad at all, not with Morgann tending him.

"Yes, Sir." Jimmy turned to Morgann. "So what's the plan?" He and the others started forward. Oz realized somewhere along the way, they'd started accepting her tactical genius as much as he had.

"Stop!" Morgann turned, her voice filled with an authority Oz hadn't heard from her before. "No one gets close to Oz on this mission but me. That's an order."

"No disrespect intended, but why are we taking him if he's not in top shape?" Mick had a head on his shoulders and followed orders. His question was right on the mark. He didn't know it yet, but Oz had recommended him for promotion.

Morgann's look didn't waver. "Because I want him with us." She turned to the map. "We're going to leave in an hour and work our way across to the cliffs, using the shelter of this depression in the land. We go as close as we can and observe. Pete, I want enough explosives with us to blow the building, but to be honest, I don't think we're going to do it. Mick and Jimmy, I need you two along primarily to go in with me if we get the chance, but bring your viewfinders so you can gather intelligence with me. Oz, you'll be backing us up on the Gatgun." She glanced at her watch. "Everyone has forty minutes to get their packs together. We meet by the West Door."

❧⟨♥⟩❧

"No explanation, just 'Because I want him with us.'" Oz laughed the minute the door to her quarters had closed behind them. "Spoken like a true leader."

"I couldn't lie. You know as well as I do that taking you on this mission is dumber than dumb. I'd make us stay here, but I can't bring myself to rely on someone else to scout the lab." She went to her closet and started pulling out gear.

"You know, you handled all of that perfectly, Morgann. The period I've been down has been good for you."

Her hands paused and she turned, her gaze searching his.

"I'm speaking as your CO here." He glanced at the clock and crossed the room. "We have time if we're speedy."

She backed away. "What do you think you're doing?"

Oz let a slow grin slide across his face. "Grounding myself." He grabbed her when she tried to skirt him and tipped her head back.

Her gaze filled with what he knew was pure desire. Her eyelids drooped and her lips plumped. She inhaled, and he knew she was fighting it.

He nuzzled her ear and growled, "We could use the bed this round." Capturing her ear, he grazed his teeth along the lobe, loving the fact he had the control to actually woo her.

She shivered and pushed at his chest. "Mission," she whispered and he knew he had her.

"We'll be quick." He pulled her shirt from her waistband. "Fast, fast, fast, Morgann. Fighting it takes up precious seconds."

She groaned and grabbed his head to kiss him.

He loved the feel of her lips on his, the small movement her body made, just a sensuous stretching of her muscles, as if she had to release the tension he created in her.

Since she was going in the right direction, he let her lead the kiss, picking her up so he could work his way across to her bed.

"Don't think I don't know what you're doing," she whispered, then bit his neck.

The sharp snip of pain fueled the remaining antidote inside him and a wave of heat rolled over him.

She pulled back as he sat her on the bed. "I thought those heat flashes were gone?" Her worry was clear.

He grinned. "Even more reason that you should ground me." He wasn't worried. He'd made it past McBain and standing in a room full of people. As far as he was concerned, he was home free.

"Oz, I'm concerned."

He pulled off her boots, then her shirt. "I made it through that whole briefing with flying colors." Pulling off her undershirt, he actually hummed at the sight of her breasts. Creamy white skin with just a sprinkling of freckles set off the perfect pink nipples.

Morgann lifted his chin. "Hello. Talking here."

He tried to rewind, but all that had been recorded were her breasts and the thoughts of what he wanted to do with them. "Morgann, I can't look at your naked body and think straight. That has nothing to do with Stasis, which I'll prove to you in two days. I have a hunger for you that is just part of me."

She went totally still.

Raising his head, Oz wondered what had just happened. He lifted an eyebrow.

She sighed and looked heavenward, as if there was someone there who might help her. "Oz, this stops the minute you're out of Stasis. It has to."

Anger shot through him, demolishing the desire in one piercing blow. "The hell it does."

"You want a straight ticket to someplace like the Omega system?" She touched his cheek and he instantly felt better.

"I'm not giving you up," he said. His rational mind called him a liar. He'd have to. There wasn't anything but misery with that choice.

"Even at the expense of your career and mine?" she asked, her beautiful eyes filled with concern and another emotion he knew to be caring. She didn't just desire him, she cared about him.

He watched the emotion in her eyes, cradling it in his heart, knowing the truth of their feelings for each other. How many times had he seen two people broken up and tossed to the farthest corners of the Inter-worlds? *Too many.*

She smiled and it was sad. "So we'll take today and tomorrow and then we'll walk away," she whispered.

He nodded, not liking it at all, but what could they do?

Except this, he thought, pulling off his clothes with jerky motions. Tossing them behind him on the floor, he climbed onto the bed.

When he kissed her again, it wasn't just hunger and desire that drove him. Pushing her back, he cherished her with every fiber of his body. Slow kisses, licks and nibbles. He was building memories of her taste, of the feel of her that had to last forever.

Running his mouth over her ribs, he brushed a hand down her stomach, pulling her underwear with it, dragging them all the way off.

He brought her foot to his mouth and pressed a kiss into the instep, meeting her gaze. Tears tracked down her face, and it took her two tries to say, "Time."

Nodding, he crawled back up and supported himself above her. She twined her legs around his hips and guided his cock to her core.

"Morgann," he said, trying to tell her this meant more to him that just the act itself, more than he knew he should say out loud.

He sunk into her, the thrust slow, as he watched her emotions dance across her face. Their bond strengthened every minute that went by. The breaking of the link between them would hurt. He worried that there would be a hole inside him where she'd been, a hole that would last forever.

Dropping his forehead onto hers, he deepened his thrusts, knowing what she needed without having to see her face. In two days, he'd become an expert on loving her.

Her body tightened, arched, and he pulled back to watch her come.

A shudder went through her, but she kept her gaze on his, struggling to keep her eyes from closing.

Her peak triggered his. He threw back his head and let the pleasure race through him, burning itself into his memory for all time.

Chapter 10

She'd locked herself in the bathroom so Oz wouldn't see her cry. Big silent sobs that shook her body and had her struggling not to scream her frustration. This was an impossible situation. Impossible.

But the mission isn't impossible. The mission will make or break your career. Concentrate on the mission, not on him. If you can't have him, you can still have your career. Don't lose both, Morgann. Don't.

When they left her quarters, Oz trailed her to the west door, his face a mask of blankness, but she knew he was as upset as she. They were a fantastic pair, the two of them, traveling through the hall as if to their death sentence.

Mick, Jimmy, and Pete stood by the portal, decked in night gear. They would be moving light, except for the explosives. Oz knelt and divided it up into four piles. Morgann let them take it. She was Commanding Officer of this mission and that meant she had some perks.

"Okay, here's how it's going to go. Jimmy, you and Mike are at point. Pete, you're on rear sweep. We're going radio-silent from the far marker out, so they won't pick us up. That means we have to stay close and tight."

"Radio silent? I don't think I've ever done that." Jimmy's worry was clear. He wasn't questioning her, he was just concerned.

"Not only are we going silent, the radios stay off." That had all four men staring at her. "They can track us by them and we need to accomplish our surveillance in such a way that tomorrow we can return to blow the lab if we don't do it tonight."

Oz let out his breath. "That means we stay within an arm's length of each other or we won't be able to see hand signals. The moons are waning and light will be scarce."

"You haven't gone on a mission without radios either," she guessed. It made her grin. She shouldn't. It wasn't funny, but the fact she'd done something Oz hadn't made her bad mood break.

"Laugh it up, SecCom," he growled, shrugging into his pack. The GatGun inside alone would have staggered her to her knees, but he barely rocked with the motion.

"Look, boys, it sounds scarier than it is. I picked each of you because you're the best in this unit and you're not going to freak out without the radios." She made eye contact with Jimmy, Mick, and Pete in turn. Mick was a rock, Jimmy reasonably steady, but Pete's gaze darted to Oz. He was their explosives expert, so they had to have him along.

"Problem Pete?" Oz asked, his voice dangerously calm.

"No, Sir."

"Didn't think so." He raised an eyebrow to ask her if she planned to get the show on the road.

Morgann took a deep breath. "Let's head out."

Turning the radios off. As simple as it sounded, he would never have thought of it. Oz shook his head, worried despite himself. The chance of something going wrong had just skyrocketed. Although she'd picked the right men for a job like this. In fact, out of the five of them, he was probably the one least suited for this. He liked communication to be only a mike click away.

But at least no one would mess up and break radio silence. They'd had one mission go to hell when someone fell and his helmet mike had been pressed on the way down. The rebels were on constant alert for the telltale radio waves that signaled their presence and had pounced.

As the two moons rose, they made the wash in four hours at a fast clip. Then they slowed into half time, skirting the ground wires and using their night vision glasses to see the laser bands that had been put at odd points to warn the rebels of company. Using hand motions, they worked as a team, with Mick showing once again how good a scout he was.

They arrived at the end of the wash, crawling up to the top to lie on their bellies in a row facing the lab. They were behind schedule, fully two hours past the latest time they'd expected. Oz was concerned about the return trip. In the daylight, they would be easily seen by the rebel transports that patrolled the area. He exchanged a glance with Morgann.

She nodded, understanding his concerns, dragging her night vision glasses up from around her neck. For a long time, she studied the building, adjusting the focus. The increased risk of their return trip had her in a whirl. He could feel it from where he lay, his thigh resting against hers. Her body tightened with each passing moment.

With his palm parallel to the ground he pushed down, catching her attention to let her know she needed to gather herself. She hissed her annoyance, her fingers catching his to smash them against the rock.

Beside him, Pete jumped, his eyes held wide at the action. Oz met his gaze and gave him a lazy smile, then held up one finger to tell Pete to give her a moment. She'd have it soon or she wouldn't. He'd bet she'd come up with something, though. She always did. Oz made sure Pete saw his complete confidence in his SecCom.

Since they'd left the base, he'd had no problems with aggression or his temper. Then again, no one had touched his woman yet.

Stress filled Morgann to the breaking point. They had to return tonight or they were screwed, but every moment she jacked around made that less of a possibility. If they were caught in daylight, she'd have to bring her team to ground until night or crawl from crevice to crevice until they were back on Trooper held land. Either way would bring them dangerously close to Oz's crash point.

He seemed fine, more Oz-like than he'd been since he'd gotten gassed with Stasis, making that calming gesture that shot her blood pressure through the freaking roof. But the very normal feel to him had her more worried. What if it signaled the end of the drug in his system?

She brushed the viewfinder over the building, hoping to find a flashing sign that said, "Set Explosives Here." The sensor grid that stretched out across the bare, cleared plain was a nightmare. How they would navigate it had her shaking her head. Maybe they should take some surveillance videos and go back to base.

She didn't want to give up.

A guard crossing checked ground transports in and out of the lab compound, but otherwise the whole complex was silent. Morgann wished she could call in fighters and have them blow the place to shreds, but with the invention of a new ground-to-air missile, those days were over, at least until another invention came along to take the violence to the next level.

She returned again and again to the cliffs behind the lab. Theoretically, they could literally lob the explosives over the cliff and blow the lab that way. Could it be that easy? The only way she would know for sure was if she went up there and took a look.

Dragging her goggles off, she flicked her gaze to Oz to assess how well he was holding up.

He smirked at her, the arrogant action intended to tell her he was better than fine.

Okay. She drew the lab into the small amount of sand covering the rock below them, putting five x's to signal where they were. He nodded once. Then she drew the cliff and met his gaze. Holding it, she drew five x's on the other side of the line.

Oz's eyes widened and he studied the surrounding territory. They would have a long trek ahead of them to circle the lab.

She raised an eyebrow. Could he make it?

Oz circled his finger in the air, giving her the head out motion.

He finally felt the first failings of his strength when they made it to the top of the cliff wall. The sun would rise in an hour and while they'd put themselves slightly closer to their home base, they were still half a day's march out.

He and Morgann shimmied to the edge to look down at the lab. One little chunk of the brittle, compressed sand tumbled over the edge and picked up other chunks, threatening to create a runaway slide before it caught on a slight edge, stopping as quickly as it started.

The lab lay a hundred feet below. Not as close to the cliff as they'd thought, but still about ten feet away. They couldn't rappel down and land on the roof. The rebels had put nets and fencing up to catch rock slides, making the path down even more difficult.

She stared over the edge for a moment, then raised her head with exaggerated slowness. The unholy light in her eyes had excitement twining through his stomach. She had the solution. Something blinding and deep built in the pit of his belly, spreading out across his whole body, only to pull into his heart and lodge there. He almost choked on it before he realized it was a combination of pride and love.

She touched his shoulder and gave him a confused look, before tilting her head at the rest of the team. He nodded to show her he'd follow.

They crawled back, Morgann pausing at an indent in the ground. Then she leaned in close and touched Oz's pack. He brought it over his shoulder and set it down lightly. She made a give-it-up motion with her finger to her palms. He took the explosives out and she pointed to the depression she'd stopped at, meeting Pete's gaze for his thoughts on her plan.

It took them twenty minutes to set the explosives, Pete checking everything once he understood what Morgann wanted to accomplish. Then they hoofed it several klicks away. They'd destroy radio silence to fire the charges, but they couldn't be close or they'd slide with the unstable cliff.

Once it blew, they'd have to run for it to get away from the area the signal came from. Sweat poured off Oz and, already, his muscles shook with fatigue. He couldn't believe he'd lost his mind enough to endanger his team by coming along. He'd been a fool.

Morgann nodded to Pete, who pushed the detonator. The angry boom of the explosives filled the air, shooting sand and rock twenty feet up. For a heartbeat, nothing happened and Oz had enough time to worry they'd put the charges too far back.

Then the cliff shifted forward, hanging for a moment in the air, separate from the rest of the ridge. In slow motion, it collapsed in on itself.

"Run," Morgann ordered and the team leapt to their feet, dashing along the ridge, scrambling to the safety of the craggy land nearby.

One last look over his shoulder showed the remains of the lab billowing up from the ruined heap smashed by the ridge. The damage had been much greater than he'd expected, the slide going all the way to the guard station across the plain.

Morgann knew Oz was in trouble halfway back to the base. He panted for breath and sweat poured from him. It was time to step in. "Stop," she ordered, breaking silence. Behind her the sun rose, showing that her whole team was ragged around the edges. "Divvy up the GatGun between you."

"I'm fine," Oz growled.

She stepped in, pissed and not bothering to hide it. He wasn't pushing her around again. "That was an order, Welty." They had a short stare down, before he rolled his pack from his shoulder and set it before him. She could almost feel his remorse at forcing his presence on the team. He'd follow her orders because of his own guilt. She didn't have time to help him. They had to return as fast as they could.

Mick, Jimmy, and Pete divided the seven parts of the heavy gun between them. Briefly, she considered abandoning it, but one glance at Oz had her discarding the idea. He'd fight her and that would delay them more.

By the time they made it to base, she supported Oz on one side and Mick had him on the other. He still propelled himself forward, but there was a lurching quality to his gait that told them all he was done.

She took him straight to MedComm. The Doc took one look at him and put him on a cot in the hallway.

Morgann knelt beside him, dismissing the rest of the team. "Are you okay?"

He nodded. "I made an error in judgment, put the team at risk."

She rolled her eyes. "Please. Let's save the melodrama until later. I need to report in."

"I fucked up," he whispered, rubbing his eyes with a hand that shook so badly she almost helped steady it.

"First of all, you did the best you could with a bad situation." She pulled down his hand to meet his gaze and knew she needed to do something fast to keep him from going overboard with guilt. The mighty Osborn Welty didn't make these mistakes. "I'm glad you were there and I wouldn't go back and change it, even if I could." She braced a hand on the wall and pressed a kiss to his cheek.

His shaking hand curled around her head and cradled her for a brief moment.

"Second of all." She pulled up to meet his brown-eyed gaze. "I love you—" her voice caught and she knew she couldn't leave it there. It wouldn't be fair to either of them to have that out on the table, then be forced to work side-by-side for the next few months until one of them was promoted and moved to another base. So she kept going, as if she'd always planned to. "—for controlling yourself when you could have destroyed the room and me. You're an excellent commander, Welty." And with that, she stood and forced herself to walk away, as if that was all that was excellent and amazing about him.

※⟨ᘓ⟩彡

He felt like a piece of his soul had ripped from his body and been trampled by a thousand feet.

She was leaving and there was nothing he could do but help her go. White waited on his assessment of this mission. If he gave his approval, Morgann would be promoted to Commander and would be whisked away within hours on a transport to Borrus. Every particle of his being didn't want to do it. He wanted to keep her by his side. But he'd spent his adult life working his way through the ranks and so had she. He knew what it meant to her, just as he knew what it meant to pursue his own dreams. Dreams they'd both give up if they stayed together.

He wanted to call her back and tell her to forget everything else, tell her she had to marry him. They could go citizen, get work that didn't have anything to do with the Troopers. But the small rational part of his brain that still functioned knew that wouldn't be fair to either of them. And dammit, she'd earned this promotion. It might kill him, but she was going to get it.

"MedTech," he growled, forcing the words from his throat. "Get General White on the Vidscreen."

✻❧(༼༽)❧✻

She traversed the base to General White's office to report in, her whole mind blank. What was she going to do? Now that she'd had him, she didn't want to give him up. And they'd be working together every single day. Side by side. Not being able to act on this magical attraction between them.

Stumbling into the command center, she found the general was out, so she sat outside his office to wait, unable to stop the whirl of her mind.

How in the hell could she be close to Oz every day and not touch him? She couldn't. Most likely, he couldn't, either. Which would mean he'd spend more time like he was now—wracked with guilt over his inability to do the right thing and leave her alone.

They were both about to end up in hell.

Hours rolled by without the general returning, but she didn't care. She needed a way out of this and she knew somewhere in her brain there was an acceptable solution. The problem was, she kept coming back to trying to figure out a way to stay with Oz. But that would lead to both their careers going into a bottomless pit and most likely married life in some god-forsaken hole smack dab in the middle of nowhere. That just wasn't acceptable, not even to be together. They'd soon grow to hate each other. It would only be a matter of time.

The general cleared his throat. She popped to her feet and saluted. "General."

"At ease." For once, the general wasn't snapping at her. "Tired, Sec-Com?"

"No, Sir. Just thinking."

"About what?"

"Tactics, Sir," she answered truthfully.

"Your Commanding Officer has been telling me since the first week you arrived that you're brilliant when it comes to strategy."

Morgann blinked, unable to stop herself from starting in surprise. Oz had said that about her? Since right after she arrived? If she hadn't loved him before, she did now.

"Didn't know, did you?" The general chuckled and led the way into his office. Pointing to a chair, he ordered, "Sit," then took his own seat. "Commander Welty is big on supporting his Troopers to his superiors."

She knew that, but she hadn't considered he'd fight for her.

"He also said you would make an excellent tactics instructor at the Military Academy on Borrus." He leaned back in his chair and studied her.

His scrutiny made Morgann sit up straighter. "Yes, Sir, that's where I want to be." But did she really? Without Oz? Well, she wasn't having Oz, so better there than here, where she'd be so close to him and yet so far away.

"I took the liberty of pulling your file." He tapped his desk screen with an impatient finger. "Your record has been spotless, and your test scores are in the top of the range." His gaze flicked up to her. "You only have to earn a promotion to be picked up by the Academy."

She nodded. She'd known that would be the case.

"I just returned from speaking with Commander Welty, and he's putting you up for that promotion."

A stab of physical pain almost had her doubling over, but she stayed upright. Oz was promoting her. It's what she'd wanted and worked so hard for, so why was she about to splinter apart?

"We spoke at length and I agree that you have more than proven your ability to lead in a variety of situations. Your final rite of passage has been the destruction of the labs and Commander Welty's assessment of your leadership skills."

He paused, which cued Morgann to say, "Thank you, Sir."

It must have been the appropriate answer, because he slid a small, plastic disk into his reader. "I have been corresponding for the last month with the Academy, and they've agreed to an immediate transfer the moment your promotion comes through, which it did when I signed off a few short minutes ago. Mick will be promoted in your place as the new SecCom."

Morgann swallowed and almost told him to *stop, back up, wait* because she didn't want to leave immediately. But this was the only way it could be, the only way to have a chance of a decent life.

The general handed her the card. "Here are your orders to report to Borrus, where you will be stationed at the Academy from this time forward."

She nodded and accepted the disk. This would solve everything. Everything. She stood before she broke down and cried right here in the general's office.

"Thank you for your service to the Troopers, Commander. The next transport leaves within an hour and I want you on it." The general smiled at the use of her new title, shook her hand and escorted her to the door. "If I didn't know better, Morgann, I would almost think you were sad to leave us."

Morgann nodded. "Yes, Sir, I will be."

In a daze, she staggered back to her quarters, her brain repeating over and over that she was leaving Oz, leaving the only man she'd ever cared for.

Opening her door on autopilot, she almost missed the piece of paper on the floor. Picking it up with shaking finger, she opened it to read, "*Morgann—good luck at the Academy. I will miss you every day. Osborn.*"

Holding the precious scrap of paper to her chest, she closed her eyes. He'd spent a week's pay to leave her a note. Paper was scarcer than any other provision on Triad and was more expensive per ounce than cloth. She would treasure it forever. It was all she'd have of him, that and the memories she knew she'd replay every night in her mind.

He'd gotten her what she wanted and she'd left, just as he'd known she would. What other choice did she have? She wasn't cut out to actually lead a team on an outpost like Triad. She would, however, be a brilliant instructor.

It had been months since she'd gone and Oz had never been more miserable in his life. He'd always thought he wanted to be an outpost commander, but now he just didn't think he could live without Morgann by his side. More and more, he realized he'd be happy in other roles, tackling other challenges.

He'd taken two months to figure out a strategy to have her and not tank either of their careers at the same time. It might backfire, and if it did, he'd leave the Troopers and go into the private sector. He refused to call her and let her know his plans. It wouldn't be fair to get her hopes up and he wanted to give her time to know her feelings for him. If she'd moved on, he was in serious trouble, but if she hadn't, and she cared for him even a tenth as much as he cared for her, she'd be his within the month.

Some things were worth sacrificing for, worth taking the chance for, he thought, as he entered General White's office to put his plan into effect.

Three months after leaving Triad, Morgann called Oz on the VizPhone. He'd been out, so she left a message. "I miss you," was all she'd said, but if she hadn't said it, she would have died. That's how she felt. Like she would implode at any minute if she didn't touch him again.

Almost two standard weeks later, he still hadn't called back, which served her right. Stirring up their feelings hadn't been wise. She didn't play games and try to convince herself he didn't care for her. What they had between them didn't just go away. She was a walking example of that, she thought, as she trudged home from teaching her beginning Tactics class.

Teaching had been harder than she thought, but this was the place for her. If she couldn't be with Oz, she would be here for as long as she could. But gods, she wished with everything inside her she could have him in her life again.

Teacher housing consisted of condos in a high rise building, like those that covered almost every inch of Borrus. She liked her small quarters. Pausing, she glanced up at the fifty story building, trying to find her window among the hundreds on the upper floors.

Her gaze roamed down again, slowly, because for some bizarre reason, she could swear that Oz was near her and she didn't want to lose the feeling sooner than she had to. Maybe she'd finally lost her mind, although she didn't think so. The sensation felt too wonderful to be a hallucination.

Tracking her gaze to the front steps, her breath caught at the sight of Oz striding toward her. She soaked him in, studying the way he moved, the play of muscles through his body, hardly believing he was here in the flesh and not a figment of her imagination.

She'd forgotten how big he was, but her neck bent back as he neared. Staring into his strong, handsome face, she said the one thing that had been circling her brain since she'd left Triad. "I love you."

One side of his mouth hitched up in a smile. "Probably not as much as I love you."

She wanted to throw herself into his arms, but she needed to make a point first. "Oh, I think you'd be surprised. I thought I'd explode from missing you and it hasn't eased, hasn't gotten any better. In fact, I think it's recently grown worse."

"I've been aching for you." He lifted a big, scarred hand and stroked her cheek. Then he pulled in a deep breath, his serious gaze making her stomach clench in worry. "I transferred to Borrus to become an assistant to Admiral Jordon."

"What?" That kind of assignment would earmark him for a lifetime of paperwork, away from the front lines. "I don't understand. I thought you wanted to run an outpost?" She didn't want him sacrificing anything for her, but oh, gods, she was glad he had come.

He shrugged one shoulder, not seeming upset in the least. "You're here." His brown eyes went amber in the setting sun. "And I'm not spending my lifetime universes apart from you."

"But your dreams—"

Ducking his head, he almost touched his mouth to hers, the very action making her shiver with a sharp spark of desire. "I would give up the Troopers for you, Morgann." He pressed his lips to hers and she had to twist her hand in his shirt to steady herself. "You complete me."

She didn't want to cry, but the emotion that swirled inside her had to go somewhere and so the tears tracked down her face in streams. Wrapping her arms around his neck, she hugged him tight. "I've never wanted anyone else but you, Oz. Never really desired another man in my life." She framed his face in her hands. "I'm sorry you gave up your dream for me."

"I'm not," he said simply. "I can be happy here." He stroked his finger across her bottom lip. "I've lived my life by my family code. Right. Honor. Family. Soul. You're what's right. You're my honor. You're my family now and you are definitely my soul."

The tears picked up speed again. "Dammit. I'm crying," she whispered, dashing them away with a hand. "I thought I'd never see you again. I thought we were lost."

"No." The word was said with a fierce finality and she knew he'd sacrifice even more to keep them together. "We're staying together. I want you to be my wife."

"Yes." She didn't hesitate. She'd said yes a thousand times in her dreams.

The desire for him that plagued her every waking moment rose up and crashed through her body like a fist. "You're living here with me starting now, right?"

His eyes narrowed as if he knew how much she wanted him. "You couldn't keep me away."

"Good," she said, taking his hand. "Let's get off the street. I have a burning need to have you in my bed, Osborn Welty."

"I thought you'd never ask." Then he swept her off her feet. Literally.

About the Author:

Leigh Wyndfield spends her free time reading anything she can get her hands on, watching movies, and skiing or hiking, depending on the season. Unable to find romances that take place on other worlds, she started writing her own. Her books have won awards and finaled in published author contests, including the PRISM, More Than Magic, the Holt Medallion, and the Dream Realm Award. Her novel, In Ice, was nominated by RT Magazine for Best Erotic Romance, won a PRISM Award, and the Write Touch Readers Award! Romantic Times calls her work, "Engrossing, enthralling and entrancing." Visit her website to learn about her books at www.leighwyndfield.com.

A Woman's

Pleasure

❧❦❧

by Charlotte Featherstone

To My Reader:

Enjoy the fantasy of a younger man teaching an older woman, *A Woman's Pleasure*! Thank you to all the readers who continually write to me, requesting more historical erotic romances! I hope this one pleases.

Acknowledgements

It is with very great gratitude, respect, admiration and affection that I thank my wonderful critique partner, Kristina Cook for her continued support, her timely pep talks and her wonderful 'red pen', not to mention her ability to keep smilin' while enduring my continued emailings of Richard Armitage fan videos. Who else could possibly understand such an obsession? You really are the best, and I value all the suggestions and comments you've provided over the years. Most of all, I value and treasure your friendship.

Chapter 1

June 8, 1848
Constantinople

Sunlight glistened off the blue waters of the Bosporus, rendering it a brilliant turquoise. The waves were gentle, rolling, rocking the ship in a slow, undulating rhythm that lulled and seduced. Like lovers in motion, the boat and the water became one, rocking in time—in tune—with the other.

Lazily fanning herself with her jeweled ostrich feathers, Isabella lay on her deck chair and let the rhythm of the water sooth her, relax her—free her. Her mind was a collage of vivid shots of naked bodies, moving, swelling in slow, erotic strokes. With the boat softly swaying, the rhythms of the water fanned the images until it felt as though it was her body moving in time with another. So vivid was the unbridled image of her naked body against another's that her breathing became ragged and harsh, and she ceased to feel the waves, but instead felt the pleasure.

"A perfect day for sailing, is it not?" her husband George, Lord Langdon, exclaimed as he looked through his binoculars. "By God, the city is astounding from this view."

"You please me, my lord, by admiring my beautiful city," Abdul Mecit, the Sultan of Turkey, murmured as he came to rest against the brass railing of his private yacht.

"I never thought I'd say this about anyplace but England," George said, "but Constantinople is the most riveting place on earth."

From their view atop the gently rolling waves of the Bosporus, Constantinople, the city where the worlds of West and East met, looked mystical and exotic. Cyprus and palm trees waved lazily in the hot summer breeze. In the distance the gold minarets of the Blue Mosque glinted in the sun. Soon it would be time for noon prayers. The bells would ring, and the city would quiet until only the chanting of the men could be heard.

Closing her eyes, Isabella listened to the waves as they slapped the sides of the boat and concentrated on the swell of the sea, letting the exoticness of this strange, beautiful land captivate her senses. Time stilled until it was only her on the boat—not George her husband, nor the Sultan and his mass of servants and courtiers. Only her and—

Feeling as though she were being watched, her eyes flew open. A man gazed back at her, one whom she had never seen before today. She would have remembered him, if she'd seen him in all the weeks since she had come to the court of Abdul Mecit.

Time stood still as they studied each other. He was not merely handsome, but beautiful, tall and broad shouldered, his hair as dark as the devil's.

His burning gaze sent her flesh tightening, her heart beating madly against her ribs.

Without a word, a smile, or even a nod of acknowledgment, he watched her, studied her from where he stood alone against the railing. The wind chose that moment to rise, to curl its way along her body and beneath the layers of petticoats, caressing her flesh. Unbidden images of this man's hands slipping beneath her skirts, of taking the exact same path the breeze had, ran through her mind, and God help her, she closed her eyes and savored the image of this man touching her while the breeze continued its journey along her body.

Sighing, she felt the mounds of her breasts rise against her bodice, heard the husky sound of whispering breath escape her pursed lips. As the image of a hand stroking her, from breast to belly, flashed before her eyes, her body arched. From the tips of her boots, to the top of her straw bonnet, the breeze enveloped her in lush coolness and the exotic scent of frankincense and jasmine, while the image before her closed eyes inflamed her body with the heat of desire.

"Your lady seems to be as affected by the delights of Constantinople as you, my lord," the sultan chuckled. "Why, it quite takes her breath away."

George sent her a glare before addressing the sultan. "She does, indeed seem to be enamored," was all he was able to reply.

When the Sultan's attention was diverted by one of his servants, her husband strode toward her with the tenacity of a commander, and heaved her unceremoniously up from her deck chair. With a cruel grip on her elbow, he maneuvered her to a quiet, isolated corner of the deck.

"What the devil has gotten into you?" he hissed in her ear as his grip tightened like a vice. "You're making a spectacle of yourself and me."

She tried to pull her arm away. "You're doing that nicely for both of us, right now. Unhand me, my lord, people are watching."

Conscious of the curious stares from the courtiers, he shook her arm and pulled her into his side so he could say in her ear, "We will speak of this tonight, in private. Go now and try not to attract any more attention. Women are to be seen and not heard, and the truth of that has never been more correct than here in the East."

With a grunt of disgust, he turned from her, leaving her alone to face the waves and the endless blue horizon. Was this it—all that a woman could expect to find in life? Disappointment and unfulfilled longing?

Isabella dearly hoped not. She didn't think she could survive another year enduring a woman's lot in life. Perhaps it was the day—her thirty-first birthday. Or mayhap she could simply no longer stomach the notion that she was merely a man's possession and little else.

Steeling herself, she willed away the bitterness edging in, and the wetness slowly pooling behind her eyes. Blinking rapidly, Isabella looked down at her gloved hands and allowed herself the luxury of shedding a tear. When she looked up, she peered straight into the gaze of the stranger. He was still watching her, but this time she could read what he was thinking. *Pity.* She turned on her heel, not wanting him to know her thoughts or feelings, which she was certain were shining in her eyes for all the world to see.

Happy Birthday to me, she whispered as she walked away. Just another year trapped in a lonely, unbearable life with nothing more tangible than the imaginings of my mind.

�﹡ﾟ❨ﾟ❩﹡ﾟ

"My dear, I wish to talk you," her husband called from the connecting room.

Sighing, Isabella squeezed the water from her sea sponge and handed it to her maid. It was time for her husband's lecture, the one he had promised was coming. He might forget a great many things, like her favorite flower, or their anniversary, but he never forgot to lecture her on the roles of a dutiful wife.

George let himself into her chamber and stopped dead when he saw her resting in the marble tub. "Good God, you're still in the bath!" George scoffed. "For the love of God, Lady Langdon, cover yourself."

How long had it been since George had used her Christian name she wondered? Their wedding night, perhaps? Had he even whispered it then, when he had taken her virginity?

The chamber door closed behind Nan, her maid, and Isabella reached for a thick towel and arose from the tuberose scented bath, sending ripples of water sloshing over the marble tub. As she covered her body with the towel, a feeling of profound sadness swept over her. In thirteen years, he had not once referred to her as anything but the title he had bestowed upon her on their wedding day.

So many years of enduring an unbearably polite and proper marriage had led her to this moment—this time of reawakening. How was it she had only recently come to the realization of how suffocating an existence it was to be a society wife? Why now, after thirteen years of never doubting her role, did she find the occupation of wife and hearth-tender so utterly confining and intolerable?

Because she had been too busy to notice what her life lacked, a quiet voice inside her whispered. She had been nothing more than a child when she had wed, barely a week past her eighteenth birthday. She had been a mother within the year, her son having been conceived on her honeymoon. Her daughter's birth had followed the very next year.

She had been so busy these past years, tending children and making a home while forging an influential place in society for her husband's politics, that she had failed to see what her life was coming to. Now, at the age of thirty-one, with her son Gordon off at school and twelve-year old Minnie starting her second year of finishing school, Isabella realized with some measure of panic that she could no longer exhaust herself in her children's lives.

Her sole duties now were to smile and nod and look beautiful and dutiful for George. She was to keep her opinions to herself and her eyes downcast in a cruel farce of subservient female loyalty and demureness.

There was no warmth to be found in her life— and no life in this shell of a marriage that she now realized was slowly smothering the life from her.

"Are you presentable yet?" her husband grumbled as he stood with his back to her.

"I have borne you two children, George. Surely you cannot find looking upon my naked body as something shocking or impure."

His shoulders stiffened when the word *naked* passed through her lips. "You're a gently reared woman, Lady Langdon. You should not be allowing anyone to see you in such an indecent state."

Stepping behind the screen, Isabella reached for her lace robe and wrapped it securely around her middle. It was not surprising that George was flustered. She couldn't remember a time when he had seen her naked. The *sessions,* as George was wont to call their carnal interludes, had occurred in her chamber with her nightgown raised to her waist and the room in darkness. The act had been perfunctory and uninspired, and George had left her alone within minutes of discharging his seed in the hopes of furthering the Langdon dynasty.

Their marital intimacies, if they could have been called such, had only been infrequent at best and had drastically decreased after the birth of their children—and inexplicably ceased two years ago.

"Lady Langdon," he growled when he saw her appear from around the dressing screen. "Your behavior today was shocking. I mean to call you on it."

Ignoring his pacing, Isabella walked to the black lacquered dressing table and reached for the silver-handled brush, inlaid with mother of pearl and emeralds, a gift from the sultan upon her arrival in his country.

"I have no knowledge what I've done that has sent you flying to the boughs, George," she said matter-of-factly, watching her husband in the mirror as she used his given name.

"You made that obscene noise on the boat this afternoon, madam! Everyone heard you. Every man looked your way."

She saw the stranger in her mind, the way he had looked at her, watched her, remembered how she had felt, knowing his gaze lingered over her throat and breasts.

"What do you have to say for yourself?"

Rousing herself from her musings, she looked at her reflection in the mirror and ran the brush through her hair. "I sighed, George."

"It was a sound of pleasure," her husband thundered. "And your posturing, good God, you were lying atop that chaise with your bosom pointed skywards and back arched as if…"

As if I were arching beneath a man during orgasm?

"You must know how you appeared," George continued. "You looked like a dolly mop lounging about in such a fashion and making those most appalling noises. What must the sultan and the valide sultana think of such a display?"

She paused, her brush still in her hand. "I sighed, George, because it was blistering hot and for the first time that morning a cool breeze waved over my entire body, and it was utterly divine. It is not easy or comfortable to suffer through six layers of petticoats on top of a heavy silk gown during the midday sun. Besides, the valide sultana," she said, thinking of the sultan's mother who was a beautiful Circassian woman, "was most grateful for the breeze as well. I'm sure it cannot be at all comfortable hiding one's face behind a veil all day."

"But that noise! Every man looked at you like you were a wanton. Even Abdul Mecit was provoked to comment."

"The sultan was by no means offended."

"You will listen to me," George barked, grasping her shoulders and turning her to face him. "You will not do such a thing again, do you understand me? You are an English lady, you are to act as one. Must I remind you that you are the representative for all English women in this country? The sultan is a very reserved and proper man, he will not tolerate such behavior in the English ambassador's wife."

"He cannot be all that proper," she muttered, giving voice to her thoughts. "He keeps a harem of women. I've heard that he has more than a hundred concubines and more than twenty children from as many as twelve women."

Her husband's face grew florid. "Where the devil have you heard such a thing? I vow I cannot begin to comprehend what has happened to you this past year. Are you..." he looked away and loosened his cravat. "Shall I send for the doctor? Perhaps the womanly change is upon you, and you are having bouts of female hysteria. I have heard of this happening even in the most biddable of women."

The change *was* upon her, but it was not the sort her husband thought. Never had she been more aware that she was a woman—a woman who was lonely, whose body cried out in the night to be touched. She was conscious of her needs, the needs her husband didn't seem to understand, or appear to care about.

She shivered with the memory of that afternoon, sailing along the turquoise waters. Never had she looked that way at a man who was not her husband. But she had looked—looked today at the stranger who took no pains in hiding behind veiled lashes and stolen glances. His body had called to her, sending heat flickering in her veins. He was tall and broad with beautiful hands that were at once unfashionably large yet elegant. She imagined those large hands traveling over her yearning body.

All that afternoon she had thought of him. And as if she already hadn't spent too many months thinking about passion, she had slipped away to privacy and started touching herself, pretending that the man she had seen on the boat was the one touching her—not her own fingers. Slowly, she had brought herself to a shaking orgasm, and she was left wondering if it was possible for a man to know a woman's body so intimately—to understand her needs so completely—that he could make her shake and cry out as she had made herself do.

For months now, she had known that she wanted more out of life. She wanted to be thought of as a woman—*wanted* as a woman.

She loved her children, adored her role of mother, but for once she would like a man to look at her and think of nothing but the sexual being she could be if she were allowed the luxury.

"There is something wrong with you," George droned on, but she drowned out his words as she ran the brush mindlessly through her hair, recalling her vision of the black-haired man with the large hands stroking every inch, every indentation of her body. She imagined him kissing her, slowly, seductively at first, then deeper, more carnally, his tongue thrusting inside her mouth as she allowed him to plunge deep inside her body.

"What have you to say for yourself, madam?"

She met her husband's dark glare in the mirror and swallowed hard. Replacing the brush atop the enameled tray, she rose and stepped around the chair, slowly untying the sash of her robe, allowing the lace to cascade down her shoulders in what she hoped was a sensual prelude to seduction. She was a dutiful wife, she would not betray her vows, but she needed more. She needed to know if her husband could come to her and be the sort of man her body was crying out for.

"Good God, what the devil are you doing? Cover yourself, Lady Langdon! No lady of breeding should be parading about her boudoir in such a fashion. Ladies such as you...." His face grew red, and his eyes began to bulge from their sockets as she stood before him, completely naked, her large breasts jutting out before him. Her sex was shaved as was the custom in the East, and she saw with some satisfaction that George's gaze dropped to her pubes, his eyes widening further.

"Ladies such as me?" she asked.

"You have been raised better, madam." He reached for her gown and hastily shielded her body. "Ladies of your rank do not lower themselves in such a fashion."

"I didn't know I was lowering myself," she muttered, crushed that he had rejected her advances. It was not the first time, but it had been the first time she had dared to brave his scrutiny and appear naked before him.

"This behavior is base and highly immoral. I won't have it, Lady Langdon, *I won't*. Need I remind you that you are a wife! Wives do not parade about in such a manner," he snapped, shoving her away. "I shall not tolerate such behavior in you. I will not!" he thundered. "Do you understand?"

She righted herself, holding the back of her vanity chair. "I understand that sex between us was nothing more than a means to procreate."

"Damn right! Ladies like you are supposed to endure the amorous advances of their husband, not embrace them. Your lot is to suffer the marriage act, not enjoy it, and a good, dutiful wife certainly does not initiate the act. Only the most skilled whore instigates sex, and I assure you, I did not marry you for you to become a whore."

She turned to gaze in the mirror. Her eyes showed her anguish. "Why did you marry me, George?"

His response was so prompt, it had to be all that there was. "Convenience and commerce. Why does any man marry?"

Chapter 2

George's humiliating words rang in her head all that evening. Even as she finished dressing, the bitterness and frustration of her cold, unloving marriage gripped her like an unrelenting vice. She felt chilled, empty, hating that the rest of her days would be spent like this—like tonight—painting false smiles on her face while inside another piece of her soul was chipped away, only to dissolve into the hollow nothingness of her body.

The rhythmic rocking of the carriage ceased, drawing her gaze back to her surroundings. Forcing the painful memories aside, Isabella steeled herself, gathering her significant self control to perform her duties as the ambassador's wife.

The door to the carriage opened and Isabella slid forward on the bench. One white gloved hand reached inside the carriage and the footman helped her descend the steps. She stopped there to gaze up at the sandstone palace with its ornate black iron and gold gates and glimmering minarets. She reminded herself that her purpose here tonight was as the English ambassador's wife, an ornament for her husband's arm. Automatically she began to function mechanically, like an automaton with its gears and wheels turning and grinding in clicking motions—moving but not feeling. Existing, but not living.

Pasting on a false smile, Isabella allowed her husband to usher her through the gates of the Topkapi Palace. Beneath curved Islamic arches studded with tortoise shells, emeralds and rubies, they walked until the *kizlar agasi*, the chief eunuch, threw open the heavy wooden door and ushered them into a long room with fluffy clouds of pink and red silks suspended from the ceiling to form billowing tents above their heads. A black lacquered table was set for an elaborate supper, and veiled odalisques, dressed in sheer silks and gold trimming, stood at measured intervals, waiting to indulge and serve every whim of the waiting guests.

George, with an iron grip on her hand that rested atop his forearm, steered her to where their chairs were placed next to the sultan. They were the guests of honor, along with the French diplomat, Monsieur Laurier.

Isabella took her seat, mindful to smile sweetly while keeping her eyes downcast as a demure and solicitous wife ought. Rage and helplessness began to suffocate her, and she forced it back down, knowing that no one would give a bloody damn, or even begin to understand what she felt. How could they, here in Constantinople, where women were worth even less than they were back home in England.

"You look l... lo... lov..." the sultan tried to speak, but then broke off and waved his hand impatiently.

"Lovely?" a deep voice said beside him, but Isabella could not see the man, nor could she very well press forward to search for the owner of the smooth, baritone voice.

"Lovely." Abdul Mecit brightened. "That is the word I search for you."

"Thank you, my sultan," she whispered, aware that George was glaring at her—his not so subtle way of reminding her to hold her tongue and behave. She ignored him and indicated the lush décor of the room. "What a lavish party. I think what I love most about your culture is the vibrant colors," she said to the sultan, motioning to the silk canopy above them. "It's like a scene out of the Alhambra." Abdul Mecit smiled, his black eyes glittering in the candlelight. "And the guns firing into the night sky was most moving."

The sultan smiled briefly. "My kadin has given me another child."

Kadin... woman. Not wife, nor lover, just his woman. "A child?" she echoed politely.

"My *kadin* has given me another daughter."

"And you fire guns whenever a child is born in the harem?" she inquired, hating the disappointment she saw in Abdul Mecit's eyes. Obviously the sultan had wanted a boy.

The sultan nodded. "The salute is five times a day for a week if the child is a boy."

"And for your daughter, my sultan?"

"For a girl child, just three days."

She smiled, tired already of constantly having to turn her lips upward. But it would not do to have the sultan discovering her thoughts, or her great displeasure. It seemed a woman's worth was the same the world round—nothing.

Abdul Mecit's inquisitive black eyes continued to watch her. Studying her thoughtfully, he brushed his fingers along his black beard and remarked to his neighbor, "She is, how do you say it English, Julian bey?"

Isabella felt her breath catch, aware of a strange sensation flickering along her skin. The man who had been on the boat that afternoon pressed forward, meeting her gaze over the sultan's narrow shoulder.

"What is the word I want, cousin?" the sultan asked.

The stranger looked up at her then and held her gaze. "Perturbed, I believe, is the word you seek."

Two thoughts struck Isabella. The first was that she had never seen eyes such as his. No Turk of her acquaintance had eyes that color. They were a hypnotizing blend of indigo and emerald, the sort of deep, vibrant blue green on the breast of a peacock. Those eyes held her captive, and she was unable to look away despite knowing that she was being far too bold.

The second thought came immediately after his gaze had raked over her in a familiar fashion. He was much too young to be looking at her in such a way.

Coloring profusely, she lowered her gaze to her lap. Dear God, she had been fantasizing about a younger man. And oh, the scandalous, wicked things she had imagined him doing to her mouth and her breasts...

She reached for her ostrich fan, and with a practiced motion, flicked it open and fanned herself, feverishly trying not to think of the way she had buried her fingers in her sex, pretending it was his large, dark hands.

"Perturbed?" the sultan finally said. "Is that what you are, Lady Langdon?"

"Nonsense," George scoffed, sending her a ferocious glare. "Lady Langdon is possessed of the most mild, even temperament. You're thrilled to be here tonight, are you not, my dear?"

"Very pleased," she murmured, still fanning herself and trying mightily to avoid the stare of the man who should have looked away from her ages ago.

"Have you met Julian bey?" the sultan asked, waving a hand to the beautiful stranger.

She didn't look up. "I have not, my sultan."

The sultan cocked one inky brow. "I am surprised. Julian bey is my representative. He acts as my advisor in all Western affairs. Your husband spends most of his days with Julian bey. Have you never seen him in the palace?"

She froze. She had never encountered him before today, but had he occasion to see her? The palace was an intricate maze of arched columns and shadowed alcoves. He could have seen her anywhere, even, heaven forbid, taking the air on her private terrace.

Her gaze flew to his face and she saw the glimmer of mirth in his strange eyes. *He had seen her.*

"Julian bey is my half-cousin," the sultan continued. She nodded and kept fanning herself, wishing she had not ordered Nan to do her corset up so tight. She felt like fainting, thinking of all the possibilities and circumstances he might have had to see her wandering throughout the palace. She particularly enjoyed the *haman*. Had he seen her in the baths—how she lounged indolently in the scented waters? Had he seen how she had pleasured herself as the steam rose around her?

The man's gaze trailed from her eyes down to her lips. He was studying her so intently that his eyes had taken on a more brilliant, glittering quality. Suddenly, she no longer felt mortified that he might have stumbled upon her most private moments—instead, she had a driving curiosity to discover if watching her from afar induced the same excitement in him, as thinking about him doing such inspired in her.

"You look confused," Abdul Mecit said with an amused laugh. "You are trying to put the pieces of the puzzle together, are you not?"

She was trying to breathe, trying to look away from those hypnotizing eyes. Trying not to think of him lying atop her with his lithe, fit body.

"Julian bey's grandmother was my aunt. His mother is my cousin, and so that is how I come to be related to him. His father is English," Abdul Mecit murmured. "Naturally all of the House of Osman was outraged when my cousin married an Englishman, but that is all in the past, is it not, Julian bey, especially since you've been gifted-"

"Enough, Abdul," she heard him whisper to the sultan. "We needn't bore the lady with titles."

"What point is a title if one never uses it?"

"Inconsequential, as I believe I have told you time and time again," he muttered, rising from the chair.

The sultan arched an un-amused brow and waved a ringed hand in the man's direction. "May I present to you, Lady Langdon, my cousin, Julian Gresham, the son of the Earl and Countess of Huntington."

He was very tall, yet lithe like a cat as he came to stand before her. Bowing low, he captured her hand in his large one and she noticed how wan her fingers looked against his tanned skin.

"Welcome to the House of Felicity."

The velvet smoothness of his voice enveloped her in a liquid warmth that seemed to flood her blood with an intoxicating languor. "Isabella, Countess of Langdon," she said, trying to stop her hand from trembling in his.

"*Bella*," he whispered, before pressing his lips to her knuckles. "Beautiful in Italian. *Guzelle* is the Turkish word for you. It, too, means beautiful."

"It is very nice to meet you," she choked out, thankful that George's attention was fully diverted by Monsieur Laurier on his other side.

"May I tempt you to take a turn about the room with me before the festivities begin?"

She found that an answer was superfluous, for he took her by the hand and placed it in the crook of his elbow. George noted her departure with a curt nod.

Julian said nothing as he led her to the opposite side of the room where a curved door, inlaid with cobalt blue tiles was cracked open. Without a backward glance, he ushered her through the opening with the press of his hot palm to her lower back—so low that one might say he was no gentleman.

They were in a circular room, richly adorned and heavily jeweled, just as every other room in the Topkapi was. Isabella kept her gaze straight ahead and saw that the grounds of the palace lay in front of them. In the breeze, Moroccan lanterns swung on tall iron hooks, while candles floated atop lily pads in and amongst the lotus flowers that were in the pond.

The scene was intimate, sultry, and she felt her blood grow thick, felt herself fight for air as her corset became tighter, squeezing her breasts until they ached to be set free.

She could smell him, the scent an unidentifiable mixture of spice. She could feel him, his broad, tall body pressing against her as he stood behind her.

Sensing a shift in the charged current she felt running between them, Isabella held her breath, not knowing what he would do—not wanting to admit what she wanted him to do.

His fingers, soft and warm, skated down her cheek to her throat. His head was bent to hers and she felt his breath ruffling the tendrils of hair that had escaped its pins. Closing her eyes she savored the feel of him so close to her—allowed herself to imagine him slipping his large, hot hand beneath the bodice of her gown. Imagined what his full lips would feel like curving around her nipple. She wanted him to draw her breast into his mouth, wanted to feel everything this man would do to her. She wanted it so much that she was not thinking rationally—only feeling—and she had never felt this much need for a man—for the touch a man—in her life. Her lips parted, and another sigh, a sigh much more erotic than that afternoon's, passed between her lips.

A sudden rise of noise and the sound of lutes playing erupted on the lawn. The fanfare became louder, yet she could not step away from him, could not stop the yearning in her blood. By the time he had lowered his head to hers and traced his fingertip along her mouth, she was trembling as violently as she had that afternoon when she had climaxed with her own touch.

"Do you believe in destiny, Lady Langdon? Kismet," he whispered against her mouth.

"Kismet?" she echoed.

"Destiny. Ours entwined."

Chapter 3

The noise of the crowd approached, evaporating the spell weaving about them. Julian cursed George Langdon's poor timing. All the guests would be upon them in seconds and suddenly he wanted nothing more than to bar the door and keep Isabella's husband at bay.

What a fool he was to be lusting after another man's wife. For six months he had been enthralled with the ambassador's wife. Six months of watching her, wanting her. Six months of wishing George Langdon to hell. This stolen moment alone with her was not enough—it was only a tease—a fleeting second that made him hungrier for the touch of her, for the feel of her beneath him.

She was the loveliest woman he had ever seen. Her pale, golden hair shone in the candlelight, making him think of the silken locks as a halo around her head. She wore it pulled back in a simple bun, and tendrils curled around her oval shaped face, snaking along her neck, touching the lace ruffle of her bodice. Her face was upturned to his, and her perfect mouth, wide and full, was the color of a ripe peach. And her eyes, magnificently large like a doe's, were focused on him. For the first time he saw they were not plain brown as he had thought, but a mesmerizing mix of brown and gold.

Her skin, which was bare to her shoulders, burned hot beneath his hand, the softness of it reminding him of rose petals dipped in cream. He had never felt anything so supple, nor seen flesh so perfect. He wanted to bend closer to her, to inhale her fragrance—the real scent of her—beneath the tuberose perfume she wore.

During the stolen moments he'd watched her from the safety of a column or a screen, he had learned that Isabella's soul was as beautiful as her face. The way she treated her servants, both English and Turkish, warmed him. He also loved the way she made every attempt to learn the language and conform to their customs, customs he knew were difficult for her to understand and accept. But she did accept his people and his culture, and God knew he coveted such kindness and understanding—the very things that had evaded him all his life.

He had come to accept the nature of his birth. Being called a half-breed—mother part Turkish and Persian— was far easier to live with than the other extraneous titles he had acquired over the years. He despised knowing that people would accept him for what he called, a Persian prince with influential ties to a Sultan and the English court, but not for the man he truly was.

He hadn't wanted to be introduced to Isabella as Prince Fatiah of Persia, or the son of an English lord. He wanted her to know him as only Julian, a man in the Sultan's employ, a man of little consequence. Everyone flocked to the prince, but he wanted this woman to come to the man.

The sound of voices became increasingly louder, drawing him back from his musings. Summoning every ounce of strength, he dropped his hand away and took one step back. The door was thrown wide, and Abdul Mecit, followed by George Langdon, entered the room. "Happy birthday, m' dear," George said gruffly as he took her hand in his and placed a kiss on her knuckles—a kiss that did not really touch her—for his lips only hovered atop her hand for the briefest of seconds before he dropped it.

A hushed silence descended the small chamber as the processional of white mares with green feather headdresses pranced on the lawn before coming to a stop before them. Harnessed to the mounts was a square platform draped in red and gold brocade. "Behold, my dear," George said with immense pomp. "Your gift." He motioned to Julian as if he were nothing but his servant, and gritting his teeth, Julian walked out onto the green lawn.

Grabbing the brocade, Julian pulled it to the side, slowly revealing the gold cage that was a miniature of the Blue Mosque Isabella was so enamored of. A collected gasp was heard from the room as the ornately decorated cage glinted in the candlelight. Inside were two magnificent peacocks. He dared a look at Isabella and saw that her expression was not one of rapture. Instead, it bore a sort of sadness that he had seen far too many times since she had come to Constantinople.

"What do you think, my dear? Are they not stunning? The green one on the left is as rare as they come. Found in the jungles of Burma he was, cost me a packet."

"Thank you, my lord," she murmured in a sad, little voice. "You are far too generous."

"True, true," George puffed with pride.

"Come," Abdul ordered, before clapping his hands. "Let us return to the room where our supper awaits. Lady Langdon, you will converse with Julian bey and inform him where you would like your present to stay. Perhaps you would care to have them brought into the salon where you could watch them through supper."

She smiled again, but Julian could discern no happiness in it, only duty. Her husband and the sultan, along with the other guests departed, leaving them alone once again.

"Caged," she said in a soft, bitter voice. "Such beautiful creatures housed in a gilded prison; to be an object of beauty, to be looked at when it pleases, and ignored when it does not."

Tossing the brocade to the ground, Julian walked to her, catching her about the shoulders and tilting her chin up with his thumb. "Tell me."

"It is a terrible life to be kept behind bars." Her eyes were glistening with tears, tears he knew were embittered. "What life is it to live in such a lovely home, to have nothing to do but fan your colors, waiting for someone to notice you?"

He sensed she spoke not only of the peacocks. "Then you know, Isabella, what sort of life it is?"

"Lonely," she said so softly and brokenly that his heart squeezed in his chest. "What point is life if we are to be caged, imprisoned, never knowing what it is to be free?"

"Do you want to be set free?" he asked, desperation filling his voice. She looked away, back to the cage where the peacocks stood motionless. "If you were mine, I would never ignore you—I couldn't. If you were mine," he said again, fanning his thumbs along her cheeks. "I would make love to you every day, every night. I would make you shudder as I fill you. I would make you scream and call my name as I bring you to orgasm."

She turned her face away. "You mustn't say such things."

"What things? That my body aches to be inside you? That I can no longer stand skulking in the shadows watching you bathe, wishing I could reveal myself to you. Wishing I could be the one to cover your body with scented perfumes."

"You have seen me," she gasped and he saw the flicker of awareness turn her eyes a warm amber.

"Yes, I've seen you and I've dreamt of you. God, you have no idea how incredibly arousing it is to watch you bathe. So many times I wanted to slip into the water and stretch you wide with my cock."

She pulled away. "Sir, I am not used to—"

"Forgive me, Isabella, but I speak as I must. I want you, and that means beneath me, your body filled with me. I ache. I burn."

"I can't... I *must not* do this. I am married, you must leave me be."

"Do you think I don't know that? I should not covet another man's wife, but I cannot get you out of my thoughts. I see you every night in my dreams. I cannot let you be, no matter how much I've struggled to do so. Why do you think I never allowed myself to come near you? Why do you think that in six months, you've never seen me in the palace? I kept my distance from you because I knew I could not resist you." He gazed down at her, and brushed his thumb across her full bottom lip. "I know how you ache, and I want so desperately to ease that ache."

She shook her head hard. "I cannot be the woman you need."

"You are the woman I want."

"I would hate myself if I allowed you such liberties." Now she looked up at him, her eyes burning. "I cannot betray my vows."

Quietly he replied, "I would have you any way you allow."

Her voice broke. "Please, you mustn't do this."

"Do you want to be free?" This time he murmured the question in her ear, allowing his breath to pass over her bare shoulder. She shuddered and pressed herself against him. "You need a man to show you what you can be, a creature of beauty and mystery. I want to be that man."

She said nothing but tilted her head, giving him more access to her alabaster throat.

He kissed the pulse there. "I would never keep you caged. I would never refuse your advances or belittle you for desiring passion—for craving my touch—for needing me to show you how a woman ought to be worshipped." He reached for her and wrapped his arms around her curved waist, crushing her enticingly full breasts against his velvet evening coat.

He knew this passion erupting between them was forbidden. She was a proper English lady—a married lady, and therefore not for him. He wanted to shout at the injustice of it as he pressed his mouth to the curve of her neck, and fisted his fingers in the heavy folds of her skirts so that his hands would not wander beneath her gown to discover how her wet, hairless quim would feel beneath his fingers.

Why had God tempted him with such a creature if she was not to be his? Why had He stolen his heart and given it to a woman who could never give hers to him?

With a whimper of surrender, she raked her hand through his hair and he moved his mouth along her décolletage, breathing hot puffs of breath along her flesh until he could feel the gooseflesh erupting along her skin. He heard her breaths, panting and urgent and he lifted his head and gazed at her. Slowly her eyelids fluttered open, and she looked at him with such a trusting, honest expression that he could only press forward to meet her mouth.

"I wanted you today—on the boat," she whispered, her beautiful eyes warm with desire. "I've thought of things I want you to do to my body—to me. I… in my dreams—my fantasies—I was with you."

"I will live out your every fantasy."

She watched him and her lips parted, and he knew that this was going to be a kiss like no other he had ever received, or ever given. Angling his head, he captured her face and watched her, felt her breath caress his lips, felt every nerve in his body tense and tighten. In silence, he allowed his mouth to hover atop hers.

"Do you want to be set free?"

"Yes." But then as he was set to touch her lips with his, she looked away, biting her lip. "But I never shall."

"If you were—"

She pressed her finger to his mouth. "I am not free, nor will I ever be."

He whispered, "What if you were? Would you come to me if you were? Would you let me show you what it is to be a woman?"

She traced his face with her fingertip, then slowly she pressed her lips to his mouth in a soft whisper of lips and breath. "Yes. I would come to you."

And then she left him standing alone in the room watching her walk away from him.

Isabella lay staring up at the white net canopy above her. The air was still outside, leaving the room overly warm. Her thin cotton nightrail was damp and clinging to her heat- slicked body. She wondered if it was the effects of the sultry night, or the memories of Julian's hard body pressed to hers that made her skin moist.

She blinked away the image of him pressing closer to her and of his large hands fisting the silk of her skirt. How beautiful he had looked towering above her, with his teal eyes boring their way into her soul. He had known her every thought, her every aching desire. And she had not wanted to hide them from him.

The gossamer web that had been woven around them was not something as fleeting as lust. It was more, something deeper and more profound. Something that made her tremble with desire, with the fear that what drew them to each other may very well be her downfall. She couldn't describe it, the intensity between them. How strange it was, to feel something so powerfully after an initial meeting.

She was being a hopeless dreamer, imagining the possibilities, the thoughts of being his lover, of allowing him to teach her exactly what a woman should be. She wanted to be worshipped by him. God, how much she wanted that. How much she had wanted him to raise her skirts and explore her. How much she had wanted to give in to her desires and allow her weakening resolve to crumble like dust around her.

But she was married... she was a mother, and he was much too young for someone like her to think about. True, he hadn't shown his youthfulness in his demeanor. In that, he was very much a mature man. She sensed somehow that he had been forced to grow up faster than most of the young men of the ton. There was a responsible, experienced aura about him that made her feel they were equals. But his face bore the youthful beauty of a man in his early twenties—so, too, did his body.

She remembered that body, all hot, hard male beneath his velvet embroidered evening coat. Remembered the breadth of his shoulders and the bulging muscles of his arms and the power of his legs as her lower body pressed against his. Even through the numerous layers of ruffled, lace petticoats she had felt his hard thighs, had wondered what it would be like to lie between something so powerfully strong.

He could easily meet her carnal needs, but what was even more surprising and perhaps alarming, was the fact that he met another need in her—a need she had not known was yearning to be met until tonight. It was the need to be understood and accepted. He had understood her, had accepted her sensual nature and sexual neediness, and most importantly he had known how she would feel seeing those lovely, proud creatures housed in their exquisite prison. He had understood *her*.

"My lady!"

Nan's cry echoed down the hall, and Isabella jumped from bed and donned her lace wrapper.

"My lady, come quick! It's his lordship."

Isabella reached for the door and was in the process of opening it when her maid came bursting in, her night cap askew and breathing labored. "What is it, Nan?"

"Fitzgibbons came to my room."

"Langdon's valet? In your room? Why?"

"His lordship, ma'am, he's having a fit. Fitzgibbon didn't know what to do. The servants, you see, they can't understand us. We need you, my lady, to order the servants to fetch a doctor."

"Take me to him," she commanded, brushing past her maid and down the hall where her husband's chamber was.

"If you please, ma'am, please don't go in there. You should order one of the servants or that eunuch that acts as a butler to send for the physician."

"I want to see my husband."

"But ma'am," Nan groaned, wringing her hands together as she fought to keep pace with her. Fitzgibbons had joined them, and was seconding Nan's opinion that she should not go into his lordship's chamber.

"Your ladyship," they both pleaded at once, but Isabella ignored them and threw open the door of her husband's room.

The first thing she saw were the two young women naked on George's bed. They were dark, exotic beauties, with long black hair and kohl-lined eyes. Their bellies were pierced and their sex shaved and decorated with a henna design. The one reached for a scrap of silk and covered herself so that only her lined eyes could be seen peering out behind the pink veil. The other whimpered and cast worried glances at George.

In some part of her brain, Isabella should have processed the fact that George was in the middle of a convulsion, but instead, she saw that he was completely naked and erect. She had never seen him naked before and she was surprised by how fit his body looked to her eyes.

Like a detached voyeur, her gaze roamed up his torso where she saw red lip marks covering his chest and phallus. The women who were on his bed had red painted lips Isabella thought, darting her eyes between her husband and his lovers. She noted that his wrists had been tied with silken bonds and that a scarf was around his neck. Had it been used as a blindfold? She had heard of such games being played to heighten one's arousal and she felt oddly removed, as if she was somehow disembodied. Her stomach rolled and she feared she'd disgrace herself by vomiting.

George let out a loud crowing noise and the sound jolted her from the mental horror and into action. Running from the room she sought the assistance from one of the palace servants. Shouting the orders in her broken Turkish, she managed to successfully send one of them for the physician from the palace.

Running back to her husband's room, she stood outside the door, listening to Fitzgibbon and Nan hurriedly whispering. Good God, she had never known that George was capable of such debauchery. How could she deal with it?

Chapter 4

The wait was so unbearably long and the silence so deafening that Isabella thought she would go mad with fear and hurt. It had been hours since the physician from the sultan's palace had arrived, and still she had not heard a word.

She had not trusted herself to return to her husband's chamber. She had not wanted to see him in such a state. In truth, it was the reality she could not face. She could not bear to look upon George and know that he desired other women over his own wife.

And she had offered herself to him. Isabella squeezed her eyes shut, not wanting to remember her humiliation or the shame that engulfed her when she recalled the pitiful excuses George had offered her. The simple truth was, he rather enjoyed sex— just not sex with her.

The sun was beginning to crest over the hills. The brilliant pink and orange rays beamed off one of the minarets of a mosque, and Isabella squinted against the brightness.

Another sunrise. Another futile, empty day.

"Ma'am?" Nan's voice was followed by a discreet knock. "If you please, ma'am-"

"Come in," Isabella replied, not waiting for Nan to finish.

The door of her chamber opened and she turned to find Nan wringing her hands together. Behind her stood Julian and another man who wore a red fez atop his black curling hair.

She was not dressed to receive visitors. She was still garbed in her nightclothes and her hair was loose about her shoulders. Gripping the collar of her lace wrapper in her hand, she brought it to her neck, the action only tightening the lace across her ample breasts.

"Mr. Julian Gresham, the interpreter, and Doctor Avev, my lady," Nan announced before curtseying.

The physician stepped boldly into her room and motioned with his hands that he wished her to remove her wrapper.

"What is it?" she croaked, stepping back from the man as she clutched her wrapper tight about her neck. "What does he want?"

"He wishes to examine you, Lady Langdon," Julian replied, his voice little more than a soft whisper.

"Examine me! Whatever for?"

"He must check to see if you carry the disease. If you do, you shall require treatment."

Her gaze flew to Julian's. He stood in the doorway, his eyes shielded by his lashes. "What sort of treatment? What disease?"

Julian said quietly, "Your husband has syphilis. It is quite an advanced case, Dr. Avev says. It's already infected his nervous system and brain. That is why he suffered a convulsion."

"Syphilis?" she hissed incredulously. "Why, that is a filthy disease that one picks up from—" she stopped herself before she could say streetwalkers and whores and women who fornicate with man after man.

No, her husband could not have such a disease. He could not! Not after George's vehement disgust for such things as women of loose morals. Had he not accused her of being such a woman? Had he not made her endure his lecture?

But she had found him in bed with two women—women who were obviously concubines—very experienced concubines. She wanted to yell her outrage. Wanted to stomp back into his room and declare with the same amount of venom that she thought him nothing but a hypocrite. While she had been the dutiful, obedient, *sexless* wife, he had been betraying his wedding vows and fornicating with God only knew how many women.

"You do understand that it is passed through sexual intercourse," Julian asked carefully, his gaze finally meeting hers. It lingered on her face before slowly descending to her breasts. He took his time studying her, and she fought the urge to shield the contours of her breasts with her arm.

Had he seen those women in her husband's room? Is that why she detected a pitying look in his eyes? Did he think she was unable to satisfy her husband's carnal desires? Did he think her not pretty enough to induce the appropriate amount of passion in her husband? She did not want to see that expression of compassion in his eyes. She felt extremely exposed and vulnerable, having George's shameful secret exposed. And damn George for making her feel shame. But what was even more mortifying was knowing that Julian must be speculating about the intimacies of her marriage bed.

"You must be examined, Lady Langdon," Julian said. "It is the only way to tell if your husband has passed it on to you."

"I may assure you, I do not have the disease."

"Why is that?"

The question hung heavy between them and Isabella felt her face flame red. "Surely you don't need the particulars. Suffice it to say, I do not have the disease."

"Why?"

He wanted her to say the words. She saw the determination in his eyes. How was it he knew her so well? How could he know this secret of hers? She set her mouth and stayed silent.

But he persisted. "Why is it not possible for you to have contracted the disease, Lady Langdon?"

He was daring her and damn him he was determined to hear exactly why she didn't have syphilis. And determined as he was to hear it, she was just as determined not tell him a blasted thing.

Turning magnificently on her heel, she gave him her back as she summoned up all the considerable pompous posturing she had learned over the years in society. Steeling her shoulders, Isabella kept her gaze on the rising sun that shone through her window.

"Leave now. It is much too bold for you to be standing inside my bedchamber. In my culture, it is not done for a man who is not a woman's husband to be in her chamber."

"How long?" he whispered and she heard the door close behind the doctor, and realized that they were now alone. His hands reached for her shoulders, and he smoothed his fingers down her arms. "How long since he has taken you in his arms and made love to you?"

"Don't," she pleaded and she hated that she could hear her resolve weakening in the word. She hated how she allowed her back to release its tension and be molded to his chest. She hated how she wanted him to press his body against hers.

"How long since you had a man inside you?" She closed her eyes and allowed herself to drown in the sensation of his face pressed into her hair.

"I released the peacocks last night," he murmured into her curls. "I would release you too if I could."

"Julian, please," she said huskily as his fingers brushed her hair over her shoulder, baring her neck.

"Have you ever had a man kiss every inch of your skin?" He pressed his warm mouth against her neck. "Have you ever had him explore every part of you with his hands, his mouth, his tongue?"

"Please," she whimpered. But was it a plea for him to stop, or to ignore her protest?

She felt him reach around her waist for the sash of her wrapper. He undid it slowly, teasing her with the movements of his fingers and his breath against her neck. Her legs shook as he slid the lace from her shoulders and kissed his way down her arm until the wrapper fell silently to the carpet.

"How long since a man has slipped your nipple into his mouth and suckled you till your womb clenches and you ache for release?" Never, she wanted to scream, but she could not. She could only gasp as Julian's large hand cupped her breast. His hot palm pressed into her soft flesh as he rubbed his hand along her nipple, sending it straining against her nightrail.

"It has been far too long, hasn't it, Isabella?"

He turned her to face him and she watched his hot gaze pass over her face down to where his hand cupped her breast. He pulled the satin ribbon that held the neckline of her nightrail together then slipped one long finger beneath the muslin and moved it aside, exposing the swell of her breast.

Unable to stand the torture, she looked down and saw how he used his fingers to feel her and send her nipple and areole puckering. Sharp stabs of need shot through her, straight to her belly, and suddenly she felt the need to curl her fingers in his hair and guide his mouth to her breast.

George had never done anything like that with her breasts. She had ached for him to explore her, but he never had.

As if he was aware of her desires, Julian lowered his head to her breast and closed his eyes, running the tip of his tongue along her searching nipple. The sharp spark of desire ignited deep in her belly and sent her knees weakening and she reached for him, her fingers biting into his upper arms—arms that felt so solid and strong beneath his jacket.

She watched as he curled his tongue around her nipple, then sipped it gently between his lips, sucking her. Arousal swept through her and she reached for his thick, silken hair and ran her fingers through it, clutching it tightly as he built the pressure up inside her. Not even her own fingers tugging at her nipples felt this arousing. Julian's mouth was pure decadence, and she encouraged him further with little moans and whimpers.

He lifted her up and turned her so that she was kneeling on the bed and his mouth was level with her breasts. He was pulling the other shoulder of her nightgown down so that the muslin was resting against her waist and both her breasts where exposed to his hungry gaze.

"How could he not have feasted on these?" he rasped as he cupped her and brought her breasts together in his hands. "I want to do so many things with these breasts. I could look at you forever. I could feast on you forever."

"Yes," she said in a long rush of breath and whispered words as he ran his tongue along both nipples. He released her, nuzzling the scented valley of her breasts before capturing one nipple between his teeth and nibbling gently so that she called out and was forced to smother the sound in his hair.

His hands slid down her waist to grasp her buttocks and he cupped her, pushing her forward so that he took her breast into his mouth and suckled her fiercely as he kneaded her bottom. His finger found the cleft of her sex through her gown and he pressed his finger against her, wetting the fabric. "Have you dreamt of a man suckling you here?"

He slid the fabric along her sex and the pad of his thumb found her clitoris. She sucked in her breath as he passed his thumb lightly over the muslin. "You'll be very sensitive with no hair, and your skin will feel supple, the finest of silk against my lips and tongue. And that makes me so damn hard waiting to see you, wanting to see what your shaven quim looks like beneath my mouth."

She moaned as he slid down her body and put his mouth to her sex, blowing hot breath through her dampened nightrail.

"You need it, don't you? My mouth down here, tasting, licking... *eating.*"

"Oh, God," she cried as she felt his mouth press against her. She felt the firm, wet tip of his tongue thrusting between her sex until he could flick her clitoris and she wanted to beg him to rip the gown from her body so that she could feel that hot, hard tongue on her skin. Thrusting her hips back so that his finger could enter her, he groaned and cupped her sex, rubbing her with his palm as it lay atop her nightgown.

"You're so bloody wet." His eyes had darkened to a glistening teal as he gazed up at her. "You yearn for it."

"I yearn for you."

"Tell me how long it has been since you've had a cock filling you?"

"More than two years." Two years of waiting and dreaming. "And before that, he hardly ever came to me. He never wanted this, never desired this with me."

"How could he have resisted?" He ran his hand along her mound as his other hand pressed into her rounded hip. "How could he not ache to be inside you? To possess you as a man should possess a woman."

"Because I am a wife," she said between breaths, knowing that she must stop this madness. "I am a mother. I should not be doing this, I should not be enjoying this, but suffering through—" she moaned as he circled her clitoris with his long, tapered finger.

"You are a woman first." She shook her head but he pressed his finger against her mouth as he continued to rub her with his hand. "A woman blossoms under a man's sexual embrace. A man wants that blossoming, to know that he alone is responsible for it."

He lowered his mouth to hers and ran his tongue along the seam of her mouth. "I wish I had you first. If I had, you can be assured that I would have allowed you to become everything you wanted. I would have given you everything you ever desired if only I could have had you in my bed. Someday I will see you shudder beneath me. One day, you will blossom under my love and care. I will wait until the day I can worship you as you want— as *I* want."

And then he brought his mouth down slow and soft against hers. Fisting his hand in her hair, he angled her head so he could taste her and she opened her mouth to him and allowed him to search between her lips with his tongue. He kissed her long and slow, his tongue moving with hers, his hand fisting and loosening in her hair.

It was a kiss with no ending, and soon she was so needy, so reckless that she was clutching him to her and rubbing herself shamelessly against his hard body and the large, erect fold of his trousers.

"You are going to need a lot of loving, Isabella. And one day," he said softly, "I will give it to you."

Reluctantly, Isabella pulled away from Julian and the temptation he was offering. What sort of wanton was she, to be seeking her pleasure with another, while her husband lay gravely ill? As tempting as the prospect was to go lie down with Julian in her bed, she could not do it. She was a married woman. She had promised, before God, to uphold her marriage vows in times of good and bad. She was not ready to forsake her word, even though her body was crying out for her to do so.

Mercifully, Julian seemed to understand the struggle within her. Tenderly he stroked her cheek with the tip of his finger. Their gazes met, and she saw the regret shining in his eyes. He did not press her, and she was thankful for that. Isabella was certain that the strength of her convictions would not rise once more if Julian chose to continue with his kisses. To resist him once had been nearly impossible, but a second time...

"I will leave you," he said, his voice husky. "I'll go immediately."

Nodding, she looked away, unable to watch him walk to the door. *Yes, go,* she silently replied. *And never come back again. I can forget you. I can forget you…*

Isabella was still repeating those words long after Julian had quit the room.

The water rippled against the prow of the ship. The tide was rising steadily and soon the ropes would slip away from the dock and the waves of the sea of Marmarma would carry the ship out to the Mediterranean and then to the Atlantic, carrying them home to England.

Two sailors in blue tunics and white breeches strode down the dock to where Isabella stood with trunks and luggage piled high around her.

"Got 'is lordship settled in 'is berth, Lady Langdon," the red-headed sailor said with a smile. "Right feisty, 'e is. Should 'ave no problems managin' the voyage back 'ome."

"Thank you, Mr. Fredricks. My thanks for tolerating my husband's temper. He is not himself."

Mr. Fredricks grinned, then winked at her before hefting a trunk containing her gowns on to his shoulder. "I'm not certain I believe that bit, my lady. I think 'is lordship is just as 'e always was. Now then, a few more minutes and we'll bring ye aboard. The moon is 'igh in the sky, and the wind is almost up enough to set us out to sea."

She nodded and curled the strings of her reticule tightly around her fingers, aware of a towering, brooding presence behind her. Julian had said not a word since he had brought her and George to the docks. It had been more than a week since he had kissed and touched her, and she found that the time she had to endure with him now, waiting for the ship to be loaded, was unbearable.

He had tried to come to her, over and over, in fact; but the truth was she had avoided him. She had scarcely left her room for fear she would run into him in the darkened halls. She had not trusted herself to deny him one more time. In fact, she knew if she were faced with his offer of a heated coupling, she would agree, without any consequences to the future.

"Right then, Lady Langdon," Mr. Fredricks announced as he hefted another trunk onto his shoulder. "I'll escort you up next."

Isabella gripped her reticule even tighter at the same time a large warm hand reached out to her, peeling her fingers from their death grip on her reticule and slowly entwining his fingers between hers.

"I regret that I was a gentleman that morning in your chamber. I should not have listened to my conscience and let you go. Had I known you would be leaving Constantinople—*leaving me*, I would have taken you right there, on your bed or against the wall. I would have made it so that you couldn't possibly leave."

She looked down at their hands and felt the same stab of regret. Secretly she wished he hadn't been the gentleman, either.

"I want to feel your lips against mine once more."

She turned and saw that they were alone on the dock, with the exception of a few sailors who were not even looking their way. George was tucked safely in bed, too weak to do more than sleep and growl demands at everyone, and the moon had slipped behind a cloud, cloaking the dock in blackness.

And she was leaving Constantinople. Leaving Julian—forever. And suddenly there was no need greater or more potent than to kiss him once more.

She allowed him to tilt her chin up with this finger, allowed him to skim his finger down her cheek. "May the wind be with you and not against you," he whispered as he lowered his mouth to hers. "May you arrive in England safe and well, your spirit unbroken."

Tears filled her eyes, and this time she did not stem their flow, but instead allowed them to fall freely. He brushed them away with his thumb and lowered his mouth further till his lips touched hers.

"May your body never forget mine."

Oh God, never! Never would she forget the feel of Julian. And then she gasped as he ran his fingertips along her breast, and despite the layers of her gown and corset, her nipple hardened.

"May your body yearn for me until I come for you. May you ache with desire and the need to feel me deep inside you." His gaze flickered to her eyes and she saw his pupils dilate in the dim moonlight. "May your heart never forget me."

And then he kissed her, heedless of anyone around them. And for the second time in her life, she tossed duty to the wind and allowed herself to feel nothing but the pleasure he gave her.

"Will your heart forget me?" she asked as she slipped out of his arms, but his hand held fast to hers and she tried to step away again, but he refused to release her.

"My heart is yours, Guzelle. Never forget it. I will come for you. It is our destiny. Believe in that, I do."

As she stood on deck, her gloved hand trembling against the railing, the wind rippling the folds of her traveling gown, Isabella watched as the dock grew further and further away, and still she could make out the lone silhouette of Julian standing alone beneath the moonlight, watching the sails of her ship fade into the black night.

"Left somethin' behind 'ave ye?" Mr. Fredricks said as he came to stand beside her.

"Yes," she whispered, looking away so that the young man would not see the tears streaming down her face. But her gaze refused to stop straying to the dock where she could still see the faint blur that was Julian. She had left something behind, her heart, and she feared her soul as well.

"All will be well, my lady. In a month you'll be back home, and everything will be back to normal and as it should be."

"How very comforting," she mumbled, realizing she could now no longer see Julian and she turned away, feeling the shame of tears, tears she could not control, tumble down her cheeks.

She did not want to go back to normal, to the way it had been for the past

Chapter 5

Mayfair, London
1851
Another meal, another evening—alone.

Isabella looked up from her blue Wedgwood plate and down the length of the long, dining table. The high gloss of the mahogany veneer was covered in an elegant white damask. All twelve of the chairs, except hers, sat empty.

She was dressed in a new rose silk charmeuse gown, complete with a champagne-colored lace flounce, and her throat was adorned with a diamond necklace that reached the valley of her breasts. Isabella felt a keen sense of disappointment that all her preparations for a special dinner at home were for naught.

"You may tell cook to serve supper, Henry."

The footman to the right of the door bowed. "As you wish, ma'am."

Raising her wine glass, Isabella sipped at the red wine, refusing to give in to the urge to fiddle with her necklace. It was a nervous habit, she knew, and one she must break if she was to venture out into society once again.

The door swung open and expecting the footman, she looked up and saw that her son Gordon was sauntering into the room.

"Allo, 'ol mum," he said teasingly before kissing her affectionately on the cheek. "You look especially lovely tonight."

She knew her eyes were alight with the love she had for her child, and her son, despite what he said to the contrary, still enjoyed seeing that love shining in her eyes. "Thank you, Gordon. Will you not take a seat?"

"I'm sorry, mother, but I can't. I promised Uncle Ferdie I would accompany him to White's tonight."

She tried to smile and remember that her son was a grown man now. He was nearly seventeen and had been the Earl of Langdon since George had passed away three and a half years ago. Ferdie, her brother-in-law, had frequently informed her it was well past time she saw to cutting loose the apron strings.

"I suppose you'll be dining out yet again with your uncle."

"I am, but I promise you that very soon you and I shall spend the entire day together, just as we did when father was alive."

Another voice added from the doorway, "And I shall join you."

Gordon looked over his shoulder and smiled. "And so you shall, brat."

"Minnie," Isabella murmured, holding out her hand to her daughter. "You look absolutely lovely in that shade of green. It goes very well with your blonde curls."

Minnie held out her wide skirts and twirled around. "Thank you, mama."

"Will you be dining with me, tonight?"

"I fear not," her daughter replied, wincing in supplication. "You haven't forgotten that tonight is Beatrice Simpson's sixteenth birthday party, have you? You promised me I could spend the night."

"Of course," she said, trying to keep the sadness from her voice. "How could I forget? You've been buzzing about it for a fortnight. Well," she said, hoping the smile she gave them appeared genuine. "It looks like I am on my own for the evening."

"We'll make it up to you, mum." Gordon flashed her his easy, charming smile. "Soon I won't have to be with uncle so much. I'm certain that once I attain my majority, Uncle will allow me more length to my leash. Good night, mum."

Isabella kissed her son on the cheek and did not give in to the urge to ruffle his golden curls. He was not a little boy.

"Good bye, mama," Minnie called with a wave as she followed her brother from the dining room.

As she watched the door close behind her children, Isabella felt the heaviness of loneliness creep into her breast. Then the door opened again.

"Mum," Gordon said, peeking around the door, his brown eyes alight with mischief. "We're glad you've gotten rid of your widow weeds. It's been far too long since you've been in mourning for Papa." He smiled. "You look much prettier in rose silk than black crepe."

She didn't bother to her hide her smile. "Thank you for noticing, Gordon."

He winked at her. "I notice everything."

The house settled to an eerie silence once the children had gone, and in solitude, Isabella ate her meal, contemplating what she was going to do to fill the rest of her days. Gordon was an earl, with an earl's responsibilities. He had no further need of the mothering she had provided him with over the years. What he needed was a man's guidance now. And although Minnie was not yet sixteen, she, too, was growing up and spreading her wings.

"If you please, ma'am," Tolland, her butler said as he held out a silver salver. "Lady Pembridge is here to see you."

"Send her in, Tolland, please."

Emma, Lady Pembridge, blew in through the door in a swishing whirl of lilac silk and pink lace. "Oh, good, just in time for dinner," she said with a gay laugh.

Emma took a glass of wine from one of the footman and winked at her from above the rim of the glass. Isabella could tell, just by the excited animation in her friend's eye, that she had a new and more than likely scandalous bit of gossip to tell her.

"Thank you, Henry," Isabella said once Emma's plate was filled with beef and Yorkshire pudding. "We will call if you are needed again."

He bowed and turned on his heel, taking the other footman with him and then closing the door softly behind them.

"How fabulous you look," Emma cried, nearly squealing with exuberance. "I vow, I thought I was going to have to bury you wearing black crepe. Now then, tell me, how does it feel to be wearing a lovely evening gown again and showing off those beautiful shoulders?"

Liberating—frightening. She had not stayed in mourning for the past three and a half years because she had mourned her husband's loss. No, the reason she kept up the charade was because she was afraid. Afraid of what her future held, afraid to leave the house and venture into the ton. Afraid of what she might want once again.

"You could not have loved him *that* much, Bella, that you stayed in mourning for an extra year."

"Six months," Isabella corrected, before sipping her wine.

"Two and one half years is the minimum required time for mourning one's dearly departed husband. George doesn't deserve to be mourned an extra day."

Emma was the only person who knew exactly what her marriage to George had been. She had confided all to Emma, except her obsession with the memory of Julian. That, her friend did not need to hear. That secret would go to the grave with her.

As Isabella sat looking down the length of the table at her friend, she was swept back to the night she had watched the dock slide further and further away. How many nights had she relived those moments, that kiss, his words…

She had not heard from him, save for one letter that he had written on behalf of the sultan, Abdul Mecit, upon hearing the news of her husband's death en route to England. Somehow, she had been disappointed that he had not renewed his sentiments—his words had been so powerful, so full of raw emotion that she was certain he had meant them to the depths of his soul, but then that was the beauty of youth. Emotions were generally felt much stronger, but alas, they were more fleeting.

"Well, I'm very glad you've decided to toss out those hideous mourning clothes and return to life. Now then," Emma said with a laugh. "What do you say about joining me at Cremore Gardens tonight?"

"Cremore Gardens! That is no place for us! It is not done for gently bred ladies to be seen at that pleasure park."

"That, my dear friend, is entirely the point. C'mon," Emma groaned, "Shed your cloak of motherly duty and enjoy a night of freedom."

Isabella laughed and shook her head. "What precisely shall we do when we arrive there?"

"Attend a very fine performance of *The Sultan's Concubine* in the red tent room."

Isabella tried for a stern tone. "I'm certain that is not the least bit appropriate."

"Of course it's not. That's why we're going."

Inside the red pavilion that was supposed to resemble a Sultan's harem, Moroccan lanterns rocked slowly from the iron beams that held up the fabric in the shape of a tent. Incense burned on braziers, an exotic mix of spice and floral and wood scents, combined with one very strange, very evocative smell that brought her back to the moment Julian had crushed her to his chest. He had smelled of that particular spice. Suddenly she yearned to know what it was. If she did, she could purchase a sachet of the herbs and set it beneath her pillow, scenting her dreams of him.

"Was this what it was like at the Sultan's palace?" Emma asked.

Isabella considered. "Well, this is a bit more Moorish than Turkish, but yes, the colors were just as vibrant and the interiors just as sumptuous."

"I wonder if we are going to witness a lot ravishing in this performance? I've always wanted to experience a wicked evening of ravishment with an Eastern despot while lounging on a divan," Emma teased.

"By the sounds of things, Emma, you will see that, and likely much more."

Isabella's gaze lingered on the stage, draped with a white silk curtain edged in gold and trimmed with lavish cascades of gold and red tassels. They had been informed when they purchased their tickets for the play that it was a magic lantern show, with the characters staying behind the curtains, their silhouettes shining through the opaque silk, while brilliant light from the gas lamps illuminated the actors.

The atmosphere of the pavilion, combined with the seductive lure of the screen left nothing to the imagination; this play was going to be nothing short of forbidden titillation.

A man, dressed in Cossack trousers, a long red tunic with yellow sash and a white turban with a large egg-shaped sapphire in its center, appeared to the right of the stage. The crowd hushed and the flickering gas lanterns fizzled above them, darkening the pavilion enough so that the orange glow from the lanterns shimmered off the vibrant silks.

"Behold fair citizens of Constantinople," the man began in a parody of a Turkish accent. "Our sultan has wed his *haseki*."

"What is a *haseki*?" Emma whispered.

"His favorite woman," Isabella answered.

"It is their wedding night," the narrator continued, "and the Sultan has come to claim his wife." A brilliant light flashed to life behind the curtain. An image of a woman, her curved waist and hip illuminated by the light shone out beyond the screen. The woman stretched along the divan while she raised her arm above her head, revealing the curved swell of a very large breast. Male hoots and whistles of appreciation for the buxom lovely rent through the air, and it was minutes before they could be quieted and the play proceed.

"Our sultan has wed a woman of great and rare beauty," the man continued, lowering his voice for dramatic effect. "She was bought at the slave market, a beauty possessed of white skin and pale hair. A beauty not of the Sultan's land."

"An English beauty," a young drunken lord bellowed.

The actor said, "And what do you think our eastern sultan will do with our western virgin?"

Isabella felt her heart begin to race and she knew it was not due to the erotic display of flesh, or the innuendo of what she would soon be witnessing. It was something else, a strange sort of awareness that she could not identify.

She felt far too warm, and her head spun as if she were about to faint. She reached behind her and gripped the bench, steadying herself, trying to fight against her racing heart.

And then she felt it, a soft brush against her fingers. She froze, tried to ignore the sensation, but she felt it again. This time, something soft and fluffy, like a feather, pressed beneath her fingers.

"I... I'm not feeling well," she mumbled to Emma as she clutched the mysterious object in her hand. "The incense, I think. I just need a moment to clear my head."

"I'll come with you. It isn't safe to be alone here, and especially in the dark."

"No, truly, I just need a moment. And there is enough light coming from the exit. I'm certain I saw a refreshment tent set up alongside this one. I shall only be a minute."

Emma said, "Don't be long, and for heaven's sake, be careful."

Isabella stepped out of the aisle, thankful that they had taken the last two spots on the bench. It would not have been easy to crawl her way over knees and legs in the dark.

Clutching whatever had been pressed into her hand, she walked down the grassy path to the exit flap of the pavilion. She had no idea what she was doing leaving the safety of her seat— she only knew she must.

Once in the light, she uncurled her fingers and saw that in her palm she held one green and one pink peacock feather. The quill had been cut away, leaving only the multi-colored eye. Attached to what little remained of the quill was a note.

Do you believe in destiny?

Chapter 6

Julian stepped out of the darkness and into the flickering gas light, waiting what seemed like forever for her to turn around and see him.

For three and a half years he had been waiting for this day. Six months ago he had returned to England, expecting her to be out of mourning for the husband who had brought her nothing but grief and heartache. He had been most disappointed and aggrieved that she had not been through grieving for her unfaithful George.

His hunger had only increased, becoming almost an obsession in the ensuing months while he waited for her to shed the safety of her widow weeds and come to him so that he could show her everything her husband should have. She had kept him waiting until he thought he would go mad with wanting.

So many times he had nearly ruined his plans by stalking up the stairs of her townhouse and demanding entrance. He had envisioned so many different kinds of welcomes, so many scenarios to pleasure her with. But he had resisted, waiting for her to come to him.

Did Isabella have any idea how damned difficult it was to come back to a society that ridiculed him and despised his mother? A society that accepted him only when they were face to face, but who scorned and laughed at him behind his back? It was damned hard, but he would walk through fire for her. He had endured these last six months in London just for her.

She saw him at last, and her eyes, wide and large, widened even more as his identity registered in her brain. How beautiful she looked, standing in the gaslight, its warm glow kissing her bare shoulders. Her skin was glowing peach and he began to feel himself harden as he thought about kissing every inch of her soft, supple flesh.

Need coiled in his belly and he took two steps to stand before her. He reached for her, his fingers curving around her shoulders, sinking into her soft skin. He was lost. "I've come for you," he growled before he crushed her mouth with his.

She went slack and crumbled into his embrace, kissing him with an open, searching mouth, clutching his hair in a fierce hold as she struggled to bring him closer while he sucked at her lips and tongue.

Wanton and willing, she told him without words that she remembered what had happened between them. Already she was rubbing her pelvis against his, searching for the pleasure she knew—*remembered*—he could give her.

Tearing his mouth from hers, he kissed a path on her cheek to her ear as the magic lantern show continued on beyond the canvas wall behind them. "Five and a half years, isn't? You must be aching for it. Are you crying for it?" he asked in a husky whisper as he ran his hands along her hips and started to pull at the silk skirt and the layers of heavy petticoats beneath.

"Julian," she panted, trying to kiss him, but he angled his head so that he could nibble on her jaw and the tender flesh of her throat. He wanted to hear her admit her need.

He groaned as his hand found the front of her drawers and he discovered, as he flattened his palm against her mound, that she had already dampened the India muslin with her arousal. "You're weeping for it, aren't you?"

"Yes," she said on a frantic, eager moan. "I ache, I burn."

"For any man, or only for me?"

She tipped her head against the wooden support at her back and looked at him with such honesty that he felt the edge of his anger melt away. His hunger, however, only raged more out of control.

"Only for you," she whispered. "I have lain awake all these nights thinking of you, dreaming of you. My body would not forget you. My heart could not, either."

"You said that if you were free, you would come to me."

"Yes."

"Are you free, Guzelle?"

"Yes."

"Then come."

He drew her into the darkness and outside of the pavilion where they were alone beneath the moon. Grasping her hand in his, he pulled her behind him and rounded the corner of one of the buildings that acted as a storage facility. They were now completely alone, and he did not bother to try the door. It was locked, and frankly he could not wait another second to feel himself sliding inside her body.

"Julian!"

His name came in a soft, startled cry from her lips as he brought her up against the stone building and pressed his body against hers. Isabella felt his hands, those large, hot hands, snaking beneath her gown, rifling up her petticoats until he found the opening of her drawers and slipped his hand inside, cupping her with his palm.

Isabella realized that nothing had ever felt this good, this ache that built and built inside her began to tighten and coil and she shoved her hips forward like an artless hussy. He met her movement with one of his own and she felt his length press into her thigh and belly. A wicked thrill shot through her when she realized how long and thick he was beneath his woolen trousers. She shivered in eager longing, just thinking of all that length thrusting inside her, filling her full of him.

He said, "Slick and wet. I can feel your arousal seeping between your swollen lips. Tell me you're ready for my tongue and cock."

She gasped, shocked, aroused by his common talk. She had never been treated as anything but a lady—by everyone. But when Julian talked to her like this, she discovered that a tiny thrill of forbidden danger slithered along her nerves and she craved more of it—craved everything he would show her, every word he would utter in her ear.

Julian pressed his cock into her hip, captured her lips between his, and began thrusting his tongue in and out of her mouth in an innuendo of what was to come. "I, too, am already wet. We are both so needy, so hungry for each other," he rasped as he tore his mouth from her and bit gently at her neck with the tips of his teeth. "Your body needs what I can give you, and Lord knows that I need—*I must*—feel your quim squeezing me, milking my climax from me."

She was mewling and writhing against him. He could feel the desire emanating from her, he only wished he could see it in her eyes, but it was so blasted dark he could see nothing. And he wanted to see, wanted to know what she looked like beneath these petticoats. He had thought about it enough during the years, it was well past time he knew.

"What color is this thatch?" he asked, his voice much too harsh as he pressed his palm harder against her and ran his middle finger between her plump, wet sex.

"Blonde," she panted and he felt her slippered foot brush his calf until her ankle was pressing into his hip.

He ran his mouth down her throat to suck at the swells of her breasts and he dipped his tongue beneath her bodice searching for her nipple so he could tongue it, but it was imprisoned behind her tight corset.

Concentrating instead on the wetness engulfing his hand, he stroked her intimately. She cried out on a gasping breath before she clutched his arms as he lightly passed his finger over her clitoris. "You could come just like this, couldn't you? You're so hot and aroused that only the little grazing of my finger on your clit would have you falling apart in my arms."

She shoved against him eagerly searching for his touch. He did not stroke her clitoris, but slowly slid his finger down to her opening, tracing the rim of her vagina with his fingertip. He did not penetrate her. He had waited too long for this moment and the only thing he wanted her to feel was his cock stretching her wide.

The image of thrusting into her tight, hot body fueled his blood, and he felt the front of his trousers dampen with his anticipation. Fumbling with the fastening of his trousers, Julian finally freed himself and was reaching for her hand when he felt her fingers curl around his cock.

He groaned and shoved himself into her hand, and she began to run her fingertips up and down his length. It felt so good to at last feel her hand pumping him.

He moved his palm so that his hand was between their bodies, and he sought her clitoris, erect and pulsating beneath the pad of his fingertip. Furiously he flicked the sensitive flesh, over and over, matching the rhythm of her hand around his shaft as she pleasured him, tossing him off like a skilled concubine.

She was panting in little breaths that made his blood pound, and he was so bloody close to spending, but he could not stop until he felt her shudder against him. So he worked her harder and even when she began to tremble and shake and arch her back, he gave her more, until she shattered in his arms and cried out his name and begged him, the word *please* a keening plea from deep in her chest.

"I shall give you what you want. I shall give it to you hard because we both yearn for it that way, don't we, Isabella? We both need it this way so that we can exorcise this imprisoned passion that is nearly consuming us."

"Yes, Julian!"

He pulled out of her hand and thrust his cock deep inside her. She was tight, so bloody tight. He penetrated her in one long stab and she groaned, a beautiful wanton sound, so beautiful that he had to hear it again, so he pulled out and entered her again swiftly, feeling the rush of wetness engulf him as he lodged himself further inside her.

Without giving her more time, he reached for her hand, bringing it above her head and against the wall so that he clutched it as he thrust up deep inside her. Harder and harder, he thrust. Higher and higher she moved up against the wall as his cock stabbed her deeper.

"Can you take more? Do you want it, all of me inside you?"

"Yes," she cried, clutching his hand as he thrust his hips upward until she could feel all of him pulsing inside. He waited till she was full of him before he began thrusting and breathing against her, and Isabella had never known something so wild and unrelenting could feel so beautiful and right.

"I'm going to fill you," he said on a hard moan, and she felt him tense and still as he ejaculated, hot and fast deep inside her. "And now I'm going to take you home and do it all over it again, the whole night through. Let me pleasure you, let me show you a woman's pleasure."

✤❧⟨ᙏᙎ⟩❧✤

Rain and wind pelted the glazed windows as another roll of thunder rumbled throughout the sky. The room was gloomy in the early morning light and Isabella found herself watching the black dots of rain shadowing along the walls and the furniture.

Bringing the paisley cashmere shawl up around her shoulders, Isabella looked away from the rivulets of rain racing down the glass and back to her desk where two peacock feathers and a torn piece of paper sat staring up at her. *Do you believe in destiny?*

How those words had haunted her. She had not slept for the past two nights thinking of those words, and recreating every frenzied moment she had spent in Julian's arms. What the devil had she done? What madness had she succumbed to—and with such terrifying ease?

Isabella did not want to contemplate what she might have done had Emma not left the pavilion in search of her. Only the fear of Emma discovering her had been enough to tear her from his arms. Only the threat to her reputation could make her see reason. And she had the very unnerving thought that it wasn't truly her own reputation she cared for, but that of her children. If she didn't have Gordon and Minnie's futures to worry about, she would have followed Julian to the bowels of Hades, if only to have him do what he had done to her all over again. That, she thought with a little shiver, was the power of Julian Gresham and the sensual hold he had over her. She would likely give up everything, ignore every edict she had ever been taught, just to share her body with a man she barely knew.

"All right, what the devil is going on?"

Isabella's gaze shot up from the feathers atop her desk. "Good grief, Emma," she cried, placing a trembling hand over her heart. "You've scared me half to death."

Emma breezed into the room, quirked a brow and took up a cushion on the settee that was positioned to the right of Isabella's writing desk. "I've given you a day and a night to tell me what is going on. Since you have not seen fit to confide in me, I have come to make it my business."

Isabella reached for the pen that lay atop the silver pen rest and mindlessly toyed with it. She needed something to occupy her nervous fingers and steady her thoughts.

"I have no notion what you mean, Emma. As I said the other night, I felt unwell. More than likely it was from all the incense being burned in that tent. I would not put it past the directors of the play to have laced the incense with opium—it seemed the sort of performance that would be heightened by such a thing."

"Opium?" Emma asked archly. "Hardly, Bella. Your hair, as you know, was in a complete state of disarray and your skirts were wrinkled."

Isabella felt herself blush. "I have already explained that I was violently ill. It is not easy, you know, being a lady while throwing up in the bushes." *It was not easy to look like a lady when you've been thoroughly seduced by a lusty, younger man who took you standing up.*

"You can tell me, you know." Emma reached out to grasp Isabella's hand. "I am your best friend, Bella. I won't tell a soul."

How could Isabella speak to her friend of what she had done? She could barely even admit it to herself.

She was ashamed—so deeply embarrassed by her actions. She had been wanton and eager and he must think her the easiest of trollops. She could not bear to think of how uninhibited she had been, the words she had allowed him to say to her—the words she had liked to hear him utter. And yet, no matter how hard she tried to convince herself otherwise, she didn't regret one second of it. She would not change anything about that primal, heated coupling. For that all too brief moment, she had felt alive—every inch of her, every nerve, every patch of skin that covered her body—all of her had trembled with passion and life. She could become addicted to that feeling. It would not be difficult to find herself dependent upon Julian and the passion he inspired in her.

But it was over. There was no reason to discuss such things with Emma because she was not going to see him again. She had ignored his letters, the one he had sent around the next morning and evening. She could not meet him as he asked. She could not risk her safe way of life.

What he was offering was something that could not last. It was best to stop this strange, almost electric spark of energy that seemed to crackle between them before it was too late. Before her heart was completely taken over by a man she could not have.

It would not be too difficult to avoid his company. He did not move in the same circles as she, so she would not have to meet him at any social events. He was younger and naturally his acquaintances would not be the same as hers. No, she was safe from him. She likely would never encounter him again.

And why did that thought further dampen her spirits?

"Dearest Isabella," Emma said with a sigh.

"Please don't, Emma." Isabella rose from her chair and clutched her shawl to her breasts. "Let it be."

"How can I when I know that you cannot let whatever it is be? You're a wreck," Emma exclaimed with a wave of her hand. "You haven't slept, that much is apparent."

"I… I'm fine now."

"You're not, and it pains me to see you this way. Furthermore it hurts me to know you feel you cannot confide in me. I may be gregarious and perhaps I do talk too freely about a great many things that a woman should not, but upon my honor, Bella, I would never betray your confidence. *Never.*"

"I know," she murmured, stopping by the window and looking down at the water puddles that were rapidly filling the ruts in the road. "I trust you, Emma. It's just that, oh, I don't know," she said, pressing her cheek to the cool glass. "I don't know how I feel about all this."

Emma replied thoughtfully, "I think it's safe to say that you feel a great deal of anxiety. It is not like you to be confused or to feel misguided. You've always known who you are and what you want."

"But I shouldn't want this," she ground out as she closed her eyes. Immediately she saw Julian behind her lids. God help her, she wanted him, wanted everything he would show her.

With a deep, fortifying breath, Isabella opened her eyes and motioned to her desk. She watched her friend pick up Julian's letters and scan them. When she looked up, Emma's eyes were aglow with delight.

"Why shouldn't you desire a man who most obviously desires you? You're a woman in your prime, Bella. You're beautiful and cultured—"

"I have had two children."

"What does that have to do with anything?"

"He is younger than me—*substantially* younger."

"All the better," Emma purred. "One cannot speak too highly of a younger man's merits in bed."

Isabella closed her eyes and tried to forget how wonderfully fit and hard Julian's body was and the strength in him. There was no denying those merits.

"Think of the stamina, my dear," Emma continued. "A younger man can satisfy women like us over and over and still, he will want more."

"He is younger than I. You must see that nothing can come of it. I have

Gordon and Minnie to think about. I cannot be having affairs with younger men, or any man for that matter and still remain respectable, no matter how much I might desire to do so." She added, "I have an obligation to my children. I must be the sort of mother that they can respect. Every decision I make must be in their best interests. My actions can affect not only my reputation but their futures as well, Emma. Don't you see that? The poor choices I make now might very well come back to haunt my children. Surely you realized that men sow their oats; women must only dream of it."

"Gordon is an earl, for heavens sake," Emma snapped. "There is very little that you could do to make some marriage-minded mother and father not desire such a match for their daughter. Gordon will be fine."

"But what of Minnie? What might my actions do to her chances of securing a marriage that she desires? What upstanding man will want to wed the daughter of the woman who has engaged in a wicked affair with a man who is younger than her?"

"So what if he is a man that you cannot see yourself being able to commit to?" Emma said, changing tack quickly. "Is that what you really want at this stage in your life anyway, another man to order you about? So what if he is younger and your liaison will end one day? It is not as though you love this man."

Isabella darted her eyes to the carpet. It would be so easy to love him. She feared she was half in love with him already. And that was totally nonsensical. She barely knew him, yet when she was with him it was as if they had been friends—and lovers—for years. There was something in his eyes, an understanding, an ability to read her thoughts. She knew instinctively that Julian could meet all her needs, the emotional ones as well as her carnal appetites. And that was the real danger Julian posed.

"You must ask yourself what you have to lose if you go to him. And what you will lose if you do not."

A knock on the door drew Isabella's attention away from Emma's probing gaze. "Come in," she called.

"'Allo, mum," Gordon said with a smile as he strolled into the room. "Oh, good day Lady Pembridge," he said, bowing before Emma. "I beg your pardon; I did not realize you were entertaining."

Isabella saw that Gordon was dressed, ready to leave on the week-long vacation that Ferdie had booked for her children. Her heart twisted a bit, knowing that she would be alone yet again.

"I was just leaving," Emma murmured, reaching for her reticule that lay atop the settee.

"You don't have to leave on my account, Lady Pembridge. I've only just come to say farewell to Mother. Minnie and I are off to tour the Lake District with our uncle. We shall be gone the week."

"The week?" Emma asked sliding her a glance. "Well, I do hope you enjoy yourself and that the weather co-operates."

"Much more than it is now," Gordon said, chuckling as he looked out the window.

"Indeed," Emma said with an affectionate smile as she tilted her head and studied Gordon. "My, you've suddenly grown up."

Gordon puffed out his chest and his chin which was cleanly shaved of blond fuzz. "I'm nearly six feet, you know."

"I noticed. You've gotten very tall. Almost a man now."

Gordon flushed a delicate shade of pink. "I like to think I'm a man already, Lady Pembridge."

Emma arched her brow and grinned at Isabella. "A man. Well, I suppose that can only mean that you will not need your mother to be traipsing after you, ensuring that you are not getting into scrapes and that sort."

"Of course not," Gordon cried, before checking his emotions. "Mother has many other duties to attend to."

"Does she? I fear your mother will not like to hear those words, my lord." Emma reached for Gordon's arm. Isabella watched as Emma settled her hand on Gordon's coat sleeve. "She has dedicated her life to you and your sister, and now you tell her she's no longer needed."

Gordon turned impetuously to his mother. "Is that true? For I would not have it so. I would have you living your life for yourself, not for Minnie and me."

Emma peered at her over Gordon's shoulder. Isabella could see that her expression was one of amusement and approval.

He said, "You must take this week to enjoy yourself, mum. I won't go if I think you will be stuck here in this house, alone. I won't go unless you promise me that you will do something that you want to do every day that Minnie and I are gone."

"You have my promise," Isabella said, kissing him lightly on the cheek. "Now go and see Lady Pembridge to the door while I find your sister."

"I mean it," Gordon said as he looked down at her.

When had he grown so tall? When had his chubby little cherub's face become strong and angular, the face of a man? When had she lost her little boy to the man who was now standing before her looking so strong and handsome and caring?

He said simply, "I want to see you happy."

Isabella forced a smile. "I am happy."

"No, you're not," he said in her ear. "But one day I will you see you happy. I've promised myself that."

Chapter 7

Isabella peered up at the sign before her as the rain fell steadily to the ground. The hansom cab had already departed, leaving her standing on the walk as men of business and foreign dignitaries bustled about her, stomping in puddles and muttering about the cursed fog and English drizzle.

She should have been shivering, what with the gray fog cloaking the air and the chill rain that fell around her, dampening her thin velvet mantalet. But instead of chilled she felt oddly warm, as she did when she drank a glass of fine champagne. There was warmth in her blood now, and a slow fire that began low in her belly.

This was it. This was the moment of truth. Could she do it? Could she leave behind her title, her duties to her family and children, and be nothing but Isabella? Could she be just a woman, or was she simply an empty shell without an identity when she removed her titles of lady and mother and society belle?

"Miss?" The doorman, dressed in black and gold livery and white gloves addressed her as he held open the heavy wooden door.

"Good day," she replied, gathering her courage and lifting the hem of her morning gown as she stepped over the widening puddle of water.

"Good day, madam," he murmured in a very polite and courteous tone. "Shall I see you to your room?"

Isabella's step faltered. It was really happening. She had crossed the threshold of Claridge's.

Surely her secret would be safe. Her face was, after all, heavily veiled and with the fog and rain, she was certain that no one had even noticed her standing in front of the hotel. They had all been in such a rush to enter the hotel or the line of carriages parked on the street.

"Your room, Madam?"

"Oh yes, room twenty-eight, please."

The doorman's eyes lit with something akin to interest. "I shall take you there myself."

It was early afternoon and much too soon for polite society to be seen stirring out of doors. It was highly doubtful that anyone of her social circle would have roused themselves this early, and in this terrible weather. She was safe. Her secret would be safe.

As Isabella followed the liveried servant through the opulent reception room to the red and gold carpeted stairs, she could not help but be impressed by the stately ambiance of the hotel. From the glimmering crystal chandelier that hung above their heads to the heavily carved banister her gloved fingers held on to, everything was meant to impress. The width of the staircase alone was impressive, easily accommodating two belled ballgowns without even the skirts touching one another. What a grand entrance one could make descending these stairs.

After reaching the top, the doorman turned left and guided her down the long hall. Isabella felt her heart beating faster and faster as the numbers grew closer. Twenty five, twenty six, twenty seven, she counted, holding her breath as she waited for the door of number twenty eight to appear. But instead of a door, they turned another corner, leading them to a double door that was inlaid with gilt moldings and rosewood panels.

The doorman fished a key from his waistcoat pocket. With a click, the lock turned and he threw open the door, ushering her through. The door immediately closed behind her and once again, Isabella heard the click of the skeleton key in the lock.

"*Wait!*" But it was too late. She could hear the retreating footsteps of the servant.

Turning around, she was met with a long corridor, carpeted in a rich Persian design. On either side of the hall were doors. Some were curiously opened, some closed. She wondered which door was number twenty eight.

Taking a tremulous step forward, she gripped the corded strings of her reticule and walked down the hall, glancing from side to side, waiting to see the gold number two and eight. Instead, she saw that each room was furnished and unoccupied. She passed a room with a dining table and chairs, and another room which appeared to be a small sitting salon. A fire burned in the grate, and she felt as though she was traveling down the corridor of the master suite wing in Langdon's country house.

A plank creaked beneath her half-boots and she paused, her nerves taut and her heart beating a skittish beat. The ticking of a pendulum clock on a demi-lune table beside her made her grip the strings of her reticule tighter. She should just leave.

But then she heard his voice behind her and she found herself frozen to the carpet.

"I thought you wouldn't come."

She stood with her back to him and the silence stretched on, an unbearable taut, static quiet that only made her nerves falter. What was she doing here? What did she know about conducting an affair?

"Can you not bring yourself to look at me?"

She would not turn and look at him.

Julian felt his gut clench, and he allowed his fingers to curl into a tight fist. She had run from him two nights ago. Had not even bothered to send a response back to him after receiving his letters. It was as if she had completely forgotten him. But he knew, somewhere deep in his soul, that Isabella could not forget him, or what they found together. That deep belief was the only thing that kept him sane these past two days as he waited, hour after hour by the window, watching for her.

He had nearly given up hope, had just been stepping away from the window that overlooked Brook Street, when he had seen the black hansom cab stop before the entrance of the hotel. And then he had seen her sitting in the cab. His body had reacted as it always did whenever she was near. He could tell just by the way she carried herself and the set of her shoulders that she was afraid. But she had come, and that was all that mattered.

He watched as she turned slowly on the heel of her boot and faced him. She wore a pink moiré long-sleeved mantelet, elegantly fitted to her waist. From beneath the deep ivory lace cuffs, he saw that her small, slender hands were encased in cream-colored kid gloves. Her fingers trembled against the strings of her reticule.

The skirt of her gown was not hooped, but lay in a pleasing shape, flaring out over her hips from her V-shaped bodice. His gaze slid up her shapely form, lingering briefly over her full, high breasts, and up to her face covered with a dark veil, to the hat that was adorned with pink cabbage roses and feathers. He could not see her face, nor the expression beneath the veil.

He extended his hand to her. "Come to me."

And she did, slowly and with an elegance that entranced him. When she was standing before him, he saw how the shadows of raindrops on the window painted a pattern on her veil. Gloomy. Depressing. But he knew when he lifted the lace from her face, he would see sunlight and beauty.

He reached for the pink ribbon that held her mantelet together and slowly pulled it until it came free in his hand. Then he removed her cloak and placed it on the chair beside him. She was breathing fast and the sound of her rapid, hurried breaths called to him, making his hunger stronger, more difficult to control. But he must control it. He had done a poor job of it the other night. He'd been coarse and frantic, and he had chastised himself for it, wondering if his roughness had been the reason behind her refusal to come to him. He promised himself that if he was ever to have another chance with her, he would not be that way again. He would cherish her, love her as a woman should be loved. She needed this, needed tender loving, the sort of passion that her husband had denied her.

They said nothing and only their hushed breaths and the sound of the rain hitting the window and the distant rumble of thunder could be heard. The shadows played along her exposed neck and the valley of her décolletage, drawing his eyes to her tight-fitting bodice.

"I want to make love to you like this, with the rain shadows dancing and streaking along your body," he murmured as he reached for her veil and slowly raised it, revealing her full lips and pink cheeks. "We will hear only the sound of the rain and our bodies atop one another. I want to hear every sigh." The veil was now raised to her eyes and he unveiled them, watching how they changed from brown to a warm, rich amber. "I want to hear every moan, every whisper, every thrust of my body inside yours. I want you to hear the sounds of passion two bodies make. I want you to know that those sounds are for me, as I make love to you."

He slipped the veil back over her hat before removing the crystal hat pin. He dropped it to the carpet and pulled the bonnet from her hair.

"I want to see you in the middle of my bed, amongst my rumpled sheets."

He was easing the shoulders of her gown down her arms and she was looking at him with such longing that he forced himself to draw out this moment for her—*for them.* "I want to see your hair fanned out on my pillow. I want to open my eyes and find you lying beside me, in my arms, and I want to see you smile. A womanly smile. A smile that tells me you enjoyed what we've done. A secret smile that lets me know you want to do it all over again. I can be anyone you want," he said against her mouth as he framed her face in his hands. "I can be the Western man who is a kind and gentle lover. The sort who has been raised to be a gentleman. I can be the mysterious Eastern man, the sort who knows the ways of love and passion. The man who has studied The Perfumed Garden and Tantra. The man who can show you the exotic ways of making love. The sort who demands that a woman take pleasure in her body."

"I want them both." Her lashes flickered then raised, revealing her amber eyes. "I want the man who is truly you."

"I am both men."

"Then I will have the English gentleman as well as the one who would show me the mysteries to be found in the East. I would have that man show me how to take pleasure in being a woman. I would have him show me how to give him pleasure."

"You would accept both?" This was what he wanted from a woman—total, utter acceptance. Acceptance of his mixed heritage and his darker skin. Acceptance of his birth, the cause of such gossip and scandal that his parents had been forced to find sanctuary in the country for years after. He remembered his devastation when a lover turned him away because he was "nothing more than a half-breed and a penniless second son." Later that woman had pulled the veil from his eyes, showing him the base, cruel nature of humankind, when she learned his maternal grandfather had made him a prince—and she came back to him.

Now all he wanted from Isabella was her acceptance of him—Julian. Not the second son of the Earl of Huntingdon. Not the sultan's cousin, or the Prince of Persia. Just Julian, the man behind the titles and the secrets.

"Yes," she said, gazing up at him, "I want both men, Julian."

No one had ever said such a thing to him. It was as if he had just been given the key to the gate of Heaven. He had always craved this unconditional acceptance and the fact that it was *this* woman, the woman who lit a fire in his belly and sent his need spiraling, that gave him this gift made it all the more profound.

"You'll not regret this. I swear you won't," he vowed to himself as much as her. "I swear it."

She whispered, "Is this wrong? Is it wrong for me, a widow, a mother, to be standing here before you offering myself? Tell me, for I can no longer separate my desires from what is right."

He pulled her close. "You have longed for this, haven't you, Isabella? You've longed for a man to show you pleasure."

She closed her eyes and tilted her head back so that she could feel more of his touch against her lips. "Yes," she said on a breathless sigh. "But not just any man. I've longed for you, Julian."

"I have longed, too. I have waited so very long for this, for you to come to me. And we have waited and longed together to become lovers. Is that not right?"

She nodded and he saw the faintest glimmer of crystal glisten against her eyelash. It twisted and knotted his insides until he thought he could not take another breath. "Is it so very hard for you to admit that you need this?"

"My dignity is all I have."

Her lips were trembling now and a tiny tear cascaded down her cheek. He chased it away with his thumb. He wanted only tears of satiation from her. He did not want this sadness, this confusion.

"All my life I have striven to be good. To be a good wife, a good mother, a..." She bit her lip and tilted her head away, giving his fingers access to her alabaster throat and the bounding pulse in her neck. "I've tried so hard to bury these feelings, to be a proper woman of my class. And I can't do it any longer. And yet I fear somehow that I have made the biggest mistake of my life by coming here."

He exclaimed, "Why, Guzelle, because for the first time you have done what you want without any thought to anyone else? That is what is a mistake, that you have never known the pleasures of indulging yourself."

"I am so selfish." Her voice sounded as though it was beginning to crumble, as if a sob would escape her parted lips at any second. "I have thought of nothing other than you and what enjoyment and fulfillment I will find in your arms. And yet everything I have worked for will be for naught if someone discovers that I've been with you. And even that thought is not enough to prevent me from coming to you, from craving your hands and lips on my body."

His heart was thudding hard and fast in his chest, and he was caught up in the honesty behind her words and the open expression in her lovely face. He never wanted the feeling to end, this feeling that wrapped itself around him when he was with her.

"You must promise me," he said as he lowered his head to hers and pressed his brow against her temple. "You must swear to me that when you are with me you will be your true self. I do not want the society hostess or the proper lady born and bred into the aristocracy. I do not want Lady Langdon beneath me. I want only Isabella, the woman I know lurks within you. Promise me and I will give you everything. I will love you, worship you. I will show you the stars and take you to heaven. But you must promise me that you will be only Isabella when you are with me."

She nodded and he framed her face with his hands. "Undress for me. Show me the woman beneath this gown and the layers of petticoats. I have waited so long to see her—to see *you*."

The skirt and bodice slipped along her hips, and he could not stop his gaze from following the slow descent. She stepped out of the gown, letting fall the layers of petticoats and the white corset dotted with embroidered flowers. The tops of her breasts peeked out at him, and he ran the back of his hand along them so that the smoothness of his nails grazed her warm, scented flesh.

"Your hair. I want to see it down." She reached for the pins, but he stayed her hand. He was overcome with the desire to be the one to let her hair down and shake it free of its pins. He wanted to be the one to run his hand through it and bring her curls over her shoulder.

The carpet muffled the sound of the hairpins falling to the floor. His hands ran through the strands and the ends slid between his fingers and over her shoulders. She had magnificent hair, the color of wheat and honey. It felt like silk, and he knew that he would soon sit behind her as she sat at her dressing table. He would brush it for her and press his mouth to her neck and the soft spot behind her ear, and he would utter erotic words, building her up, increasing her need so that she would be entranced by the sensuality created between them.

"The rain is letting up, and it is time," he said as he lifted her into his arms. "Come to my bed, Isabella. Come to me and let me make love to you in the way I have dreamed of."

Chapter 8

Julian's arms felt strong beneath her as he carried her to his bed. He had unbuttoned his linen shirt, allowing her to feel the hot skin of his corded neck beneath her lips. Aware of the steely strength in his shoulders, she slid her fingers beneath the opening of his shirt and caressed his chest. His flesh was taut over the thick muscle, warm and scented with the smell of eastern spices and man.

She knew that she only had but a week to indulge herself with him. So feeling brave, Isabella threw caution to the wind and allowed her hand to slide further into his shirt. Cupping his breast, she discovered his chest was nothing but chiseled muscle, as unyielding as rock and as contoured as a sculpture. She ran her finger along his nipple and felt it grow taut and erect, pressing urgently beneath her finger.

Tilting her head back, she looked up into his face and saw that he watched her with unblinking eyes. She could not help but think once more how beautiful and mysterious were his eyes, his irises turning to a brilliant, glistening shade of teal.

He reached the bed and instead of tossing her on it, he gently placed her atop the blankets and followed her down until his body half-covered hers. His weight sank them both deep into the mattress. She should have felt smothered by his strength and the strong, large bulge of his arousal pressing eagerly at her pubes. But she felt only desire and comfort and a strange sense of safety and rightness.

He said, "I was too anxious the last time. I did not take my time to explore you as I should have—as I wanted."

She covered his sculpted mouth with her finger, stopping his words of regret. "You gave me what I needed, Julian. And I needed you so fiercely, and somehow you knew that. My body has not stopped crying out for more of it."

His eyes darkened further and his lashes lowered. He was busy untying the strings of her petticoat, and she became mesmerized by the beauty and elegance of his long, dark fingers pulling and tugging and freeing the bow. Her breathing became rapid and she felt the light brush of his knuckles along her belly as he parted the cotton over her hip.

"I want to give you more, Isabella. I want to savor you, to kiss and lick every inch of you."

Her womb clenched and the muscles of her vagina tightened in yearning.

"I want to tongue you," he said in a deep, provocative voice. Then he flicked the tip of his tongue between the seam of her lips. "Everywhere. Your lips, your neck, your breasts, your rounded belly. *Your quim*," he growled, sending a wicked, forbidden tremor throughout her limbs. "I want you to tell me your desires. I want to know what you want me to do to you."

When her corset was off, he tossed it to the side of the bed where it fell to the floor in a heap with her petticoats. As she lay beneath him, clad in only her chemise, she felt his wide palm slide up her calf, then thigh, nearly engulfing her flesh in his hand. He caressed her to her hip, running his hand appreciatively up and down the rounded contour.

He reached up above her head towards the lamp, and she froze, stiffening beneath him. It was a silly response, but she could not hide it nor could she look away from his gaze that studied her so quizzically.

"Please don't," she whispered, seeing how his hand was against the bed curtains. "It always happened in the dark. I don't want it to be dark, not with you. I.. .I want to see you—*us*."

"I would never want you in the dark, Isabella. You were made to be seen beneath a man."

"I want see you, too," she said, slipping her hands beneath his shirt. He helped her tug the linen over his shoulders. When his head pulled free, his hair was mussed, and she ran her fingers through it, thinking how rakish he looked.

Sliding his hand beneath her pillow, he raised himself slightly above her. It was then that she saw how beautiful he was—how strong—how wonderfully muscled beneath skin that was a rich tawny brown. Her gaze skimmed down to his belly fashioned out of the same hard muscle.

Black silky hair ran in a straight line from his navel, disappearing below the waistband of his black trousers. Her gaze slipped lower and she noticed that his trousers were tented with a formidable erection. He was a young stallion in his prime, and her stomach curled in a knot, knowing she was going to have him covering her with this hot, hard, *very* male body.

"You're beautiful," she said on a sigh, sounding awed even to her own ears. "You feel like steel beneath this soft skin."

He moved higher above her, sending his chest muscles bunching and she then saw the black mark that rested on his chest above his heart.

"What's this?"

"A tattoo," he mumbled as he nuzzled her neck. His fingers sought and found the silk tie holding her chemise and he tugged the ends of the bow taut, freeing it and allowing her chemise to gape open. She barely registered the fact that he was parting her shift, preparing to bare her breast to his gaze.

"A Saracen's sword," she said, gazing at the curved shape and the intricate engraving on the blade as she traced the outline of the tattoo with the tip of her finger.

"My family's crest. I hope it does not offend you."

"Indeed not. But why would the Huntington crest be an Eastern sword?"

He shook his head. "Later, my sweet. I'll tell you everything later. Right now my attention is consumed with seeing these breasts and tonguing your nipples."

She let out a deep satisfied sigh as he pulled her chemise from beneath her. Julian looked down between their meshed chests and studied Isabella's lush body. She was naked and the rain drops on the window dappled shadows on her skin. He saw the reflection of a crystal drop snake over the roundness of her hip. He traced it with his finger until it ran down her thigh, racing to the shadow of her apex.

His heart was beating fast, his breathing coming in short harsh pants. It was so damn hard to control the hunger that was stirring violently inside him. But he was determined to hide the truth from Isabella. He might feel like he was going to expire from waiting for release, but he'd be damned if he would show that weakness. He could not bring her to orgasm after orgasm if he allowed himself to plunge deep inside her, satisfying his own appetites.

So instead, he acted as though he had all the time in the world to bring her to release. And with his cock protected inside his trousers he would be safe to explore her silken body. He had waited so long to see her naked beneath him, he was not going to forgo one second of it to his urgent, rampant cock.

His palm roved to her softly rounded belly and the suppleness of her flesh reminded him of silk and rose petals. Her body was almost luminescent in the gray afternoon light and he watched how the dark rain clouds outside his window cast shadows along the hollows and curves of her body.

Her breasts which were lush and womanly pressed beneath him. Every once in a while the wind and the splattering of rain hitting the window would drown out her breathing and he would find himself holding his own breath as he waited to hear hers once again.

She stirred restlessly, her knee sliding up to shield her shadowed sex and he held her still before slowly raising his gaze to hers. "Don't hide anything from me. You're beautiful."

"I've had two children," she said quietly, her skin turning a warmer shade in the gray light.

"You have the body of a woman. Where you are soft, I am hard. Where you will take delight in my hardness, I will take delight in your softness." He pressed his forehead to hers. "Your body will fit perfectly with mine."

And he meant every word. She was amazingly lovely and utterly arousing in her voluptuousness. He always admired curves in a woman—indeed it was his preference—but there was something about Isabella's large breasts and rounded hips that made him think that she was the most enticing woman ever.

Raising himself on his elbow, he moved just enough so that he could see her completely. Perfect, full breasts with rose colored nipples and large dusky areoles greeted him and he brushed his hand along the outside of her breast, watching as it gently swayed, beckoning him to play with it.

"I want to touch your breasts and suckle them." He let his gaze slowly meet hers. "Do you want that?"

She nodded and reached for his hand, placing it atop her breast. But before he could take her nipple between his thumb and finger, she reached for his head, bringing him to her so that she could offer her breast to his mouth. "Suckle me," she whispered into his hair.

She arched so beautifully, like a taut bow, when he curled his tongue around her distended nipple. Her fingers gripped his hair and her head was thrown back by the time his hand was palming her and his mouth was slowly and steadily devouring her nipple. He was frantic to suckle her hard, but she was so wanton beneath him as he teased her that he could not allow himself to indulge his lust. So instead he suckled her slowly, with slow, erotic tugging motions, savored her taste, the feeling of her nipple lengthening and hardening in his mouth, the sounds of her passion whispered between her parted lips.

Her hand flew to her belly and he allowed his palm to slide down below her rib cage to lie atop her hand. She must have felt her womb clench, that was why she placed her trembling fingers atop her belly. And suddenly he wanted to bring her to orgasm while he suckled her. He wanted to feel her belly contract as she came and he wanted her to feel her womb contract as he brought her to orgasm with his mouth.

"You're going to come for me with just suckling, Isabella. I want to hear your cries of pleasures as you feel my lips drawing your nipple deep into my mouth."

She gasped as he nuzzled his mouth against her nipple, making it harder, making it strain against his lips before he mouthed his way from her breast to the soft, scented valley between, only to capture her other waiting nipple between his lips.

On a hiss she arched into his mouth, and he covered her hand more forcefully until he could feel the flesh of her belly quivering, and he could imagine her sex trembling and aching for his cock. Finally he could almost sense her arousal seep from her body and onto her thighs. And still he sucked and sucked until she was gasping and gripping his hair and her breasts were swaying wantonly with desire and the need for release.

"Oh, God, Julian," she murmured, "you are so beautiful like this."

"While I'm tonguing your pert nipples, or when I'm drawing you deep into my mouth and sucking you hungrily?" he lifted his head to ask, then went back to mouthing her nipple which was now red and swollen. He blew against it and watched the areola crinkle in response and her nipple jut out even more. His cock pulsed at the sight and he felt a dribble of come seep out and roll along his shaft. With a groan, he grasped her breast and teased his lips with her nipple before he drew it into his mouth, suckling her deeply, over and over again.

"I never knew…" She trailed off, her body tightening, her hand clenching on her belly. "I never thought…"

"Sssh," He felt her belly contract beneath his hand and he saw her lashes begin to flutter. "Let it come to you. Savor this. Love this," he said against her mouth as he saw her orgasm wash over her.

The shattering and splintering of mind and body had barely settled before Isabella felt Julian slide down the length of her, his tongue burning a path down her midriff to her belly. *I want to tongue you…* his words filtered through her mind, and she rubbed her thighs together, feeling the slickness pooling between them.

If this were any other man, she might have been ashamed of her response and what she wanted him to do to her with his mouth and hands. She might have been mortified to find her legs spread and Julian's hard, muscled thigh riding her mound. Any other man might have made her feel less of a woman because of her body's imperfections. But Julian made her feel wanton and cherished. Julian made her feel as though she were the most beautiful, desirous woman in the world.

She would not allow her fears and society's dictates to come between her and her passion for Julian. She wouldn't let anything take away from the beauty of what he was giving her. There was no shame. No humiliation.

His thigh was riding against her, and she could feel the woolen fabric abrading her sex. She was so wet that his thigh seemed to slide along her and he pressed forward—harder—rubbing intimately against her clitoris with his knee, and she gripped the bed sheets tightly in her fists.

"Not the sheets, Guzelle," he said, reaching for her hand. "These sheets shall not be the ones to bear your passion. I will. Score my back with your nails. Pinch my shoulders with your fingers. Tug my hair as you ride my thigh. I don't care," he said, his voice husky. "I just want to feel the pleasure coursing in you."

"Julian, oh, God," she screamed as one hand snaked its way through his hair, and her other hand bit into his shoulder.

He looked up from her belly and smiled wickedly. "I want to tongue you." She arched beneath him, but he pinned her still with his heavy thigh and held her steady with his burning gaze. "I want to tongue your quim. And I want you to watch as I do it."

Then he was sliding down her, and his big hands were gripping her bottom, angling her sex to his mouth, and then he was greedily lapping at her, and she watched him make love to her with his lips and tongue. His eyes were closed as if he were savoring a rare, exotic dish. And the way his tongue slowly slid up the length of her made her ache to hold him there.

But soon she was so restless. He was going too slow and she rubbed against him, struggling to find the right rhythm, the right pressure that would make her shatter once more. And he ignored her, doing what he pleased with his tongue in slow, stroking, flicking movements.

And then, just when he moved his tongue against the spot that ached, she moaned and felt two of his fingers sink deep inside her, drawing out her arousal, then sinking inside again. She groaned, a deep guttural sound of need and release, then he set his tongue to her clitoris and pressed against it, making it throb. His furiously fast rhythm had her nearly convulsing and crying out his name. He continued to lick and murmur soft words of passion as she climaxed beneath him.

Slowly, she floated back down to earth. And she opened her eyes and felt no shame gazing at him, thinking of how handsome he looked making love to her in such a way.

She also saw that his erection was still thick and protruding from behind his trousers. Her fingers, shaking still from her climax, reached for his waistband and unbuttoned his trousers.

He sighed.

"Touch me, Isabella. God, I need to feel your hands on me."

She did, stroking her hand up and down the long, thick length of him, watching in amazement as the already distended veins filled more, coloring the head of his penis a dusky plum color. She felt the shaft widen in her palm and gripped him harder, stroking him more determinedly, knowing that she wanted him thick and hard plunging inside her.

"Faster. Work my cock with that pretty hand."

She did as he asked and she watched him, knowing that despite her inexperience, she was giving him what he wanted. Julian could barely breathe as he watched her work him with her hand. When a drop of pearl-colored fluid leaked out the slit of his sex, her tongue came out and moistened her lip, and all she could think of was taking his swollen tip into her mouth and tasting him.

Julian's groan caught her attention and her gaze flew to his. She knew he had guessed her thoughts as she watched him catch the drop on his thumb and bring it to her lips.

She did not hesitate to accept what he offered. With a flick of her tongue, she captured the drop and tasted him.

"Another time we will pleasure each other this way," he whispered, his eyes closed, as if he were concentrating very hard. "I will teach you all about fellatio, and I will show you the ways we can mutually pleasure each other. But right now I'm so close,"

And then he straightened away from her and tore off his trousers. His erection soared to the ceiling, and she tried to capture it again in her hand, but he evaded her touch and settled himself between her thighs. "Another time," he promised, "I will release myself in your hand, or along these beautiful breasts. But this afternoon, I want to be buried deep inside you."

And then, with the sound of the rain on the windows and their husky breaths their only accompaniment, he lowered himself atop her so that her breasts scraped his chest and their eyes were locked together, and then he sunk himself deeply inside her.

He did not ask if she could take all of him, for he knew she could. He was so deep inside her, he felt her pulsating around him. And when he began his dance of enter and withdraw, and he heard each gasp, each creak of the bed with his measured strokes, he knew that he had found the one person who matched the passion in his veins.

He looked down at Isabella, at her hair fanned out against the white pillow, down to her breasts which swayed and brushed his chest, down to the blonde thatch that meshed with his black hair, to the sacred place where he joined inside her. The beauty of it hit him all at once, and he realized that he had never before thought of the act of intercourse as a magical dance. But as he watched himself enter her, watched as she took him—his length, his thickness—deep inside her, he knew he was watching something much more profound than two bodies seeking pleasure.

As if to confirm his thoughts, he looked up and saw their reflection in the cheval mirror that sat in the corner of the room. His body, so much harder and darker than hers slid along her curves, and he saw how her hips moved with his, saw how his hips undulated with each stroke of his cock deep inside her until they moved together as one.

"Look and see us."

Her head moved against the pillow, and her eyes went wide with wonder and desire as she studied their bodies sliding along one another in the reflection of the mirror. He slowed his rhythm till it resembled an unhurried rising and falling of hips and legs, breasts and breaths.

They watched their bodies moving slowly together, and after a long while, Julian lowered his face to hers and kissed her cheek. "You look perfect beneath me, as I knew you would."

Isabella placed her palm up against Julian's. They stayed like that, palm to palm, for long seconds. Then he entwined his fingers through hers and brought it back behind her head as he thrust deeply into her.

She had never felt this connection with George when he had been atop her. She had never felt this—this oneness of mind, body and spirit. As they looked into each other's eyes, as his hand gripped hers tightly and his body slid along hers, Isabella knew that she would never, ever, feel this connection with anyone else.

"Don't close your eyes. I want you looking into my eyes as you come. Show me everything, Isabella. Hide nothing."

And then he stabbed her deeply, and she fought to keep her eyes open as she trembled beneath him. She was shaking and shattering in his arms and he thrust up into her once more and poured his seed deep inside her.

"I saw such beauty in your amber eyes," he murmured as he pressed her close to him and slowly pushed himself inside her once more. "I saw your pleasure. A woman's pleasure. And it was the most beautiful thing in the world."

Chapter 9

Daylight had turned to dusk and Julian was disappointed that he could no longer see the gold highlights running through Isabella's hair. Sliding his hand through her tousled curls, he watched the silky strands slip between his fingers, glimmering in the last vestiges of light.

A profound sense of rightness filled him when he saw the corner of her mouth curve into a hint of a smile. She was sleeping on her belly, arms thrown above her head, and her hair, wild from their coupling, shielded part of her face. When he brushed it aside and kissed her temple, her smile deepened and she purred seductively in her sleep.

"That is what I've been waiting to see," he said against her brow. "That secret smile that tells me you want to do everything we've done all over again."

She murmured something before cuddling up to him, molding her soft body into his. As he lay looking down at her slumbering face, he trailed his fingertips down her bare shoulder and arm, allowing himself to feel possessive of her.

She belonged to him. Never had the sensation been stronger then it was now that she was lying sexually replete in his bed. He had the taste of her on his tongue, the essence of her on his fingers, the feel of her printed on his soul. *She was his.*

Never had a woman given herself so completely to him—*Julian*. Many women had tumbled with the forbidden half-breed son of a disgraced earl; many more had fucked the prince. But Isabella had not, and that was the allure of her. She knew nothing of his background or the fact that his father had caused a scandal by divorcing his first wife in order to marry his pregnant lover, a lover, the ton had taken great delight in noting, who was not even an Englishwoman.

Isabella was also unaware that his mother's father had come all the way to England from Persia to bestow Julian with the title of prince of Persia and bequeathing to him a wealth that rivaled the queen of England.

But Isabella only knew him as Julian, the part Eastern man whom she had taken as her lover. In his bed, they were only Julian and Isabella. But he was not fool enough to think that the way they were now could be the way they stayed forever. Eventually she would have to know that he was a prince, albeit a prince with little chance to take the throne. He would also have to tell her of the scandal his parents had created. She would have to know that he was only tolerated in society because of his royal title, nothing more. She would have to understand that any association with him could mean disparaging comments behind her back.

And that was when the fear crept into his soul. He wanted to believe that Isabella was above succumbing to the cruel, taunting behavior of the ton. He wanted to believe so damn much that she could ignore the jeers and thinly veiled innuendoes and love him despite it all. But that belief was beginning to waver.

He knew her well enough now to know that the title would not induce her to stay at his side. There was also the possibility that she might not wish to be seen with him, not because of what might happen to her own reputation, but of the damage his reputation might cause to her children. He had only one weapon in his arsenal to keep her ensnared. His ability to arouse and please her would keep her chained to him.

He frowned at that thought. He didn't want what happened between them in bed to be the only thing they shared. He wanted more from this woman. He wanted everything she had given George, everything she gave to her children.

He knew he was being a selfish bastard when he saw the image of young Gordon Langdon flash before his eyes. He remembered the way the young man had proudly held himself as they'd been introduced by a mutual acquaintance at a coffeehouse a few weeks before. He had been struck by the level of Langdon's maturity, and the dignity and pride shining in the eyes that reminded him so much of Isabella's. *By God, she has done well in raising this boy.* That had been his first thought when Gordon had shaken his hand in a firm, gentlemanly grip.

But his only thought now was that he was terrified that he could not compete with her children. He felt a bit sick admitting that he was jealous of her son and daughter. It wasn't right. And yet he could not help feeling resentful. He suddenly wanted Isabella to fight for *them*—for this love that he knew existed beneath the passion.

For once, he wanted someone to fight for him.

Wiping a hand across his face which already bore a shadow of whiskers, he fought off the choking sensation of his younger years. Suddenly he was back at Harrow being sneered at by the other boys because his mother was despised by all of society. She was the Eastern whore who had come between his father and the woman who had been his first wife and the child she had borne him. His heir—his *rightful* son, not the child who was considered his half-breed son borne of a whore.

How he hated those boys. How he hated the women who began to flock around him after his grandfather had given him the title of Prince Fatiah. He hadn't been good enough for them when he was nothing more than Julian Gresham, the second son of the Earl of Huntingdon. No one had wanted him then. Not even Cassandra, the girl he had loved so desperately, the girl who had made him hope in a future for himself—no, not even Cassandra had fought for him. She'd tossed him aside for his brother when she was old enough to understand that he would not be able to give her what his brother could. And to add insult to injury, he had found her one night in his bed, after he was made a prince. His brother's damned wife, in his bed, begging him to come to her. Begging him to believe that she had loved him all along, but had been forced by her father to marry his brother. He had tossed her out his room without so much as a sheet to cover herself.

After that he realized that his worthless royal title and his pile of gold made him the most sought after man of the ton. Everyone wanted him. No, that wasn't true. No one wanted *him*, they just wanted the prince and whatever they could manage to get out of his royal highness. They didn't even care that it wasn't an English royal title. All they cared about was the possibility that he might have some influence or gift in his possession. Men wanted the power they thought he had, and the women wanted his wealth and the title of princess. But neither sex had wanted anything from *him*.

As he lay looking down at Isabella, he knew that she was not one of those women. She wanted him, he knew that, but somewhere deep inside that frightened and hurt little boy refused to let go of the fear he hid within his soul.

Isabella's stomach made a gurgling protesting sound, and he realized for the first time how late it was. Sliding away from her warm body, he forgot about his fears and reached for his trousers. He would order a meal and nourish her then take her back to his bed and love her the night through. In the morning he could tell her everything she needed to know, but tonight he would not speak of it. Tonight he was only Julian.

✾❀✿❀✾

"How were you able to acquire this magnificent wing of the hotel? It must have put a considerable dent in your pocket book."

Julian shrugged and Isabella found herself wondering that a mere second son of an earl could afford such luxuries. The entire east wing belonged to him as well as an army of servants who were utterly discreet and at his beck and call. She'd been impressed to awaken late in the evening to find that the dining room had been set for an intimate dinner.

"These rooms are fit for a king," she said, her voice sounding a trifle awkward.

"But what of a princess?" he asked, grinning devilishly. "Do you think a princess could find pleasure living here?"

"What woman wouldn't?" she murmured, wondering why he would ask such a question. *He's probably using every farthing his father left him in order to procure these rooms for our wicked, illicit tryst. And I should feel guilty about that, making him a pauper and all so that I can feel him atop me.*

"But you are not just any woman, are you, Isabella?" he asked, drawing her gaze back to him. "You are unique. I've never met another like you."

"I wouldn't say that. There is really nothing all that original about me. I am a politician's widow. I was borne and raised to be a man's possession, to tend his hearth and pour his evening tea and keep my duties limited to society luncheons and boring discussions of fashion and medical cordials."

He gazed at her. "You're wrong. I've never met a woman with such a capacity for love and kindness. You have a zest for living that not even George was able to curtail. I'm drawn to your goodness, your kindness and that zest I know is beneath the society veneer. Physical beauty can be fleeting, but inner beauty only glows brighter over time."

His words were probably the nicest thing anyone had ever said to her, and she could not help but feel that they were said from the heart. And if they were speaking from their hearts, she was in very grave danger of opening up hers and allowing everything to spill out of it.

One week. That was all she could allow herself.

He said, "You crave adventure, do you not? I saw you numerous times at the bazaars and it was as though you had lived your whole life in Constantinople—you navigated them with such ease."

She sighed wistfully, thinking of those days back in Turkey where everything was brilliant and scented and full of life. "I adored Constantinople. When George accepted the post of ambassador. I was thrilled. It took quite a bit of convincing for him to allow me to accompany him."

"And how did you manage to prevail upon him?"

"I made the very sound argument that it would set a good example to appear as a loving couple, giving the allure to the Turkish people of English family harmony."

"Clever minx," he said with an admiring smile. "You preyed upon his political agenda, the westernization of the east."

"Indeed," she said, smiling back and taking pleasure in his appreciation for her intelligence.

"Have you a desire to travel anywhere else?"

"Oh yes, Tangier, Marrakech, Romania. I think I'm bit of a nomad."

"What are your thoughts of Persia?"

"Persia." she let the word slip from her tongue, savoring it, conjuring up images of a world where the Western nations had not been able to penetrate or inflict their ways upon a culture whose doors had been firmly shut to outsiders. "Yes," she said, meeting his gaze. "I daresay I could fall in love with Persia. It is steeped in history and mystery. It has also been forbidden to outsiders, and I'm afraid that the notion of the forbidden does excite me."

"Does it?" he asked, his voice now a seductive purr. "I shall have to keep that in mind."

She shivered, seeing the intent in his eyes. And she looked away. He was forbidden, and damn it, he excited her. Far more than what she should allow.

"How do you feel?"

His question dragged her thoughts away from more dour thoughts, and Isabella looked up from her plate of eggplant and pilaf and met Julian's searching gaze. Determined not to feel shy, she smiled and said, "Invigorated? Alive? I'm not certain just how to describe what I feel. I only know that I never knew how liberating it could be to indulge in sexual pleasure."

He grinned before settling his lips around his champagne flute. "There is more, so much more, you know. We touch Heaven when we put our hands on another. There are no rules in Heaven, Guzelle. Nothing is forbidden. Nothing is forbidden between us."

Her skin tingled, and she suppressed a shiver as she began to wonder how much more there could be. After their initial lovemaking, they had fallen asleep in each other's arms. She had awakened to the feel of Julian suckling her breast and his fingers searching between her sex. Before she knew it, he pulled her atop him and ordered her to ride him. And how she had ridden him.

Heat kissed her cheeks and she pulled the gaping neck of Julian's shirt tighter around her throat. His eyes flickered along her body and she saw the primitive satisfaction in them.

"I like seeing you in my shirt, knowing that nothing lies between your naked skin but the linen that bears my warmth and scent. It makes me feel as if you truly could be mine."

She moved a few grains of rice around her plate with her fork as she avoided his gaze. She could not be his. A permanent position as his mistress was out of the question, and marriage was even more impractical for he was much too young to be wed to a thirty-four-year old widowed mother of two.

Deep down she thought that he was only satisfying his lust and passions. The flame that flared between them would soon flicker to embers. It was only natural. And even though their liaison would end in time, she could not in all conscience allow herself to see it through to its natural conclusion. She had a feeling that this passion she felt for him would not die swiftly in a week, and a week was all she could give him—for her own sake. She would not endanger Minnie and Gordon's reputation because she wanted—*needed*—her carnal appetites appeased. And she could not risk her heart, although, deep down she knew her heart was already lost.

"How old are you?" she asked, unable to stop thinking about the matter of his age.

"Six-and-twenty, but I fail to see why it matters."

So he had been only twenty-three when she had first caught his interest in Constantinople. Triumph flooded through her like the warmth of a fine wine. What a coup for a woman of her age to have captured the carnal interest of a young, virile man. What woman of her years did not wonder about her attractiveness? What woman of her circumstance did not question if she still had the power to entice a man that was not her husband to her bed? How many other unsatisfied wives in London wished they could trade places with her in the bed of this man?

"The first time I saw you I knew I had to have you." Julian set his champagne flute atop the table and considered her across the length of the table. "There was nothing that could have stopped the wheels of fate from turning. Destiny is a mysterious thing. One must not fight it, but embrace it without question. Don't fight our destiny, Isabella. Accept it."

Isabella watched as Julian's long fingers reached for the brass bell that sat atop the table. With a flick of his wrist, the little bell rang against the brass and an army of liveried servants opened the door of the dining room and marched in, clearing away the dishes and the white tablecloth. When the door closed behind them, Julian rose from his chair and with a stride that reminded her of a panther, he prowled around the table and made his way to her.

"That first day you walked off the boat, the sun was shining and you were wearing a blue muslin gown with a lace mantelet. The wind was gusting and lifted the edge of the cloak away from your bodice, revealing the swells of your breasts. I became instantly, almost painfully aroused. I imagined what your breasts would look like, how large they would be. I saw your breasts cradling my cock, and I promised myself that I would make that vision come true. I would see your breasts with my shaft thrusting between them."

With each one of his measured steps, her skin began to feel stretched, and butterflies began to flutter and circle madly in her belly.

"The longer I watched you, the more I wanted you. And I thought myself the biggest bastard because I was standing on the dock watching you, arm in arm with your husband, with the hardest erection I've ever had in my life. And as you got closer, I envisioned touching you everywhere. I saw myself filling you in every way and every place a man can fill a woman. And somehow I knew—*I felt*—that you were made for me. That you could fill the empty part in my soul. I did not question the feeling. I accepted it without reservation, believing that two souls meant to be together will find each other when the time is right. And that was the time, Isabella, when my soul knew it was bound to yours."

She was trembling, fearing that she understood what he meant about destiny and fate, and souls seeking their mates. She believed him, believed in the mysterious powers of destiny. But her future could not be with Julian, no matter how much she might wish it.

He was standing before her now, his trousers tented with a formidable erection that was level with her eyes. Swallowing thickly, she found she could barely breathe, could barely take her eyes off his trousers and from imagining what it would feel like to take him in her hand and run her tongue up the long length of him.

"After I left you that first day, I went straight home and tossed off like a school boy."

Her head shot up, and her heart did quit beating when she saw sexual desire in his eyes. "I thought only of your body and your face, and it aroused me as I have never been aroused before. I did not think of you as the ambassador's wife. I did not think of you as a mother, or someone who was too old for me to find pleasure in. I only thought of you as a woman."

"Why?" she croaked, her voice dry.

"Why did I want you? Why do I still want you?" he asked, and she saw that his fingers had slipped to the fastenings of his trousers and he was unbuttoning them slowly, one at a time. "I want you because you are a woman who knows what she desires. There are no coy games between us. You desire what I desire. You need what I need. You aren't ashamed of those needs. You don't pretend that you don't have them. I have never met another woman who was so honest. I certainly have not met with a woman my own age who could arouse or satisfy me like you do. Age means nothing," he said, and he opened his trousers and allowed his phallus to spring free. "The only thing that matters is this, the passion and the friendship that I know we're building between us. I don't want a milkwater miss that I must step carefully around. I don't want some schoolroom girl who will faint and wish to die of shame when I put my tongue to her clitoris and suck it. I want a woman whom I can ask to do anything. A woman who will do it because she wants to and because she enjoys it, not because it is her duty to suffer me, or endure the marriage bed. I want a woman who will ask me to pleasure her as she desires. I want a woman who will become aroused and not horrified when I am beyond thinking straight and I forget myself by using words like cock and cunt."

He reached for her and pulled her up to stand before her, and she realized that those words, those base, carnal words did have a place to titillate the senses. She knew enough now to know that there was room for soft, romantic loving, and fierce carnal pleasuring. She had experienced both with Julian—craved both—and she found beauty in both things knowing that mutual pleasure was the only thing that mattered.

"I want a companion," he murmured, his eyes holding her gaze steady. "I want someone who shares my interests and who can discuss any topic with intelligence and thoughtfulness. I want a friend with whom I can laugh and spend time with. I want a woman who will accept me for the man I am, not the trappings of my circumstance, or my birth—but just me. I want a lover who will come to my bed and share with me all the pleasures to be found between a man and a woman. I want the elegant lady and the insatiable concubine who finds the forbidden exciting. I want you, Isabella."

"But you cannot—" She broke off on a quiet gasp as he reached for the hem of his shirt that she was wearing and raised it to her waist, then up over her head, pulling it from her shoulders before he tossed it carelessly to the ground.

"You, Isabella. No other woman. I wanted you three years ago and my desire for you has not abated. No other woman can give me what I want. No other woman has ever cared enough to ask what I want. But you did."

He lowered himself into her chair and spread his legs wide, capturing her knees with his thighs. He was shirtless, and she watched as the thick bundle of muscles in his belly flinched and constricted. The muscles of his chest danced and she studied the tattoo above his heart, feeling her body begin to tingle in appreciation.

His erect phallus throbbed through the opening of his trousers and she studied it with a deep hunger, heedless of the fact that she was standing shamelessly naked before him.

"You asked me this afternoon to show you what I desire. I wish to tell you, Isabella. I wish for you to pleasure me as I've dreamt all these long years."

She knew what he wanted, what he would ask for as he reached between the parted folds of his trousers and gripped his phallus in his tanned hand. He slid his palm up and down the shaft, pleasuring himself slowly, expertly, and she watched him, and he watched her as she studied the way he found pleasure with his hand.

She lowered her body so that she was kneeling before him as if she were a servant set to do his bidding. But there was no shame in her subservient posturing. There had been more shame in her subservience to George. In fact, she felt rather powerful like this, because it was obvious that Julian was struggling with his self-control. His hand had tightened around his shaft, and a muscle jumped and flickered in his jaw as he gritted his teeth, watching her kneel before him.

And it was then that Isabella knew a woman could wield immense power in the bedroom. She could make herself a man's slave, kneeling before him, pleasuring him as he commanded, while slowly turning the table on him so that he was enslaved to her. No, there was no shame, no humiliation in kneeling before Julian, or wanting to be submissive to him and his pleasure.

"You know what I want, don't you?"

She nodded and pressed forward, feeling the prickly hairs of his legs brushing the sides of her breasts as she insinuated her body between his thighs.

"Tell me what you think I want you to do to me."

She allowed her eyes to slowly trail up his body, taking in every hard contour and muscle, allowing herself to feel her body growing warm and wet and anxious, anticipating the moment when he would cover her body with his.

He hadn't touched her, yet already her vaginal muscles were clenching, as if preparing for his deep invasion.

"What you want is fellatio," she whispered huskily.

His breath rushed out of his chest as she reached for the waistband of his trousers and pulled the black fabric down his slim hips. He was now naked and magnificently aroused. And she realized that she was anxious to perform this act for him. She wanted to discover what he would feel like in her mouth. She wanted to watch his expression as she pleasured him. She had never done such a thing, but she wanted desperately to do this for Julian.

"That is what you want, isn't it, for me to take you into my mouth?"

"Yes, Isabella," he half-drawled, half-groaned, and she felt his fingers thread through her hair and cup the back of her head. "I want you to suck my cock. And I am going to sit back and enjoy watching you do it."

Chapter 10

She set her tongue to him and trailed it up his long shaft. She groaned, a husky sound that came from the back of her throat. He was so hard, yet the flesh that covered him was so soft, like the most expensive silk or velvet. And the taste of him, salty, male, utterly unique, filled her mouth, and she closed her eyes and opened to him, allowing the tip of him inside her.

"I want this," she purred, nuzzling her lips against the throbbing vein that ran the length of him. "I want to feel this pulsating in my mouth."

"Like it pulsates in your cunt?" he growled as he thrust forward, filling her mouth with more than just the head of him. She sucked him vigorously, allowing the rhythm of his hips to guide her. She knew she was driving him to the brink when she felt his hand fist in her hair.

Julian's thighs tightened around her hips, and he nudged her closer so that she could take more of his straining cock into her mouth. Good God, no woman had ever been able to pleasure him so completely. No woman had ever sucked him so thoroughly, nor so wantonly. As he studied her, her mouth moving along him, he realized that he had never felt so weak, or so much at a woman's mercy as he felt at Isabella's. But the truth was, this woman had gotten to his heart, and the intimacy of the act only bound her tighter to him.

She was working his cock with such enthusiasm that he nearly came seconds into it, but he closed his eyes and forced himself to find control. He did not want this to end. He was going to be selfish tonight, indulging in his fantasies.

He was going to possess her in ways that George never had. He was going to mark her for his—*tonight.*

Grasping a handful of her hair, he tilted her head gently back so that he could see her pink tongue snaking up and down the length of his thick shaft and curling around the swollen head. His cods tightened and as if she instinctively knew, she cupped his sac, fondling him in her palms as she made love to his prick with her mouth.

He was content to sit back in his chair, like a pasha being pleasured, watching her, studying the way her mouth looked atop him, and the way her lashes fluttered against her cheeks as her sexual need began to heighten. How bloody powerful it was to sit back and take his pleasure, to do nothing other than watch and direct her with pressure from his hand. How dominant he felt sprawled out in his chair as she worked his cock with an eager, inexperienced mouth.

She would allow him everything tonight, he knew that, could tell just by the way she was moaning and shifting her weight restlessly on her knees. She was aroused just by pleasuring him, and he was violently aroused himself.

"I am so eager to please you," she murmured between flicks of her tongue.

"How eager? So eager that you would give your body over to me?" She looked up at him, through a veil of golden lashes, and he saw her pupils dilate, but he did not think it was in fear, but rather curiosity, and perhaps arousal.

"I want you to do everything to me that you have ever thought about."

"Everything?" he asked, brushing her mouth with the tip of his cock, coaxing her to take him between her swollen lips. Her lip trembled and she ran a shaking hand down her smooth ivory thigh. He grew thicker, imagining that elegant hand snaking between her thighs and playing in her plump folds. Their gazes met and locked and he felt his fiercely held desire begin to unravel.

"You would deny me nothing?"

"Nothing, Julian."

"What if I wanted to feel my cock between your breasts? Would you let me?"

"Yes."

His gaze drifted down her throat and then to her breasts. "Offer them to me."

She did and the sight of her breasts in her hands and her fingers stroking her pebbled nipples was more than he could bear. He brought her forward and gripped his cock, stroking it between the soft valley of her breasts.

"What if I wanted to come on them?" She gasped as he put his hands to her breasts and squeezed them so that they gripped his cock like her sheath. He pressed his mouth to her ear and thrust his hips once more, filling the valley of her breasts with his prick. "What if I want to come in your mouth?"

She didn't have to answer him, for he knew that she would bring him to orgasm and keep him inside her mouth until he was limp and spent.

"Another time," he whispered. "For now, I want you to pleasure me as you pleasure yourself. I want to hear my name on your lips as you come. I want you to know that I am here, watching you pleasure yourself with your hand."

Her fingers snaked between her thighs, and she widened her legs enough to allow him to watch her hand sink between her plump thighs and her fingers part her pink lips. He pumped his shaft in his hand.

"Tell me what you are thinking of," he asked, his voice shaking with need as she spread her sex wider, showing him how wet and aroused she was.

"Your mouth on me," she whispered, then she moved her middle finger lower and pressed deeply. "I love the way it feels. I love the way you look as your tongue is pleasuring me. I am thinking about how much I need to feel something inside me."

"My finger, perhaps?"

"Yes, or this beautiful cock," she purred, closing her fluttering lashes, and putting her mouth on his phallus.

He groaned, watching her insert another finger inside her quim as her thumb worked her clitoris, and her mouth worked his cock. And he watched, so very aroused, as she built herself up, as well as him, milking him with her mouth, seducing him with forbidden visuals of self pleasuring.

He was too close and he did not want to lose control yet. So he rose from his chair and stood before her, then lifted her up from her knees and placed her atop the table so that her bottom was on the edge, and she was opened to him while she continued to pleasure herself.

"Put your feet on my shoulders."

She did as he asked and then he sunk three fingers deep inside her. He found the rigid little spot at the back of her vagina, and her eyes went wide. He curled his fingers forward in her tight sheath, reaching for the little spot that The Perfumed Garden said gave a woman her most powerful orgasm.

He felt her getting wetter, and she was so responsive, so open to lovemaking and her own sensuality, that he could pull this from her this female ejaculation that he craved giving her.

"Deeper," she said in a dark, husky voice as her fingers furiously stroked the little pearl hidden in the crest of her curls. He captured a taut nipple between his teeth and tugged, making her wetter as he worked diligently to arouse her.

"Oh, God, yes, Julian! *Yes!*"

And then she was coming all over his hand and between his fingers and her body was vibrating against him. And while she was still shaking, he pushed his cock deep inside her, finishing her off so that she sheathed him with more of her arousal.

She lay back on the table, her back arched, her hands thrown high above her head, her thighs splayed wide like a wanton goddess, and he took her hard and watched her breasts bouncing with the rhythm of his strokes. Thrusting and retreating, he reached for her hips, pressing his fingers into her flesh so that he could grip her and bring her down as he thrust his cock upwards, filling her with his entire length.

And still she gasped and moaned, begging for more, needing more. His finger searched for her clitoris, and he found it to be erect and swollen and he flicked it, making her arch.

As he watched himself enter her body, then slide out, his shaft glistening with her desire, he felt the primitive, overwhelming need to mark her as his. He wanted to take her—hard—so that she would never forget the feel of him thrusting deep inside her.

Watching his possession of her made him wild, reckless, and forgetting that he was not with her in a dream, he lowered her legs to the table and reached for her, bringing her up so that her breasts where against his chest.

"I want to fuck you from behind."

Her eyes went wide, but he turned her over, his hand covering her bottom as he positioned her before him and tilted her hips back so that she was exposed to his gaze.

"Julian!" Isabella heard the arousal and need in her voice as Julian, stood behind her as she knelt on the table.

He thrust hard and she heard his breaths harsh behind her, and she looked over her shoulder and saw that his gaze was fixed on where he was busying entering and retreating from her.

"I love the way you can take me, Isabella, the way you allow me to watch you taking me." His gaze flickered up to hers. "You take me as I am, without question. Without hesitation. No one has ever given me so much of themselves, and I cherish it."

His hands fell lower on her hips and he showed her how to rotate them, giving them both more pleasure. And soon, she was lowering her body to the table, taking gratuitous joy in the way her nipples brushed against the polished wood and she imagined that he was beneath her and she was rubbing her nipple against his lips, and he was teasing her with the hard tip of his tongue, and she smiled secretly at the image of teasing Julian.

"Look at me, Isabella," he commanded as he thrust into her. "See what strength you give me."

And then his body went taut and she felt him become stiff, and she saw how his expression hardened into a fierce scowl as he splashed his seed deep inside her. And then, while he was still inside, he sought her clitoris and rubbed it between his thumb and finger as he lowered his head to her back and kissed her in small, soft kisses.

"You make me the strongest of men, Isabella. A woman's pleasure is a man's pleasure. Never forget that."

While Julian slept, Isabella slipped from bed and paced the room. Something was happening, something she swore wouldn't happen, something she could not quite bring herself to believe was happening so fast. But as she looked over her shoulder and saw Julian sprawled out in bed, naked to the waist, she could not deny what she felt in her heart. She was falling for him, and if she were being completely honest with herself, she was more than likely already in love with him.

Nibbling on her fingernail, she looked away from Julian's magnificent body, now relaxed and reposed in slumber, and saw her clothes piled atop a chair in the corner. She could dress quickly and sneak out, like a thief in the night. She could simply leave before the week was out and not have to worry about these feelings. She could stamp them out, she was sure of it. She just needed distance—distance from Julian, from the desire she felt whenever she looked at him.

Standing before the chair she gazed down at her clothes, remembering how Julian had disrobed her. How wanted she had felt—how desired. She wondered if she would ever feel that again, or would she be forever doomed to replay the events in this room in order to keep her warm inside.

"Guzelle?"

The word was a question, and it was uttered in a very quiet, very stern voice—a voice that held no trace of sleep.

She spoke in a whisper. "I must go. It is very late."

Julian said, "You told me this afternoon while I was holding you in my arms that you were free to come to me. You said your children were gone for the week."

"Even so," she said, unable to untangle the shift because of her shaking hands, "I think it best if I go."

The mattress creaked, and she heard his footsteps atop the carpet. His hands reached for her shoulders and skimmed down her arms. Snaking his arms around her waist, he lifted her up and brought her to the window that faced Brook Street. Pulling back the curtains, he pressed her forward so she could see them together in the window's reflection, Julian standing behind her, his hand brushing her hair over her shoulder, baring her neck.

"Look outside, Isabella," he murmured, and he reached for her hands and brought them together, holding him with one of his, high above her head so that it rested against the wood casement. "What do you think is going on out there in the streets of London?"

She scanned the street that should have been quiet at this time of night and noticed the carriages and hansom cabs rumbling down the cobbles. Gas lamplights flickered along the street, casting a golden haze that penetrated through the shroud of drizzling fog. She saw a woman step out from beneath the shadow of an alcove as a gentleman strolled down the street, his fashionable walking stick stabbing the cobbles while his opera cape billowed out behind him. He was obviously making his way back from the theatres.

"Do you think he sees her yet?"

Her eyes darted to the man, his face concealed by the brim of his top hat. The woman emerged fully from the shadows, the train of her green satin gown trailing silently along the walk until she pressed her back against the lamppost and thrusting her bosom forward in a seductive pose. The woman's gloved hand slid slowly up her belly and brushed the curve of her breast as an enticement. The man slowed his gait as he came upon the wanton creature.

She should not be doing this, taking part in this game of his. She told him she needed to go, and she should, but Julian had waylaid her, and now she could not move, nor take her eyes off the couple below her.

"What do you think he wants to do to her?" Julian asked darkly, and she felt his tongue stroke her neck.

The gentleman was unbuttoning the woman's pelisse and running his hand along her breast concealed behind a white ruffled blouse. Isabella swore she felt the touch, then Julian's long fingers were drawing tiny circles along the side of her breast, and her nipples constricted in yearning and her breasts grew heavy with the need to have those large, dark hands cupping her from behind. Had Julian ever needed to solicit the services of a prostitute? Had he visited the East-End brothels or the more elegant and tasteful establishments in Trevor Square?

"What would you do to her?" she asked him, her voice a husky whisper.

"Nothing that I would do with you," he murmured in her ear. "I would merely fuck her, taking my own pleasure. But with you, I would take my time, savoring you, pleasuring you in the most wicked ways possible. There are so many wicked, forbidden things that I have yet to show you."

"Show me," she said on a breathless moan as he cupped her breasts. "Show me every forbidden thing."

"What do you think is going on behind these fashionable doors? Have you any idea, Isabella?" His manhood had grown hard and he pressed it against her bottom. "I want to take you like this," he whispered in her ear. "I want you to watch the streets and know what is happening behind those doors. I want to show you. I want you to be a part of it. Now, spread your legs and bend forward."

She did as he asked, but he held her hands still in his, as if she were a captive, but he easily positioned her as he wanted and slipped his erection inside her, slowly moving in and out in a rhythm that made her burn for more. He caught her swaying breasts with his free hand and cupped and squeezed them before sliding his hand against them, growling when he watched them swaying wantonly in the reflection of the glass. And she knew he liked watching such a display, because she felt him swell even more inside her.

"Behind those doors, Isabella," he murmured while he played with her breast, watching his movements in the glass, "repression is being shed. Passion is being explored, sex, in all its forms are being discovered." She gasped as he kept up his slow assault on her body and she felt a quickening in her womb as he playfully slapped at her breast. "There is tender lovemaking between lovers, fucking between whore and patron. There is every perversion and vice you can think of."

Julian bent forward, angling his head so that he could slip her nipple between his lips. And Isabella looked down, watching her nipple being compressed between his teeth, before his tongue flicked along the distended red tip, and all the while he stroked her slowly and steadily with his cock.

Julian was watching her intently as he continued to lave her nipple, and she felt her vagina clench, holding him deep inside her. His iris became a richer shade of teal, and he brought more of her nipple into his mouth.

Her gaze fluttered to the street, and she saw that the gentleman below them was leading the lady of the night away from her lamppost. Where would he take her? On the street in the dark? Up to his room or his carriage? Did he have a wife? A family? But Isabella saw that he did not take the woman far, only into the reaches of the shadows. She saw a flash of the woman's stocking-clad leg as her skirts were raised, and then the motion of bodies finding pleasure.

"He's fucking her," Julian growled in her ear as he thrust deeper into her. "He can't even be bothered with a bed. The setting is titillating and his pleasure will be expedient. But every now and then it is pleasurable to take risks, to make the act carnal and fierce."

"Would you take me like that, Julian—in a dark alcove on a street?"

"Would you want me to? Do you want to be taken like that?"

"I… I don't know," she gasped as she felt his finger circle the tight bud between the cleft of her bottom. "I don't think I would want what I find with you to be reduced to something unfeeling."

"What is happening in this room?" Julian asked softly, continuing to slowly stroke her with his cock and his finger. "Loving or fucking?"

Her body stiffened. This was loving. For her it was the truth. It might just be carnal pleasures for Julian, but for her it was the most intimate, loving embrace she had ever experienced.

"What is this to you?" he asked, his voice suddenly sounding raw. "Are you that gentleman, and me, I am that whore?"

"How could you think such a thing?" she gasped.

"What do I mean to you, Isabella? Am I just a dalliance to amuse you? Am just a young buck to pleasure you until a rich, older man comes by and offers you a respectable arrangement?"

Hadn't she tried to think of Julian as a flirtation, as something that would end, that *she* could end?

"If this is fucking," he said, thrusting inside her again, "then I want you to leave tonight. If this is lovemaking, I want you to turn around and look at me."

Time seemed to still. Isabella forgot that she was standing naked in front of a window, where anyone might happen to look up from the sidewalk or a passing carriage and see her being ravished. She forgot that she was a widow and a mother and a lady of breeding who should be mortified to be seen doing such things. She forgot everything save for the feeling in her heart, the sickness in her belly when she thought of what she had shared with Julian being nothing but empty mating to fulfill her carnal appetites.

She had found so much more with him than she ever expected. Not only had she found physical pleasure, she had found a spiritual connection as well. He met her needs both in and out of bed, and that was something she could never have said about George.

He released her wrists and she felt him pull away, his sex sliding out of her, causing her to feel empty and alone. It was the same feeling she experienced when George had discharged his seed and rolled over, leaving her alone in the dark. She did not want that. She did not want what Julian had given to her to be reduced to what her husband had done to her. That had been fucking. This... she dropped her arms and slowly, she turned around to face him, and her heart twisted when she saw his anguished expression.

"I hardly know what I'm saying, but I know that these moments have been too beautiful to attach such a cold, carnal word to them," she whispered, trailing her palm over his heart and the tattoo that lay above it. "I have never felt such beauty. I have never been loved in such a way." She looked up and met his eyes. "But I think that this really isn't what you're asking me, is it?"

He looked at her with eyes that for the first time were unreadable. "I need to know what you feel, Isabella. Am I a passing fancy, or do I mean more to you than a few evenings of sex and pleasure?"

"Of course you mean more to me than what we find in bed," she said. "But you must understand that what we have cannot last."

His eyes narrowed and she had never seen him looking quite so dangerous before. "Why can't it last?"

"Julian, you must see. You must know that I came to you because my children were gone for the week. It was the only time that I could reasonably come to you."

"So you're planning to leave, when—when I was sleeping?"

"I had every intention of leaving after this week was up," she mumbled, feeling like a heartless hussy. "I didn't—*I don't*—want to hurt you."

"Don't bother," he snapped, stalking away from her and reaching for his trousers.

"Julian, I never meant.. that is to say…"

"You never meant for me to fall in love with you?" he said viciously as he pulled his trousers up over his hips. "Or you never meant for me to make love to you. Or perhaps you meant for it to happen once, but certainly not on the dining room table while you were on your knees."

Her heart swelled with the knowledge that Julian had fallen in love with her, yet that euphoria suddenly vanished, and she felt used and dirty after his very unsubtle reminder of how she had allowed him to pleasure her. "You're making this into something very ugly."

"Well, isn't it?"

"Julian, please. You're young. This is just an infatuation, a passing fling that you will tire of very soon. This love you feel, It's… *puppy love.*"

"Don't you dare!" he roared wheeling on her. "Don't even think to speak to me in such a way—like I'm a goddamned child. I am not your son. I am not a little boy who has a crush. Do not insult me, Isabella. I know my heart. I've known it for three years. I've spent the last three damned years hoping that one day you'll return my affections. Perhaps *you* feel an infatuation, but do not accuse me of loving you falsely. I am a man, damn you, and I feel like a man. I love like a man."

She swallowed hard and forced herself to meet his gaze. "You know that I cannot… I cannot be your mistress."

"Who said I'm offering you carte blanche? I don't want you as my mistress. I want more from you than that. I want the devotion you gave to George. I want the love you give your children. I want you completely and selfishly in my bed, giving me everything you are, and everything you have inside you."

"Julian," she murmured, allowing her fingers to caress his mouth.

"Can't you love me, Isabella? Can't you be my wife?"

"I… I don't know," she said, looking away from him.

"What if I weren't a second son?" he sneered as he pulled away from her touch. "What if I were filthy rich? Would you agree then? Would your friends approve of us then? Would *you* approve?"

"Julian, I'm older—"

"I will not allow for age difference. That is irrelevant."

"It is not, Julian. You're forgetting that you will want children. I am thirty-four, well past time for bearing children."

"The queen is still bearing Albert's children, and she is your age. And you're right, I will want children," he said, looking down at her, his chest heaving with anger. "But I want those children to be *our* children. I want my babies to be born to you, no other."

"You don't understand, Julian. After Minnie, I never conceived again. I'm not sure—"

"The matter of children does not concern me," he said decisively. "If it is our destiny, you'll bear me children. If it is not, then it is not meant to be. Besides, I can and will love your children as my own."

"You could love another man's children?" she asked skeptically.

"Of course I would. What sort of man do you take me for? I don't resent them. They are a part of your life, and I would love them because you love them. I would love them because they are a part of you. I would do anything to win them over. Just tell me what I need to do to win you."

Despite his impassioned words, Isabella reached for her discarded clothes and clutched them to her body. "I just can't," she mumbled, thinking of her children and trying not to think of how her heart was slowly dying. "You will just have to accept—"

"I'm a prince," he announced, interrupting her. "You will be a princess. You will have unlimited funds and homes in Persia and England. Your daughter will be given a dowry to rival any royal princess, and she will have her pick of husband."

A prince. Her mind reeled with shock and horror and the room began to swim before her eyes. She focused on the Saracen sword tattooed to his breast, sickened by what she had done and what she had allowed to happen.

He said bitterly, "My mother's father was a younger son of the Persian king. When I was eighteen he gave me my title of Prince Fatiah of Persia. The Saracen sword is the crest of his family—my mother's family. The title has little ruling power, but it came with wealth, with riches beyond your belief. Does that win you over?"

She glared at him. Now he was standing before her with his princely hauteur and his accusations. She would have railed at him for thinking that she could be swayed by such material things as a title and money, but the images of what they had done, the reminders of how she had been, filtered through her mind and she felt ashamed and mortified.

"What have I done?" she cried, running towards the door. "I have behaved so wantonly, so commonly, and all this time you were a prince. Oh, God," she groaned, "a prince."

She reached for the door but Julian's dark hand pressed it closed before she could slip through. "Your actions were perfectly fine when you thought I was nothing but a second son. You weren't ashamed then."

"But that was before I knew…" His hand slid away from the door, and she met his gaze. "That you were a prince."

"So you would have behaved differently, then, had you known I was a prince? Tell me, had you known before I asked you to stay with me, would you have stayed? Would you have agreed to be my wife? Would you have acted like all the other women who have ever tried to tempt me into marriage?"

He moved away from her, his head slowly nodding. "I see everything now, madam. You can love the prince. You can marry the prince, but you can only fuck the half-breed."

"Julian—"

"I asked you to be only Isabella when you were with me. You gave your word you would. Since Lady Langdon with her high morals and slavish duty has returned, please leave."

"Julian—"

"Leave and don't come back until you can come to me as Isabella. The Isabella who wanted me, *Julian*. The Isabella who can be with me without being ashamed. The Isabella that I have loved so desperately. I don't like this woman—this Lady Langdon. She makes me feel like a male whore."

"Julian!"

"Goodbye, Lady Langdon," he declared. "Perhaps one day you will be able to put aside your duty and come to me of your own free will. But I shall not hold my breath. We both know that duty will always win out."

She hated herself for what she was allowing him to think. It was not because he was a half-breed. It was because of her children. But she didn't say that, because it was better for her if he thought her uncaring and cruel. He would not pursue her this way. He would not come after her and threaten her resolve—a resolve that would be too weak.

"I will not be coming back."

"I am not surprised," he shot back, not bothering to look at her. "After all, it was Julian who proposed. Not the prince."

Isabella allowed the footman to hand her into the hansom cab. As she settled against the cool leather squabs she folded her hands in her lap and stared out into the night. The crack of the whip echoed through the silent night and the carriage lurched forward.

Unconsciously she raised her eyes to the window that overlooked the street and saw through the thin fog that Julian stood shirtless, looking down at the cab. Unable to stem her tears, she allowed them to spill from her eyes and cascade down her cheeks. What a cold emptiness she felt sweeping through her body. She felt heartless, soulless. As the carriage clattered down the cobblestones, she covered her face with her hands and sobbed. How was she ever going to live without him? How could she go to bed night after night alone and cold, knowing that one day he would find another to love? Knowing one day that some woman would take her place in his bed and his heart?

"What am I to do?" she shouted at the heavens, not caring the driver might hear her. "Tell me. For I do not know the right answer."

But the heavens remained eerily silent and Isabella wept the entire way home.

Chapter 11

A week later, Julian found himself nursing a snifter of brandy in a quiet corner of White's, contemplating his life and what the devil he was going to do with it. A week ago it had been so easy—he'd had it all planned. He was going to seduce Isabella and make her enthralled with passion and him—so enthralled that she would never leave him, or wish to be with any other man. And then he was going to marry her and spend the rest of his life with her.

Well, his plans had come to naught. She hadn't loved him. This affair had been one-sided, and it was only his emotions that were engaged.

Male voices and laughter floated over to him, and Julian looked up from the glowing embers in the hearth to see the young Earl of Langdon take the chair beside him.

Gordon looked so much like his mother, he thought, returning his gaze back to the fire as a knot of loneliness and heartsickness twisted his insides. He missed her, missed touching her and seeing her laugh. He'd do anything to get her back, but he knew that until Isabella gave up her notions of being what she termed a respectable lady, he didn't have a chance in hell of touching her.

"You don't mind if I join you, do you?" Langdon asked, settling himself into the chair.

"Not at all, provided you won't be put out by my lack of conversation" Julian said. "I am not feeling very sociable at the moment."

Langdon fixed his gaze on him, and Julian found himself staring into Isabella's amber eyes. "Then we shall be bosom bows, for I am in no mood to be solicitous, either."

Julian motioned the waiter for a second glass. When it arrived, he poured young Gordon a hefty snifter of brandy and saluted him. "To melancholy."

"To melancholy," Langdon grunted, before swallowing the entire contents in one gulp. "An acquired taste," Julian drawled, smiling to himself when saw how Gordon tried to conceal his grimace of distaste. Refilling Gordon's glass, he advised, "You might want to savor this one."

Young Langdon flushed and pulled at his cravat. Julian studied him from the corner of his eye, wondering what had prompted the young man to join him in the corner of the club far away from the gaming and drinking and the discussion of politics.

"Is it true?" Langdon asked, "that you're a prince?"

"I fear so," Julian said.

"Why didn't you say something, that day we met at Stowe's coffeehouse. You said you worked with my father in Constantinople, but nothing of your royal connections."

"I did work with your father." Julian sighed. "I am a man, nothing more. I want to be accepted for what I am, not who I am. When I met you, I wanted you to know me only as someone who knew your father, someone who respected your father's innate ability to handle tricky foreign affairs."

Langdon nodded and peered down into his snifter. "I understand, sir. A title does not make a man, although many—especially the ladies— seem to think that all one needs is a fortune and a title to be of consequence."

"A very astute observation for one so young."

Gordon declared, "I have decided that no woman shall have me because of my title or fortune or my connections in the House of Lords."

Julian wondered what this was all about. This was, after all, Isabella's son. Perhaps he was acting as an emissary. He decided to impart a bit of information. "Like you, Langdon, I have no wish to be married for my title. Besides, my title does not come with any real ruling power. My wife would be a princess, true, but the chance of her ever becoming a queen is so far removed as to be impossible. My fortune, on the other hand, is very real, and I'm afraid, not to mention deeply mortified, that its sum has been accurately bandied about."

Gordon whistled. "That much, eh? The Persian king must have been very wealthy."

Julian inclined his head. "But I am more than my sum parts— like you, Langdon. I shall confess my curiosity," Julian began, purposely lowering his voice. "What exactly is it that has you finding solace here with me?"

Gordon turned his head and met his gaze. "What has you taking solace in this corner?"

Julian studied the way the flames made the brandy in his glass glow warm and amber. The color reminded him of Isabella's eyes and he sighed, knowing he was lost.

"Women troubles, if you must know," Gordon grunted inelegantly when Julian didn't answer his question.

"Ah, yes, the fairer sex. They do give a man fits now and then, do they not?"

"They do."

Julian wondered at the strange, almost impassioned expression in young Gordon's handsome face. For one so young, he was most mature in this regard. Had Gordon fallen as hard as he had? If it was the same pain that Julian was feeling, young Gordon would likely not survive it.

"May I ask you a question, sir?"

The tone was respectful, and made Julian look up. "Ask your question, Langdon. Although I am not certain I shall be able to provide you with a useful answer."

"Do you understand women?"

Julian crossed his leg and reached for his brandy. He used to think he had a fairly good understanding of the opposite sex. He had been able to look beneath their smiling faces and read the machinations and stratagems they had in regards to him. He used to think he had known what women wanted, and he used to think he knew how to give them what they desired.

It was painfully apparent that he didn't understand a blessed thing. Ever since he had awakened to find Isabella preparing to leave he'd been out of control. He hadn't understood a damn thing, save for the fear that had gripped him when he realized that she meant to leave him. He could not fathom how she could so easily walk away from what they had shared—what they had found in each other. But he would not speak a word of this to Gordon or any other soul.

"Perhaps you might tell me what troubles you, Langdon."

Gordon shifted his weight to his left hip and leaned over the arm of the wingback chair. "What would you do, sir, if a woman did not want you?"

Julian stiffened. "That would depend."

"Sir?"

"On how much I wanted her to want me."

"I see," Gordon mumbled, then sunk back into his chair.

"If I wanted her very much," Julian began, focusing on the yellow and orange flames that leapt from the coal in the hearth, "I would stop at nothing to gain her attention. I would do whatever I needed to in order to gain her trust and her love." He slid his gaze back to Gordon and noticed that the young man's lips were pursed tightly. "Are you certain that this woman does not want you? Women often play these sorts of games. They think it keeps us interested by suspense."

"This woman is not the sort to play games, sir," Gordon growled. "This woman is a lady."

"I see," he mumbled, wondering just what woman they were now discussing. Something had changed in young Langdon's eyes, and Julian felt his hair stir on his nape. Suddenly, this conversation felt very personal.

"What if the woman is afraid? Could that be possible?" Gordon asked, piercing him with his amber eyes. "What if the lady in question is afraid to admit her love and her desire? What if she fears ridicule and the harm it might cause to those she loves."

"If her love and desire for the man is strong enough, then she should not fear telling him. If she truly loved this man she would not allow anything to come between them," Julian growled. Somehow Gordon had found out about Isabella and him.

Gordon persisted. "What if she thinks that duty comes before everything. What if she fears losing her family, what then? Is that a strong enough inducement to renounce love?"

"I would not allow her to lose her family. I would do everything in my power to protect her and those she loves. If the lady is worth it, I would risk anything to be with her."

"That is the nature of my question, sir. Is the lady worth it?"

"The lady?" Julian pressed himself into the leather squabs, shrinking back like a bloody coward from Gordon's all-seeing gaze. Bloody hell, he was boy, nothing more. He had nothing to fear from this youngling. Gordon could know nothing of his affair with Isabella. Julian had made certain of that. He had sheltered and protected her reputation with meticulous care. No one knew that she had shared a night in his company and his bed. And he was damn certain Isabella would never have discussed something like this with her son.

Gordon's gaze never wavered. "I should tell you now, sir, that I never went on the trip to the lake country."

"And why should that interest me?"

"Because I saw you, sir." He knew Gordon saw the shock that flittered across his face. Julian couldn't hide his response to the pointed insinuation. "I saw my mother enter Claridges, and I saw you waiting at the window. I saw your face when she emerged from the cab. I stayed the entire day and night, waiting in the lobby for her to return. When she came down the stairs I knew something was wrong. And when I saw you standing at the window... well, I reasoned it all out."

Julian took a deep breath and tried to focus on a plan. What would he say to young Gordon? How could he deny it? Did he even want to deny it?

"I might be younger than you, sir, but I know what it means when a man keeps a woman that late into the night in his hotel room."

Unable to formulate the appropriate response for the first time in his life, Julian just sat in his chair, studying the flickering flames and wondering what Isabella would say or do once she discovered the fact her son had learned of her affair with him.

"I love my mother, sir." Gordon's voice throbbed with barely controlled emotion in Gordon's voice. "She has not had an easy time of it these past years—even before—" Gordon swallowed hard and fiddled with his neckcloth. "Even before my father died, this life was not easy for her. After I came to my title, I vowed that I would protect her. I promised myself that I would see her happy—and not the sort of restraint my father insisted upon. I want to see her smile, I want to hear her laugh. And I have not seen that these past days, sir."

Julian met his gaze and they studied each other for a long while. "What is it you want, Langdon?"

"I want the truth, sir. I want to know if you care enough about my mother to take the risk. Or were you just amusing yourself with her while you're in London?"

His hand fisted tightly in his lap. "I have never amused myself with your mother."

Gordon let out a rush of breath. "Then why have you left her miserable?"

"Because," he said between set teeth, "she does not return my affections." *Because she cannot bear to see you or your sister hurt. Because she believes that she has a duty to fulfill, and that duty means not causing a scandal. That duty means marrying someone of her own age and suffering through the same sort of marriage she had with your father.*

Gordon heard what he didn't say. "It is because of us, Minnie and me," he whispered, his eyes widening in alarm.

"I've said too much," Julian mumbled, gripping the arms of his chair and standing slowly. "We should not be discussing your mother. We should not even be discussing such things at all."

"Sir," Gordon countered, standing. "A moment please. You said that my mother did not return your affections. What... what affections are those?"

"The deepest, most abiding love," Julian said softly, not caring that he was speaking to his lover's son in such a way. Gordon might be all of seventeen years, but his maturity was much beyond that. Gordon understood the ways of men, Julian could tell that, he could see the understanding in the young man's eyes. Isabella had the same expressive eyes. So easy to read. So easy to love.

"She feels the same for you, sir," Gordon murmured, reaching for his arm and gripping it tightly. "I know. I can tell. I... I saw the way she looked at you when she was in the carriage. She was crying, sir. I... I know what lies in her heart, and I swear I want her to reach out and take what she deserves. She did not deserve my father or his treatment," he hissed, and Julian stepped back, shocked by Gordon's vehemence against his father.

"I saw him, you know," Gordon continued in a low, angry voice. "I saw him in a carriage with a lightskirt. I heard him with his friends in his study, talking about his women. He should not have had women—he had my mother who did everything to please him. And I hated him as I watched him. I hated what I saw him do to my mother. She deserves a life, sir. A life of happiness and love. She just needs to understand that she deserves it. You said you would never give up on a woman if you wanted her enough. I am asking you, sir, to not give up on my mother."

"Does she know you are here?" Julian asked.

"No, and she will not find out. I would not shame her by telling her I know about the two of you. And furthermore, I know you would never shame her either."

"I wouldn't."

"My mother has accepted an invitation to Lady Pembridge's ball tomorrow evening. I am to escort her. Perhaps we will see you there, sir."

Julian nodded slowly. "Indeed you will."

Emma's ballroom was filled to overflowing with the cream of the ton. In the center of the fray was Emma, their gracious, not to mention, flirty host. Surrounding her were the most seasoned lovers of the ton. As Emma's closest friend, Isabella felt compelled to watch over the gregarious creature. Emma had a habit of taking her flirting too far. Now she had one hand on Isabella's arm and the other on the arm of a middle-aged man. "What do you say, Lord St. John, to seeing Lady Langdon out of mourning?" Emma said in light teasing voice.

"It is very good to have you out in Society once again, Lady Langdon," St. John replied with a polite inclination of his head.

Isabella murmured, "Thank you, my lord."

"Is she not looking very well?" Emma asked of the men gathered around. They all nodded, and one lecherous beast pressed close to Emma and whispered,

"But not as well as you, you teasing little minx.'

Isabella swallowed hard and resisted the urge to fiddle with her emerald necklace. The way the man was eyeing Emma made Isabella extremely uncomfortable, especially with Gordon standing nearby talking with his friends.

"You do indeed look rather ravishing, Lady Langdon," Mr. Scott whispered, pressing into her. "How long has it been?" he murmured seductively.

"I beg your pardon," she said on a gasp, and saw how the man let his gaze roam lazily down her bosom.

"How long has it been?" he said with a leer. "Since you've been out in society, I mean." Isabella snapped her fan open and furiously beat the air before her, not caring that it was the height of impropriety.

He didn't take the hint. "You take my breath away," he breathed urgently against her ear, and she sent him a sidelong glare, but he only smiled and moved a fraction away from her. "Later," he murmured with smug confidence.

"Mum," Gordon whispered in her ear. "Shall I fetch you a glass of punch?"

She looked up at her son with a sense of a relief. "That would be wonderful."

"Lady Langdon," a very deep voice said behind her. "May I request the next dance?"

"Lord Powell," she replied when she whirled around and saw the man standing behind her. "Why, I would be delighted, my lord."

Alastair Powell was a harmless man and a good conversationalist. He was a much safer choice as a companion than Mr. Scott, who had been brazenly staring at her bosom for the past forty minutes.

"Shall we, then?" Lord Powell asked, offering his arm. With a smile, she excused herself from Emma's court and allowed Powell to usher her to the dance floor.

"You are looking very fine this evening, Lady Langdon," Powell said stiffly as he gathered her in his arms, taking care not to hold her too closely. "It has been a long time since we have danced."

"I believe it was the Carson soiree, where we last danced."

"Indeed, right before Langdon carted you off to the east. How did you like the east, by the way?" he asked, finally meeting her gaze. "I heard it's positively hedonistic."

She flushed and fixed her gaze over his shoulder. "Actually, it was rather lovely."

"Hmm," he mumbled, and she heard the vibration in his chest as he twirled her around.

"So, what have you been up to?" she asked. "Gordon tells me you're still very active in parliament."

"Quite right," he said brightening.

"I believe he was mentioning something about a brilliant speech you made in the Lords. A motion, I believe, favoring the Turks and encouraging the government to side with them against the Russians?"

Powell's gaunt face grew radiant. "You've the right of it, madam. I see you still are very interested in politics. As I recall, you were an invaluable asset to Langdon and his political endeavors."

She felt her body stiffen and she was unable to meet his gaze, knowing what she would see shining in them.

"Do you know how damned difficult it is for a diplomat to find a suitable wife, one with a brain that functions?" he asked.

She smiled, a faint pained smile, and scanned the room. She could not do this again. She could not pretend to feel where she did not, love where she did not, perform a duty which would only smother what was left of her spirit.

Suddenly Powell halted on the dance floor and his hands fell from her waist. "Bloody hell, he has some nerve," Powell grunted, and the dancers slowed and the crowd grew quiet.

"His royal highness, Prince Fatiah of Persia," Emma's butler announced.

Isabella knew the second her breath froze between her lips. She made a soft sucking sound and she tried to hide it, but Powell looked down at her and arched his brow.

"Probably haven't met his highness yet," Powell grunted as the dancing resumed its pace. "Bloody pompous half-breed. His mother was nothing, you know. Her father was a younger son of the Persian king, her mother the sister of a crazed Ottoman Turk Sultan. His father was the only decent factor in the whole mix. That was, until he caused a scandal and married his eastern inamorata."

"My lord, it is not polite to gossip," she chastised, unable to keep her gaze from straying to where Julian was cutting a swathe through the ballroom.

"It is not gossip, but fact. Everyone will tolerate him to his face, and scorn his back. The truth of the matter is, no one believes he is a man of breeding. Title or no, he is still a half-breed."

"He is rich, surely that is inducement enough to make the feckless members of society bring him into their fold," she snapped, despising Powell for his pompousness and feeling ill because Julian had not even bothered to look her way.

"Well, there is that," Powell said. "Some industrious gentleman will sacrifice his daughter and suffer the stigma of tawny grandchildren— if for nothing but getting his hands on part of the Persian dynasty. I understand that his wealth is not just in currency, but very rare jewels and gems that would fetch a bloody fortune at Sotheby's. Any man would send his daughter to the slaughter for a chance at that."

Isabella felt a retch in her throat. God help her, she could not smother the sound, or hide her disgust. Is this what the ton truly thought of Julian? Is this why he was enraged with her, for thinking she wanted the prince—just like everyone else wanted the prince? Now she could understand why Julian had never bothered to tell her of his title—for wasn't she just like the rest of society, painting a false face? He hadn't wanted to be used for his title. He had only wanted to be desired as a man, and heaven help her, she had hurt him, destroyed his faith in her.

Powell took hold of her elbow. "The dance is finished, my dear, shall we walk to the refreshment table?"

She drew away. "I think I shall return to Lady Pembridge."

"Allow me to escort you."

Isabella's gloved hand trembled atop Powell's sleeve. As they approached Emma and her circle of admirers, she saw the dark head of Julian towering over everyone. Beside him stood Gordon, his blond curls glistening in the candlelight. Their heads were bent together, and she tilted her head to get a better look. Oh God... they were... talking.

Powell asked, "What is it, my dear? Have you changed your mind about a refreshment?"

She searched for the right words, tried to slow her reeling thoughts, but then Julian looked up and met her gaze. She felt that gaze flicker along her body and then his gaze strayed to her right, and fixed on Powell. Isabella watched the warmth in his eyes die before he lowered his lashes and bent his head, listening to whatever Emma was prattling in his ear.

Walking leisurely through the couples, Isabella felt anger sear her breast. What the devil was Emma saying to him to make him smile so? Was Emma flirting with him? Damn the coquette, had she no morals. Of course she didn't. This was the friend who had actually encouraged her to seek her pleasure with a younger man. No doubt Emma was sizing Julian up, thinking of the delightful ways they could spend the evening.

"Your highness, what a wit you are," Emma cooed. "You have a very clever, skilled tongue, or so I am told."

Isabella was now standing among Emma and her admirers, and she heard Emma's remark and could not help but snap in her ear. "Do remember darling, this is not Cremore Garden."

Emma glared at her. "And your meaning?"

"Double entrendres are amusing in so few places. A ballroom is not one of them."

"Mum," Gordon said then cleared his throat. "Have you met Prince Fatiah yet?"

Isabella's gaze flew to Julian, and she studied him, seeing how his jaw locked and his eyes grew narrow.

He began, "I am afraid—"

"Yes," she said, cutting off his denial, and she saw his eyes go round. "In Constantinople. He was invaluable as our interpreter."

Powell swung his head and stared at her, as did Emma.

"Lady Langdon," Julian murmured, bringing her hand to his mouth. "It is very good to see you again."

"Yes, it is very good," she said, looking at him and thinking how strange it was to be in a room so full of people and yet feel as though only the two of them existed. "It feels almost like a lifetime since we have last met."

His nostrils flared and his gaze slipped to her throat and the cream swells that were revealed by her low cut gown. "It feels the same for me as well, like a lifetime."

"Mum," Gordon murmured, capturing her attention. "Would you care to take a stroll? Lord Cavendish expressed a notion to see you. You remember

Lord Cavendish, do you not, he was one of Papa's dearest friends."

"Yes, of course," she smiled sadly. Duty again was taking her away. "Please excuse me."

Julian bowed as she past him, and she felt heat paint her cheeks red. "You don't look well, mum," Gordon grumbled. "I'm taking you home."

"What?" she asked, shocked. "I am not going anywhere save for back to the ballroom." How dare he drag her out and back home—especially since Julian was here and she ached for the sight of him, her body hungered for his. Just like an opium addict hungered for the drug, she hungered for Julian.

Gordon continued to pull her along. "I'm taking you to the carriage."

"Gordon, I am not a child."

But he ignored her protest, tugging her along and out into the night where their carriage was awaiting them at the bottom of the stairs.

She planted her feet on the walk. "Young man, I am not going anywhere."

Gordon opened the door and motioned his head towards the carriage interior. He grinned as bright as a mischievous child caught stealing an extra sweetmeat.

"Good evening, Isabella."

At the sound of that voice, Isabella's gaze flew to the carriage, only to see Julian sliding forward on the bench, his dark hand reaching out to her. She met Gordon's eyes, a myriad of questions in her expression.

"I approve, Mum. Minnie approves. You deserve this, your prince."

She was speechless, stunned. She stood outside dressed only in her evening gown, without her cloak, staring between Gordon and Julian.

"I want you to go with him," Gordon whispered in her ear. "I want you to be happy, and you're not happy without him. He'll make you happy, mum."

And then Julian was helping her into the carriage, and Gordon was closing the door and rapping against the side to set them in motion. Julian did not set her on the seat beside him, instead he brought her to his lap and wrapped his arm around her waist and tilted her head so that she was looking at him through the soft carriage lamp light.

"My God, you take my breath away," he rasped, his eyes scouring her face. "I could have ripped Powell out of your arms when I saw him pawing you during that waltz. You're mine."

Elation swept through her and she stroked her finger along his lips. "I could have throttled you for allowing Emma to flirt with you."

"This past week has been hell without you," he murmured against her throat. "Everywhere I looked I saw you, smelt you, remembered you. I could still feel you against me when I was laying in bed."

"It is the same for me. When you looked at me across the ballroom my body came alive and I felt... yearning... no... hunger, *fierce hunger* for the touch of you."

He looked up and studied her face as he ran the back of his hand against the upper swells of her breasts. "I am here to touch, Guzelle."

"I am here, too, Julian—me—Isabella."

He kissed her softly allowing his lip to drag across hers. "This is not puppy love, Isabella. This is love in its most honest form. You have my heart—forever."

"And you have mine," she gasped as he crushed her mouth with his. Slowly he kissed her, raising the heat, the urgency until he was gripping her head in his head and thrusting his tongue in her mouth. He tore his mouth away from hers and buried his lips in the valley of breasts, licking and nuzzling and sucking the swells as they inched higher and higher above her bodice.

"I am taking you to Claridges for the night," he murmured against her. "I am undressing you at the dressing table, and then I am going to brush your hair. I have dreamed of brushing your hair and whispering in your ear, and I am going to make love to you right there, so that you can watch me worship you."

She moaned as he pulled her bodice down enough to suckle her nipple. "I want to sleep the night through with you," she said on a soft intake of air. His hot hand ran beneath her skirt and petticoat, only to grasp her thigh above her garter. "I want to wake up in your arms. I have never done that, you see, and I want to open my eyes and see the morning sun streaking into the room, and I want to look over and find you sleeping beside me."

"You will," he whispered as his hand spread her thigh and his fingers sought her wet folds. "You will see me like that every day of our lives. Now," he said, "I want to see you atop me, making love to me as you look into my eyes."

"You are my destiny," she whispered in awe as she felt his fingers slide inside her. "I will never doubt that again."

"Remember that, will you, when you think of our ages, and society." Julian pressed a kiss into her hair. "Just remember what we have between us—a bond that age and color and class will never destroy. There is no bond more powerful than this one, Isabella. Kismet, never question it, only accept it. And know that you are loved and desired by a man who will never stray, who will never refuse your advances. A man who will show you a woman's pleasure for the rest of your life."

Epilogue

Persia, 1852

"Mama," Minnie yelled from the long corridor. "I cannot believe that we shall be living for the next year in a palace."

"Hmm," Isabella murmured as she set her swollen feet atop the red silk stool and gently fanned herself with her peacock fan that resembled a feather duster.

"When Papa claimed to be a prince, I had no idea he meant, well, a *true* prince."

"Neither did I, dearest. I will admit to be taken aback by the whole business. One does not become a princess at my age."

Her daughter scoffed, "Mama, you're not old."

"I feel old," Isabella grumbled as she settled herself deeper into the chair and stroked her swollen belly.

"Nonsense." Minnie turned in a circle, studying the whitewashed walls that were decorated with jewels and mosaics. "Mama, do you think Papa knows any princes who would marry me?"

"I do not," a deep, melodious voice answered from the door. "Besides, you are much too young to be thinking of marrying, Minnie."

Isabella smiled as her husband and her son walked into the room. True to his word, Julian had taken her family into his heart, loving them as if they were his own. Not surprisingly, Gordon and Minnie had accepted Julian just as readily, and the four of them had become a family.

"Your mother looks tired," Julian grumbled as he walked towards her.

"Actually, I just sat down for a few minutes of rest."

"You should be resting in a bed," he murmured in her ear. "with your husband."

"Do you mean that insufferable prince that is always hanging about making certain that I am not taxing myself?"

"The very one."

"I would like to rest in *his* bed," she whispered as she watched Julian's dark hand caress his child safe inside her.

"Your prince would do anything to make you happy."

"He has." And when she looked up from Julian's teal eyes, she saw that Gordon and Minnie had already left the room.

"You have raised two very wise children," Julian said with wickedness in his voice. "Let us hope this child shall be as intuitive and know when to depart the room."

"Indeed," she said, wrapping her arms about Julian's neck. "Now then, show me how a Persian prince goes about seducing his princess."

"It is very wicked."

"Oh, how delightful."

"Very forbidden."

"Even better," she said with a grin.

"It is very loving."

She placed her hand along his cheek and smiled into his eyes. "That, Julian, is the best of all."

Julian murmured, "Do you know, my love, I never could stomach the notion of being a prince. But now that I have seen you in my bed, surrounded by silks and jewels and eastern riches, I can say, with some fondness, and a good deal of wickedness, that it is very good to be your prince."

"Well, you might have said something before, you know," she grumbled. "It is rather unnerving discovering that I've been cavorting with a prince like a common strumpet."

"He likes you as a common strumpet," he murmured. "And he loves you as Isabella."

"A woman's lot in life," she sighed, laying her head against his chest. "It is quite the most decadent thing in the world. I will never again question mine."

About the Author:

Charlotte Featherstone is an incurable dreamer and hopeless romantic. She loves to write steamy stories that represent those mystical bygone days of corsets and rogues. When not day dreaming she can usually be found surfing the net under the guise of research and chatting with her critique partner about her next 'masterpiece'. Occasionally, when she comes back to the twenty-first century, Charlotte can be found reading, writing and generally avoiding any duties attributed to 'Domestic Godesses'.

Charlotte would love to hear from her readers and invites them to visit her at charlottefeatherstone.net *to see where her fantasies will take her next.*

Men you've been dreaming about!

Secrets

Satisfy your desire for more.

*F*eel the wild adventure, fierce passion and the power of love in every **Secrets** Collection story. Red Sage Publishing's romance authors create richly crafted, sexy, sensual, novella-length stories. Each one is just the right length for reading after a long and hectic day.

Each volume in the **Secrets** Collection has four diverse, ultra-sexy, romantic novellas brimming with adventure, passion and love. More adventurous tales for the adventurous reader. The **Secrets** Collection are a glorious mix of romance genre; numerous historical settings, contemporary, paranormal, science fiction and suspense. We are always looking for new adventures.

Reader response to the **Secrets** volumes has been great! Here's just a small sample:

"I loved the variety of settings. Four completely wonderful time periods, give you four completely wonderful reads."

"Each story was a page-turning tale I hated to put down."

*"I love **Secrets**! When is the next volume coming out? This one was Hot! Loved the heroes!"*

Secrets have won raves and awards. We could go on, but why don't you find out for yourself—order your set of **Secrets** today! See the back for details.

Secrets, Volume 1

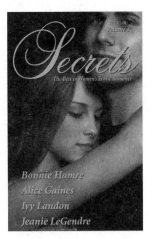

Listen to what reviewers say:

"These stories take you beyond romance into the realm of erotica. I found *Secrets* absolutely delicious."

—Virginia Henley,
New York Times Best Selling Author

"*Secrets* is a collection of novellas for the daring, adventurous woman who's not afraid to give her fantasies free reign."

—Kathe Robin, *Romantic Times* Magazine

"…In fact, the men featured in all the stories are terrific, they all want to please and pleasure their women. If you like erotic romance you will love *Secrets*."

—*Romantic Readers* Review

In *Secrets, Volume 1* you'll find:

A Lady's Quest by Bonnie Hamre

Widowed Lady Antonia Blair-Sutworth searches for a lover to save her from the handsome Duke of Sutherland. The "auditions" may be shocking but utterly tantalizing.

The Spinner's Dream by Alice Gaines

A seductive fantasy that leaves every woman wishing for her own private love slave, desperate and running for his life.

The Proposal by Ivy Landon

This tale is a walk on the wild side of love. *The Proposal* will taunt you, tease you, and shock you. A contemporary erotica for the adventurous woman.

The Gift by Jeanie LeGendre

Immerse yourself in this historic tale of exotic seduction, bondage and a concubine's surrender to the Sultan's desire. Can Alessandra live the life and give the gift the Sultan demands of her?

Secrets, Volume 2

Listen to what reviewers say:

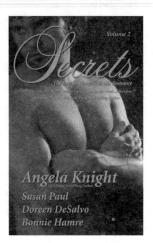

"*Secrets* offers four novellas of sensual delight; each beautifully written with intense feeling and dedication to character development. For those seeking stories with heightened intimacy, look no further."

> —Kathee Card, *Romancing the Web*

"Such a welcome diversity in styles and genres. Rich characterization in sensual tales. An exciting read that's sure to titillate the senses."

> —Cheryl Ann Porter

"*Secrets 2* left me breathless. Sensual satisfaction guaranteed… times four!"

> —Virginia Henley, *New York Times* Best Selling Author

In *Secrets, Volume 2* you'll find:

Surrogate Lover by Doreen DeSalvo

Adrian Ross is a surrogate sex therapist who has all the answers and control. He thought he'd seen and done it all, but he'd never met Sarah.

Snowbound by Bonnie Hamre

A delicious, sensuous regency tale. The marriage-shy Earl of Howden is teased and tortured by his own desires and finds there is a woman who can equal his overpowering sensuality.

Roarke's Prisoner by Angela Knight

Elise, a starship captain, remembers the eager animal submission she'd known before at her captor's hands and refuses to become his toy again. However, she has no idea of the delights he's planned for her this time.

Savage Garden by Susan Paul

Raine's been captured by a mysterious and dangerous revolutionary leader in Mexico. At first her only concern is survival, but she quickly finds lush erotic nights in her captor's arms.

Winner of the Fallot Literary Award for Fiction!

Secrets, Volume 3

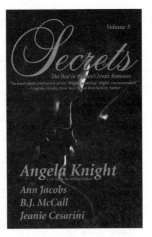

Listen to what reviewers say:

"*Secrets, Volume 3*, leaves the reader breathless.
A delicious confection of sensuous treats awaits
the reader on each turn of the page!"

—Kathee Card, *Romancing the Web*

"From the FBI to Police Detective to Vampires
to a Medieval Warlord home from the Cru-
sade—*Secrets 3* is simply the best!"

—Susan Paul, award winning author

"An unabashed celebration of sex. Highly arousing! Highly recommended!"
—Virginia Henley, *New York Times* Best Selling Author

In *Secrets, Volume 3* you'll find:

The Spy Who Loved Me by Jeanie Cesarini

Undercover FBI agent Paige Ellison's sexual appetites rise to new levels
when she works with leading man Christopher Sharp, the cunning agent who
uses all his training to capture her body and heart.

The Barbarian by Ann Jacobs

Lady Brianna vows not to surrender to the barbaric Giles, Earl of Harrow.
He must use sexual arts learned in the infidels' harem to conquer his bride.
A word of caution—this is not for the faint of heart.

Blood and Kisses by Angela Knight

A vampire assassin is after Beryl St. Cloud. Her only hope lies with Decker,
another vampire and ex-mercenary. Broke, she offers herself as payment for
his services. Will his seductive powers take her very soul?

Love Undercover by B.J. McCall

Amanda Forbes is the bait in a strip joint sting operation. While she per-
forms, fellow detective "Cowboy" Cooper gets to watch. Though he excites
her, she must fight the temptation to surrender to the passion.

**Winner of the 1997 Under the Covers
Readers Favorite Award**

Secrets, Volume 4

Listen to what reviewers say:

"Provocative... seductive... a must read!"

—*Romantic Times* Magazine

"These are the kind of stories that romance readers that 'want a little more' have been looking for all their lives...."

—*Affaire de Coeur* Magazine

"*Secrets, Volume 4*, has something to satisfy every erotic fantasy... simply sexational!"

—Virginia Henley, *New York Times* Best Selling Author

In *Secrets, Volume 4* you'll find:

An Act of Love by Jeanie Cesarini
Shelby Moran's past left her terrified of sex. International film star Jason Gage must gently coach the young starlet in the ways of love. He wants more than an act—he wants Shelby to feel true passion in his arms.

Enslaved by Desirée Lindsey
Lord Nicholas Summer's air of danger, dark passions, and irresistible charm have brought Lady Crystal's long-hidden desires to the surface. Will he be able to give her the one thing she desires before it's too late?

The Bodyguard by Betsy Morgan and Susan Paul
Kaki York is a bodyguard, but watching the wild, erotic romps of her client's sexual conquests on the security cameras is getting to her—and her partner, the ruggedly handsome James Kulick. Can she resist his insistent desire to have her?

The Love Slave by Emma Holly
A woman's ultimate fantasy. For one year, Princess Lily will be attended to by three delicious men of her choice. While she delights in playing with the first two, it's the reluctant Grae, with his powerful chest, black eyes and hair, that stirs her desires.

Secrets, Volume 5

Listen to what reviewers say:

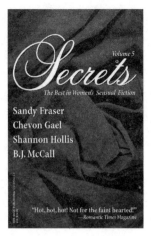

"Hot, hot, hot! Not for the faint-hearted!"

—Romantic Times Magazine

"As you make your way through the stories, you will find yourself becoming hotter and hotter. *Secrets* just keeps getting better and better."

—Affaire de Coeur Magazine

"*Secrets 5* is a collage of luscious sensuality. Any woman who reads *Secrets* is in for an awakening!"

—Virginia Henley, *New York Times* Best Selling Author

In *Secrets, Volume 5* you'll find:

Beneath Two Moons by Sandy Fraser

Ready for a very wild romp? Step into the future and find Conor, rough and masculine like frontiermen of old, on the prowl for a new conquest. In his sights, Dr. Eva Kelsey. She got away once before, but this time Conor makes sure she begs for more.

Insatiable by Chevon Gael

Marcus Remington photographs beautiful models for a living, but it's Ashlyn Fraser, a young corporate exec having some glamour shots done, who has stolen his heart. It's up to Marcus to help her discover her inner sexual self.

Strictly Business by Shannon Hollis

Elizabeth Forrester knows it's tough enough for a woman to make it to the top in the corporate world. Garrett Hill, the most beautiful man in Silicon Valley, has to come along to stir up her wildest fantasies. Dare she give in to both their desires?

Alias Smith and Jones by B.J. McCall

Meredith Collins finds herself stranded overnight at the airport. A handsome stranger by the name of Smith offers her sanctuary for the evening and she finds those mesmerizing, green-flecked eyes hard to resist. Are they to be just two ships passing in the night?

Secrets, Volume 6

Listen to what reviewers say:

"Red Sage was the first and remains the leader of Women's Erotic Romance Fiction Collections!"
— *Romantic Times* Magazine

"*Secrets, Volume 6*, is the best of *Secrets* yet. …four of the most erotic stories in one volume than this reader has yet to see anywhere else. …These stories are full of erotica at its best and you'll definitely want to keep it handy for lots of re-reading!"
— *Affaire de Coeur* Magazine

"*Secrets 6* satisfies every female fantasy: the Bodyguard, the Tutor, the Werewolf, and the Vampire. I give it Six Stars!"
— Virginia Henley, *New York Times* Best Selling Author

In *Secrets, Volume 6* you'll find:

Flint's Fuse by Sandy Fraser
Dana Madison's father has her "kidnapped" for her own safety. Flint, the tall, dark and dangerous mercenary, is hired for the job. But just which one is the prisoner—Dana will try *anything* to get away.

Love's Prisoner by MaryJanice Davidson
Trapped in an elevator, Jeannie Lawrence experienced unwilling rapture at Michael Windham's hands. She never expected the devilishly handsome man to show back up in her life—or turn out to be a werewolf!

The Education of Miss Felicity Wells by Alice Gaines
Felicity Wells wants to be sure she'll satisfy her soon-to-be husband but she needs a teacher. Dr. Marcus Slade, an experienced lover, agrees to take her on as a student, but can he stop short of taking her completely?

A Candidate for the Kiss by Angela Knight
Working on a story, reporter Dana Ivory stumbles onto a more amazing one—a sexy, secret agent who happens to be a vampire. She wants her story but Gabriel Archer wants more from her than just sex and blood.

Secrets, Volume 7

Listen to what reviewers say:

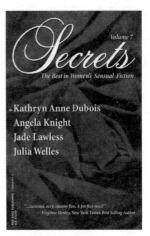

"Get out your asbestos gloves—*Secrets Volume 7* is... extremely hot, true erotic romance... passionate and titillating. There's nothing quite like baring your secrets!"

—*Romantic Times* Magazine

"...sensual, sexy, steamy fun. A perfect read!"
—Virginia Henley,
New York Times Best Selling Author

"Intensely provocative and disarmingly romantic, *Secrets*, *Volume 7*, is a romance reader's paradise that will take you beyond your wildest dreams!"
—Ballston Book House Review

In *Secrets, Volume 7* you'll find:

Amelia's Innocence by Julia Welles

Amelia didn't know her father bet her in a card game with Captain Quentin Hawke, so honor demands a compromise—three days of erotic foreplay, leaving her virginity and future intact.

The Woman of His Dreams by Jade Lawless

From the day artist Gray Avonaco moves in next door, Joanna Morgan is plagued by provocative dreams. But what she believes is unrequited lust, Gray sees as another chance to be with the woman he loves. He must persuade her that even death can't stop true love.

Surrender by Kathryn Anne Dubois

Free-spirited Lady Johanna wants no part of the binding strictures society imposes with her marriage to the powerful Duke. She doesn't know the dark Duke wants sensual adventure, and sexual satisfaction.

Kissing the Hunter by Angela Knight

Navy Seal Logan McLean hunts the vampires who murdered his wife. Virginia Hart is a sexy vampire searching for her lost soul-mate only to find him in a man determined to kill her. She must convince him all vampires aren't created equally.

Winner of the Venus Book Club Best Book of the Year

Secrets, Volume 8

Listen to what reviewers say:

"*Secrets, Volume 8*, is an amazing compilation of sexy stories covering a wide range of subjects, all designed to titillate the senses. ...you'll find something for everybody in this latest version of *Secrets*."

—*Affaire de Coeur* Magazine

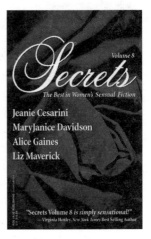

"*Secrets Volume 8*, is simply sensational!"
—Virginia Henley, *New York Times*
Best Selling Author

"These delectable stories will have you turning the pages long into the night. Passionate, provocative and perfect for setting the mood...."

—*Escape to Romance* Reviews

In *Secrets, Volume 8* you'll find:

Taming Kate by Jeanie Cesarini

Kathryn Roman inherits a legal brothel. Little does this city girl know the town of Love, Nevada wants her to be their new madam so they've charged Trey Holliday, one very dominant cowboy, with taming her.

Jared's Wolf by MaryJanice Davidson

Jared Rocke will do anything to avenge his sister's death, but ends up attracted to Moira Wolfbauer, the she-wolf sworn to protect her pack. Joining forces to stop a killer, they learn love defies all boundaries.

My Champion, My Lover by Alice Gaines

Celeste Broder is a woman committed for having a sexy appetite. Mayor Robert Albright may be her champion—if she can convince him her freedom will mean a chance to indulge their appetites together.

Kiss or Kill by Liz Maverick

In this post-apocalyptic world, Camille Kazinsky's military career rides on her ability to make a choice—whether the robo called Meat should live or die. Meat's future depends on proving he's human enough to live, man enough... to makes her feel like a woman.

Winner of the Venus Book Club Best Book of the Year

Secrets, Volume 9

Listen to what reviewers say:

"Everyone should expect only the most erotic stories in a *Secrets* book. …if you like your stories full of hot sexual scenes, then this is for you!"

— Donna Doyle Romance Reviews

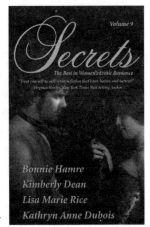

"*SECRETS 9*… is sinfully delicious, highly arousing, and hotter than hot as the pages practically burn up as you turn them."

— Suzanne Coleburn, Reader To Reader Reviews/Belles & Beaux of Romance

"Treat yourself to well-written fiction that's hot, hotter, and hottest!"

— Virginia Henley, *New York Times* Best Selling Author

In *Secrets, Volume 9* you'll find:

Wild For You by Kathryn Anne Dubois

When college intern, Georgie, gets captured by a Congo wildman, she discovers this specimen of male virility has never seen a woman. The research possibilities are endless!

Wanted by Kimberly Dean

FBI Special Agent Jeff Reno wants Danielle Carver. There's her body, brains—and that charge of treason on her head. Dani goes on the run, but the sexy Fed is hot on her trail.

Secluded by Lisa Marie Rice

Nicholas Lee's wealth and power came with a price—his enemies will kill anyone he loves. When Isabelle steals his heart, Nicholas secludes her in his palace for a lifetime of desire in only a few days.

Flights of Fantasy by Bonnie Hamre

Chloe taught others to see the realities of life but she's never shared the intimate world of her sensual yearnings. Given the chance, will she be woman enough to fulfill her most secret erotic fantasy?

Secrets, Volume 10

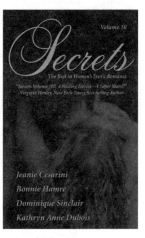

Listen to what reviewers say:

"*Secrets Volume 10*, an erotic dance through medieval castles, sultan's palaces, the English countryside and expensive hotel suites, explodes with passion-filled pages."

—*Romantic Times BOOKclub*

"Having read the previous nine volumes, this one fulfills the expectations of what is expected in a *Secrets* book: romance and eroticism at its best!!"

—*Fallen Angel Reviews*

"All are hot steamy romances so if you enjoy erotica romance, you are sure to enjoy *Secrets, Volume 10*. All this reviewer can say is WOW!!"

—*The Best Reviews*

In *Secrets, Volume 10* you'll find:

Private Eyes by Dominique Sinclair

When a mystery man captivates P.I. Nicolla Black during a stakeout, she discovers her no-seduction rule bending under the pressure of long denied passion. She agrees to the seduction, but he demands her total surrender.

The Ruination of Lady Jane by Bonnie Hamre

To avoid her upcoming marriage, Lady Jane Ponsonby-Maitland flees into the arms of Havyn Attercliffe. She begs him to ruin her rather than turn her over to her odious fiancé.

Code Name: Kiss by Jeanie Cesarini

Agent Lily Justiss is on a mission to defend her country against terrorists that requires giving up her virginity as a sex slave. As her master takes her body, desire for her commanding officer Seth Blackthorn fuels her mind.

The Sacrifice by Kathryn Anne Dubois

Lady Anastasia Bedovier is days from taking her vows as a Nun. Before she denies her sensuality forever, she wants to experience pleasure. Count Maxwell is the perfect man to initiate her into erotic delight.

Secrets, Volume 11

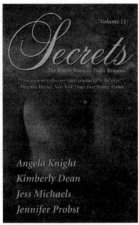

Listen to what reviewers say:

"*Secrets Volume 11* delivers once again with storylines that include erotic masquerades, ancient curses, modern-day betrayal and a prince charming looking for a kiss." **4 Stars**

—*Romantic Times BOOKclub*

"Indulge yourself with this erotic treat and join the thousands of readers who just can't get enough. Be forewarned that *Secrets 11* will whet your appetite for more, but will offer you the ultimate in pleasurable erotic literature."

—*Ballston Book House Review*

"*Secrets 11* quite honestly is my favorite anthology from Red Sage so far."

—*The Best Reviews*

In *Secrets, Volume 11* you'll find:

Masquerade by Jennifer Probst

Hailey Ashton is determined to free herself from her sexual restrictions. Four nights of erotic pleasures without revealing her identity. A chance to explore her secret desires without the fear of unmasking.

Ancient Pleasures by Jess Michaels

Isabella Winslow is obsessed with finding out what caused her late husband's death, but trapped in an Egyptian concubine's tomb with a sexy American raider, succumbing to the mummy's sensual curse takes over.

Manhunt by Kimberly Dean

Framed for murder, Michael Tucker takes Taryn Swanson hostage—the one woman who can clear him. Despite the evidence against him, the attraction between them is strong. Tucker resorts to unconventional, yet effective methods of persuasion to change the sexy ADA's mind.

Wake Me by Angela Knight

Chloe Hart received a sexy painting of a sleeping knight. Radolf of Varik has been trapped for centuries in the painting since, cursed by a witch. His only hope is to visit the dreams of women and make one of them fall in love with him so she can free him with a kiss.

Secrets, Volume 12

Listen to what reviewers say:

"*Secrets Volume 12*, turns on the heat with a seductive encounter inside a bookstore, a temple of naughty and sensual delight, a galactic inferno that thaws ice, and a lightening storm that lights up the English shoreline. Tales of looking for love in all the right places with a heat rating out the charts." **4½ Stars**

—*Romantic Times BOOKclub*

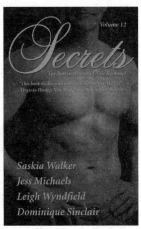

"I really liked these stories. You want great escapism? Read *Secrets, Volume 12*."

—*Romance Reviews*

In *Secrets, Volume 12* you'll find:

Good Girl Gone Bad by Dominique Sinclair

Reagan's dreams are finally within reach. Setting out to do research for an article, nothing could have prepared her for Luke, or his offer to teach her everything she needs to know about sex. Licentious pleasures, forbidden desires… inspiring the best writing she's ever done.

Aphrodite's Passion by Jess Michaels

When Selena flees Victorian London before her evil stepchildren can institutionalize her for hysteria, Gavin is asked to bring her back home. But when he finds her living on the island of Cyprus, his need to have her begins to block out every other impulse.

White Heat by Leigh Wyndfield

Raine is hiding in an icehouse in the middle of nowhere from one of the scariest men in the universes. Walker escaped from a burning prison. Imagine their surprise when they find out they have the same man to blame for their miseries. Passion, revenge and love are in their future.

Summer Lightning by Saskia Walker

Sculptress Sally is enjoying an idyllic getaway on a secluded cove when she spots a gorgeous man walking naked on the beach. When Julian finds an attractive woman shacked up in his cove, he has to check her out. But what will he do when he finds she's secretly been using him as a model?

Secrets, Volume 13

Listen to what reviewers say:

"In *Secrets Volume 13*, the temperature gets turned up a few notches with a mistaken personal ad, shape-shifters destined to love, a hot Regency lord and his lady, as well as a bodyguard protecting his woman. Emotions and flames blaze high in Red Sage's latest foray into the sensual and delightful art of love." **4½ Stars**

—*Romantic Times BOOKclub*

"The sex is still so hot the pages nearly ignite! Read *Secrets, Volume 13!*"

—*Romance Reviews*

In *Secrets, Volume 13* you'll find:

Out of Control by Rachelle Chase

Astrid's world revolves around her business and she's hoping to pick up wealthy Erik Santos as a client. Only he's hoping to pick up something entirely different. Will she give in to the seductive pull of his proposition?

Hawkmoor by Amber Green

Shape-shifters answer to Darien as he acts in the name of the long-missing Lady Hawkmoor, their hereditary ruler. When she unexpectedly surfaces, Darien must deal with a scrappy individual whose wary eyes hold the other half of his soul, but who has the power to destroy his world.

Lessons in Pleasure by Charlotte Featherstone

A wicked bargain has Lily vowing never to yield to the demands of the rake she once loved and lost. Unfortunately, Damian, the Earl of St. Croix, or Saint as he is infamously known, will not take 'no' for an answer.

In the Heat of the Night by Calista Fox

Haunted by a century-old curse, Molina fears she won't live to see her thirtieth birthday. Nick, her former bodyguard, is hired back into service to protect her from the fatal accidents that plague her family. But *In the Heat of the Night*, will his passion and love for her be enough to convince Molina they have a future together?

Secrets, Volume 14

Listen to what reviewers say:

"*Secrets Volume 14* will excite readers with its
diverse selection of delectable sexy tales ranging
from a fourteenth century love story to a sci-fi
rebel who falls for a irresistible research scientist
to a trio of determined vampires who battle for
the same woman to a virgin sacrifice who falls in
love with a beast. A cornucopia of pure delight!"
4½ Stars

—*Romantic Times BOOKclub*

"This book contains four erotic tales sure to keep readers up long into the night."
—*Romance Junkies*

In *Secrets, Volume 14* you'll find:

Soul Kisses by Angela Knight

Beth's been kidnapped by Joaquin Ramirez, a sadistic vampire. Handsome
vampire cousins, Morgan and Garret Axton, come to her rescue. Can she
find happiness with two vampires?

Temptation in Time by Alexa Aames

Ariana escaped the Middle Ages after stealing a kiss of magic from sexy
sorcerer, Marcus de Grey. When he brings her back, they begin a battle of
wills and a sexual odyssey that could spell disaster for them both.

Ailis and the Beast by Jennifer Barlowe

When Ailis agreed to be her village's sacrifice to the mysterious Beast she
was prepared to sacrifice her virtue, and possibly her life. But some things
aren't what they seem. Ailis and the Beast are about to discover the greatest
sacrifice may be the human heart.

Night Heat by Leigh Wynfield

When Rip Bowhite leads a revolt on the prison planet, he ends up struggling
to survive against monsters that rule the night. Jemma, the prison's Healer,
won't allow herself to be distracted by the instant attraction she feels for Rip.
As the stakes are raised and death draws near, love seems doomed in the heat
of the night.

Secrets, Volume 15

Listen to what reviewers say:

"*Secrets Volume 15* blends humor, tension and steamy romance in its newest collection that sizzles with passion between unlikely pairs—a male chauvinist columnist and a librarian turned erotica author; a handsome werewolf and his resisting mate; an unfulfilled woman and a sexy police officer and a Victorian wife who learns discipline can be fun. Readers will revel in this delicious assortment of thrilling tales." **4 Stars**
— *Romantic Times BOOKclub*

"This book contains four tales by some of today's hottest authors that will tease your senses and intrigue your mind."

— *Romance Junkies*

In *Secrets, Volume 15* you'll find:

Simon Says by Jane Thompson
Simon Campbell is a newspaper columnist who panders to male fantasies. Georgina Kennedy is a respectable librarian. On the surface, these two have nothing in common... but don't judge a book by its cover.

Bite of the Wolf by Cynthia Eden
Gareth Morlet, alpha werewolf, has finally found his mate. All he has to do is convince Trinity to join with him, to give in to the pleasure of a were-wolf's mating, and then she will be his... forever.

Falling for Trouble by Saskia Walker
With 48 hours to clear her brother's name, Sonia Harmond finds help from irresistible bad boy, Oliver Eaglestone. When the erotic tension between them hits fever pitch, securing evidence to thwart an international arms dealer isn't the only danger they face.

The Disciplinarian by Leigh Court
Headstrong Clarissa Babcock is sent to the shadowy legend known as The Disciplinarian for instruction in proper wifely obedience. Jared Ashworth uses the tools of seduction to show her how to control a demanding husband, but her beauty, spirit, and uninhibited passion make Jared hunger to keep her—and their darkly erotic nights—all for himself!

Secrets, Volume 16

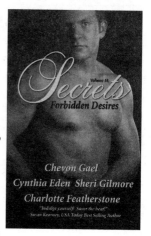

Listen to what reviewers say:

"Blackmail, games of chance, nude beaches and masquerades pave a path to heart-tugging emotions and fiery love scenes in Red Sage's latest collection." **4.5 Stars**
—*Romantic Times BOOKclub*

"Red Sage Publishing has brought to the readers an erotic profusion of highly skilled storytellers in their Secrets Vol. 16. ... This is the best Secrets novel to date and this reviewer's favorite."
—*LoveRomances.com*

In *Secrets, Volume 16* you'll find:

Never Enough by Cynthia Eden

For the last three weeks, Abby McGill has been playing with fire. Bad-boy Jake has taught her the true meaning of desire, but she knows she has to end her relationship with him. But Jake isn't about to let the woman he wants walk away from him.

Bunko by Sheri Gilmoore

Tu Tran is forced to decide between Jack, a man, who promises to share every aspect of his life with her, or Dev, the man, who hides behind a mask and only offers night after night of erotic sex. Will she take the gamble of the dice and choose the man, who can see behind her own mask and expose her true desires?

Hide and Seek by Chevon Gael

Kyle DeLaurier ditches his trophy-fiance in favor of a tropical paradise full of tall, tanned, topless females. Private eye, Darcy McLeod, is on the trail of this runaway groom. Together they sizzle while playing Hide and Seek with their true identities.

Seduction of the Muse by Charlotte Featherstone

He's the Dark Lord, the mysterious author who pens the erotic tales of an innocent woman's seduction. She is his muse, the woman he watches from the dark shadows, the woman whose dreams he invades at night.

Secrets, Volume 17

Listen to what reviewers say:

"Readers who have clamored for more *Secrets* will love the mix of alpha and beta males as well as kick-butt heroines who always get their men."
4 Stars

—*Romantic Times BOOKclub*

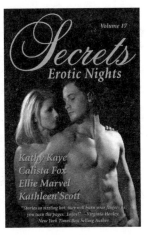

"Stories so sizzling hot, they will burn your fingers as you turn the pages. Enjoy!"
—Virginia Henley, *New York Times* Best Selling Author

"Red Sage is bringing us another thrilling anthology of passion and desire that will keep you up long into the night." —*Romance Junkies*

In *Secrets, Volume 17* you'll find:

Rock Hard Candy by Kathy Kaye

Jessica Hennessy, the great, great granddaughter of a Voodoo priestess, decides she's waited long enough for the man of her dreams. A dose of her ancestor's aphrodisiac slipped into the gooey center of her homemade bon bons ought to do the trick.

Fatal Error by Kathleen Scott

Jesse Storm must make amends to humanity by destroying the computer program he helped design that has taken the government hostage. But he must also protect the woman he's loved in secret for nearly a decade.

Birthday by Ellie Marvel

Jasmine Templeton decides she's been celibate long enough. Will a wild night at a hot new club with her two best friends ease the ache inside her or just make it worse? Well, considering one of those best friends is Charlie and she's been having strange notions about their relationship of late… It's definitely a birthday neither she nor Charlie will ever forget.

Intimate Rendezvous by Calista Fox

A thief causes trouble at Cassandra Kensington's nightclub, Rendezvous, and sexy P.I. Dean Hewitt arrives on the scene to help. One look at the siren who owns the club has his blood boiling, despite the fact that his keen instincts have him questioning the legitimacy of her business.

Secrets, Volume 18

Listen to what reviewers say:

"Fantastic love scenes make this a book to be enjoyed more than once." **4.5 Stars**
—*Romantic Times BOOKclub*

"*Secrets Volume 18* continues [its] tradition of high quality sensual stories that both excite the senses while stimulating the mind."
—CK²S Kwips and Kritiques

"Edgy, erotic, exciting, *Secrets* is always a fantastic read!"
—Susan Kearney, *USA Today* Best Selling Author

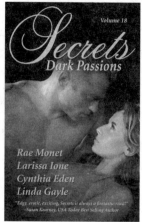

In *Secrets, Volume 18* you'll find:

Lone Wolf Three by Rae Monet

Planetary politics and squabbling over wolf occupied territory drain former rebel leader Taban Zias. But his anger quickly turns to desire when he meets, Lakota Blackson. Focused, calm and honorable, the female Wolf Warrior is Taban's perfect mate—now if he can just convince her.

Flesh to Fantasy by Larissa Ione

Kelsa Bradshaw is an intense loner whose job keeps her happily immersed in a fanciful world of virtual reality. Trent Jordan is a laid-back paramedic who experiences the harsh realities of life up close and personal. But when their worlds collide in an erotic eruption can Trent convince Kelsa to turn the fantasy into something real?

Heart Full of Stars by Linda Gayle

Singer Fanta Rae finds herself stranded on a lonely Mars outpost with the first human male she's seen in years. Ex-Marine Alex Decker lost his family and guilt drove him into isolation, but when alien assassins come to enslave Fanta, she and Decker come together to fight for their lives.

The Wolf's Mate by Cynthia Eden

When Michael Morlet finds Katherine "Kat" Hardy fighting for her life in a dark alley, he instantly recognizes her as the mate he's been seeking all of his life, but someone's trying to kill her. With danger stalking them at every turn, will Kat trust him enough to become The Wolf's Mate?

Secrets, Volume 19
Released July 2007

Affliction
by Elisa Adams

Holly Aronson finally believes
she's safe and whole in the
orbit of sweet Andrew. But when
Andrew's life long friend, Shane,
arrives, events begin to spiral out
of control again. Worse, she's
inexplicably drawn to Shane. As
she runs for her life, which one
will protect her? And whom does
she truly love?

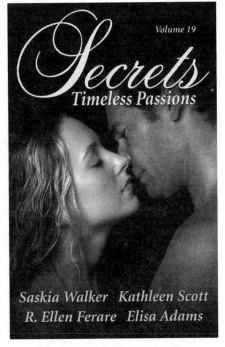

Falling Stars
by Kathleen Scott

Daria is both a Primon fighter
pilot and a Primon princess. As a
deadly new enemy faces appears,
she must choose between her duty
to the fleet and the desperate need
to forge an alliance through her marriage to the enemy's General Raven.

Toy in the Attic
by R. Ellen Ferare

When Gabrielle checks into the top floor of an old hotel, she discovers a life-
sized statue of a nude man. Her unexpected roommate reveals himself to be
a talented lover caught by a witch's curse. Can she help him break free of the
spell that holds him, without losing her heart along the way?

What You Wish For
by Saskia Walker

Lucy Chambers is renovating her newly purchased historic house. As her
dreams about a stranger become more intense, she wishes he were with her
now. Two hundred years in the past, the man wishes for companionship and
suddenly they find themselves together—in his time.

Secrets, Volume 20
Released July 2007

The Subject
by Amber Green

One week Tyler is a hot game designer, signing the deal of her life. The next, she's on the run for her life. Who can she trust? Certainly not sexy, mysterious Esau, who keeps showing up after the hoo-hah hits the fan!

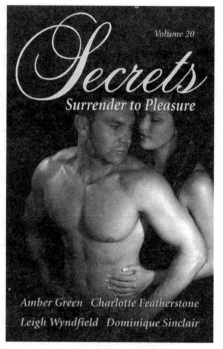

Surrender
by Dominique Sinclair

Agent Madeline Carter is in too deep. She's slipped into Sebastian Maiocco's life to investigate his Sicilian mafia family. He unearths desires Madeline's unable to deny, conflicting the duty that honors her. Madeline must surrender to Sebastian or risk being exposed, leaving her target for a ruthless clan.

Stasis
by Leigh Wyndfield

Morgann Right has a problem. Her Commanding Officer has been drugged with Stasis, turning him into a living, breathing statue she's forced to take care of for ten long days. As her hands tend to him, she suddenly sees her CO in a totally different light. She wants him and, while she can tell he wants her, touching him intimately might come back to haunt them both.

A Woman's Pleasure
by Charlotte Featherstone

Widowed Isabella, Lady Langdon is tired of denying her needs and desires. Yearning to discover all the pleasures denied her in her marriage, she finds herself falling hard for the magnetic charms of the mysterious and exotic Julian Gresham—a man skilled in pleasures of the flesh. A man eight years her junior. A man more than eager to show her *A Woman's Pleasure.*

The Forever Kiss
by Angela Knight

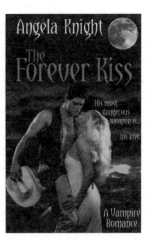

Listen to what reviewers say:

"*The Forever Kiss* flows well with good characters and an interesting plot. ... If you enjoy vampires and a lot of hot sex, you are sure to enjoy *The Forever Kiss*."

—*The Best Reviews*

"Battling vampires, a protective ghost and the ever present battle of good and evil keep excellent pace with the erotic delights in Angela Knight's *The Forever Kiss*—a book that absolutely bites with refreshing paranormal humor." **4½ Stars, Top Pick**

—*Romantic Times BOOKclub*

"I found *The Forever Kiss* to be an exceptionally written, refreshing book. ... I really enjoyed this book by Angela Knight. ... 5 angels!"

—*Fallen Angel Reviews*

"*The Forever Kiss* is the first single title released from Red Sage and if this is any indication of what we can expect, it won't be the last. ... The love scenes are hot enough to give a vampire a sunburn and the fight scenes will have you cheering for the good guys."

—*Really Bad Barb Reviews*

In *The Forever Kiss*:

For years, Valerie Chase has been haunted by dreams of a Texas Ranger she knows only as "Cowboy." As a child, he rescued her from the nightmare vampires who murdered her parents. As an adult, she still dreams of him—but now he's her seductive lover in nights of erotic pleasure.

Yet "Cowboy" is more than a dream—he's the real Cade McKinnon—and a vampire! For years, he's protected Valerie from Edward Ridgemont, the sadistic vampire who turned him. Now, Ridgmont wants Valerie for his own and Cade is the only one who can protect her.

When Val finds herself abducted by her handsome dream man, she's appalled to discover he's one of the vampires she fears. Now, caught in a web of fear and passion, she and Cade must learn to trust each other, even as an immortal monster stalks their every move.

Their only hope of survival is... *The Forever Kiss*.

Romantic Times Best Erotic Novel of the Year

It's not just reviewers raving about *Secrets*. See what readers have to say:

"When are you coming out with a new Volume? I want a new one next month!" via email from a reader.

"I loved the hot, wet sex without vulgar words being used to make it exciting." after *Volume 1*

"I loved the blend of sensuality and sexual intensity—HOT!" after *Volume 2*

"The best thing about *Secrets* is they're hot and brief! The least thing is you do not have enough of them!" after *Volume 3*

"I have been extremely satisfied with *Secrets*, keep up the good writing." after *Volume 4*

"Stories have plot and characters to support the erotica. They would be good strong stories without the heat." after *Volume 5*

"*Secrets* really knows how to push the envelop better than anyone else." after *Volume 6*

"These are the best sensual stories I have ever read!" after *Volume 7*

"I love, love, love the *Secrets* stories. I now have all of them, please have more books come out each year." after *Volume 8*

"These are the perfect sensual romance stories!" after *Volume 9*

"What I love about *Secrets Volume 10* is how I couldn't put it down!" after *Volume 10*

"All of the *Secrets* volumes are terrific! I have read all of them up to *Secrets Volume 11*. Please keep them coming! I will read every one you make!" after *Volume 11*

Finally, the men you've been dreaming about!

Give the Gift of Spicy Romantic Fiction

Don't want to wait? You can place a retail price ($12.99) order
for any of the *Secrets* volumes from the following:

① **Waldenbooks and Borders Stores**

② **Amazon.com or BarnesandNoble.com**

③ **Book Clearinghouse (800-431-1579)**

④ **Romantic Times Magazine** Books by Mail (718-237-1097)

⑤ Special order at other bookstores.

Bookstores: Please contact Baker & Taylor Distributors, Ingram Book
Distributor, or Red Sage Publishing for bookstore sales.

Order by title or ISBN #:

Vol. 1: 0-9648942-0-3	**Vol. 8:** 0-9648942-8-9	**Vol. 15:** 0-9754516-5-0
ISBN #13 978-0-9648942-0-4	ISBN #13 978-0-9648942-9-7	ISBN #13 978-0-9754516-5-6
Vol. 2: 0-9648942-1-1	**Vol. 9:** 0-9648942-9-7	**Vol. 16:** 0-9754516-6-9
ISBN #13 978-0-9648942-1-1	ISBN #13 978-0-9648942-9-7	ISBN #13 978-0-9754516-6-3
Vol. 3: 0-9648942-2-X	**Vol. 10:** 0-9754516-0-X	**Vol. 17:** 0-9754516-7-7
ISBN #13 978-0-9648942-2-8	ISBN #13 978-0-9754516-0-1	ISBN #13 978-0-9754516-7-0
Vol. 4: 0-9648942-4-6	**Vol. 11:** 0-9754516-1-8	**Vol. 18:** 0-9754516-8-5
ISBN #13 978-0-9648942-4-2	ISBN #13 978-0-9754516-1-8	ISBN #13 978-0-9754516-8-7
Vol. 5: 0-9648942-5-4	**Vol. 12:** 0-9754516-2-6	**Vol. 19:** 0-9754516-9-3
ISBN #13 978-0-9648942-5-9	ISBN #13 978-0-9754516-2-5	ISBN #13 978-0-9754516-9-4
Vol. 6: 0-9648942-6-2	**Vol. 13:** 0-9754516-3-4	Vol. 20: 1-60310-000-8
ISBN #13 978-0-9648942-6-6	ISBN #13 978-0-9754516-3-2	ISBN #13 978-1-60310-000-7
Vol. 7: 0-9648942-7-0	**Vol. 14:** 0-9754516-4-2	
ISBN #13 978-0-9648942-7-3	ISBN #13 978-0-9754516-4-9	

The Forever Kiss: 0-9648942-3-8 ISBN #13 978-0-9648942-3-5 ($14.00)

Red Sage Publishing Mail Order Form:

(Orders shipped in two to three days of receipt.)

Each volume of *Secrets* retails for $12.99, but you can get it direct via mail order for only $9.99 each. The novel *The Forever Kiss* retails for $14.00, but by direct mail order, you only pay $11.00. Use the order form below to place your direct mail order. Fill in the quantity you want for each book on the blanks beside the title.

_____ *Secrets* Volume 1   _____ *Secrets* Volume 8   _____ *Secrets* Volume 15

_____ *Secrets* Volume 2   _____ *Secrets* Volume 9   _____ *Secrets* Volume 16

_____ *Secrets* Volume 3   _____ *Secrets* Volume 10   _____ *Secrets* Volume 17

_____ *Secrets* Volume 4   _____ *Secrets* Volume 11   _____ *Secrets* Volume 18

_____ *Secrets* Volume 5   _____ *Secrets* Volume 12   _____ *Secrets* Volume 19

_____ *Secrets* Volume 6   _____ *Secrets* Volume 13   _____ *Secrets* Volume 20

_____ *Secrets* Volume 7   _____ *Secrets* Volume 14   _____ *The Forever Kiss*

Total _____ *Secrets* Volumes @ $9.99 each = $_____

Total _____ *The Forever Kiss* @ $11.00 each = $_____

Shipping & handling (in the U.S.) $_____

US Priority Mail: UPS insured:
  1–2 books .... $ 5.50   1–4 books $16.00
  3–5 books .... $11.50   5–9 books $25.00
  6–9 books .... $14.50   10–21 books $29.00
  10–21 books $19.00

SUBTOTAL $_____

Florida 6% sales tax (if delivered in FL) $_____

TOTAL AMOUNT ENCLOSED $_____

Your personal information is kept private and not shared with anyone.

Name: (please print) _____

Address: (no P.O. Boxes) _____

City/State/Zip: _____

Phone or email: (only regarding order if necessary) _____

Please make check payable to **Red Sage Publishing**. Check must be drawn on a U.S. bank in U.S. dollars. Mail your check and order form to:

Red Sage Publishing, Inc.   Department S20   P.O. Box 4844   Seminole, FL 33775

Or use the order form on our website: **www.redsagepub.com**

Red Sage Publishing Mail Order Form:

(Orders shipped in two to three days of receipt.)

Each volume of *Secrets* retails for $12.99, but you can get it direct via mail order for only $9.99 each. The novel *The Forever Kiss* retails for $14.00, but by direct mail order, you only pay $11.00. Use the order form below to place your direct mail order. Fill in the quantity you want for each book on the blanks beside the title.

_____ *Secrets* **Volume 1**	_____ *Secrets* **Volume 8**	_____ *Secrets* **Volume 15**
_____ *Secrets* **Volume 2**	_____ *Secrets* **Volume 9**	_____ *Secrets* **Volume 16**
_____ *Secrets* **Volume 3**	_____ *Secrets* **Volume 10**	_____ *Secrets* **Volume 17**
_____ *Secrets* **Volume 4**	_____ *Secrets* **Volume 11**	_____ *Secrets* **Volume 18**
_____ *Secrets* **Volume 5**	_____ *Secrets* **Volume 12**	_____ *Secrets* **Volume 19**
_____ *Secrets* **Volume 6**	_____ *Secrets* **Volume 13**	_____ *Secrets* **Volume 20**
_____ *Secrets* **Volume 7**	_____ *Secrets* **Volume 14**	_____ *The Forever Kiss*

Total _____ *Secrets* Volumes @ $9.99 each = $_____

Total _____ *The Forever Kiss* @ $11.00 each = $_____

Shipping & handling (in the U.S.) $_____

US Priority Mail: UPS insured:
  1–2 books .... $ 5.50   1–4 books $16.00
  3–5 books .... $11.50   5–9 books $25.00
  6–9 books .... $14.50   10–21 books $29.00
  10–21 books $19.00

SUBTOTAL $_____

Florida 6% sales tax (if delivered in FL) $_____

TOTAL AMOUNT ENCLOSED $_____

Your personal information is kept private and not shared with anyone.

Name: (please print) _____

Address: (no P.O. Boxes) _____

City/State/Zip: _____

Phone or email: (only regarding order if necessary) _____

Please make check payable to **Red Sage Publishing**. Check must be drawn on a U.S. bank in U.S. dollars. Mail your check and order form to:

Red Sage Publishing, Inc.   Department S20   P.O. Box 4844   Seminole, FL 33775

Or use the order form on our website: **www.redsagepub.com**